ONCE IS NOT ENOUGH . . .

Marcus was silent for a moment, and then he stunned Beka by leaning forward and kissing her with fervor. He wrapped one big hand around the curve of her shoulder and the other around the back of her head, pulling her in close as his lips pressed firmly against hers, both soft and rough at the same time. Heat blossomed between them, roaring up out of her core like a wildfire, fierce and magical and completely unexpected.

The kiss only lasted a minute or two, but it felt like an eternity of bliss. Beka felt strangely bereft without his arms around her.

"Wow," she said, blinking rapidly.

Marcus gave her a wicked grin. "Sorry about that," he said, clearly not sorry at all. "I just wanted to thank you for giving me a way to reconnect with my brother. I never would have thought of it like that." He paused, and then added, his smile widening, "Not being a flaky New Age nut, and all."

Beka rolled her eyes, pleased that her idea had gone over so well. And wondering what on earth she could suggest next to elicit the same reaction . . .

WICKEDLY WONDERFUL

DEBORAH BLAKE

BERKLEY SENSATION, NEW YORK

THE BERKLEY PUBLISHING GROUP
Published by the Penguin Group
Penguin Group (USA) LLC
375 Hudson Street, New York, New York 10014

USA • Canada • UK • Ireland • Australia • New Zealand • India • South Africa • China

penguin.com

A Penguin Random House Company

WICKEDLY WONDERFUL

A Berkley Sensation Book / published by arrangement with the author

For information, address: The Berkley Publishing Group,
a division of Penguin Group (USA) LLC,
375 Hudson Street, New York, New York 10014.

ISBN: 978-0-425-27293-0

PUBLISHING HISTORY
Berkley Sensation mass-market edition / December 2014

PRINTED IN THE UNITED STATES OF AMERICA

10 9 8 7 6 5 4 3 2

Cover art by Tony Mauro.
Cover design by Sarah Oberrender.
Interior text design by Kelly Lipovich.

*To the daughter of my heart, Jennifer Holling-Blake.
I couldn't be prouder or happier if I'd birthed you myself.
Thank you for allowing me the privilege of being your
mom. (And thank you to Jo Holling for sharing.)*

*And to Nancy Holzner.
For all the advice, cheerleading, and chats about writing.
Not to mention the opera. It's great having a fellow
author in the neighborhood. More or less.*

*To Robin, for being there at the beginning,
and to Chris, for being there now.*

And to Ellen. Just because.

ACKNOWLEDGMENTS

No man is an island. And while authors may *occasionally* wish that they could have a nice quiet vacation on a deserted island, most of us are pretty happy to have one or two special people around the rest of the time.

I am particularly blessed by the people who share my life. Elaine Spencer is a gem among agents, and The Knight Agency is a gem among agencies. I couldn't be happier than to be in such company. (Welcome to the world, Cora! Your mom rocks!) And when I was imagining the perfect editor for my books, I'm pretty sure there was a picture of Leis Pederson in my head. In fact, everyone at Penguin/Berkley has been fabulous and I plan to take them all to the island with me (my copyeditors get an extra mai tai).

Writers need a lot of things to be successful, but very high on that list are the folks who read, and reread, and re-reread the many drafts of any book, offering helpful suggestions, endless encouragement, and sometimes just listening to you whine about how it is never going to be right. Huge thanks to my fabulous critique partner, Lisa DiDio (who is way more brilliant than I am) and also to Judy Levine (ditto), Alex Bledsoe (also ditto, dammit), and anyone else who was forced to sit through the various versions of this book and any other. Thanks for not putting me out of my misery when I asked you to, and just handing me chocolate instead.

Many thanks to my friends and family for all the encouragement, and especially to my sisters, Sarah and Becky, who were part of the inspiration for giving the Baba Yagas sisters to share their paths. Sisters are the best, even if sometimes they live far away, and you only get to see them if you can travel through a magical doorway. (Or, you know, get on a plane.) Love you both more than I can say.

And last but not least, a huge thank-you to all the wonderful readers of my Llewellyn nonfiction books on witchcraft, who kept saying, "When do we get to read a novel?!"

Now. You're welcome. And thanks so much for making this trip with me.

NE

MARCUS DERMOTT WATCHED the sunrise from the wind-swept deck of his father's fishing boat and wondered if the sea had changed, or if it was him. When he was a boy, growing up on this very boat, the sight of the water being painted with light could make his heart sing, no matter how troubled the rest of his life was. But all he felt now was numb. Numb, and a little bit cranky. The ocean might be beautiful, but it was the last place he wanted to be.

He'd planned to spend his life in the Marines, far away from the restless sea and the memories that came with it. He'd sure as hell never planned to come back to this damned boat. Or to his father. *Especially* to his father. But as the master sergeant who'd trained him liked to say, "Life is what happens while you are making other plans."

Turns out that twelve years in the Corps was all he had in him. Three tours in Afghanistan had sucked him as dry as the desert sands, and as much as he missed the action, and the close bond with the other men in his unit, his head just wasn't in the game anymore. He'd been around long enough to know that if you didn't get out when that happened, you were dangerous to yourself and to everyone around you.

So he'd finished out his time, packed his kit bag, and headed home. One of the guys who'd gotten out a year before him had invited Marcus to work with the extreme adventure vacation company he'd started, and that seemed like as good an idea as any in the post-exit blur Marcus had been in. But life had had other plans there, too, apparently.

"Are you going to stand there daydreaming all day, boy?" a low-pitched voice snarled in his ear. Even the musical Irish lilt couldn't make his father sound like anything other than a bear with a sore paw. "We finally start catchin' some fish after pullin' up empty nets day after day, and you can't bestir yourself to lend a hand? I thought you came back here to help me, not to stare at the sea like you've never seen it before. It's the same ocean it always was—waves and salt and finally, dammit, some fish. So move your ass and check the lines, will ya?"

Marcus sighed. He and his father had never gotten along, and twelve years apart hadn't helped that in the least. When he got the call telling him his father had cancer, Marcus had hoped that maybe if he went home to help out, they could move past their differences. But the past had its barbs in them too deep, and the present was as cold and gray as the ocean. He didn't see either one of those things changing anytime soon.

THE RED-GOLD GLOW of the rising sun turned the sea into a fire of molten lava that belied the cold Pacific waters of Monterey Bay. Beka Yancy didn't mind, though; her wet suit kept her reasonably warm, and it was worth braving the morning chill to have the waves mostly to herself.

Soon enough there would be plenty of people around, but for now, she reveled in her solitary enjoyment of the frothy white lace overlaying blue-green depths, accompanied only by the sound of the wind and the hooting laughter of a nearby pod of dolphins. She gave a chortling greeting in dolphin-speak as she went by.

Beka paddled her surfboard out until the pull of the ocean overruled the calm of the shore and she felt herself settle into that peaceful space she only found when there was endless water below her and infinite sky above. On land, there were human beings and all their attendant noise and commotion; here, there was only the challenge that came from pitting herself against the crushing power of the rolling waves.

The fresh scent of the sea filled her nostrils, and a light breeze tugged playfully on a strand of her long blond hair as she steered in the direction of a promising incoming swell. But before she could angle herself toward it, her board jerked underneath her as if it had suddenly come to life, and she had to grab on tightly with both hands as it accelerated through the water at impossible speeds, cutting through the whitecaps as if they weren't even there.

What the hell? Beka held on tighter, ducking her head against the biting teeth of the icy spray that washed over her. Through squinted eyes, she could barely make out what looked like a pale green hand grasping the end of her surfboard, gossamer webbing pressed against the bright red surface of the board. A powerful tail with iridescent feathery ends undulated just beneath the water, only occasionally breaking through the surface as it stroked forcefully through the ocean.

Mermaid! Beka thought to herself. But the identification of her mysterious hijacker raised more questions than it solved. She doubted the water creature meant her any harm; they normally stayed far away from Human civilization, preferring to hide in their own territory concealed by ancient magic within a two-mile-deep underwater trench. And Beka was friendly with most of the local non-Human residents, on the rare occasions that she saw them.

Still, she was glad of the small knife she wore in a waterproof sheath strapped to her calf, carefully disguised from sight with a tiny glamour that kept the other surfers from noticing it. Not that she really expected to need it, as she had other defenses much more powerful than cold steel, but she'd discovered long ago that it paid to be prepared for the unexpected. It came with the territory, when you were a Baba Yaga.

Most people had never heard of the Baba Yagas. Those who recognized the name were usually only familiar with the legendary witch from Russian fairy tales: a curved-chin, beaky-nosed crone with iron teeth who lived in a hut that ran around the forest on giant chicken legs, flew through the air in an enchanted mortar and pestle, and ate small children when they misbehaved.

Some of that had even been true, once upon a time. Certainly, the Baba Yagas were powerful witches, gifted with the ability to manipulate the elemental forces of nature. Even the tales about the huts and the odd form of transportation had been true, back when the Babas had been found only in Russia and its Slavic neighbors. Things were done a little differently these days though.

Beka might have been the youngest and most inexperienced of the three Babas who lived in the United States, but she was still more than a match for a single Mermaid. So it was with more curiosity than trepidation that she sat up straight on her board when they finally reached their destination.

A swift glance around showed her that the Mermaid had brought her quite some distance from the shore, only barely visible as an ochre-colored smudge on the horizon behind her. Two or three miles out at least, then, a guess reinforced by the sight of a commercial fishing boat moving ponderously through the steely blue sea, dragging its gnarly mesh of nets behind it like a stout wooden bride with a too-long train. Red and blue buoys bobbed on the surface, giving the nets a festive look. Up on the bow of the boat, two men argued about something she was too far away to overhear; luckily, they were looking at each other, and not at her.

Beka jumped as the Mermaid surfaced without a sound, her auburn hair turned almost black by the wetness that slicked it back from her face, green eyes bright with fear as she started speaking almost before her lips reached the open air. The now-risen sun glittered off shimmering scales and glinted on sharply pointed teeth.

"Baba Yaga, you have to help me!" The Merwoman's head swiveled anxiously between the boat and Beka. Beka was about to reply, something about it being good manners to ask first before dragging someone out into the middle of the ocean, when a large cerulean tear rolled down the woman's sharp cheekbone and she added, "My baby—my baby is caught in the net!"

Damn it to Dazhdbog, Beka thought. That was bad. Not just for the poor, defenseless Merbaby, who was much too young to be able to change shape or breathe outside of its natural watery environment, but also for the water peoples—the Mer and the Selkies—who had successfully hidden their existence from Humans since the rest of the paranormal races had retreated to live in the Otherworld; this situation could be catastrophic for that closely held secret.

And since the Baba Yagas, while acting independently, ultimately reported to the powerful and volatile High Queen of the Otherworld, a failure on Beka's part could be catastrophic to her, as well. The Queen had once turned a half a dozen handmaidens into swans during a fit of pique; Beka had no desire to discover if she looked good in feathers.

"What was your baby doing out here in the open waters?" Beka hissed, trying not to panic. It wasn't that she wasn't sympathetic, but she'd been trying her best to avoid any major issues since her mentor, Brenna, the Baba Yaga who'd raised and taught her, had retired to the Otherworld a few years ago and left her to handle things on her own. After years of being told by the elder Baba that she wasn't "quite ready yet," a tiny inner voice seemed to have taken up residence inside Beka's head, constantly whispering the same thing.

"Why aren't you in the trench with the rest of your people?" Beka slid into the cold water, barely noticing the chill as she tried to figure out how she was going to rescue the Merbaby without being seen by the men on—she peered up at the clean white side of the boat—the *Wily Serpent*.

The sea creature tightened her grip on Beka's surfboard, gazing at the nets with terror in her wide-set eyes. "Didn't you know?" Her head bobbed up and down with the waves as she flapped her long, elegant tail in agitation. "There is a problem with our home; all the life there is being poisoned by something our healers have been unable to detect. The plants, the fish, even some of the people have become sickened by it. All the Mer and Selkies must move to a new place closer to land to escape the contamination, and my little one got away from me in the confusion."

She let go of the board to grasp Beka's arm. "Please, Baba Yaga, I know I should have watched him more closely, but please don't let him die."

Not a chance, Beka thought grimly. Then she gritted her teeth as she realized the boat had stopped its lazy forward motion and come to a halt. The mechanical screech of a winch disturbed the quiet sea air as the nets slowly started being drawn in toward the boat's hull. Pain accompanied the sound as the Merwoman realized what was happening and unconsciously tightened her grasp, webbed fingers turning into claws.

"Oh no," she said, seaweed-tinted tears flowing faster now. "It's too late."

Beka shook her head. "Not yet, it isn't," she said, and set off swimming with strong, purposeful strokes toward the slowly rising mesh of ropes. "Stay here," she ordered, tossing the words over her shoulder. Then she swam as if a life depended on it.

As she drew closer to the boat, she could see that it wasn't as pristine as she'd thought; a blue-black crust of barnacles marred the deep green bottom half where it met the water, and the white paint on top was dull and peeling. For all that, though, the boat itself seemed solid and well constructed—as, alas, did the net that was slowly but relentlessly being pulled in toward its home.

Beka took a deep breath and dove under the water. Thankfully, since she spent so much time in the ocean, she had long ago done magical work that enabled her to keep her eyes open even without protective goggles. Through the gaps between the ropes, she could see the Merbaby clearly, swimming in desperate circles round and round the ever-shrinking space. His tiny pale green face was splotched with crying, although any sound he made was lost in the metallic grinding of the winch as it pulled the purse seine in tighter and tighter. As he spotted her, he shot over to her side of the net, making soft *eep*ing noises like a distressed dolphin.

Beka swam up to the choppy surface to gulp another breath, then down again; the trip was noticeably shorter on the way back, and she knew she was running out of time. It was tempting to use magic to blast through the net, but she was afraid that she might accidentally hurt the child, and magic often didn't work well underwater, so in the end, she simply pulled out her knife and sawed away frantically at the tough fibers.

Twice more she had to dart above to take a breath, but after the last time, her efforts paid off; she had cut a ragged hole not much more than two feet long, but large enough for the small Merbaby to exit. The fish within were already bolting toward freedom, brushing her with their tickling fins as they flashed past.

She gestured for the Merbaby to come closer, only to realize that while she had been fighting with the robustly woven strands, the child's tail had become entangled in a section of net, and he was trapped, unable to get loose from the seine's unrelenting grasp.

Cursing soundlessly, Beka raced to get one more deep lungful of air, then threw herself toward the hole and eeled her way through the impossibly small opening. Frantically, she fought the sinuously twining ropes until the little one was free and she could shove him through to the other side. Only to find herself trapped in the quickly contracting net and rapidly running out of time and oxygen.

WO

"THERE'S SOMEONE IN the net!" Kenny yelped, screeching to a halt by Marcus's side. "Oh my god! We caught a mermaid!"

Gripping the side of the boat with both hands, Marcus peered in the direction where Kenny pointed. *Sonofabitch—there* was *someone in the net. Well, SHIT.* The rough brown strands were being pulled inward, but most of the mesh was still underwater, where he could just make out a vaguely female form struggling to get loose.

Without thinking, he pulled off his sneakers and dove into the icy water. The shock of it almost drove the breath from his lungs, but he didn't let that slow him down. Once in the water, he swam freestyle as fast as he could, using his military training to keep his target in sight every time he raised his head up over the waves. Once he got closer, he stopped, treading water, and assessed the situation.

Marcus couldn't believe his eyes. Instead of the shimmering fish he'd expected, he was staring at the impossible— a gorgeous woman in a wet suit holding a knife, its sharp edges clearly responsible for the brand-new opening in the net he had so meticulously mended not three days ago. A net that *had* until a few minutes ago contained the only decent catch they'd made in weeks. It was a great pity, because she really was stunning, but he was going to have to kill her.

Probably by strangling her with his bare hands. As soon as he'd rescued her, of course.

He could see that she had almost managed to get loose but hadn't been able to hold the hole open and free herself from the tangles of the net at the same time. She struggled to keep her head above water, ducking underneath the surface in between breaths to hack at the stubborn strands surrounding her. Marcus closed his eyes and dived under, grabbing the knife out of the woman's hand and slashing by feel alone at the slit she'd made, enlarging it enough that he could reach through and grab her.

He pulled her out, dropping the knife so he could get one arm around her slim waist and use the other to propel them toward the surface as fast as possible. Even so, he was gasping for air when his face broke through the waves, and the woman had to finish coughing up seawater before she could turn to him and say, "Hey! That was my favorite knife!"

THE CREW HAULED Marcus, the woman, and the remains of the net up onto the deck. Before he'd even had a chance to catch his breath, he heard his father's gruff voice say, "Marcus Henry Dermott, what the hell have you done now?"

Only his da could hold Marcus responsible for some mystery woman slicing through their net. Of course, given half a chance, the old man would blame him for everything from the weather to the lack of fish to the high price of beer in their favorite tavern.

For a brief moment, Marcus actually found himself wishing he was back in the dusty, arid deserts of Afghanistan. Yes, people had been trying to kill him there, but it was still a lot more restful than being trapped on the memory-haunted boat he grew up on with the tough, brutal old fisherman who shared his name and way too much unpleasant history.

The two men who made up his father's regular crew looked on with wide eyes. Chico had been with his father for as long as Marcus could remember; an illegal immigrant who had come across the border thirty years ago, around the time Marcus was born, he was as tough as shark hide and about as pretty. But he was dependable and knew how to fish, and that was all Marcus Senior cared about.

Kenny, on the other hand, was a weedy kid barely out of his teens who had more enthusiasm than experience. He'd only been working the boat for about six months, after Marcus's father had chased off yet another in a long line of crewmen who got tired of being cursed at in a strange mixture of Gaelic, Spanish, and English.

Kenny peered down at their visitor with open curiosity. "Um, are you okay, lady?" His Adam's apple bobbed up and down like a buoy on rough waters. "You're not a mermaid, are you?"

The woman stood up with a Valkyrie's warrior grace despite the mangled fibers still wrapped around her bare feet. "Sorry," she said in a voice that sounded like music. For a moment, Marcus could have sworn he smelled fresh strawberries on the salty breeze. "Not a Mermaid. Just an innocent passing surfer girl, I'm afraid."

Marcus's father snorted and spat on the deck. He had no time for people who used the sea for play instead of work.

"Not so innocent," Marcus pointed out, crossing his arms over his chest and ramping up his stare to a level that used to make the men under him drop and give him twenty without even being asked. "You sabotaged our net, and we lost the better part of the first good haul we've had in a very long time. What are you, one of those crazy Greenpeace idiots?"

His father let loose with a truly impressive stream of profanity at this, but their unexpected passenger seemed unimpressed. Probably didn't understand most of the words under his father's anger-heavy Irish accent, which was just as well. Marcus was about as furious as he got, but he still didn't believe in swearing at women.

Bright blue eyes looked from the hole in the net to him and back again as a slight flush slid over tanned cheekbones. "Look, I'm really sorry about your net, and the fish and everything. But there was a baby . . . dolphin trapped in it, and I had to get the poor thing out before you killed it." The blue eyes widened in an attempt to look innocent, but Marcus wasn't buying it. He'd had a kid in his unit that used to give him the same exact look, usually when he was caught doing something illegal, immoral, or both.

Marcus scanned the waters on either side of the boat. "I don't see any dolphins. Haven't seen any all morning, for that matter."

The woman hummed a little under her breath and made an odd swiveling motion with her hand before turning toward the bow and pointing. "They're right there," she said confidently.

And damned if there weren't a half a dozen dolphins, including a small one, right where he could have sworn the sea was empty a minute ago. *Weird*. He was usually more observant than that—old habits die hard, and after three tours in the Marines, all of them spent in places full of snipers and killers disguised as civilians, he still hadn't learned to stop watching everything and everybody in the nearby vicinity.

"I don't give a crap if there was three nuns and the Virgin Mary in them damned nets," his father snarled, gray beard bristling. "You don't go cuttin' a hole in a man's equipment. Who the hell is going to pay to get that mess mended, I ask you? And who's going to pay for all them fish I lost?" Righteous ire painted a wash of red over his father's too-pale face, but Marcus could see the shakiness in his bull-like stance.

"Da," Marcus said, in a slightly softer tone, "why don't you go up to the wheelhouse and figure out exactly how much you think we lost. Then I'll escort this crazy tree hugger back to whatever asylum she escaped from and she can write us a check to make up for the damage." He made a small gesture with his head, and Chico nodded behind his father's back, then put one hand on the old man's arm.

Marcus Senior shook it off. "I know what you're doing, Mark-boy. No need to coddle me." But he headed off toward the small cabin nonetheless, Chico on his heels, both of them moving slower than the slight heave of the ship required.

Marcus clapped the still gape-mouthed Kenny on the shoulder, shoving him gently toward the damaged netting. "Why don't you collect whatever fish we did manage to get and put them on ice in the hold? We'll be heading back in now; no chance of any more fishing today, thanks to her." The boy went back to work reluctantly, looking back over his shoulder as he walked away and almost tripping over a coil of rope.

Forcing himself to unclench his fists, Marcus turned back to study his mystery woman. Her hair was long, almost to the middle of her back, and he thought that when it finished drying it would probably be a natural blond; she had the coloring of a true California girl. Slim and tall, she wore her wet suit like a second skin that clung to curves in all the right places. He swallowed hard, hit by a sudden burst of desire that welled up out of nowhere. He hadn't had any interest in women since he'd gotten back from the war—figures he'd finally rediscover it in the presence of some nutcase they'd fished out of the sea.

A thought struck him. "Hey, how the hell did you get all the way out here?" He gazed around, but the ocean was empty; no boats but the *Wily Serpent* anywhere in sight. Not even a dinghy.

She strolled over to the rail as if she owned the place and pointed over the side. A scarlet surfboard with a black dragon painted on it bobbed tranquilly in the calm sea, occasionally rubbing up against the side of the boat like an affectionate cat.

Marcus shook his head. "Are you kidding? You got all the way out here on a surfboard? No way." He shaded his eyes with one hand, looking for a lurking vessel full of delusional do-gooders. "You must have had friends who brought you out here. Did they just abandon you?"

A smile tugged at the corner of full lips. "No friends," she said. "It must have been a rogue wave. I was surfing closer to land, and before I knew it, I was out here."

Oh, for the love of Pete. She wasn't even trying to come up with a good lie. What a flake.

"Fine," he said. "That's your story and you can stick to it. But don't think that I'm going to let you get away with destroying my father's property and ruining our fishing just because you've got some cockamamy idea in that pretty head of yours about saving endangered turtles or poor, defenseless sharks from the mean fishermen."

God, he hated flakes. That type could get you killed, whether you were on the battlefield or on a boat. And the most dangerous ones were the flakes who didn't know they were flakes. He'd be doing her a favor by teaching her that there were consequences for your actions.

"You're going back to the shore with us," he said. It's not like he could leave her out here in the middle of nowhere on a surfboard anyway. Rogue wave, my ass. "And then I am going to escort you home, where you can write me out a check to cover the cost of the damage to the net and the lost fish."

He scowled at her to make sure she got his point. "My father may be a rude, grumpy pain in the ass, but he works hard to make a living. Being a fisherman isn't an easy life, especially when . . ." He caught himself. It was none of her business anyway. ". . . when crazy blond nutcases decide to cut holes in our net. I hope you've got money to pay for this, or you're going to find yourself in jail."

He glared at her, hands on his hips, waiting for tears to well up in those big blue eyes. Instead, she merely shrugged one neoprene-clad shoulder and said, "That's fair. Do you mind if we pick up my surfboard first?"

Off the starboard bow, he could swear he heard a dolphin laugh.

BEKA FOUGHT BACK the mental image of Mr. Stick-up-his-butt hopping wetly around on deck and saying *ribbit*. The Baba Yaga who'd raised her had stressed the importance of never misusing her magic. But man, was it tempting. That deep voice of his would sound quite nice on a frog. Although it would be a shame to waste those broad shoulders and craggy good looks. Too bad he didn't have a personality to go with them.

You'd think she'd purposely set out to ruin his day. Of course, she couldn't exactly explain what she *had* been doing, so she'd just have to give him some money and hope that he'd let it go at that. At least the Mermaid and her son seemed to be long gone, so Beka had done something right. Too bad she'd screwed everything else up in the process. As usual. Maybe her mentor had been right, and she simply wasn't ready to be out on her own. The old Baba probably would have figured out a way to save the little one without ever alerting the fishermen to her presence.

Still, she thought, brightening a little as her naturally cheerful disposition reasserted itself, she *had* actually gotten the job done. Now she had a lovely boat ride back to the shore, with the glorious ocean all around her. Sunlight glinted off the green-blue water with its dancing waves. The salt-laden breeze ran soft fingers through her hair as she sat on the prow. Warm sun caressed her skin where she'd peeled back the top of the wet suit, and her companion was quite nice to look at as long as he didn't actually speak.

"Do you have a name?" he asked.

So much for that.

"A number of them, in fact," she said with perfect honesty. She always tried to speak the truth if possible; there was power in words, and it didn't do to misuse them. "You can call me Beka. Beka Yancy."

He hesitated, and then stuck out one large, calloused hand. A tingle ran through her as she took it. "Marcus Dermott. The charming gentleman you met before is my father, Marcus Senior."

A scowl marred his otherwise attractive visage. "I'm helping him out temporarily. This is his boat." Something about the way he said it made her think he'd rather be anywhere but here, doing anything but this.

"He's sick, isn't he?" she said softly. Even without the heightened sensitivity of a Baba, she would have noticed the obvious pallor under the older man's weathered skin, and the way his well-worn clothes hung on a frame that looked as though it had lost much of its original bulk. "What's wrong with him?"

Marcus stared at her, then out at sea. "Advanced lung cancer. He'd been fighting it for a few months before I got home from my last tour of duty. Trying to work this boat with only two crew, one of them barely out of school." Beka could see the muscles in his shoulders bunching up under the dark tee shirt he wore.

"I'm sorry," she said. Babas didn't suffer from Human illnesses much; one of the benefits of being a powerful witch. But that didn't make it any easier to watch the people around you suffer. Her mentor used to warn her away from close friendships with Humans, said they were too fragile and short-lived for folks like them. Beka was almost thirty but still looked like she was in her early twenties. Yet another reason not to get attached—sooner or later, someone would notice. But that didn't mean she didn't like Humans. After all, she'd been born one.

Marcus shrugged, still not looking at her. But his shoulders hunched a little more, making a lie of his casual tone. "I told him that the cigarettes would catch up with him someday. He tells me he quit a couple of years ago, but I guess it was too late."

Something about that rang strangely. "He told you? You didn't know?"

"I did three hitches in the Marines," he said. His back straightened as if just saying the word made him stronger. "Only got out a little while ago. While I was trying to figure out what I was going to do with myself, some busy-body called to tell me my father was sick. So I came here to pitch in. Not that the old man wants my aid."

He snorted. "You should have seen his face when I showed up. Cursed that doctor up, down, and sideways." A crooked grin relaxed the grim lines set into his face and startled Beka into realizing he was actually quite hand-some. If you liked your men tough and muscular and just a little scruffy around the edges. Which she didn't, thankfully.

She turned a little so she could see his face better, enjoying the light touch of the spray on her skin. All Baba Yagas were in tune with the elements, but each tended to be drawn more strongly to one in particular. Her sister Baba, Barbara Yager, who had just relocated to New York State, was tied to the earth. Beka, on the other hand, was water all the way. Although she traveled around as Babas did, she slept the most soundly when she could hear the ocean singing a lullaby through her open windows.

"How long had it been since you'd seen him?" she asked, more because she was enjoying the deep rumble of his voice than out of any desire to know. Soon they'd be onshore; she'd pay him off and then she'd never see him again. An odd shivery melancholy ran through her at the thought, but she shrugged it away.

Marcus swiveled to face her, his visage settling back into its customary wall of stone. For a minute, she thought he wasn't going to answer her.

"I left the day I turned eighteen," he said. "Joined up that week, and haven't been home since. Until now."

"You said you did three tours." Beka thought about what little she knew about the military. "That's twelve years, isn't it?" She blinked. Babas were solitary creatures, for the most part, except for the time they spent training their replacements (usually about fifteen or sixteen years, for most, although Beka's mentor had stuck around for a lot longer, since she didn't trust Beka to manage on her own). But Beka knew that Humans usually valued family as much as the Selkies and the Merpeople did. "You couldn't get back here to visit in all that time? That's so sad."

Marcus stood up abruptly, his large shadow blocking out the sun. "Not really," he said shortly. "We don't get along."

Beka opened her mouth to say something, but he stalked off toward the port side and didn't say another word to her until the *Wily Serpent* glided into the harbor as smoothly as its name.

THREE

MARCUS LEFT HIS father and the guys unloading the few fish they'd managed to salvage and stowed Beka and her surfboard into his battered ancient Jeep. During the trip back into shore, Beka's hair had dried to reveal its true color, a golden yellow the color of sunshine. In rippled down her back like silk, smelling faintly of summer memories and shining in the bright morning light. For some reason, it kept catching at his vision out of the corner of one eye, distracting him.

There was something generally sunshiny about her, in fact. She seemed to radiate a kind of cheerful glow that both attracted and annoyed him. He couldn't pin down exactly why that was, which *also* attracted and annoyed him. Thank goodness he'd be rid of her soon. His life was complicated enough. And he was kind of used to the gray that colored everything in his world since he'd gotten home, as though he'd been wrapped in slightly dingy cotton wool.

He parked in a spot off Highway One, with the ocean on one side and a steep bluff on the other. There were no houses in sight, but this was where she'd instructed him to bring her. What the hell was the woman playing at now?

"I thought you said you lived near here," he said, not trying to hide his scowl.

Beka nodded, sliding out of the Jeep and grabbing her board. She gestured to the bluff. "I live up there, at least for the moment." She cast a wicked grin in his direction. "You can wait down here for me if you want."

"Not a chance." He looked at the nearly vertical path that cut into the sandy incline. "You carry your surfboard up and down that thing?"

"Just about every day," she said, tucking it under one arm effortlessly and heading toward a path. Her wet suit hung around her hips, revealing a simple white one-piece suit and lots of toned, tanned girl. He tried not to watch her perfect butt as he followed her up the hill.

Marcus stopped at the top of the bluff to get the lay of the land. At first glance, there was nothing much there—a few windblown trees, a patch of ragged land more weeds than grass, and . . .

"Is that a *school bus*?" he asked. It had the right shape, but the entire thing was painted with a mural of an underwater seascape of blues shading into aqua and greens, complete with colorful fish, playful seals and dolphins, and a scantily clad mermaid wearing an enchanting smile. He walked around to look at the other side, bemused, and found a sinuous sea serpent with crimson, orange, and yellow scales curling in and around the windows. Whoever had done the painting was wasted on buses; the entire effect was so realistic, he felt like he could swim right into the world in front of him. A tiny shiver ran down his spine.

"That's my home; at least, its current incarnation," Beka said with another one of her sideways smiles. "A little flashy, I know, but it looked that way when I inherited it from my foster mother." An eye roll accompanied the statement. "Some people got way too attached to the sixties."

Marcus shook his head. *Great. A flake from a long line of flakes. It figured.* He was much more impressed by the improbably well-preserved Karmann Ghia with a surf-board rack on top, parked alongside a shiny black Vespa motorcycle. *Nice toys for a crazy surfer girl. Maybe she has a rich father. At least then he wouldn't have to worry about taking her food money to pay for this morning's mess.*

"I'll go get you the money," Beka said, echoing his thought as she headed toward the door to the bus. Marcus followed her in, more out of curiosity than distrust.

His eyes widened as he hit the top of the stairs and looked down the length of the converted school bus. Unlike the fanciful outside, the inside was as tidy as any barracks, although considerably more attractive.

Pale wood paneled all the surfaces—floor, walls, and ceilings—giving it the feel of a shipboard cabin. The many windows along the side allowed in plenty of light, lending an airy ambiance to a space that might otherwise have felt claustrophobic. There was a tiny bathroom, an efficient galley, and a living area that included a rag rug and a futon that probably doubled as a bed.

Well-crafted maple bookshelves ran along the walls, inter-spersed with cabinets and cupboards that kept everything not in use neatly stowed away. A cast iron stove between the liv-ing area and the kitchen stood cold and unused at the moment, thrusting its chimney through the roof of the bus.

The few decorations he could see all continued the nautical theme: strands of shells hung like wind chimes, a decorative driftwood sculpture, blown glass globes, and the kinds of odds and ends you might find beachcombing. The futon cover was some soft woven material in shades of blue and green that reminded him of the ocean.

The only jarring note was a collection of knives and a few swords that ran along the top of the walls above the windows; some of them looked brand-new, and others as if they might have been salvaged from the wrecks of ancient ships, but all of them appeared to be sharp and ready for use. Maybe she was expecting to be boarded by pirates.

"Nice place," he said, not commenting on the cutlery. "It's not what I expected."

Beka snorted, wrinkling her straight nose and revealing a couple of adorable freckles he hadn't noticed before. "You were expecting a lot of tie-dyed throw pillows, billowing incense, and some pot plants, maybe?"

Actually, he had been. The reality was a lot more cheerful and appealing than he'd anticipated (sharp-edged weapons aside), and he couldn't quite make it mesh with the mental image he'd formed of the girl so far. So which one of them was misleading?

"Was the interior like this when you inherited it too?" he asked. Maybe the foster mother she'd mentioned had been the tidy one. Although the outside of the bus screamed hippie, and he'd never met a tidy hippie. He loved California, but the state had more flakes than a bowl of Raisin Bran.

Beka shook her head. "No way. We've been changing things around ever since my foster mother moved out about two years ago. It used to be a lot more cluttered." A dimple flashed as she grinned. "And there were, in fact, tie-dyed pillows."

We. Oh. So she didn't live alone. Marcus wasn't sure why that fact hit him so hard, especially since he didn't intend to ever see her again after today.

Of course someone that gorgeous had a boyfriend. Maybe even a husband, although a glance down at her slim left hand didn't reveal a ring. The only jewelry she wore was a tiny gold dragon necklace and matching earrings; odd accessories for a surfer, but clearly sturdy, since they'd survived her tangle with his father's nets.

What the hell. "We?" he asked, not really wanting the explanation.

She laughed, a sound like bells. "Oh, sorry, I haven't introduced you." She gave a sharp whistle. "Hey, Chewie, come say hi!"

For a moment, Marcus was baffled; it wasn't as though there was any place for someone to hide in the open space of the bus. Then a large shape lumbered up from behind the futon and shambled over to sit in front of Beka like a gigantic walking mountain of black hair and gleaming teeth.

"Jesus!" Marcus said, taking an involuntary step backward. The thing had to weigh at least two hundred pounds, maybe more, and its head was almost as high as his waist, even sitting down. "What is that?"

Beka tutted, leaning down to pat the monster on its furry head. "This is Chewie. He lives with me. Be nice, now."

Marcus couldn't tell if she was talking to him or to the dog, but the creature put out one massive paw to shake. Blinking a couple of times, Marcus took it, mindful of the tough claws.

"Er, hello, Chewie," he said politely.

"Woof," the dog said back.

"Chewie is a Newfoundland," Beka explained. "They're great water dogs. They swim better than we do, and even have webbed feet. They're often used for water rescue, and the breed started out as working dogs for fishermen."

"Uh-huh." Marcus tried to imagine what his father would say if Marcus brought him a huge black dog to help out on the boat, and failed miserably. Instead, he commented on the dog's unusual name. "Chewie—I guess you named him for Chewbacca in *Star Wars*. I can see why; they're both gigantic and furry."

Beka giggled. "I never thought of that. Actually, Chewie is short for Chudo-Yudo. Also, he chews on stuff a lot, so it seemed fitting."

"Chudo *what*?" Marcus said. The dog made a snuffling sound that might have been canine laughter.

"Chudo-Yudo," Beka repeated. "He's a character out of Russian fairy tales, the dragon that guards the Water of Life and Death. You never heard of him?"

Marcus shook his head. "My father used to tell the occasional Irish folk tale when I was a kid, but I'm not familiar with Russian ones at all. Sorry."

"Oh, don't be," she said cheerfully. "Most of them were pretty gory, and they hardly ever had happy endings."

"Right." Marcus looked at the dog, who gazed alertly back with big brown eyes, as if trying to figure out if the former Marine was edible or not. "So, you named him after a mythical dragon from a depressing Russian story. Does anyone get eaten in that story, just out of curiosity?"

Chewie sank down onto the floor with a put-upon sigh, and Beka shook her head at Marcus. "Don't be ridiculous. Of *course* people got eaten. But don't worry; Chewie hasn't taken a bite out of anyone in years. He's very mellow for a dragon." She patted the massive dark head fondly.

"Don't you mean he's very mellow for a dog?" Marcus said with a chuckle. He had to admit, the animal seemed completely laid back. Maybe the dog was a hippie too.

Beka looked startled for a second, then caught herself. "Oh, right. That's what I meant." The dog gave another snort, drooling a little on her foot in the process. "Could you turn around, please?"

Marcus raised one eyebrow in question. "Excuse me?"

She made a little spinning gesture with one finger. "Turn around. I'm going to get your money now, and I don't want you to see where I hide my stash. You can just go outside if you're afraid to turn your back on me."

Right. Big, bad Marine is afraid to turn his back on the skinny blond surfer chick. Not likely. Even when the chick in question had a whole lot of sharp pointy objects on her walls and a ginormous hound from hell. He turned his back on her and crossed his arms. "So, do you actually have a job, then?" he asked, as she padded on bare feet across the floor toward the cupboards in the rear. He could feel the dog's hot breath on his knees like the wind out of the desert.

Muttered words and an odd series of clicks floated up from the end of the bus. *Weird. She must have some kind of safe. Somehow she didn't seem like the type. Hell, the door to the bus hadn't even been locked when they'd gotten here.*

"I make handcrafted jewelry and take it to Renaissance fairs and farmer's markets and places like that," she said, suddenly right behind him again.

Marcus tried not to jump. How on earth did she move

like that? The elusive scent of fresh strawberries teased his nostrils again, oddly titillating. It didn't smell like the too-fruity fake smell of some overly perfumed shampoo—more like the first lush strawberry of the season, warm from the sun and filled with impossible sweetness. Everything about this woman confused him, and he *hated* to be confused. He spun around, hand out for a wad of cash, and gazed in amazement as she dropped a half a dozen gold coins into his outstretched palm.

"And I do some diving and salvage work on the side," she added. "These came off a wreck in the Gulf of Mexico. I'm not sure what they're worth, but they ought to more than cover the cost of mending that tiny hole in your nets, as well as a few lost fish." She tossed long, silky strands of golden hair over her shoulder, her expression wary and defensive.

Marcus realized that she was waiting for him to argue with her again, or say something insulting about someone who makes a living selling crap—that is, crafts—at fairs, and treasure hunting. He'd been about to do just that, truth be told, but he closed his mouth with a snap.

Behind her cheery disposition and irritating in-your-face attitude, he suspected there lurked someone who was used to being criticized. Stormy depths hid behind those bright blue eyes. He'd had young guys in his unit like that; sometimes half the bluster was just a defense against being told they were lacking in some way. And hell, at least she'd paid him for the trouble she'd put them through. The coins she'd given him would more than make up for the day's wasted trip. Assuming they were real. Although looking at the decorations on the walls, he didn't doubt her story of being a diver, even if he thought half of everything else she'd told him was a lie.

No point in hanging around any longer, no matter how nice the scenery was (and he didn't mean the inside of the bus either). There was no place in his life right now for women, especially not gorgeous, eccentric ones whose worlds were so far from the one he inhabited, they might as well be on two different planets. He had a responsibility to his da, no matter how much he might dislike the old man. And as soon as he'd fulfilled that obligation, he'd be long gone. If he never saw another fish, or another ditzy California environmentalist, it would be just fine with him.

He closed his fingers over the coins and nodded brusquely. "Thanks. And do us both a favor and stay away from my father's boat. I've got enough to deal with without having to worry about you crazy Greenpeace people. We're just honest fishermen trying to make an honest living. I suggest you do the same."

He turned on his heel and stalked out the door, almost running to get away from the feeling that he didn't truly want to leave at all.

"WELL. THAT WAS rude," Beka said. That didn't stop her from crossing to the window to watch him walk away. No harm in looking. And it wasn't as though she was likely to have the chance again. Besides, just because she was a powerful witch didn't mean she couldn't appreciate a nice butt when she saw one.

"Man's clearly got issues," Chudo-Yudo said, padding over to stand next to her and giving her leg an affectionate nudge that almost knocked her over. "But he's kinda cute."

Beka rolled her eyes. "What the hell do you know about cute? You're a dragon." She resolutely tore her gaze away from the sight and went to flop down on the futon instead.

"I know that you hardly ever pay attention to men, even when they treat you a lot better than that guy did," Chudo-Yudo said, opening the mini-fridge with his teeth to fetch out his latest bone. "And I also know that you hardly took your eyes off that one the whole time he was here. Hence— cute." He crunched on the bone loudly.

Beka would have argued, but what would be the point? It was true. There was something about the man that pulled at her core . . . despite the fact that he was cranky, unpleasant, and couldn't stand anything about her. Thank goodness she was never going to see him again.

Chudo-Yudo lifted up his head and a second later, a knock on the door made her heart skip a beat. But something told her it wasn't a stick-up-his-butt fisherman, coming back to borrow a cup of sugar.

In fact, when she opened the door, her visitor was revealed to be a slim, dark-haired man clad only in a pair of shorts. He dripped wetly on her doorstep, smelling faintly of salt and sea and mystery. When Beka came down to meet him, he bowed low in respect, his pale form bent almost to the ground. A ragged piece of seaweed was caught behind one ear like a ribbon, tangled in his ebony curls.

"Baba Yaga," he said, his tone formal as he handed her a roll of something that wasn't quite parchment, but still looked ancient and weighty, for all that it, too, dripped salt water on the ground beneath. "I bring you greetings and salutations from the Queen of the Merpeople and the King of the Selkies. They hope that you will meet them this e'en at tide's turn, down upon yon beach." He gestured gracefully toward the ocean that waited just across the highway, its heartbeat as dependable as the waxing and waning of the moon.

Damn, Beka thought. *So much for staying out of trouble.*

"I see," she said to the messenger, although clearly she didn't. "Please tell them that I will be there."

She'd spent the last two years avoiding anything that would call for her to draw on her powers as Baba for anything more urgent than averting the occasional tidal wave or quieting an earthquake, so she could be sure of not screwing up. Something told her she'd finally run out of time.

OUR

A LOW MOON hung over the deserted beach, casting eerie shadows over windswept sand. A few days past full, its pallid globe danced in and out of scudding clouds, playing at hide-and-seek with a group of friendly stars. A little way offshore, a whale breached, sending a spume of water into the sky to add to the fun.

The night air held a tiny bite of cold as it crept in off the water, and elusive scraps of fog wandered to and fro as if looking for the party. At her feet, a crab edged sideways toward a safer section of sand. Beka wished she could do the same.

The moon hid its face for one long moment, and when it returned, a half a dozen figures had materialized out of the frothing surf. They walked out of the sea as if they strolled out of another world, one of mystery and magic and strange enchanting beauty. Which was more or less the truth of the matter, as it happened.

The two in front had the kind of presence that caught the eye without intending to; an upright stance, a high-held head, a regal stare that said, *Look, these ones are important. Special. Do not presume to bother them.*

It wasn't anything they did or said, simply who they were. The guards who walked behind each of them were nothing; a habit, perhaps, a display of power, or merely the caution of the long-lived. But the two in front . . . it was just as well that the beach was empty at this late hour, because no one seeing them could have mistaken them for anything less than what they were: royalty out of legend, risen up upon a shore not their own.

On the left, the Queen of the Merpeople wore a gown of green and blue that swirled around her ankles, the pointed tips of the hemline dragging over her bare, slightly webbed feet as they slid effortlessly across the crusted sand. A silver belt entwined her slender waist, and a bejeweled diadem twinkled atop the crimson flame of her hair.

To her right, the King of the Selkies strode in muscular grace. His attire was more muted: brown and gray with tiny glints of light from layered scales, as though his pants and tunic had been crafted from some exotic deep-sea creature whose subtle armored shell could be formed into everyday attire. No crown sat on his straight black hair, but he carried a scepter in one hand with a large emerald at its tip.

Beka took a few steps forward and executed a sweeping bow. Strictly speaking, a Baba Yaga didn't need to bow to anyone except the High Queen of the Otherworld, before whom all paranormal beings bowed (at least, all those with any sense of self-preservation). But as her mentor always said, it never hurt to be polite.

"Your Majesties," she said. "You wished to speak to me?"

Queen Boudicca inclined her head slightly. "And so we did, Baba Yaga. We have need of your services, and have come to ask for your aid." Her pale face was proud and stern in the moonlight, but worry haunted her almond-shaped green eyes. The Irish lilt in her voice bespoke the Celtic origins of both the underwater races who had migrated to the New World along with those who once believed in them.

King Gwrtheyrn growled an agreement, sounding like a bull seal warning off a rival. "We tend to our own, most times," he said. "With no need of meddling from those who left us behind when they fled this plane of existence. But the Babas have always been a friend to our people, and I'm not ashamed to say that the Selkies are in dire want of a friend, just now."

"And the Merpeople as well," Boudicca said, shaking her head a little at her fellow royal. "After all, it was my woman who came and told us the tale of the Baba Yaga rescuing her child this day, which put the idea into our heads in the first place."

The King snorted, waving one hand in that "settle down, woman" motion that was the same both above and below the sea.

"Are the mother and her baby okay?" Beka asked, trying to avert an argument. The King and Queen might share an underwater kingdom, but they (and their people) spent more time squabbling than a school of tiger sharks. Sometimes with as messy results. "I couldn't see them from the boat once I was aboard, so I hoped that meant they'd gotten away without any further problems."

Boudicca gave a narrow, pointy-toothed smile. "Both are doing well, thanks to you, Baba Yaga. But the same cannot be said for our people as a whole. We face a calamity the likes of which we have not experienced since our ill-considered move to these shores."

Beka could feel her heart rate pick up. "The Merwoman I met said that something had happened to the water in the trench and you'd been forced to relocate all your subjects. Is that really true?" It wasn't that she'd thought the Mermaid was lying, exactly; it just didn't seem possible. And then, of course, a large, attractive fisherman had distracted her from the issue.

The King's austere face creased with concern. "It is true, Baba Yaga. Something poisons the fish, the plants, and the more vulnerable among us. Two children have already sickened greatly, and others show signs of ill health. Our wise men and healers can find no reason for this, our mages have tried all their tricks, and yet, the problem persists."

Boudicca sighed, head drooping as though the weight of the delicate crown she wore was suddenly too heavy to bear. "After one of the eldest of our tribe died suddenly, it was finally decided that we had no choice but to leave our homes. We found another deep trough, closer in to the shore, and we have cast all the magical protections around it that we can, in hopes of keeping the Humans away."

"But the trench where we have always lived was never discovered by the air dwellers; it appears on no map, and no diver has ever returned from its treacherous depths." The King's slightly predatory smile made Beka shudder, although she made sure to hide the movement. "This new place is visited from time to time by those they call scientists. We cannot safely stay there forever."

"And so it is we turn to you, Baba Yaga," Gwrtheyrn said in formal tones. His voice took on the cadence of one about to invoke the Old Rites: magic and tradition that bound as tightly as any chains.

Beka glanced wildly around the beach, as though some miracle might come dashing through the fog to carry her off, out of the danger of obligations she might not be able to fulfill. But none was forthcoming.

Boudicca laid one long-fingered hand over Gwrtheyrn's, and their heavy gazes filled with the magnitude of their request. The temperature on the beach seemed to drop, and Beka shivered.

"We ask, Baba Yaga, that you undertake the task of discovering the cause of this mysterious illness that afflicts our lands and our peoples, and if it is possible, cure it. Find a way for us to return to our homes before it is too late and the air dwellers discover us."

The Queen's mellifluous voice rang with the power behind her words. It was a Baba Yaga's job to maintain the balance of the elements, if she could. In this day and age, that was nearly impossible, but if someone who knew enough to ask requested a Baba's help, and made the correct bargains, tradition insisted the task be undertaken.

As if hearing her thoughts, the King added, "We promise

you three boons, should you accomplish this difficult undertaking. A boon for you, a boon for a friend, and a boon for a stranger, should you find one such in need of our aid. These things we promise."

Boudicca repeated after him, "These things we promise." And then they said it together, "These things we promise. And so the bargain is made. And so shall it be done."

A chime rang through the air, as clear as though the stars above had all rung like bells in unison. Beka felt the magic tremble down from her head to her toes, touching her essence and wrapping the invisible strands of destiny around her with a silken inevitability.

"I will do my best," she answered them, bowing again. And was glad they could not hear the tiny voice, far down inside, that said, *But will your best be good enough? Or will you fail all these people, dooming their races to death?*

CHARLIE KELLY WATCHED from the edge of the road as his driver backed the anonymous white van oh-so-carefully down to the decrepit-looking dock. It wouldn't do to have an accident with the current cargo aboard. Charlie wasn't exactly holding his breath as the tires ground their methodical way down to the abandoned cannery, but he didn't breathe deeply again until the van came to a gentle halt.

The moon overhead cast a welcome light over the Stygian darkness; no doubt the reason why his contact had insisted they meet tonight. Charlie hated all this cloak and dagger crap, but under the circumstances, he didn't have much choice.

There were too many people depending on him, and all those damned government regulations and budget cutbacks were forcing him to take drastic measures in order to prevent mass layoffs that would compromise the safety of the plant he ran. This was really the only way to cope—people kept their jobs, he kept his year-end bonus, and nobody got hurt.

Hell, it was practically a public service, the way he saw it. And it was perfectly safe, no matter what anyone said; the containers were tightly sealed and the ocean was huge. It wasn't as though anything one guy did could really affect it. Everything would be fine. As long as he didn't get caught.

Which was why he and his two most trusted guys were the only ones who knew about this little cost-cutting measure. Them and the man they were here to meet, that is.

Charlie peered into the distance, finally hearing the sound he'd been waiting for. The muffled thrum of a powerful engine running at the lowest speed possible barely disturbed the silence of the empty site. A large speedboat, painted a black so deep it blended with the night, eased up next to the dock and slid to a stop so smoothly it barely caused a ripple in the water. An equally dark figure jumped lightly onto the splintered wood dock and had a rope slung loosely around a crooked post before Charlie could even take a step forward.

"You're late," Charlie said in a low growl. There was something about the diver he'd hired that just set his teeth on edge, although he could never put a finger on exactly what it was.

But it hadn't been easy to find someone willing to drag a bunch of unmarked containers down into the Monterey Trench where they would be out of harm's way and safe from discovery. In fact, the guy had actually found him, although how he'd known that Charlie was looking to hire someone, the diver had never quite gotten around to explaining.

Arrogant son of a bitch, and tight-lipped to boot. Of course, for Charlie, the latter was a quality he needed in the person he hired, and outweighed the first, so he just put up with the man.

The new arrival shrugged. "I'm here now. Shall we get these t'ings loaded before the dawn is upon us?" The diver's good looks and charming Irish accent did nothing to conceal the steel edge under his tone. Something in his gut told Charlie that this was a dangerous man. Of course, who else would you hire for illegal dumping?

Charlie's two flunkies did most of the hard work of moving the unmarked canisters from the back of the van onto the dock, but the diver put them all onto the boat himself, swinging each large, unwieldy container effortlessly through the air and setting it down just so. Muscles rippled under the tight black tee shirt he wore, and he never lost his expression of mild amusement.

When they were done, and Charlie had handed him an envelope bulging with cash, the man flashed a grin as bright as the moon up above and jumped lightly back into the boat.

"A pleasure doin' business with you, to be sure," he said. Something cold lurked behind the sparkling eyes, making Charlie long to be back home, tucked safely in his bed.

"Yeah, you too," Charlie said gruffly. "Same time next month?"

The man shrugged. "And why not, then? The money's good and the work is easy." His smile tilted sideways, giving him a sudden predatory look, like a barracuda who'd been masquerading as a tuna. "And like you say, the ocean is large. What harm could come of it?"

His laughter hung over the water long after the boat was gone from view.

BEKA STOOD AT the end of the harbor dock and took a moment to appreciate the view. Not the ocean, although its green-blue surface shone like glass under the early morning sky. Nor was she admiring the orderly row of boats, all preparing to set sail for a day of fishing, their decks swarming with purposeful men, the air filled with shouting and slightly blue with the coarse language they used freely in the company of their own.

No, Beka was taking in the unexpected magnificence and grace on the boat directly in front of her as Marcus Dermott methodically scrubbed the deck and fittings of the *Wily Serpent*. It was obvious that particular boat wasn't heading out to sea this morning; Marcus was the only one to be seen on board, and the bustling activity of the other ships was notably absent on the *Serpent*.

Dressed in only a pair of denim cutoffs, Marcus looked even larger and more imposing than he had the previous day. Muscles formed by hard work rippled across his broad back as he faced away from her, and his large hands moved quickly and easily across the deck's surface. Beka had a momentary flash of what those hands might feel like on her body and felt a blush heat her face. What was it about this man that pulled at her so?

He was attractive, yes, but not in a way that would grab your eye from across a room. It was more that he was somehow so self-contained within his skin—masculine and strong and real in a way that was rare in the world where Beka spent most of her time. No fun-seeking surfer or Renaissance fair reveler, this one. He was clearly a man who'd lived a hard life on his own terms, and he bore the scars to prove it. To Beka's mind, they only added to the attraction.

Of course, the wavy brown hair, flashing hazel eyes, and strong chin didn't hurt either.

Alas, she couldn't stand there all day staring at him. Sooner or later, someone would notice and ask her what the hell she was doing. Besides, she was on a mission. Not one she had a lot of faith that she'd succeed at, but she had to try. Maybe he'd gotten over being mad about the net.

And maybe fish could fly.

Beka walked down to stand next to the boat and cleared her throat loudly. "Good morning," she said in as cheerful a voice as she could muster. "Can I talk to you?"

Marcus straightened up and turned around, dropping his sponge into a bucket of water with a splash. "Oh, for the love of god," he growled. "What are *you* doing here?"

Beka sighed. She'd known this wasn't likely to be easy. "Nice to see you again too," she said. "I came to hire you. Well, the boat. I can explain, if you'll give me five minutes."

Marcus crossed his arms over his lightly furred chest, an expression she couldn't read lurking at the back of his eyes. "You have three," he said. "I have work to do. Thanks to you, I have to mend a net before we can go back out."

Beka had to resist the temptation to snap her fingers and fix the hole in the net herself. It wasn't all *that* large, and she could have persuaded the fibers to grow back into one another in the time it took her to draw another breath. She might be the youngest, newest Baba Yaga in the States, but she was plenty powerful. A dangerous combination, her mentor always said. So Beka had learned to be cautious with her magic. But, oh, she was so tempted to see the look on his face when he went to repair a perfectly good net.

Still, that would raise too many questions. And she had work to do too.

Three minutes. Fine. "I've got a lead on a salvage job," she said, speaking quickly and trying to bend the truth rather than break it. After all, she *was* trying to salvage the Selkies' and Merpeople's home. "And I need to do some diving in the area where you were out fishing. I know that most fishermen tend to have a route they use, so I figured that meant your boat would be the only one that went out to that part of the ocean regularly."

He opened his mouth, a *no* clearly forming on his lips, and she hurriedly added, "I wouldn't interfere with your fishing. You could drop me and a dinghy and come back for me when you were done for the day. You'd hardly even notice me."

A tiny smile tugged at the corner of his mouth. "I doubt it. I can't imagine a circumstance under which you would be anything less than noticeable."

Beka wasn't sure how she was supposed to take that, but his comment had her heart beating faster despite her uncertainty.

She pulled out a bag with some gold coins in it, like the ones she'd given him the day before. "I'd pay you well for the ride out there and back."

The smile disappeared, vanishing behind the cloud of his usual black scowl. Thick brows pulled together as he moved in an effortless leap from the ship to the dock, leaving him suddenly standing only inches away. "Are you insane? You want me to just *drop you* in the ocean?" he asked. "Put that away. It's not happening."

Beka felt his nearness like an electric humming in her blood, and his anger washed over her in a magenta-hued rush of emotion. She returned his glare, with interest. "It's not like I took the gold out and flashed it at you," she muttered. "What the hell are you getting so worked up about?"

"I'm not talking about the gold," Marcus said through clenched teeth, his tone even and measured, as if he were talking to a not-very-bright child. "I'm talking about the fact that you think I would leave you out alone in the middle of the ocean. Diving by yourself is dangerous."

Beka rolled her eyes. Of course, she couldn't tell him why she'd be as safe in the sea as she would be in her own bed, but still, he could have a little faith. And a lot less crappy attitude.

"I dive by myself all the time," she said, matching his tone. "What's more, I am an accomplished surfer, and that can be a lot more dangerous. I assure you, I know what I'm doing. I just need to hitch a ride on a boat to do it, that's all."

"Not a chance in hell," Marcus said. "You're a damned menace. Look at what you did yesterday, getting yourself all tangled in our net trying to save some baby dolphin. You could have been killed!" Suppressed fury made his hands tighten into fists. "I am not going to allow you to go out there and finish the job. Not on my boat. Not on my watch."

"Fine!" Beka couldn't believe the nerve of the guy. Who the hell was he to tell her what she could and couldn't do? "I'll find another ship to take me out. Or I'll rent a motorboat and just take myself." *Ass.*

"The hell you will," he said, in slightly lower tones. "You know perfectly well that a motorboat will just drift away while you're underwater, and no other fisherman is going to leave his territory just to take you diving."

She opened her mouth to speak, and he added, "Besides which, I plan to have a little word with the other captains. I grew up on this harbor, and I know just about everybody around here. Believe me, by the end of the day, there won't be one person willing to have you. So you might as well give up this cockamamy idea and go home. There's no treasure worth risking your life for."

Beka closed her mouth with a snap. She couldn't believe she'd actually been attracted to the man. He was a bossy, stubborn jerk. Counting to ten under her breath, she forced herself to speak calmly.

"You must find it hard to work a boat with that handicap," she said, meeting his steely gaze with one of her own.

"What handicap?" Marcus asked, a puzzled look on his face.

"The stick you've got up your butt," Beka said with a sweet smile. "I imagine it makes bending over kind of difficult." And she swiveled on her heel and marched off down the dock, refusing to look back. If she never saw Marcus Dermott's face again, she'd be a happy, happy woman.

MARCUS WATCHED THE most infuriating woman on the face of the earth stomp away from him and wished he could call her back. There was no point, of course. Even if she didn't hate his guts. He chuckled a little at her "stick-up-the-butt" comment. No one could argue with her nerve, at least, even if her common sense was seriously in question.

He couldn't believe she actually thought he would agree to take her out to the middle of nowhere and just leave her there, much less support her plan to dive without a safety partner. The woman really was crazy. Which was a pity, since he couldn't seem to stop thinking about her. Last night, his dreams had been haunted by images of a beautiful, long-legged blond enchantress who had somehow soothed and aroused him at the same time. Too bad that in person, she just made him livid.

He'd thought for a moment, when he fished her out of

the sea the other day, that the universe had gifted him with some kind of miracle. Not that he believed in miracles. But still, there she was, dripping with salt water, like Aphrodite risen from the waves. Instead, she was turning out to be more of a curse. He could almost hear the universe laughing at him.

First, she'd sabotaged their net—he still hadn't figured out if he bought the idea that she was rescuing a dolphin, or if she really was just one of those crazy activist types as he'd initially thought. Now, she wanted to rent his father's boat to go out on a suicide mission? So not happening. He'd lost enough men during his years in the war. No one else was ever going to die on him; not if he could help it.

His father . . . well, that wasn't under his control, as much as he wished it was. The old man would either beat the cancer or he wouldn't. All Marcus could do was stick around, here in the last place on the planet he wanted to be, and try to keep the stubborn mule from working himself to death while he fought the disease. It would also be good if Marcus could keep himself from giving in to the impulse to strangle his father before the cancer could kill him. That, and maintaining a fishing boat that had suffered from long years of neglect, was enough to have on his plate.

There was no way he was going to allow Beka to risk her life—and the life of everyone around her, since that was the way the flaky ones worked. Most of the time, they didn't kill themselves; instead, it was the innocents around them that died. Like his brother.

Marcus sucked in his breath as the old grief eddied around him like a riptide, all unexpected waves and downward pull. It was one of the reasons he'd stayed away so long. In the desert, he could go days, sometimes weeks, without thinking of the younger brother who had been his shadow from the day he was born until the day he died, lost over the side of this same ill-fated boat when Kyle was only fifteen.

Now that shadow haunted him in all the silent moments, only eclipsed for a brief time by the bright light that Beka brought with her, captured like a rainbow in her sunshine-colored hair, temptress smile, and sparkling blue eyes.

There was no way he would risk that light going dark. Not on his watch. Never again.

FIVE

BEKA WAS SO mad, steam rose out of her damp footprints on the dock until she noticed what she was doing and reined herself in. That was the problem with magic if you were a Baba Yaga; it was a part of you, like the beat of your heart or the flow of blood through your veins. If you weren't careful, it seeped out, spilling over into the mundane world.

Not that most people would notice. Back in the old days, in the Old World, magic was accepted and people knew it when they saw it. These days, folks were more likely to explain it away with logic, or suspect a lurking camera crew and Hollywood illusions. Still, she needed to be more careful.

Her sister Baba, Barbara, laughed at her cautious nature and perpetual worrying. Beka thought Barbara was amazing and wished she could be more like her—tough and decisive, not caring what anyone else thought or believed. Maybe when she'd been a Baba for as long as Barbara had been . . . But probably not. At least not as long as her foster mother's voice drifted like fog through the back of her head, telling her she still wasn't *quite* getting it right.

Like now. She'd made a promise—and not just any

promise, but one with a magical commitment behind it, writ like words carved into stone—and now she had no way to keep it. She couldn't believe she'd failed before she even started.

At the end of the pier, she stopped outside the harbormaster's office to pull herself together, tucking shaky hands into the pockets of her patchwork cotton skirt. Through an open window, she caught the tail end of a heated discussion, two voices raised in head-butting dissent. One of them sounded familiar, with a slight Irish brogue under the bulldog growl.

"I've told you," the voice said. "I'll pay my mooring fees when I've caught something to pay them with. It's not my fault the damned fish aren't showing up where they're supposed to."

"It's not my fault either, Dermott," the other voice said. It was tenor rather than bass, and less filled with ire than the loud Irish rumble, but there was no trace of weakness there either. "Nobody else is catching fish, but they're all paying what they owe. You're behind three months already. I can't just let you keep docking your boat here for free." There was the clear sound of a deep inhalation. "Why don't you ask your son to help you? He just got out of the service, right? He's probably got some money stashed away—nothing much to spend it on over where he was. Get him to pay your mooring fees."

"The hell I will!" This bellow was probably heard halfway down the dock. Beka winced a little, standing just outside.

"It's bad enough the boy has put his life on hold, coming back here to take care of me when I never asked him to. I'm sure as hell not going to take his money too. You'll just have to wait." There was the sound of boots clomping against a wooden floor, and then the slamming of a door.

Beka peeked around the side of the building. Marcus's father stood by the door he'd just crashed shut behind him, leaning against the wall next to it and holding one hand to his chest. His breathing sounded rough and uneven, and his face was white except for the flush of anger riding his sharp cheekbones.

"Are you okay?" Beka asked, stepping around the corner. Behind her back, she made a gesture that pulled a bottle of water out of her fridge on the bus. That trick didn't work when she was in the ocean—too much water could inhibit magic unless you prepared for it in advance— but here on land, it barely took any effort at all. She held the bottle out to the older man. "Here, I haven't even opened this yet. You look like you could use it."

The elder Dermott glared at her from his piercing eagle eyes but took the bottle anyway, gulping down half its contents along with a pill from a container in his pocket. After a few minutes, his color looked better and he had enough breath to thank her grudgingly.

"You're that idiot girl we brought up in the nets yesterday, aren't you?" he said, looking at her more closely. "What the hell are you doing down here? If you came thinking you could sue me, don't bother. There's nothing to win."

Beka suppressed a sigh. She could see where Marcus the younger got his charm and good manners. "Actually," she said, "I came to offer your son a job. Well, both of you, really, since I wanted to hire the boat. But he turned me down flat."

One graying eyebrow rose toward the battered cap perched above it. "Hire the boat? You want to go out fishing?" He looked unconvinced. "Is this one of them Greenie tricks?"

"Not at all." Beka was suddenly struck with an idea. She dug the bag of gold coins out of her pocket and held it out. "I want to hire someone to take me out to that stretch of water so I can go diving on a wreck I heard about. I'm willing to pay."

The old sailor gave her a dubious glance that turned thoughtful when he looked inside the pouch she'd handed him. "Huh. I never heard of no wreck out there." He looked into the sack again, poking at the coins with one gnarled, black-rimmed fingertip, before gazing into her eyes. "You know how to dive, do you, girly?"

Beka laughed. "How do you think I got what's in that bag?" She gave him her most earnest smile, although it mostly seemed to go unnoticed. "I won't get in your way, I promise, and you can still fish while I'm diving."

"Huh." Dermott thought for a moment, bouncing the little bag up and down in one hand. "You'll sign a waiver afore you come on board? Sayin' I'm not responsible if anything happens to you?"

She nodded, trying not to look too eager.

"And if there happens to be something down there, I get ten percent as a bonus," the old man added. "Only fair, seeing as how you couldn't get out there otherwise."

Beka bit back a laugh. She kind of liked the greedy bastard. At least he wasn't pretending to be looking out for her. And it wasn't as though she was expecting to actually bring up anything valuable. "You bet," she said. "Have we got a deal?"

Dermott tossed the bag into his left hand, spat into his right, and held it out for her to shake. "We've got a deal. Although I've got to tell ya, my son ain't gonna be too happy about it."

A grin hovered around her lips, despite her attempts to hold it back. "Consider that *my* bonus," she said. *Mr. Crankypants was going to have a cow.*

KESH DROPPED THE last canister into place in a deep crevasse and swam easily toward the surface, completely unaffected by the depth or the change in pressure. He was a creature of the ocean, and magical to boot, and this had been his home, not too long ago. Now it was the blighted landscape of his revenge—home to no one at all.

He laughed as his sleek head crested the waves, changing instantly from his seal form to that of a handsome, dark-haired Human man. As a man, he slid over the side of the boat as gracefully as he had eeled his way through the tangled gray-green seaweed and jagged brown underwater rock formations of his former kingdom. Kesh was a prince of the Selkie people, equally comfortable above and below the ocean, unlike some of his kind.

He pointed his black speedboat in the direction of land, the first rays of the rising sun glinting off its menacing prow as it sliced through the waves like a weapon, innocuous now that that its deadly cargo had been tucked away to leak its perilous Human poisons into the lifeblood of the sea.

Kesh's striking face reflected brooding thoughts, twisting his attractive features into something more revealing of his own inner landscape, as jagged as the rocks below. The much-gloried eldest son of the King of the Selkies, Kesh had always enjoyed a life of privilege and self-indulgence.

The Selkies, although not immortal, enjoyed long lives. Kesh's father had been king when they'd made the long ocean journey from the coves and inlets of Ireland to these new and welcoming shores. It was only now that Gwrtheyrn was feeling his advancing years and contemplating passing on his crown to one of his offspring.

But not to Kesh. Stormy gray eyes narrowed, remembereing another time and seeing in his mind's eye an ornate and elegant chamber under the sea, instead of the current vista of dawn-lit sky and choppy waves. More garden than throne room, fronds of kelp rose toward the towering ceilings amid sea anemones blooming in hues of crimson, orange, and brilliant iridescent pink. Mother of pearl chairs were scattered around the open space, where courtiers swam or sat or floated in place, their cheerful voices echoing off carved stone walls.

Kesh had stood proudly with his younger brother, Tyrus, and their six sisters, each lovelier than the last. Their black hair and smoky eyes clearly showed their bond to one another and to the King, graying now, and less agile than in his earlier years, but still as powerful as an old bull seal. He sat at ease atop a throne encrusted with the glittering jewels and gold from a hundred sunken ships; symbolic not just of his position, but also of the Selkies' mastery under the sea.

Kesh's sensuous mouth curved upward in a small, mostly hidden smile as his father had—finally, finally, finally—made official his announcement of an heir, set to take over the throne in a year's time. But his amusement had turned to confusion, and then blood-boiling fury, as he heard the name that slid like a tiny, biting fish from between his father's lips. Tyrus. Not Kesh. Tyrus.

There must be some mistake. "Father," he'd said quite reasonably. "I am the eldest son. Surely you mean for me to inherit the kingship. I have been waiting so long. So patiently. I might have killed you years ago as you slept or hunted or dived to the unexplored depths. But I waited instead for this day. Where is my reward for my patience?"

King Gwrtheyrn had gazed at him, a stony expression on his hawk-nosed face, a hint of something that might have been sadness in his deep-set eyes. "I said what I meant to say, as I always do. Your brother shall ascend to the throne, where I know I can depend on him to do his best for our people.

"This title bears with it more than glory, Kesh. It holds in its essence an obligation to the weighty needs of all our people. And nothing about your behavior over the last many, many years has led me to believe that you would put the interests of others before your own."

His father sighed, a gust of sorrow and disappointment that swirled in the water like the ink from a wounded squid. "I am sorry. I know how much you wished for this. But it is not to be."

In a less watery realm, Kesh's ire might have ignited the air. Here, he simply spoke through gritted teeth, trying to ignore the excited muttering of the crowds around him. "But father, I have trained all my life for this role. You yourself taught me all the arts of kingship, that I might someday assume your mantle. I do not understand."

Another sigh, gustier than the last. Gwrtheyrn sat up straight, dropping his acid words into the calm, clear waters that surrounded them. "My son, you know I love you, as I love all my children. But your playboy behavior and callous disregard for your subjects have been the topic of many a discussion between the two of us. Yes, I have endeavored to teach you the ways of leadership, but you only learned the parts you enjoyed—the ways of war, the outward pomp and ceremony.

"Never the true skills needed by a king; wisdom in decision making, planning for the future, care for others, mastery of self. These, too, are part of a ruler's skills, and you chose not to bother with them. You made this choice for yourself long before I came to this painful decision. I have waited many years, hoping you would prove me wrong, that you would mature into a wiser, kinder Selkie. But I grow old in this unforgiving chair, waiting for changes that will clearly never happen." The King stood and the entire court fell silent. Not a breath stirred the crystalline waters.

"It is done," Gwrtheyrn had said. *"Your brother shall inherit the throne. You will bow your head to him, your new sovereign, as you have bowed your head to me. Or you can leave this kingdom and find yourself another home. These are the only choices you have left yourself."* Heavily, his father had sunk back onto the throne, as if all the weight of the deep, deep sea had suddenly rested itself on his broad shoulders.

Kesh remembered glaring at his father, imagining a light of triumph in his brother's eyes, since there would have been triumph in his own, had things been different. His sisters all gazed at the floor, tears like precious pearls dripping down pale, downcast faces. Betrayal sat like ashes in his mouth. A shark's sharp teeth gnawed bitterness into his gut and soul, lodging there in perpetual motion, chewing an unceasing path of anger and sorrow and despair to his very core.

Without a word, he'd turned his back on the people who'd turned their backs on him, vowing never to return. If he could not be a king under the sea, he would make a place for himself on the land. There was power aplenty to be had there, for one who was handsome and charming and as cunning as the treacherous sea.

And if he could not have the kingdom for which he had long waited, no one would.

BEKA SPAT THE regulator out of her mouth as she reached the surface, treading water beside the faded white dinghy while she handed her collection bags up into a pair of waiting hands.

As expected, Marcus had been less than happy about his father's decision to allow Beka to catch a ride out to where she wanted to explore. In the end, he'd only agreed to allow her aboard if she brought a buddy to keep watch as she dived. She figured that was a small enough concession to make, all things considered, and asked Queen Boudicca for the loan of one of her Mermen who was the most familiar with Humans and their ways.

Beka knew Fergus slightly from the beach, where he assumed the guise of a man in order to indulge his un-Merman-like love of surfing. They got along well enough, and he'd been happy to help out, since her mission involved his people. Now, clad in shorts and a tee shirt that said SURFERS DO IT IN WAVES, he peered over the gunwale of the boat with furrowed brows.

"Sun says it's past two," he said. "Your Human friends said they would be back about now. Best you wrap it up for the day, eh?" His shaggy red-brown hair blew into his face, and he pushed it back with one slender hand.

"They're no friends of mine," Beka said, scowling as she allowed him to help her back into the boat. "Or I wouldn't have had to give them a bag of gold coins to bring me out here." *Not to mention arguing for what seemed like an hour with the world's most stubborn man first. Although it had been fun to watch his hazel eyes spark and flash.*

Fergus shrugged. Money meant little to the undersea folk; they mostly traded for what they needed. Gold coins were just one more shiny object in the world below. "Never you worry about that," he said. "I'm sure the Queen will replace them for you, since you were doing her bidding."

"I am *not* doing anyone's bidding," Beka reminded him, shrugging out of her oxygen tank, pulling off her wet suit, and piling them neatly out of the way. "I am doing my job as a Baba Yaga, that is all."

"And how are these bags full of kelp and dead fish going to help you do it, Baba?" he asked, opening one of the airtight sacks and peering inside. "Are you sure you need all these fish? I could use a snack."

Beka smacked his hand away gently. "I don't think you want to be nibbling on those fins," she said as she tucked the samples safely away with the rest of her gear. "They seem to have died from whatever is causing the flora and fauna down in your home to sicken. I'm going to take them, and everything else I gathered, to a lab for examination. I'm hoping they'll be able to tell me what is causing the problem."

Fergus tilted his head and looked at her quizzically out of almond-shaped green eyes. "Cannot you simply do magic to reveal nature's secrets?"

"Could any of your magicians get answers to this malady that way?" She knew the answer to that, of course. It was a resounding NO. "When I am in the water, I can sense the *wrongness* of the area. I can feel the plants and animals crying out in pain. But I can't tell what's causing it." She shook her head. "I've never come across anything like this before."

"I am certain you will figure it out," Fergus said, his lanky body relaxed against the side of the boat. "You are the Baba Yaga."

Beka bit her lip, wishing she had his confidence in her abilities. "I don't know, Fergus. Maybe we should contact the old Baba and ask her to come back and take a look. I know that the Queen of the Otherworld insisted that it was time for Brenna to retire, but with all her experience, she could probably find the answer in half the time."

He surprised her by shaking his head vigorously. "No. Don't do that. You will solve this. You don't need to call that one back." A shadow crossed his eyes, turning their brilliant green to muddy olive.

"You'd rather have me than her?" Beka asked. She couldn't imagine why anyone would prefer an inexperienced, barely competent Baba to one who had been doing the job for hundreds of years. "Why?"

Fergus gazed at the water, a somber expression on his normally cheerful face. "I do not wish to speak badly of the woman who raised you, or insult the Baba; she did her job well, of that there is no question." He hesitated, two careful breaths that spoke more than words. "But I much prefer you, all the same. There was something . . . not quite right about the old Baba, toward the end. Many of us felt it."

Beka could feel her eyebrows climbing in the direction of the blue skies above. "Well, Babas have never been known for their ability to fit in with the other races, Human or mystical, but my foster mother always seemed to me to do it better than most. She was not warm and cozy, exactly, but she took good care of me, long after any other Baba would have simply left me to manage on my own."

Fergus shook his head, shaggy hair flopping into his face. "On the surface, yes, she always appeared benign. Especially for a Baba Yaga. But there was something dark underneath all those layers of long batik skirts and jangling beaded necklaces. Something wrong hiding just out of sight, like the fleeting glimpse of a predator you see out of the corner of your eye, right before it pounces and gnaws on your bones." He gave her a rueful smile. "I know you think I am talking foolishness, but I still ask of you, as one who calls you friend, do not bring back the old Baba."

Beka blinked, pleased that the Merman considered her a friend. She still thought she was out of her depth, and as likely to fail as not, but his faith in her gave off warmth like the sun overhead. As for the other . . . clearly, he was talking nonsense.

"I'll do my best," Beka said. She saw the *Wily Serpent* approaching from the open ocean, a ramrod-straight figure standing in the bow. She could almost see his scowl from here.

"But I'm not sure what I'll do if the lab at the university can't find whatever is poisoning the water. I will keep diving, searching for clues, but honestly, I'm baffled. Everything looks fine, and yet, there is something very, very wrong down there. And the closer I get to your home, the worse the *wrongness* gets."

"I am sure that you will find your way to the answer before long," Fergus said firmly. "You are the Baba Yaga."

Yes, she was. And that was part of the problem. She really wasn't sure she wanted to be.

SIX

"YOU'RE BROODING," CHEWIE said as they sat outside the bus a couple of days later. A glowing quarter moon hung bright in the sky overhead, and cool, salty breezes blew in from the ocean across the highway. A small bonfire burned in the fire pit before them, its sparks spitting defiance at the stars.

Despite the beauty and peace of the night, Beka was definitely in a funk.

"I'm not brooding," she said, poking listlessly at a log with a pointed stick.

The giant Newfoundland huffed, his breath igniting the stick and sending the flames roaring upward for a moment. "You are brooding," he said, plopping onto the ground by her camp chair with a thud that rattled the entire bluff. "And it is getting on my nerves. You should make s'mores. That would cheer you up."

Beka dropped the stick rapidly into the fire. "S'mores would cheer *you* up. And I'm not brooding. I'm just thinking, that's all."

"About that hunky fisherman?" Chewie said, perking his ears up.

She rolled her eyes. *Yes.* "No, not about the hunky fisherman. Well, at least not mostly." *Although it did seem ridiculously difficult to stop thinking about him. Three days on that damned boat together, and he not only tortured her during the day, but haunted her dreams as well. It hardly seemed fair.*

"To be honest, Chewie, I'm not sure I can do all this."

"Do what?" the dragon-in-disguise asked, baffled. "Sit under the stars and drink chardonnay?"

Beka sighed. "No, I mean *this*." She waved her hand around, indicating the bus and everything it represented. "Maybe I'm not cut out to be a Baba Yaga after all."

Chewie sat up so suddenly a roosting flock of birds was startled out of a nearby tree. Their indignant caws rained down like fall leaves as they flew away.

"What the hell are you talking about?" he said, staring at her. "You're the Baba Yaga—there is no 'cut out for' or 'not cut out for.' Brenna chose you and trained you, and here you are." Concern filled his soulful brown eyes. "Maybe you just need to have a little drink of the Water of Life and Death. It sounds like you need a boost."

Beka scuffed the dirt with one bare toe. "Hasn't anyone ever chosen wrong?" she asked. "In all the history of the Baba Yagas, did none of them ever pick the wrong girl to train as her successor? Because I have to tell you, Chewie, I'm pretty sure that Brenna made a mistake when she chose me. I'm just not good enough."

"I don't ever remember hearing of such a thing," Chewie said, his tone thoughtful. "There have been some pretty strange Babas through the years, but hell, strange is practically a part of the job description. And Brenna clearly thought you were good enough, or she wouldn't have left you in charge of a third of this benighted country."

"Ha," Beka said, shaking her head. "Brenna stayed around to keep training me a lot longer than most Babas do. Barbara told me that her mentor sent her out on her own when she was nineteen. I was almost twenty-eight before Brenna left, and even then, the Queen of the Otherworld had to order her to retire, or she'd still be here."

Chewie cocked his head, looking at her thoughtfully. "Has it ever occurred to you that Brenna's reluctance to leave had more to do with her than it did you and your skills or lack thereof? After all, even she admitted that you were an extremely powerful witch."

"Powerful, yes," Beka said, ruefully. "Careful and wise, not so much."

The dog huffed again, this time without the pyrotechnics. "Man, you sink one submarine and you spend the next ten years second-guessing yourself. I think Brenna was too hard on you. And now that she's not here, you've taken over the job. Cut yourself a little slack, will you?"

Beka knotted her hands together in her lap, looking down at them instead of at her companion. "I'm thinking of cutting myself a lot of slack, actually, Chewie. Like, as in giving it up altogether."

Chewie's jaw fell open. "What? You can't just quit being a Baba Yaga!"

"I can, actually," Beka said quietly. "The change isn't final until a Baba has been drinking the Water of Life and Death for twenty-five years. That won't be until my thirtieth birthday, in a couple of months. If I stop using it now, my extra powers will eventually wane and I'll go back to aging at a normal rate. I'd be a regular Human again."

"Why the hell would you want to be that?" Chewie bellowed. "You are so much more than that now. And people are depending on you. The world needs Babas, and there are too few of them as it is."

"Lots of reasons," Beka said. She tried to concentrate on the sound of the waves, which always soothed her, but tonight, they seemed to have lost their magic. "I don't feel like I'm doing a very good job at being a Baba. I haven't been able to make any headway in solving the Selkies' and

Merpeople's problem. And once you are permanently a Baba . . . well, you know, Babas can't have children of their own. Sometimes I think I might want that."

Chewie rested his massive head on her thigh. "You've only been working on the water issue for a few days; it is too soon to say you have failed. Besides, do you really want to give up *magic*?"

She didn't say anything. If she knew the answer to that, she would have made this decision long ago.

He gave a bone-scented sigh and rubbed his jowl affectionately against her leg. "I can't tell you what to do, Beka. I can just tell you that I would be very sorry if you weren't my Baba. I've kind of gotten used to having you around."

Beka blinked back unexpected emotion. "Thanks, Chewie. That's really sweet."

He was quiet for a moment, and then said, "You know what's really sweet? S'mores, that's what." He gazed up at her with an innocent expression. "Just sayin'."

PEWTER-EDGED CLOUDS SCUDDED across a sky that bled crimson, making the rising sun look sickly and dull. Restless waves lashed the barnacled hull of the boat as Marcus stood guard over the port side where it was tied up to the dock, ignoring the spitting rain with the practice of someone who'd spent most of his youth on the sea.

His breath caught in his throat when he saw Beka walking toward him. Her long blond hair was pulled back in a practical braid, and her gear was slung over one shoulder; she looked cool, and competent, and not at all like the flaky hippie chick he'd snared in his nets less than a week before. He had to remind himself that underneath the current illusion there still lurked the girl who lived in a painted bus and made a living selling jewelry to people dressed as knights and wenches. It wasn't fair that even in the sullen light of an overcast morning, she still shone like the sun.

At her heels, Marcus saw an even less welcome sight—the

ever-cheerful Fergus, trotting along behind her with his own equipment, grinning through the drizzle at something she'd just said. Marcus wasn't an idiot; he recognized the stupidity of resenting the very person he himself had insisted she have join her. But apparently having Beka around did something to sabotage the rational part of his brain, because there was no denying that every time he saw her with Fergus, his fingers twitched just the slightest bit with the urge to shove the weedy redhead into the water.

Marcus wasn't even sure they were a couple. He just knew that the two of them joked and laughed together in a way that was diametrically opposed to the constant arguments and head-butting standoffs that seemed to be the only way she and Marcus communicated. And he knew that it bothered him, although he couldn't for the life of him figure out why. It wasn't as though he was at all interested in her. She lived to make his day a misery, and he couldn't wait to be done with her.

Then she was, standing in front of him, bare feet planted firmly on the rough wood dock, a quizzical look on her face.

"I wasn't expecting a welcoming committee," she said. "Good morning."

Marcus shook his head. "It's not, actually, in case you hadn't noticed. The weather is miserable, and likely to get worse. Not a good day to be out on the water."

Beka just stared at him with blue eyes as bright as the sky should have been. "So you're not going out today?"

He snorted. "Oh, we're going out, all right. It would take more than the possibility of a bad blow to get my father to give up a day of fishing." He muttered under his breath, "Stubborn old jackass." The man was going to get them all killed. You'd think he'd learn. Hell, you'd think *Marcus* would learn.

"Just because my da is insane doesn't mean we all have to be. It's not going to be safe to dive; I suggest you skip it today." He pointed down the dock the way she and Fergus had just come. "Why don't you go home and string some beads or something. Your imaginary treasure will wait for you."

Beka narrowed her eyes, and Fergus stifled a laugh, turning it into an unconvincing cough.

"I don't think so," she said in an unruffled tone. "If it is safe enough for you to go out, then it is safe enough for me. The water's much calmer under the surface anyway."

Marcus gritted his teeth. Why did the woman always have to be so difficult when he was just trying to keep her safe? "Maybe it will be calmer for you, but what about poor Fergus here? He'll be stuck in a tiny dinghy with no place to hide from the storm, if it comes. Surely you don't want to put him in danger."

To his surprise, Fergus gave a loud, barking laugh, sounding for all the world like one of the seals who often greeted the boat on its way out of the harbor. "Oh, don't worry about me, lad. I'm not afraid of getting a little wet."

Beka snickered, although Marcus didn't see anything funny about the two of them risking their lives for some sunken treasure that almost certainly didn't exist.

Fine. He'd tried being reasonable. Now he was just going to be himself. He hadn't led dozens of men across a war-torn country just to be thwarted by a skinny blond surfer girl in cutoffs and a curve-hugging red tee shirt.

"Forget it," he said, crossing his arms over his chest and blocking their way onto the ship. "You're not going out with us today and that's final."

"What's final?" his da asked, appearing over his shoulder like the ghost of fishing trips past. The older man's face was paler than ever, with a pasty green undertone that owed more to chemotherapy than it did to the choppy water of the harbor. "What the hell is the holdup? We were due to cast off five minutes ago." Bushy white brows waggled aggressively in Beka's direction. "I told you, girl. You slow us down, you can't come."

Beka beamed at the old curmudgeon, as unimpressed by his bluster as always. "Hey, don't blame me, Mr. Dermott. I got here right on time."

She tilted her head in Marcus's direction. "Your son seems to think he gets to say who does and doesn't get to ride on your boat." She gave Marcus a sly look out of the corner of her eye. "Is that true?"

Oh, nicely played. Dirty pool, but nicely played. Marcus could feel the muscles in his neck tighten as the situation slid out of his control.

"No, he damned well does *not* get to say who comes on my boat," Marcus Senior growled. "Get the hell out of the way and let the girl come aboard, Mark-boy. We're burning daylight."

Marcus glanced dubiously at the sky, where any kind of light was in short supply, but he knew when he was beaten. "Fine," he muttered, putting out a hand for Beka's gear. "But if we get to the spot where you want to dive and I don't think it's safe, you're staying on the goddamn boat."

Beka shrugged tanned shoulders. "We'll see." She looked past him to where Chico and Kenny were standing, watching the show. "If it's too rough to dive, Fergus and I will just help around the ship." She cast Kenny a particularly sunny smile, and the poor kid almost fell overboard. "I'm a pretty quick study; you guys just point to where you need me, tell me what to do, and I'll do it."

Marcus watched in amazement as Chico's weathered face split into a grin. Kenny he understood; the kid was young, and Beka looked like a mythic goddess risen from the sea. But Chico was a grandfather, slow moving and even tempered. He sent most of his wages to his family back in Mexico, and Marcus had never seen him even so much as glance at any of the half-naked women who decorated the beaches and piers of Santa Carmelita. But one smile from Beka and the ugly old bandito just twirled his long mustache and cleared off a place for her to put her gear as they motored slowly out of port.

If he didn't know better, he'd say she'd cast a spell on all of them—his crabby father, the taciturn old Hispanic, and the starry-eyed young twerp currently gaping at her with a face like a guppy. Thank god Marcus was immune, or they'd all be in a world of trouble.

TWO HOURS OUT of port, the seas were rougher, the skies were darker, and the rain had turned from drizzle to deluge. Marcus tried one more time to convince his father to turn around and take them back in, but the stubborn old man had only said, "You catch more fish in bad weather than good, boyo," and went off to sit in front of the sonar screen, glaring at it grimly as it continued to reflect an empty ocean. At least that way he was in the cabin, out of the chilly rain, Marcus thought, and went to deal with his other problem.

Surprisingly, Beka hadn't put up much of a fight when they'd reached her proposed dive site and Marcus had insisted that the water was too wild for her to go in. She'd just raised an eyebrow at Fergus, who had taken a long, hard look over the side and slowly shaken his head.

"Well, crap," she'd said with a shrug. "At least I tried."

Marcus tried not to be put out that she'd paid more attention to one headshake from her pal Fergus than to a whole slew of reasonable arguments from him. And then he'd tried not to be even more annoyed by the way she and Fergus had both pitched in as promised, helping to batten down everything on deck and prepare the nets in case a school of fish miraculously appeared out of the wind and mists. As with her diving, her movements were controlled and efficient, and she seemed to have no trouble keeping her footing on the slippery, wave-swept deck.

She and Fergus finished up the last of the tasks he'd given them and came over to join Marcus in the bow of the boat. He caught another whiff of strawberries and sunlight, although it should have been impossible to smell anything but sea and salt and fish guts. As always, it made his heart race, and he had to take a deep breath of briny air to clear his head.

Fergus gave him a piercing look accompanied by a wry smile, and then gazed out over the churning ocean. "Does your father really think we will find fish out in this tempest?"

Marcus sighed. "I don't know if he believes it, or if he is just too stubborn to give up. Anyone with any sense either didn't go out today or went back early, so if we catch anything, we'll get prime dollar for it. I suspect he needs the money." He eyed Beka, who wore a slightly guilty expression. "Either way, the fish haven't been running in their usual patterns or showing up in the places they would normally be at this time of year, so I don't know why he thinks bad weather is going to change anything."

Under his red hair, slicked back with rain until it looked much darker than usual and currently dripping down the back of his neck, Fergus's face was thoughtful as he gazed at the watery surface before them.

"There is truth in that, undeniably," he said in the slightly formal way he had of speaking. Marcus thought it sounded like he came from some foreign country, except he didn't have an accent. "We have noticed that as well. The fish are not where they are supposed to be, and they are turning up in the oddest spots instead."

"We?" Marcus asked, a little suspicious. "I thought you said you didn't fish much." *Could the man be spying out his father's fishing routes for some rival?*

Beka and Fergus exchanged wordless glances; Fergus blinked wetness out of his eyes with absurdly long lashes. "Er, us divers, I mean."

Uh-huh.

Beka stirred restlessly beside him, distracting in her nearness. "If I can find us some fish, do you think your father will agree to go back in?"

Marcus snorted. "Sure. Why, do you have some hidden up your sleeve?"

Fergus rolled his eyes, gesturing at Beka's skimpy attire. "And where in that ridiculous getup do you think she could hide so much as a pea?"

Beka smacked his arm playfully, causing an electric

buzz to zing through Marcus's chest for a moment. "Not exactly," she said.

"There doesn't seem to be much point to the question, then, does there?" He glowered at Beka, tired of the rain, the boat, and the memories that always seemed to haunt him on days like this. If he had a magic wand, he'd wave it and fill the hold with fish so he could go sit on the shore with a cold beer and try to forget.

Surprisingly, Fergus's normally merry face suddenly took on a look of alarm. "What are you thinking of, Baba?"

"Baba?" Marcus said, looking from one to the other. "I thought your name was Beka."

"It's kind of a nickname," she said, kicking Fergus lightly with one bare foot. "We don't usually use it in public."

Well, that answered that question, didn't it? Not that he cared.

Fergus cleared his throat. "So, *Beka*, how exactly did you plan to find these elusive fish?" He looked pointedly at Marcus, who got the curious feeling that there was some subtle communication going on that he was missing.

Beka's expression became serious, too, and she turned toward the open ocean as she spoke, so the wind nearly snatched her words away.

"I'm going to ask someone who knows, of course," she said, and leaned dangerously far over the bow.

SEVEN

BEKA GAVE A piercing whistle that she knew would travel a long way over the open water. At the same time, she added a silent magical call and sent it out in all directions. A few minutes later, she got an answer, as a pair of gray dorsal fins cutting their way through the equally gray waves headed rapidly in their direction.

She heard a low chuckle from her left and a gasp of surprise from her right but ignored them both to pay attention to the two dolphins now keeping pace with the slowly moving ship. But she'd have to get closer if she was going to get any useful information. Marcus was going to have a fit.

"I know what I'm doing," she said, and before he could stop her, she grabbed one of the ropes they used to tie on to the dock and flung it over the side. She clambered down it, ignoring the splintery fibers that gnawed at her fingers, and the cold spray from the turbulent sea. Above her head, she caught a brief glimpse of Fergus, holding Marcus back when he would have climbed down after her. *Good. She was already pushing the limits anyway. No point in having him discover she spoke fluent Dolphin.*

"*Baba! Baba!*" the dolphins chortled joyously, squirting water through their blowholes to add to the already raucous ocean spray that dampened Beka's face and clothes.

"Hello, my friends," Beka responded, approximating the mammals' whistles and clicks the best she could. "I am looking for some fish. Do you know where I can find some fish?"

A few minutes later, she climbed back over the bow of the boat, her arms aching from hanging on to the rope. Rough hands hauled her the rest of the way onto the deck and set her down with a thud that rattled her teeth.

"Are you out of your damned mind?" Marcus's face was white and his body was as rigid as stone. "Are you trying to get yourself killed? What the *hell* were you thinking, climbing over the side of a moving boat in the middle of a storm?"

Before she could answer, he swung around and stalked away from her, barely suppressed fury vibrating from his aura like a Human manifestation of the squall that raged around them.

"I was fine," she muttered to the air. "Jeez."

Chico detached himself from the shadow of the cabin, where he'd apparently been watching the entire time. Fergus nodded at him in greeting. Beka gave him a small, tight smile, still feeling the smart from Marcus's scolding.

"He was just worried about you, *senorita*," Chico said, patting her on the arm. "You should not take his yelling so personal, eh? He has his reasons."

"What kind of reasons could justify him screaming at me like that?" Beka fumed. "I was perfectly safe."

Chico shrugged. "Maybe you were, maybe you weren't. What you did, perhaps it was a little foolhardy. Boats can be dangerous places."

Fergus slung one arm companionably around her shoulders, lending her some much-needed warmth. "You have to remember, Ba—Beka, not everyone knows how tough you are." He smiled to take the sting out of his words.

"You frightened him," Chico said in his soft, quiet voice. "That is why he shouted at you."

He looked around to make sure Marcus was out of earshot. "When he was seventeen, his younger brother died in a storm much like this one, swept over the side of this very boat. It was the three of them and me, and some new *idiota* his father had hired because no one else wanted to work for such a difficult man. The boy, Kyle, was just fifteen. He loved the sea, and working on the *Wily Serpent*, and most of all, he worshiped his *hermano*. Followed Marcus around like a puppy, that one."

Beka tried to envision Marcus as a boy and failed. "What happened?"

Chico gave a classic Latino shrug. "The new one, *el estupido*, he pull on the net at the wrong time. The boy, he fell in the water and got tangled up with the net. By the time we pulled him out, there was nothing anyone could do. The boy was *muerto*, yes? So you see, I think, why it was not so good for you to take such a chance as you did, *seniorita*." He patted her on the shoulder again and walked away.

"Well, crap," Beka said. "I screwed up again." She hadn't thought about how it might look to Marcus; just jumped right in because she'd thought she'd figured out how to solve their problem. And ended up creating an even bigger one. Brenna was right; she was always leaping first and then thinking things through afterward.

Fergus hugged her, tapping his pointy chin on the top of her head before letting her go. "You didn't know about his brother, Baba. It was not as though you tried to upset him on purpose."

"Yeah. Try telling him that." Beka blinked back tears that vanished into the company of their raindrop brethren. She sighed. "Well, I suppose it would be foolish to waste the information, especially since Marcus will probably never let me on the boat again."

She ducked around the cabin and stuck her head inside. Marcus Senior was slumped down in his seat, but he straightened up when she knocked on the open door and came in.

"What do you want?" he asked. "You can't come hang out in here just because it's getting a little wet out there."

Beka ignored that, since he clearly knew that she'd been out in the rain working with the men all this time. She cut to the chase. "I can tell you where the fish are," she said. "If you're tired of staring at that empty screen."

A little color came into the old fisherman's face, but he looked unconvinced. "How could you possibly know where the fish are, when even I can't find them?" He scowled at her.

"A dolphin told me."

Marcus Senior's mouth dropped open, revealing an uneven set of tobacco-stained teeth. "This is no time for jokes, missy."

Beka stared at him, refusing to look away. "No joke. I promise you, I really do know where the fish are. Look at it this way—what do you have to lose by going where I tell you to? It's not like there are any fish here." She pointed at the blank radar screen.

"This is crazy," the old man said, but he tapped the edge of the wheel with his fingers anyway. "So, where did the *dolphin* tell you to go?"

WITH MARCUS AND the other two men wrestling the haul of fish into the *Serpent*'s hold and his father gleefully piloting the ship back toward shore, Beka and Fergus met at the starboard side, away from all the action. The storm had, if anything, picked up in intensity, and the small vessel wallowed in the choppy seas, seeming to make barely any headway as it headed for home.

"That was risky," Fergus observed in a mild tone. "You usually work so hard to maintain the illusion of normality; I cannot believe you would take the chance of speaking to dolphins when anyone could see."

Beka shrugged, so wet she thought she might turn into a Merperson herself if they didn't get back to land soon. "You know Humans; they'll find a rational explanation for anything they can't readily understand. And there are plenty of stories of sailors who are helped by dolphins." She sighed. "I know I probably shouldn't have done it, but I didn't like the way Mr. Dermott was looking, and he wasn't going to take us in until he'd caught some fish or the sun fell into the ocean."

Fergus was silent for a moment, looking out at the water through knowing eyes. "Baba, I do not like this storm. There is something . . . uncanny . . . about it."

She bit her lip. She would have liked to have disagreed with the Merman, but she'd been thinking the exact same thing herself.

"It does have a malicious feel to it, doesn't it?" she said, peering out across the open seas as if she could see through the roiling clouds and livid waves to whatever—or whoever—had caused them. "But who could create such a storm, and why would they do it?"

The faintest trace of webbing was visible between Fergus's fingers as he pushed sopping hair back from his forehead. "It seems to have worsened since this morning, and no one else is mad enough to be out. Perhaps it is aimed at this boat, or someone on it." He smiled slyly at her. "A Baba Yaga could make such a tempest."

"I'd hardly try to sink the ship while I was on it," Beka said. "Although if Marcus was out by himself and I was onshore, I could see why you might be suspicious." A tiny laugh slipped through tense lips. "So who besides me could do it? As far as I know, there are no other Babas anywhere around, so that means someone else supernatural."

Fergus looked uncharacteristically grim. "The Queen of the Otherworld could do it without dropping a stitch of her knitting."

"Yes, but why would she?" Beka asked, trying to envision the ethereally beautiful and dangerously unpredictable High Queen of the Otherworld doing anything as mundane as playing with yarn. "As far as I know, I haven't done anything to upset her, and these Humans have nothing to do with her."

"Well," her companion said thoughtfully, "my own

Queen could do it, or the King of the Selkies, or a few of the more powerful magicians of our kingdoms. But I cannot imagine what reasons any of those would have to send such a deluge either."

A particularly assertive wave curled itself over the side and lashed at them with bitterly cold fingers. The old boat rocked unhappily, its timbers creaking. Beka shivered.

"That's it," she said. "I'm going to have to do something about this, or we're never going to make it back to the shore." Apprehension chilled her even further; weather magic wasn't her strongest suit. Visions of a silver submarine, slowly tumbling to the ocean floor, threatened to weaken her resolve.

"Thank Manannán," Fergus said with a heartfelt sigh. "I thought you would never offer."

Beka gave a shaky laugh. "What are you worried about? You can always jump overboard and return to your natural shape."

He shook his head violently. "And explain to my Queen that I let the Baba Yaga drown? No, thank you very much. You can take care of a little squall like this; I have seen you surf higher waves without effort or fear."

She snorted, feeling inexplicably buoyed by his unshakable faith in her abilities. "Okay, okay." She peered around the deck; it looked as though Marcus's father was still in the cabin, and the others were occupied with their fish-wrangling duties. "Why don't you go keep an eye out, and make sure no one comes over here while I'm doing my thing?"

Fergus nodded, and walked toward the stern, leaving Beka to gaze out over the pewter-colored sea. She stiffened her spine and reminded herself that water was her element. And she was a Baba Yaga, dammit. The natural world was hers to command. Hopefully there were no submarines down there anywhere . . .

She closed her eyes, ignoring for a moment the sway of the deck and the bite of the spray. Throwing her arms up in the air, she pulled power from her core, visualizing it glowing yellow like the unseen sun and sending it dancing out amid the pelting raindrops. Farther and farther, her magic pulsed out from the boat in every direction—out and up and down, calming the wind, soothing the ocean, singing a lullaby of comfort to the angry clouds above.

A whistling babble of dolphin voices prompted her to open her eyes again. Next to the boat, a pod of about a dozen lithe gray bodies frolicked in a sedate sea, the blue-green surface reflecting the sunlight as it broke through the dispersing clouds. Beka let out a sigh almost as gusty as the vanishing winds. She'd done it!

"Wow," said a voice behind her, and she spun around to see Marcus coming around the curve of the boat, Fergus at his heels. The Merman looked relieved when he saw Beka leaning casually against the side. Probably because he couldn't see her shaky knees.

"I can't believe how fast that storm blew over," Marcus continued, scanning the horizon with one hand over his eyes. Even soaking wet and covered with fish scales, Beka thought he was the handsomest man she'd ever seen. *You're an idiot, Beka Yancy. He can't stand you, you can't stand him, and yet you can't stop mooning over him. Get a grip.* She braced herself for him to start yelling at her again.

But it didn't happen.

Instead, he took a deep breath and said, "I owe you an apology."

Beka nearly fell over. "What?" she said. Maybe quieting the storm had done something to damage her ears.

Marcus gritted his teeth. "You heard me. I'm sorry for yelling at you before." He paused, probably trying not to do it again. "You startled me, climbing over the side like that. I was, well, I was worried about you. And when I'm upset, I yell."

He nodded his head in Fergus's direction. "Your boyfriend here reminded me that you are an experienced diver and surfer, and you wouldn't have done something like that if you hadn't been sure you could do it safely. I still don't understand how dolphins could possibly have told you where we could find fish. It sounds like something out of the ridiculous stories my da used to tell us when we were kids. But since we've got a hold full of fish, I can't exactly argue with the results." He shrugged, massive shoulders moving up and down like a mountain during an earthquake. "So I'm sorry, and thank you. I still think you're a crazy woman, but I shouldn't have lost my temper."

Beka blinked. "That's one of the worst apologies I've ever heard, but I'll accept it." She laughed and added, "And Fergus isn't my boyfriend; he's just a surfing buddy who offered to lend a hand."

An unreadable expression crossed Marcus's craggy face, and he opened his mouth to say something, but he was interrupted by Kenny, who appeared from the front of the boat, looking alarmed. His waterlogged tee shirt clung to his skinny chest, the beer logo on the front slowly bleeding red dye into the white cotton expanse behind it.

"Marcus! Marcus!" Kenny skidded to a stop in front of the larger man. "Come quick! Your father collapsed—I'm not sure he's breathing."

EIGHT

MARCUS SIPPED AT the cup of insipid hospital coffee and resisted the temptation to get up and pace around the drab, almost empty cafeteria. Its beige walls, beige tables, and beige food were getting on his nerves.

His father was still in the emergency room, being treated for exhaustion and dehydration, but otherwise fine. They'd both had to suffer through a lecture on chemotherapy patients not overdoing things from a resident who looked about sixteen, and then Marcus's father had unceremoniously kicked him out of the treatment room.

"There's no need for you to sit around and watch fluids drip into my arm," Marcus Senior had said in his usual tactful manner. "Go down to the cafeteria and ogle a nurse or something. You're getting on my nerves."

Marcus knew that it was hard for his father to appear weak in front of him, but that didn't make any of this easier to take. The truth was, he didn't know why he was here at all, putting up with his old man's bad temper and lousy attitude again after all these years. It wasn't as though they liked each other. Hell, they hadn't exchanged one word since Marcus ran away to join the Marines the day he turned eighteen. Until the day he'd gotten that call from his father's doctor, Marcus hadn't even been sure that his da was still alive. Or if he cared, one way or the other.

And yet, here he was, sticking to the old man like a burr under a horse's saddle; trying to make sure he made it to his chemo appointments and followed the doctor's instructions. Not that anyone short of God Almighty could have gotten Marcus Senior to rest and take it easy. It was like trying to make a shark sit up and beg for treats.

Much to his dismay, it turned out that Marcus cared after all. Even though seeing the old man brought back all the anger and grief. Even though they didn't get along, no matter how hard he tried to keep the peace. Somewhere in his heart of hearts, it seemed that he wanted a relationship with his father after all. Hell of a time to figure that out.

Marcus scrubbed at gritty eyes with the heels of his hands. They'd been up and out at five in the morning, and he hadn't slept well the night before. Or the night before that. It was ironic that he'd slept just fine in the middle of a war zone, but ever since he'd gotten home, it seemed like every little noise had him wide awake and twitching at nothing. And sometimes his nightmares made it seem like he was right back in the midst of it all. It didn't help that he and his da got on each other's nerves so much, he'd taken to spending half his nights bunking on the boat, which wasn't exactly built for comfort.

Still, it was only temporary. Either his father would get better and Marcus could leave and get on with his life, or the cancer would beat the old man when nothing else could, and Marcus would leave and get on with his life. Either way—another six months or a year, max, and he was out of here. And not a moment too soon.

"Marcus!" a tenor voice said happily, jarring him out of his funk. "What are you doing here?"

He looked up to see a too-thin boy with a baseball cap perched at a jaunty angle over his bald head and an ashy undertone to his dark skin. Despite his obvious ill health, the youth radiated enthusiasm and goodwill. Tito was a frequent visitor to the chemotherapy unit; at twelve, he was battling leukemia with a grace that made Marcus like him from the first moment they'd met. He always took the time to talk to the boy when they were in the waiting room at the same time.

"Hey, Tito, good to see you," Marcus said. "I hope you're not here for the coffee. That stuff will stunt your growth, you know."

Tito chuckled, sliding into one of the empty chairs at the table and waving his bottle of water as evidence to the contrary. "No way, man. I had to come get my levels tested before my next session, and my mom wanted to grab something to eat while we were here." The boy lowered his voice. "She pulled another double shift at the plant, and I don't think she remembered to pack enough lunch for both shifts."

Marcus had met Tito's mother, too, of course. Candace Philips was a single mom who tried hard to balance spending time with her sick son with working extra hours at the town's last remaining fish processing plant to help pay for his treatments. She was also unrelentingly cordial to Marcus's father, no matter how crabby and rude the old man was.

"Look, Mom," Tito said as his mother walked over to the table, a half-empty tray in her hands. A limp tuna sandwich and an apple barely made a dent in its faded blue plastic expanse. "Marcus is here!"

"Mr. Dermott," Candace corrected him, and mustered a tired smile. "Hi there."

"Hi yourself," Marcus answered, getting up to pull out a chair for her. "And Marcus is fine; Mr. Dermott is my father."

Candace sat as though her legs might not hold her for another moment, eyeing her dinner with a notable lack of enthusiasm. Marcus didn't blame her.

She looked around the room. "Is your father here?"

"Emergency room," Marcus said shortly, then held up a hand when she looked alarmed. "He's fine. We were out in a storm and he pushed a little too hard. They're pumping him up with fluids and balancing his electrolytes, and then he gets to go home."

"You were out in the boat in that storm?" Tito's eyes looked even bigger in his gaunt face. "Wow. That must have been something." He turned to his mother. "You know, Marcus promised to take me out fishing sometime. On his dad's boat. That would be so cool."

Marcus smothered a grin at the boy's enthusiasm. It had been a long time since he was that excited about going out on the water, but he could remember what it felt like as a boy. There was something magical about being out on the ocean.

"I'm sure he didn't mean it as a promise, Tito," Candace said, with the tone of someone who had been let down one too many times. Marcus didn't know what the story with the boy's father was; just that he had never heard one mentioned.

Tito's face fell. "Oh, sure. I didn't mean to be pushy or anything."

Marcus couldn't stand the look of disappointment. "Hey, I have an idea," he said.

The other two looked at him, one with blank exhaustion, the other with budding excitement.

"What?" Tito asked.

"Well, if your levels check out okay, and your mom says it is all right, what about coming out in the boat with me tomorrow?" Marcus had no idea what had possessed him to offer. Since he'd gotten back, he'd studiously avoided emotional attachments of any kind. There was too much collateral damage when you got close to people. But this wasn't a war zone, and Tito was just a sick kid.

"Really?" Tito said, a wide grin showing off a mouthful of white teeth. His mother looked torn between hope and fear.

"Sure, why not?" Marcus said recklessly. "The doctors told my father he had to take a day to rest before he could go back to work, and I've got this woman who is paying us to bring her out to a dive site, so I have to take the boat out anyway. She can only dive for a couple of hours, so we

wouldn't be out that long. You wouldn't get too overtired."
Marcus found himself looking at Tito's mother as eagerly
as the boy was.

Candace tried to appear stern, but an indulgent smile
played around the corners of her chapped lips. "*If* his levels
are good, and *if* you don't keep him out too long, I suppose
it is okay," she said. Gratitude shone out of shadow-haunted
brown eyes. "You're sure it is no trouble? I have to work
most of the day, but I can drop him off at the dock on my
way in and then he can go to my mom's house afterward."

Marcus high-fived Tito over the top of the table, trying
not to notice how thin the boy's hands were. "No trouble at
all, ma'am. I hope you like fish, because we're going to do
our best to catch you a few for dinner."

"That would be great," she said. "We used to be able to
bring home a fish here and there from work, but since the
catches lately have been so small, there simply isn't anything extra."

"My father has been saying this is the worst year he can
ever remember, and the other guys all pretty much agree."

Candace shook her head, looking grim. "It's bad, all
right. There are so few fish being brought in, they're talking about shutting down the plant. There's some guy who
has been bugging the owners to sell; he wants to turn the
space into luxury waterfront condos or something." Her
full lips pressed together. "The owners are third gener-
ation. They don't want to lose the place. They know the
locals need the jobs. But they may not have any choice if
the fish don't start running again soon."

She gave a sideways glance toward her son, blinking away
tears before the boy could see them. "I don't know what I'll
do if I lose that job. We need the health insurance to pay for
Tito's treatments. As it is, I'm barely covering the copays."

Marcus wished there was something he could do. He'd
heard stories from the other fishermen about how tough
things had been—for years, really, but even worse now.
Men like his father were having to go farther and farther
away to catch fish, sometimes being away from home for

days as they competed with fishermen farther up the coast for a dwindling supply of fish. But if the plant closed, that would be a disaster for everyone.

Still, if there was one thing he'd learned in the service, it was that there was no point in fretting about the things you had no control over. As his old sarge used to say, "Figure out what you *can* do, then f-ing do it!"

So Marcus gave Tito his biggest grin and said, "I guess we're going to have to find us some fish, isn't that right?" And he was going to do it, too, even if he had to beg Beka to talk to her damned dolphins again. He'd never live it down, but it would be worth it to see a smile on Tito's and his mom's faces.

BEKA WAS GLAD to hear that Marcus's father was okay, and just as happy to discover that the *Wily Serpent* wasn't going to head out to sea until the very reasonable hour of ten o'clock. That meant she could actually get in a morning of surfing, which she'd been pining for. It wasn't as though she wasn't spending every day in the ocean; hell, during yesterday's storm she thought she might have absorbed half of it through her skin. But that wasn't the same thing as catching a wave and riding it halfway up to the sky.

Something about challenging the wild, untamed foamy sea made her feel completely alive, and for just a while, let her stop worrying about who and what she was, and just *be*.

She was so eager to breach the blue-green depths, she must not have been watching where she was going as she moved purposefully toward the surf. Another body slammed into hers, two boards tumbling down to batter them both. A gallant hand reached down to help her to her feet, and she found herself gazing into the face of a god.

Or maybe a movie star. It was California, after all, and anyone that good-looking was likely to be famous, or on his way to being so. He reminded her a bit of that guy who'd played a private detective, and then James Bond. His dark hair was smooth and silky looking, and his gray eyes gazed at her with admiration and no little amusement. After days of Marcus's clearly expressed disdain and annoyance, it was kind of nice to see a man look at her that way. Even if she had just run him down with her surfboard.

"Oh, hell," she said. "I'm so sorry."

"I'm not," her victim said with the flash of a dimpled grin. An Irish accent made the simple words pleasantly exotic. "Otherwise, we might never have met."

Something about him tugged at her senses. "I'm Beka," she said, tilting her head to get a better look as she sat up straight. "Have we met before?"

The dark-haired man gave her a hand up, then leaned over to kiss her fingers with a gallant bow. "Not as such, Baba Yaga," he said. "But you know my father, Gwrtheyrn, King of the Selkies. I am Kesh, and I am very pleased to make your acquaintance."

Ah, a Selkie. No wonder he gave her tingles. Of the supernatural kind, anyway. Not like the tingles she got around Marcus. Dammit. Why couldn't she be attracted to the gorgeous guy who actually seemed to like her?

"Um, me too," she said. Suddenly she felt self-conscious, out cavorting on the beach when she was supposed to be working on solving the Selkie and Merpeople's problem. "I hope you don't think I'm goofing off; really, I've been out diving every day, trying to find out what is wrong with the water in the Selkie home, and I'm going out again later today. I just had a couple of hours first and thought I'd come catch a wave or two. It helps me think, you know what I mean?"

Kesh didn't seem at all disturbed by what might have been interpreted by some as a frivolous distraction. Of course, he was obviously a surfer, too, so maybe he understood how addictive it could be. A little farther down the beach, the froth danced up on the wet sand in beckoning invitation.

"So, are you making any progress?" Kesh asked casually as they picked up their boards and strolled closer to the water. Seagulls practiced aeronautical displays overhead, alert for the tasty tidbits dropped by early morning donut eaters.

Beka bit her lip. "Well, it's too soon to say for sure. Like I said, I've been diving every day, and taking samples from a few different spots. I can't get down as deep as your home crevasse, of course, but I've collected kelp and other sea life from nearby and sent it off to a lab to be tested. I'm just waiting for the results."

"Oh?" Kesh put one warm hand on her arm to steer her around a curly-haired toddler who was chasing a small dog, both sets of stubby legs churning up sand as they went. "Which lab?"

"The one at the university," Beka said. "I have a friend there."

She gazed at him, impressed all over again by how attractive he was. He didn't make her skin hum and buzz the way Marcus did, but he was having an actual conversation with her, instead of yelling, which made for a nice change.

"You can tell your father I'm doing everything I can," she said, not quite beseeching. "I haven't seen anything obvious to tell me what is going on, and my magical senses just tell me there is *something*, but I'm sure I'll get to the bottom of this soon. Then your people will be able to return to their homes."

White teeth gleamed in a tanned face as he gave her a charming smile. "Not to worry, darlin'," he said. "I've got complete faith in you. Now how about we see which one of us can catch the largest wave? The loser can treat the winner to dinner tonight, after you get in from your diving." Brown eyes twinkled at her. "That way, even if I lose, I win."

KESH WATCHED BEKA walk away carrying her board tucked under her arm. She turned around at the edge of the road and waved, and he gave her a big grin, not letting it slide into the sneer that lurked behind it until she was gone from view.

A lovely girl, she was. Pretty to look at and all heart and earnest Human emotion. Not at all like the Baba Yaga who preceded her, thank the gods. Now that one, she would have been tough to fool. But this silly girl? He already had her wrapped around his finger.

That Brenna, she was a piece of work, she was. She and Beka had used this as a home base the last few years before the Queen of the Otherworld had dragged Brenna kicking and screaming into retirement, and he'd seen her do a thing or two that the High Queen might not approve of, had she but known.

Not that Brenna wasn't still poking her nose in, behind the scenes. She and Kesh had found a few small mutual goals, and she'd even given him advice on how to deal with the current Baba.

According to Brenna, her replacement was insecure and uncertain of her abilities. Which was a damned good thing, as far as Kesh was concerned. There was no way he was going to let one inexperienced Baba Yaga ruin his carefully laid plans.

The discovery that she'd been poking around had initially alarmed him, and he'd engineered this meeting on the beach to find out how far she'd gotten. And while he wasn't happy about the samples she'd taken, it was clear that she had no clue as to what he'd been dumping in the ocean for the last few months. He'd just have to make sure she never found out.

One way or the other.

For the moment, his plan was simple: he'd take advantage of her vulnerability, woo her and stay close so he could keep track of her progress, and sabotage it as necessary. Kesh thought that, lacking confidence as she was, it would be easy to distract and mislead her, while charming her into trusting him completely.

In fact, he'd had a rather brilliant flash after meeting her in person. She was, after all, stunningly pretty, and sooner or later he would need to take a mate to give him heirs for this new kingdom he was building on land. There were a few women among the Selkies he'd persuaded to follow him when he left, but none of them particularly appealed to him for the long term. If he played the game just right, he could not only exact his revenge, but also end up with the massive powers of a Baba Yaga to add to his own.

Of course, if that didn't work, he could always kill her.

INE

BEKA AND FERGUS got to the *Wily Serpent* just before ten. Marcus was already there, along with an unexpected guest.

"Hey, Beka," Marcus said, nodding his head neutrally at Fergus. "I hope you don't mind, but I'm bringing along a friend of mine today. This is Tito. He gets chemo with my da, and I've been promising him a day out on the water. Thought I'd take advantage of my father not being around, and take Tito out to watch you dive. The two of us can throw a line in while you're doing your thing."

There was something eager and a little vulnerable about the way he asked; after all, he could have just *told* her the boy was coming. It was his father's boat. But it was clear to Beka that he wanted the boy to have a good time. And if that meant a truce for the day, it was just fine with her.

"Hi Tito," she said, climbing on board and stowing her gear out of the way. "I'm Beka, and this is my dive buddy Fergus. Nice to meet you."

The boy stuck his hand out politely and shook hers, then extended it to Fergus, his eyes bright as stars in the night sky. "That's cool," he said, looking down at Fergus's hand and turning it sideways so he could get a better look. "You have little webs between your fingers. Does that help you swim?"

Marcus cleared his throat, looking embarrassed. "Tito, dude, it's not polite to comment on people's, um, oddities." He shrugged an apology at Fergus, who just laughed.

"I do not mind," Fergus said, grinning at the dark-skinned boy. He leaned down and whispered, "Can you keep a secret? I am actually a Merman from an undersea kingdom; that is why I have webs between my fingers." He held up one bare foot and said in a more normal tone, "Toes, too, see?"

Tito's face was a study in conflicting awe and disbelief. "I never heard of a Mer*man*," he said, dubiously. "I thought there were only Mer*maids*. And they're made up."

Fergus snorted. "If you do not have any Mermen, how would you get more Mermaids, eh? As for made up, well, maybe they are, and maybe they are not." His grin grew wider, and the boy matched it with one of his own.

"If you're a Merman, how come you don't have a tail?" he asked.

"Because then your friend Marcus might mistake me for a big fish and bring me in to market," Fergus said with a laugh. "I do not think I would like that."

"I'm finding something fishy about this whole story," Marcus said, but he was smiling too. "You're as bad as my da with the ridiculous fairy-tale nonsense. Let's get this show on the road, shall we?" He turned to Beka and Fergus. "I gave the guys the day off, since we were just going out for a few hours so you can dive. Can you give me a hand casting off?"

Tito gave Fergus one more admiring look and trailed Marcus up to the front cabin. The other two started releasing the ropes that kept the ship attached to the dock.

"Really?" Beka said under her breath to Fergus. "A Merman from an undersea kingdom?"

Fergus winked, eyes twinkling in multiple shades of green like the changeable ocean. "He did not believe me, did he?" He coiled the last rope neatly and used a gaff to push the boat away from the old wooden dock. "And it made him smile. I think this is a good thing."

Beka sighed. She hoped the boy was winning his battle, but either way, she was all in favor of giving him a great day out on the water if that's what made him happy. The fact that Marcus was going out of his way to help the kid made her see him in a different way. Maybe he wasn't such a grumpy pain in the butt after all.

Of course, that might mean he was only that way around *her*, which was kind of a drag. But considering that when he'd met her, she'd just sliced a big hole in his net and let all his fish get away, and then followed that up by bribing his father to let her use the boat when Marcus didn't want her to, she supposed she shouldn't be surprised he wasn't all that pleased to have her around. Maybe she should have baked him cookies or something. Or had Chewie bake them . . . she sucked in the kitchen.

Once at the dive site, Marcus stopped the engines and he and Tito came back to watch Beka and Fergus put on their wet suits and double-check Beka's tanks. They double-checked Fergus's gear, too, even though they'd both done so before they'd gotten on the boat. You couldn't be too careful when you were diving. If Beka got into trouble, Fergus had to be ready to jump into the water at a moment's notice; even a five-minute delay could be fatal. Of course, as a Merman, he didn't really need any gear, and Beka wasn't all that likely to get into trouble she couldn't handle, but still, when there were witnesses, it was best to go through the motions.

"Wow," Tito said, bouncing up and down on his toes. "That looks so cool. Are you going to find pirate treasure down there?"

Beka and Fergus exchanged looks. Of course, the supposed sunken wreck she was going after didn't exist. Or rather, there was a theoretical ship that had been lost in that area many years ago, but she had no real expectation of finding anything from it—she wasn't even looking. But seeing the expression on Tito's too-thin face, she was suddenly determined to bring up *something* a twelve-year-old boy would find exciting.

Marcus raised a quizzical eyebrow. He'd seen her hauling up small bags, but he had no way of knowing she'd been collecting specimens instead of booty.

Crap. Where the heck was she supposed to find treasure?

"Well, not exactly," Beka said cautiously. "I'm following up on a legend about a Spanish ship that was sunk by pirates, though, and there was supposed to be a lot of gold on board. So you never know. All I've found so far are bits and pieces that might turn out to be something."

Marcus rolled his eyes. "Don't get your hopes up, Tito, my man. We're a lot more likely to catch a nice tuna to take home to your mom than Beka is to magically stumble on some pieces of eight."

Oh, bite me, Mr. Crabbypants. With a smile at Tito and a glare for Marcus, Beka lowered herself into the effervescent waves of the welcoming sea. She was going to bring back something cool for that boy if she had to swim back to shore to get it.

MARCUS STIFLED A laugh at the expression on Beka's easy-to-read face. She might be a slightly delusional hippie nutcase, but at least she was an open book—exactly what she appeared to be. Everything she thought was written across her lovely countenance for all to see. Especially when she was pissed at him, which was most of the time.

He couldn't really blame her; he'd been so angry at her in the beginning, when she'd pulled that idiotic stunt with the net and then taken advantage of his father's weakened state and empty bank account to get the old man to allow her back on the boat. She still made Marcus crazy most of the time, but he had to admit—to himself, if not to her—part of that was because he couldn't seem to shake the unreasonable attraction he felt whenever she was near. At least if he kept her at a distance, he'd never have to worry about anything foolish happening between them.

Besides, she was just so much fun to tease. He loved watching her narrow her gorgeous blue eyes at him, as if her glare could magically turn him into a toad with its icy sapphire defiance. He shouldn't have made fun of her lack of progress, though; he'd peeked into one of her bags a couple of days ago, and it had been filled with scraps of seaweed and a dead anemone. Not exactly the treasure she'd been seeking. She'd probably just brought up something so she wouldn't look bad in front of him and the crew. Unless she really *was* crazy. With that girl, it was hard to tell.

Still, she was being damned nice to Tito, which made up for a lot of crazy in Marcus's book. Both she and Fergus were patiently answering the boy's endless questions about their gear, how a dive worked, why it took two of them, and, of course, pirates.

"Can I try diving?" Tito asked Beka. His eager face glowed with admiration as he gazed at the statuesque blonde in her formfitting wet suit. Marcus didn't blame him for that, but he held his breath as he waited for Beka to make a promise he wouldn't be able to let her keep. There was no way a sick, inexperienced boy was going to dive off this boat.

But he needn't have worried. "Sorry, dude," she said, shaking her head. "Divers train for a long time before they ever do the kind of thing Fergus and I are doing." One slim finger tapped petal pink lips. "Can you swim pretty well?"

Tito nodded. "Sure."

"Then maybe someday you and I can go snorkeling instead. We can do that in relatively shallow water, where it won't be so cold and we'll only stay in for a little while, so you don't get overtired." She gave him a mock-stern look, a weak second cousin to the fierce glower she usually aimed at Marcus. "As long as your mother says it is okay, that is."

Tito grinned, his teeth gleaming white in his dark face. "Marcus, too, right?"

Marcus and Beka exchanged glances, and she fought to cover a grimace. "I guess so," she said reluctantly. Marcus coughed to cover his snort of laughter. Clearly, she hadn't thought that one through. Typical. Good intentions, but not much planning. Beautiful, sexy, and kind . . . but still a flake.

Too bad, because he found the first three traits amazingly

appealing. But nothing on this planet would make him put up with the last one.

Once Beka was in the water, he and Tito did some fishing off the opposite side of the boat. Unfortunately, as with so many other occasions of late, the fish just weren't there. It was as if something unseen had driven them all away. Marcus took it as a personal slight, especially on a day when he had promised a seriously ill boy a treat.

Tito didn't seem to mind, but Marcus nearly bit Beka's head off when she finished up and came over to ask them cheerfully, "So, how was the fishing?"

"Lousy," he growled, then tried to paste a less disgruntled look on his face when Tito blinked up at him in surprise. "How was the treasure hunting?"

Beka shrugged one tanned shoulder, revealed now that she'd unzipped her wet suit down to her slim waist. The simple white one-piece suit underneath was as alluring on her as a more provocative bikini might be on any other woman, and he had to force himself to drag his eyes back up to her face. Where he was fairly sure he saw a twinkle in the azure depths as she caught him staring.

"Nothing very interesting, I'm afraid. Too bad about the fishing though." She got a thoughtful look. "Why don't you keep at it for a few minutes?" she suggested. "I think Fergus wanted to take a quick dive before we go, anyway."

"Please, Marcus, just a little while longer," Tito begged. Marcus didn't have the heart to say no, although he didn't see what difference another half an hour would make. Still, the boy had more animation than Marcus had ever seen before, and the ashy undertone to his skin was less obvious than usual. Clearly, being out on the water agreed with him.

Marcus had a sudden yearning to make this kind of outing possible for other sick kids; a morning out in the fresh air in the midst of the soothing waters of the bay, with dolphins occasionally coming to frolic alongside the boat, far from the acrid medicinal scents and bleak beige realities of the all-too-necessary hospital.

He snorted under his breath at his own foolishness; he

was getting as bad as Beka. It wasn't as though he was going to stick around long enough to get involved with something like that, even if he wanted to take on the responsibility. Which he didn't. Just thinking about all the things that could go wrong made his gut clench, like back when he had men to protect from flying bullets and roadside ambushes.

A glance toward the port side of the boat showed him an unwanted glimpse of Beka and Fergus, their blond and red heads close together as they whispered about something that made Beka flash that sunshine smile that was so rarely aimed at him. He turned back to answer one of Tito's never-ending questions, and a splash told him that Fergus must have gone into the water.

"Be right back," he said to the kid, and wandered casually over to where Beka was standing, looking over the side of the boat.

"Thanks," he said, gruffly, not used to having any conversation with her that wasn't an argument of some kind. "For being so nice to Tito, I mean. I know he was probably annoying you with all the 'How come you have to wear a special outfit?' and 'Do the fish nibble on your toes?' "

Beka laughed, a sound as silvery as a salmon's flashing belly. "He's great, Marcus. And I think you're really sweet for bringing him out here. All those questions just mean he's thinking, and that's never a bad thing. I didn't mind at all."

Sweet. Nobody had called him sweet in . . . well, maybe never. He was a lot of things: loyal, tough, dependable— but sweet? Hardly. Marcus could feel a flush spread over his cheekbones. *She thought he was sweet.* He didn't know whether to be flattered or appalled.

He was about to answer, probably with a sentence that was both stupid and clumsily polite, when he noticed something odd: Fergus's gear, including his neatly folded wet suit and carefully checked air tanks, sitting next to Beka's tanks on the damp deck. Marcus glanced around; no Fergus. *What the hell?*

His mouth was opened to ask her about it when a panicked yell from Tito had him sprinting across the boat instead, his heart beating almost as rapidly as his pounding footsteps.

"Marcus! Marcus!" Tito yelled as he wrestled with a fishing pole that was suddenly bent almost double as it dipped down toward the water. "I think I caught a fish! What do I do now?"

Beka had followed him over at a slightly more sedate pace. "Way to go, Tito!" She gave a tiny shake of her head as Marcus moved to grab the pole away from the boy. "You can do it!"

Taking the hint, Marcus stood behind Tito and put one hand on the pole to take some of the pressure off, and used his other hand to steady Tito as he hauled mightily on the rod.

"That's it," Marcus said. "You've got it. Keep reeling in. Slow and steady. Pull up on the rod, then reel in a little more. You're doing great."

Beka grabbed the hand net and had it ready to slide under the wriggling pumpkin orange fish as the guys worked together to heave it over the side of the boat. Tito was beside himself with joy, jumping up and down and whooping as Marcus gently removed the hook from the fish's mouth.

"That's one of the best looking cod I've ever seen," Marcus said. The thing was longer than Tito's arm. "That's going to make one heck of a dinner, kiddo."

Marcus laid the fish out on the deck and started to clean it, only glancing up briefly as Fergus climbed back on board and stood dripping to receive a high five from Beka. The former Marine shook his head in bafflement. There was definitely something odd going on here, but damned if he could figure it out.

"Nice cod," Fergus said, padding over to stand next to him. "Beka said the boy is pleased. That is good."

"Yeah, it is," Marcus said, peering up at the other man suspiciously. "You wouldn't happen to know how a fish miraculously appeared as soon as you went for your little swim, would you?"

Fergus just smiled, showing teeth that looked slightly

pointed in the glare of the bright midday light. "The boy is happy, yes? This is what matters."

Marcus shook his head. He was clearly losing his mind. What did he think the other man was, some kind of fish whisperer?

"Right." Marcus put the cleaned fish on ice. "I guess we might as well head in now." He hesitated, thinking about how terrific Beka—and Fergus, of course—had been with Tito.

"You know, Tito's mom said she was working until late. I was just going to drop him off with his grandmother. Maybe we could all go back to dock and then I could cook some of this nice fish up for dinner?" He was talking to Fergus, but his eyes kept straying to a glowing Beka as she chatted with Tito, who was reenacting the entire fish-catching adventure, complete with exaggerated hand gestures.

Fergus shrugged, what looked like genuine regret on his face. "That sounds very pleasant, and I am quite fond of cod. But I am afraid that Beka already has other plans."

"Other plans?" Marcus asked. A cloud seemed to blot out the sun.

"Indeed," Fergus said, obviously unaware of the effect of his words. "I believe she has a date."

"A date," Marcus repeated. Of course she had a date. She was a beautiful, fun-loving woman. Of course men asked her out. Not men like him, of course. But still, it was absurd for him to be so shocked. "Probably with some surfer or hippie New Age tree hugger."

Fergus gave him a blank look from under red brows. "Why would anyone hug a tree?" He gazed from Marcus to Beka and back again, and comprehension spilled into his eyes, along with a sympathetic look that Marcus chose to ignore. "And yes, she told me they met while surfing. They seem to have much in common."

Of course they did. Marcus stifled a sigh and resisted the impulse to throw the ice chest into the sea. *And he and Beka had nothing in common at all. What the hell had he been thinking?*

EN

BEKA GAZED AT the food spread out on the blanket in front of her and blinked rapidly a couple of times, a mystified look on her face. "When you said a picnic on the beach, this isn't quite what I envisioned."

Kesh surveyed the feast he'd assembled, awash with smug satisfaction. Smoked salmon, oysters, caviar, chilled lobster—all the glorious gifts of the sea, along with a few more landlocked pleasures, including a couple of bottles of expensive champagne. He was a prince of the Selkies; he knew how to dazzle a woman. And Human women were especially easy to dazzle. If the Irish accent and suave good looks didn't get them, flattery and charm would. The Baba Yagas might be the most powerful witches on the planet, but they were still, on some level, just Human women. In the beginning, anyway. And this Baba Yaga was still very young.

"Only the very best is good enough for such a beautiful, gracious creature as yourself," Kesh said with a flourishing bow. He could feel her falling under his spell already.

Beka gave him a curved crescent of a smile that seemed more amused than awed, the expression on her face hidden momentarily by the silken fall of her loose blond hair. "I'm afraid I'm a bit underdressed," she said, waving a hand to indicate her simple but colorful batik wraparound skirt and red scoop-necked tank top. "If I'd known we were dining at the Ritz, I would have worn my diamonds."

Taken aback for a moment, Kesh rebounded by pouring her a crystal goblet full of effervescent nirvana. "You look lovely no matter what you wear, Baba Yaga. And I would be happy to adorn you with the pearls of a thousand oysters, if you but say the word."

Beka choked a little on her champagne. "Goodness. Do those kinds of lines usually work for you?" The twinkle in her eyes took the sting out of her words.

He gave her a rueful grin. "They do indeed, darlin', but I fear that my attempt has failed to impress you. For that I am sorry. I have no wish to offend."

She laughed, helping herself to a cracker heaped with caviar. "Oh, I'm impressed, Kesh. This is a delightfully over-the-top picnic, and I intend to enjoy every bite. But you can save the flowery sentiments for someone they're better suited to. I'm not a 'pearls of a thousand oysters' kind of girl."

Kesh studied her in the moonlight, rethinking his original approach to wooing her. She truly was lovely, her golden hair shimmering almost silver in the moon's enchanted light as she lounged across from him on the raw silk blanket. It would be a shame to have to kill her. He would just have to take a slightly subtler tack.

"Tell me," he said, gazing intently at her over the rim of his glass, "how goes the search for the solution to my people's problem?"

Her relaxed posture tensed, legs pulled in and tucked under her skirt, shoulders hunching as she hugged her knees. "Not all that well, I'm afraid. There still isn't anything obvious that I can see."

Pouring more wine into her goblet, Kesh favored her with his most sympathetic look. "Oh? That is a pity. And all those Merpeople and Selkies depending on you." He shook his head. "You have no idea what is poisoning the water?"

Beka put down the piece of lobster she'd been about to eat. "I've brought samples from a variety of spots to a friend of mine at the University of California at Santa Cruz. They have some amazing, state-of-the-art labs there, and I'm expecting him to call me with the results within a couple of days." She gave him a strained smile. "You can tell your father I'm working on finding the answer as fast as I can."

Kesh saw no point in mentioning that he and his father hadn't spoken in six months, and popped a delicate oyster into his mouth instead. It tasted of the sea, salty and smooth with the essence of the ocean. He gazed longingly for a moment at the waves whooshing quietly against the shore before yanking his attention back to his companion. This was his place now, and he was not going to lose it. In the end, he would rule it, taking it one piece at a time until he owned it all. Destroying the sea he'd come from and could no longer have would simply be an amusing sideline.

"Once you find out what is contaminating the home waters in the trench, what do you intend to do about it?" he asked, as if only out of idle curiosity. "Do you have some kind of plan?"

Even in the darkness of the summer night, he could see the blush that stained her high cheekbones a becoming pink, like the inside of a shell.

"Well, it depends on what is causing the issue, of course," she answered.

Kesh shrugged. "Surely it is some Human taint, brought about by their encroachment on our world." A hint of bitterness crept out to color his voice. "We should never have allowed them to drive us so far into the depths, hiding like frightened fish from the relentless teeth of the shark. We are the predators here, not they."

"I wouldn't call Selkies predators," Beka said. "They're tough and strong, and beneath the sea they are a match for almost anything, but fortunately, they are a peaceful race."

"And see where that has gotten them," Kesh sneered. "Chased from their own homes by the poisons of others."

Beka put a comforting hand over one of his, scooting closer to him on the blanket. "We don't know that's true," she said. "I know you're worried about your kingdom, but I promise you, I'll do everything I can to help."

Kesh draped his arm loosely around her shoulder and gave her his most charming smile. "Perhaps we can work together on the problem, my dear Baba. I have a feeling that we would make a wonderful team." His chuckle echoed across the sand and into the warm night, and below the moon-kissed waters, small creatures scurried to hide in the safety of the reef's jagged landscape.

FRONDS OF KELP danced coyly around her ankles the next day as Beka floated far enough below the surface that only a faint light filtered down to illuminate her task. Not that she needed much light for what she was about to attempt. Only her own powers and some luck. A lot of luck, probably.

Collecting samples wasn't getting her anywhere. It was time to try something a little less passive and a little more Baba Yaga. Magic. The very thought made her stomach churn and shoulders tighten under their slick neoprene covering; her breath reverberated harshly through the regulator between her lips.

Calm down, Beka, she ordered herself sternly. *You've spent years training to do this. Even Brenna admitted that you have power. The other day you calmed a crazy-ass storm. You can do this.* She tried not to think about how difficult it was to work magic under this much water or to hear Brenna's voice echoing in the back of her mind, tone pitying. *"Don't worry, dear, you'll get the hang of it eventually. I'm sure you will."*

The Selkies and the Merpeople couldn't wait for eventually. They needed her to fix this now. So water or no water, she was going to try.

There was no way to use any of her magical tools down here, and she didn't have the luxury of time to spend getting into the right mind-set, as she normally would for anything this tricky. But she didn't intend to try to fix the entire crisis right now—just see if she could mend one small part of it. If that worked, she'd come up with a way to address a larger area.

The biggest problem was that she still didn't know what she was dealing with. Knowing the cause to any issue always made it easier to come up with a solution. But since she was still no closer to finding the answers, she was desperate enough to try anything. Despite the tingles of fear and trepidation that made her fingers shake as she wrapped them gently around a limp and pallid pink starfish.

Even in the dilute light trickling down through the layers of water, she could see that its color was off, and it drooped in her hands instead of being taut and muscular. Poor thing. Its life energy had dwindled so low she could barely sense it, although she could feel the mysterious illness it carried like a low-voltage buzz humming through her fingertips.

Carefully, slowly, she pulled a strand of elemental power through her core and out into the palms of her hands. The water around the starfish took on a golden glow as her magic flowed into its body. For a moment, a breath, a heartbeat, Beka thought she could sense it working, and her pulse raced. Then the small creature shuddered and died, the last of her magic sliding uselessly into the darkness of the murky water.

Beka opened her hands and let the sad little body drift away, down to the bottom far beneath them. It had probably been on the verge of dying before she got there. There was too much water for undirected magical work. She knew these things were true. But she couldn't help feeling the weight of its passing as more evidence that Brenna had been right, and she just wasn't ready to be a Baba Yaga.

And maybe she never would be.

"THAT'S IT, I quit," Beka said as Fergus used one strong arm to help her over the side of the *Wily Serpent*. Her bare feet hit the deck with an emphatic thud, wet suit dripping salt-water rain onto the worn wooden planks.

Marcus straightened up from tidying nets around the corner from where they stood, telling himself it didn't count as eavesdropping if you simply happened to be there.

"Still nothing?" Fergus inquired, his tone sympathetic but not surprised.

Marcus snorted to himself, stifling the sound. He'd told her there was no damned treasure down there.

"Nothing that I can find, anyway. Although clearly there's *something*, or I wouldn't keep coming across fish and plants that were dead, or soon to be." She tossed her collection bags onto the deck with a frustrated thump. "I'm tired of gathering up masses of blighted kelp and three-legged starfish. Even without them for evidence, I can sense the damage to the ecosystem—I just can't pin down what the hell is causing it. I am checking different sections to see if I can find anything out of the ordinary and finding nothing. Nothing except bits and pieces of sea life that are dying or warped for no obvious reason. I keep collecting samples for the lab to look at, but if they can't give me answers, I'm at a dead end. And my powers are no help at all. It's driving me crazy!"

Wait. What the hell was she talking about? *Kelp and starfish? Damage to the ecosystem?* Marcus felt like he'd opened a straightforward ship's log and fallen headfirst into a mystery novel instead. What the hell did dead fish have to do with sunken treasure?

Beka's voice was muffled, as if she'd dropped her head into her hands. "I'm failing your people, Fergus, and the others too. I'm so sorry."

"Maybe this laboratory will find the answers we seek," Fergus said. "If not, you will think of something else. You are the Baba Yaga."

"Hmph," Beka said. "That's the current theory, anyway." Marcus could hear her gusty sigh from where he stood. "Regardless, there's no point in my diving anymore until we get the results back from the lab. You might as well head home for now."

"Are you certain?" Fergus asked, but even Marcus could tell the other man was relieved. "I would like to see my wife and children again, and check on my little son. He was one of the babes affected by the illness, and part of my reason for volunteering to help. If you are assured that you will not need me further for the moment, I will gladly return to my family."

"Go with my blessing," Beka said. "I'm sorry we don't have a cure for your son yet. What are you going to tell their majesties?"

"I will tell them the truth: that you are working diligently on the problem and will soon have a solution," Fergus said gravely.

Marcus almost fell over. Fergus was married with children, there was some kind of illness, and now they were talking about *royalty*? Were they using some kind of code? Clearly, there was something going on here that had nothing to do with salvage. And he was going to find out what, dammit.

ONCE THE BOAT pulled into port, Marcus walked Beka and Fergus to the end of the pier. Fergus nodded at him and gave Beka a friendly peck on the cheek before walking off with a lanky, confident stride, leaving his diving gear sitting in a heap at Beka's feet.

Marcus indicated the equipment. "He's not going to need that anymore?" Marcus had decided, probably against his better judgment, to give Beka a chance to explain herself. She might be flaky, but in the week they'd spent together, he'd never gotten the impression that she was a liar. If anything, she'd gone to great lengths to dance around the truth. Maybe there was some kind of reasonable explanation—although for the life of him, he couldn't think of what that might be.

"You'll be relieved to know that you're rid of me at last," Beka said, giving him a smile that didn't quite have its usual radiance, although it tried gamely. "I'm giving up on the diving for now, although there's always the chance I might need to go out again at some point. Tell your father I'll drop off the final payment tomorrow."

"Didn't find what you were looking for?" Marcus asked, the very personification of innocence.

She rolled her eyes at him. "I think you know I didn't. Are you going to say 'I told you so' now?"

"I'd rather take you for a beer," he said, enjoying the look of shock on her sun-burnished face. "And have you tell me exactly what's going on here."

Beka opened her mouth, then closed it again without saying anything after taking a careful look at his expression. He stood there patiently, arms crossed, in what his men used to call the "Hell can freeze over before I move" pose. There'd never been a marine who didn't eventually cave when faced with that pose, and Beka was no different.

Finally, she heaved a sigh, glanced at her waterproof diving watch, and shrugged in defeat. "I'm meeting someone later, but I guess I have enough time for a beer."

Marcus tried not to grind his teeth at the thought of the someone she was meeting; no doubt her mysterious surfer pal again. None of his business, after all. Even though his heart sometimes whispered that it would like it to be. He stowed the diving gear back on the boat and escorted her to his favorite bar, the Cranky Seagull.

Inside, it looked like what it was: a working sailor's tavern. No frills for tourists, no cute pink umbrellas in the starkly utilitarian glasses. But the beer was cold, the bartender minded his own business, and nobody cared if you smelled like fish at the end of a long day at sea. The dusty floor, the long wooden bar, and the massive beams in the ceiling had all come from the bodies of long-dead ships, sailing now only in the dreams of hard-drinking men. Since he'd come back to Santa Carmelita, the Cranky Seagull was the only place that had felt remotely like home.

"Nice," Beka said as they grabbed a beer each and a table toward the back, away from the rowdy bunch playing five-card-draw with a tattered deck. Marcus gave her a sharp look, thinking she was insulting his favorite watering hole, but she was gazing around with a slight grin, admiring the aging sepia prints of ancient seafaring men and their long-ago catches.

"It is," he agreed, impressed by the way she seemed to fit in wherever she went, even here, where she should have stuck out like a sore thumb. Beauty among the beasts. But she just waved at the drunken card players, gave the bartender a thumbs-up as she took her first swallow of the house brew, and settled in across from Marcus as if they'd been coming there together forever. He had to remind himself that he was there to get the truth, not to watch the way the dim lights made her blue eyes glisten like the summer sky outside. The subtle aroma of fresh strawberries teased at his nostrils, even in the midst of the yeasty, beery smell of the bar.

Might as well get to the point, he thought. "So, are you going to tell me what the hell you're really up to?"

She choked a little on a swallow of beer, those miraculous eyes widening with alarm. "What?"

Marcus looked at her steadily across the splintery table, which bore witness to the history of those who'd sat there before them in deep-carved initials and the names of ships and women, indistinguishable from one another with the passage of time.

"I overheard you and Fergus talking on the boat," he said bluntly. "I didn't understand most of it—something about dying kelp and some mysterious illness, and people depending on you to find some kind of answers—but it was enough to make it pretty damn clear that you were never diving for buried treasure. So I want to know what you were looking for; the truth, this time, if you please."

Beka's face went blank for a moment, then she sighed, took one last gulp of beer, and set her mug resolutely down on the table. "Fine," she said. "But I have to warn you, there are secrets involved here that aren't mine to tell. I'll explain what I can, and I won't lie, but there are things I'm not free to speak about. If you can accept that, I'll share what I can."

Marcus set his jaw, but nodded. It was a place to start, anyway. "So, not buried treasure," he repeated.

"That wasn't exactly a lie," Beka said, a tiny smile playing at the corner of her lips. "If I can find the answers I'm looking for, they will be worth more than gold to the people involved. And the answers are most certainly buried—at least, I haven't been able to find them."

The moment of frivolity slid away, leaving her expression solemn and her eyes shadowed. "There is something wrong with the water down there," she said. "Plants and fish are being affected, and some people have gotten ill too. We don't know why, or how to fix it, and that's what I was trying to find out."

"Who's 'we'?" Marcus asked. "Are you working for the government? Is that why I haven't heard anything about this? Are they covering this up?" He thought about the load of fish he'd delivered to market a couple of days ago. "Hey! Am I poisoning people with the few fish I'm bringing in?" He started to rise from the table, suddenly furious, but she waved a placating hand in his direction and he subsided. For now.

"Sort of, no, no, and definitely not," she said, the laughter in her voice calming him more than her words. "The fish closer to the surface, the ones you're catching, seem to be fine. It's the plant and animal life deeper down in the sea trenches that seem to be affected."

He opened his mouth, and she added, "And don't ask me how that is affecting people, because that's one of the things I can't tell you. They're . . . a special group."

So she sort of worked for the government, and there was some kind of secret underwater experiment that had run into trouble? He'd heard rumors about that kind of thing when he was in the Marines, but hell, you heard all kinds of bizarre rumors about new weapons and super-soldiers and government experiments when you were in the military. Mostly they didn't amount to much. But maybe he'd stumbled onto something real. Or maybe it was all as foolish and delusional as the fairy stories his father used to charm his younger brother with, getting him so wrapped up in the so-called magic of the sea that he forgot to watch out for its grim reality.

"Okay, so let's say that for the moment, I'm taking your word about all this. Why is it your job to fix it? You're a hippie chick jewelry-making surfer girl. Why aren't there a bunch of government geeks looking into it with submersibles and an army of scientists?"

Beka sighed, suddenly looking ten years older. "Believe it or not, it really *is* my job to fix it. I've got some, um, special skills. And the responsibilities to go with them." She gazed steadily at him. "I'm thinking you know a little something about how that feels."

That he did. And the project must be so hush-hush that they'd brought in one troubleshooter instead of a larger group that would have been harder to keep on the down low. Hell, she'd fooled him into thinking he was just another flaky California blonde, so there was something to that plan. Although to his credit, he'd had a feeling something wasn't quite right about her all along. He just hadn't known what it was.

"So you haven't made any progress at all?" he said, feeling more than a hint of sympathy. He'd hated failing at a mission. That's one of the reasons he'd rarely let it happen. The few truly spectacular failures still kept him up at night, replaying endlessly in his head as though he could somehow change the outcome even now.

One shoulder, clad in the simple white sundress she'd pulled over her bathing suit before leaving the boat, moved up and down. "I've got a bunch of samples from different places, taken over a variety of days. Hopefully they'll tell me something I can use to help—"

As if on cue, her cell phone vibrated. She pulled it out of the pocket of the dress, looked at the caller ID, and said apologetically, "That's my friend from the lab, actually. I have to take this. Sorry."

She bent her head over the phone, hiding it under a fall of sunbeam hair. Marcus watched her face, more out of habit than any expectation of learning anything, so he saw the moment when the blood drained away, leaving her almost as pale as her sundress.

"What?" she said. And then, "You're kidding me." A pause for the person on the other end of the phone to speak some more. "All of them? You're sure? Was anyone hurt?" Pause. "How long before you are up and running again? *Shit*." That last word was uttered in a heartfelt gust of breath. "Okay, Bran. Thanks for letting me know. And I'm sorry."

She closed the phone gently and laid it down on the table as if it were a pet snake that had suddenly turned around and bitten her without warning.

"I take it there's a problem?" Marcus said, his voice gentler than usual when dealing with Beka.

She wrapped both hands around her beer mug. He could see the slight tremor she used the action to try to hide. "That was my friend Bran; he works at the university lab where I brought all my samples. He'd given them to some of his students as an extra-credit project. They were hoping to have the results this week." She heaved a sigh. "He just called to tell me that the lab burned to the ground late last night. Took everything I collected with it. I'm going to have to start all over again."

"*Shit*," he echoed, taking a swig of his own beer. "That sucks. Do they know what caused the fire?"

"Could have been an accident; some student forgetting to turn off a piece of equipment that then overheated," she said, discouragement etched into her face as deeply as the names on the table between them. "Or maybe even arson. I guess they're considering all the options."

"Could it have anything to do with your project?" Marcus asked. He knew as well as anyone how much collateral damage the government was responsible for, one way or the other.

Beka's jaw dropped. "Mine? Why would anyone burn down a whole lab to stop me from getting my test results?"

"You'd know that better than I would," he said, his voice dry. It hadn't escaped him that she had only told him a fraction of what he'd wanted to know. "But it is worth considering." *If for no other reason than if the fire was in fact targeting Beka's work, she could be in danger.*

"There was that storm," she said, "but I don't see how that could have anything to do with this." She shook her head, a strand of golden hair drifting into the nut-brown contents of her mug. She yanked it out with a scowl and dried it on her dress, unmindful of the stain. As usual, Marcus had no idea what she was talking about.

"Besides, nobody knows I'm here except the people who sent me," she added.

"And me," Marcus pointed out. "And whoever saw you going out on my father's boat every day, if they knew about this secret job of yours." He wanted to reach across the table and shake her awake. "You're too trusting, Beka."

"And you're too suspicious," she snapped. "I have bigger worries right now. Like what am I going to do about getting more samples? Not only do I have to find another lab to do the tests, I have to collect all the material again. Which would have been easier if I hadn't just sent Fergus home." She bit her lip.

Something that looked suspiciously like a tear trembled at the edge of her dark gold lashes, and Marcus heard himself say, "I'll help you."

He wasn't sure which one of them was more surprised.

ELEVEN

KESH SHOOK HIS head. "How unfortunate," he said to Beka in his even, lightly accented voice, only the slightest hint of a smile escaping to swim sharklike around the edges of his lips when she wasn't looking. "All that hard work lost. Such a pity."

Beka made a face, staring out over the darkening bay. The lingering remnants of another splendid sunset cast a copper glow on the gentle ebb and flow of the waves and picked out golden highlights in her hair. Kesh took a moment to admire her as he congratulated himself yet again for finding such an elegant solution to a tricky situation. His father should have made him king after all. The senile, crusty-gilled old fool.

"It's a disaster, that's what it is," Beka said gloomily. She didn't even move away when he slid closer and put one comforting arm around her. "I'm right back where I started, with nothing to show for it. Your father and Queen Boudicca are going to think I'm the most incompetent Baba Yaga in the history of Baba Yagas. Gah."

"Surely not," Kesh said in his best imitation of kindness. "I doubt that even the old Baba could have solved this problem." He shuddered a little at the thought of the former Baba. He was not afraid of much on sea or on land, but that one . . . she made his spine twitch. "It is merely one of the mysteries of the wide world, destined to remain unsolved. The Selkies and Merpeople will adjust to their new homes. The weak will die, as they always have. No one will blame you."

Now she shifted, backing off to stare at him in amazement. "*I* will blame me," she said. "And it doesn't matter, because I'm not giving up."

It was Kesh's turn to stare. "Surely you are not serious. You told me yourself that all your hard-won bits and pieces are gone, swallowed up in a fire. And there is no guarantee they would have shown you anything even if they had not been. You have no clues, no answers. Your helper has returned to his rightful place in the sea. It is time to accept the inevitable and move on to other things." He put one hand on her knee to suggest what those things might be.

Frustratingly, she ignored him as if he had not spoken. Kesh was not accustomed to being ignored.

Beneath his calm exterior, his temper boiled like lava, although nothing showed on the surface except his usual boyish charm. If the twinkle in his deep eyes suddenly hinted at sparks as hot as the blaze he had started in the laboratory, Beka seemed not to notice.

"I've been thinking about this ever since I got the phone call from Bran," she said, animation returning to her tone as she spilled her plans out as if they were pearls instead of the foolish schemes of an inexperienced girl who had no idea what she was up against.

"I'm going to dive and get some more samples, but this time, instead of just sending them to a lab, I'm going to do some magical experiments on them as well. Maybe I'll be able to determine something that way. Just because I couldn't get a handle on the problem underwater, where working magic is more difficult, doesn't mean I won't be able to sense something pertinent once I'm in the school bus, with all my tools."

"How clever," Kesh said through gritted teeth. "But how will you dive without your Merman assistant?" He tilted his sleek head, the picture of regretful disappointment. "I would take you out myself, but of course, I have no boat sufficient for such a task."

"Oh, that's no problem," Beka said. A slight breeze off the water picked her hair up, making it float around her shoulders in silky waves. "Marcus said he'd help me."

The copper goblet Kesh was holding made a slight crunching noise, covered up by the sound of the breakers hitting the beach. He set it down out of sight, lest Beka spot the finger-shaped indentations now marring its classic lines. "Oh?" he said, not quite growling. "I thought the two of you did not get along."

Beka shrugged, taking a sip from her own goblet and nibbling on a bit of salmon, her usual healthy appetite obviously returning as she cheered up. "I'll admit, when I first met him, I thought he was a jerk. I would gladly have run him down with my Karmann Ghia, if I hadn't thought it would dent the poor baby. But it turns out he's got hidden depths."

Kesh snorted. The only hidden depths he was interested in were the ones where he could conceal his unexpected rival's dead and mangled body.

"No, really," Beka said, blissfully ignorant of the sudden homicidal turn of her companion's thoughts. "He's taking care of his sick father even though he can't stand the man; you've got to give him credit for that. He spent twelve years in the Marines, and Chico, that's the sailor who's been with his dad for years, told me that Marcus has all kinds of medals stowed away in his gear that he never tells anyone about."

"Medals, foolish Human tokens," Kesh muttered under his breath. "Let him kill a whale with only a spear and his bare hands, and then tell me of shiny medals." His sharp teeth pulled a raw clam from its shell, tearing it into shreds that he swallowed to wash the bitter taste out of his mouth. This was not going as he had planned.

"And he took this boy with cancer out on the boat for the day. I couldn't believe how patient Marcus was with him."

"It almost sounds as though you *like* this Human," Kesh said with a sneer. "You are the Baba Yaga. He is not for one such as you."

Beka blushed, or perhaps it was just the reflected light from the bonfire he had built from piles of gnarled and crooked driftwood, glowing off her high cheekbones. "Don't be ridiculous. He still treats me like I'm an annoying, ditzy pest that he only puts up with because he has to. And I know he's not planning to stick around forever; he's told me a bunch of times that he's only here for as long as his father needs him. But I had to tell him at least part of the truth, and he's willing to help me because he thinks that whatever is causing the problem in the water might be related to why the fish aren't showing up the way they're supposed to. Enlightened self-interest, I guess you could call it."

"Self-interest indeed," Kesh scoffed. "That is the only reason Humans do anything. Has it not occurred to you, *Baba*, that almost all of the imbalances that you are called upon to fix in nature are caused by Humans? And that this one is likely to have been as well. Why clean up their messes for them? Why not simply let them reap the rewards of their callous disregard for our beloved oceans?"

Beka's lovely face showed her every emotion, as usual: shock, sadness, doubt, and a touch of reluctant agreement. Kesh pounced the moment he saw it.

"There are many of us who feel that the Humans have been allowed to wreak destruction on the seas for far too long. Perhaps, instead of running around picking up after them as if they were children who never learned to play responsibly with their toys, you might consider joining with those of us who would punish them for their harmful ways instead, and teach them better manners when they are guests in places that do not belong to them."

"Us?" Beka said, a touch of sharpness in her voice that caught him by surprise. "Who is *us*?"

Kesh shrugged. "Some are my people, or other denizens of the magical places under the sea, where we water dwellers were forced to stay behind when most of the paranormal creatures of the world passed into the greater safety of the Otherworld during the great exodus. Others are magical folk who stayed here by choice, or visit periodically from the Otherworld, although those grow fewer every year as the Humans encroach even further on the rare untouched places left for our kind."

"I see," Beka said slowly. "And what kind of 'punishments' do you and your friends use to teach these pesky Humans better manners, pray tell?"

Sensing a sudden hint of danger, Kesh backpedaled rapidly. "Nothing drastic, my dear Beka, I assure you. Merely little things, like driving the fish away from their established routes, so that the fishermen will get discouraged and go find some less dangerous trade to ply, one that does not involve the careless and wasteful deaths of thousands of dolphins and turtles and others of our marine brethren, as well as an ongoing threat to all Merpeople and Selkies."

"Look, Kesh, I don't approve of some of the techniques that commercial fishermen use," Beka said, looking troubled. "But there are Humans who are trying to change things so that such tragedies don't happen as often. And many of these fishermen are good people, just trying to support themselves and their families in the way they learned from their fathers. If you drive the fish away, those families will suffer."

"And what of the suffering of our families?" Kesh rebutted, letting more anger into his voice than he'd intended. "Are you too Human to care about them too?"

Beka rocked back as if he'd slapped her, and he immediately softened his tone. "I apologize if my words seem harsh, dear one; I am simply concerned for the well-being of my people."

Not the fools who had stayed behind to follow his father like a mindless school of fish, of course, but those who had more wisely chosen to throw their lot in with him. There were not many, as yet, but once he could demonstrate that he was a strong leader, capable of inflicting harm upon their enemies, more would come. They would carve out a new kingdom upon the parched dry land until he could build up enough strength and numbers to return to wrest his rightful place as king under the sea from the hands of his weakling brother. One way or the other, the Baba Yaga would help him with that plan, whether she intended to or not.

"I understand that, Kesh," she said, patting him on the arm. "But depriving the fishermen of their livelihood isn't the way to go about it. Please tell me you'll send the fish back where they belong."

She gave him a bright, encouraging smile. His fingers itched to slap it off her face, but he smiled back charmingly instead. "As you wish, darling Baba. I am certain that if we work together, we will be able to come up with solutions that will satisfy us both, and still keep those entrusted into your tender care safe from Human carelessness."

An innocent sideways glance accompanied his next question. "No doubt you have some clever plan to fix everything, if you cannot find the answers through your exploration of the damaged areas near the trench where once my people swam so freely?"

He knew she did not. And when she once again began to doubt herself, and her ability to solve the problem, he would be there to console her, whispering his own clever suggestions in her ears.

Beka scratched her nose pensively. "Actually, I was thinking about that earlier, and I had an idea. It's kind of a long shot, but I thought I would start doing some research on the kind of damage I've been finding on the plant and animal life, and some of the symptoms that have been showing up in the children and elderly sea people who have been affected by this poison." She perked up again as she put her plan into words. "Maybe I can find records of similar instances, something that will give me a clue to what would cause this kind of mutation. I'm not sure why I didn't think of it before; I guess I was just so certain I'd be able to figure it out right away. Still, it gives me another avenue to follow, and that's good, right?"

Kesh raised his glass to her. "You astonish me, my dear Baba," he said with complete honesty, and no little irony. "I had no idea you had it in you."

This was bad. Very, very bad. If she started looking in the right direction, it would not take her long to find the answers she sought. And that would be the ruination of all his careful plans. How very unfortunate indeed. Such a pity.

He reached into the basket of food he had packed so carefully for their romantic picnic on the beach and pulled one special container from underneath the extra black linen napkins folded into intricate, dainty shapes and the last unopened bottle of vintage California wine.

"We should celebrate," Kesh said solemnly, placing the beautiful lacquered box on the blanket in front of Beka. He opened the lid with a flourish, displaying the glistening red fish that lay inside on a tranquil bed of light green seaweed salad. Together, they glowed like jewels under the rising moon. "I brought this especially for you. It is a delicacy prepared by my finest chefs." He smiled almost as brightly as the moon itself. "I caught the fish myself, as a gift."

Beka ducked her head, hiding her answering smile behind the golden fall of her long hair. "Thank you, Kesh. I'm honored." She held out the box in his direction so he could take a piece.

"Oh no, darling Baba," he said, soft as the whispering undertow that hid beneath the calmest surface. "I brought that for you. I would not think of depriving you of one precious morsel." He leaned forward and plucked a delicate sliver of fish out of the container with slender, slightly webbed fingers. "I insist you eat every last piece," he said, placing it into her mouth with tender care. "I promise you, it will change your life."

BEKA CLOSED THE final collection bag carefully and placed it in the waterproof sack with the others in the bow of the dinghy. As she turned to sit down again, she took a moment to look across the small vessel at her companion.

Marcus was so large, he seemed to take up most of the space in the tiny boat. Not that there was an extra ounce of fat on him, but between his height, wide shoulders, and broad chest, not to mention all those muscles, he took up a lot of room. The power of his personality only added to the impression.

Yet he was also amazingly graceful. She'd already seen him moving around the *Wily Serpent* in the carefully orchestrated dance of the fisherman, but underwater, he'd been a revelation. Although Marcus told her he hadn't dived since he'd left home at eighteen, it was clear he hadn't forgotten a thing. He'd gone down with her the first two times so she could show him the blighted patches of giant kelp, and other evidence of the poisoned area, and he'd had no trouble keeping up with her even when they dove to the very edge of the depths she could handle. As a Baba Yaga, that was very deep indeed.

Now they both sat and recovered from their efforts, Beka with her wet suit rolled down to her waist over a crimson one-piece suit, and Marcus in only tiny trunks that hugged his slim hips and lean bottom in a way that made it easy for Beka to wait for the *Serpent* to return from its rounds and fetch them on its way home. She glanced at him from beneath lowered lashes and surprised him looking back at her the same way. They both laughed, a little sheepishly.

"Thanks for all your help today," she said, shifting carefully to sit across from him. "I've got enough new samples to make another start on some of the research I want to do, although I'll definitely want to go back down again tomorrow if that's okay with you."

Marcus scowled, but for once his grim expression wasn't aimed at her. "I can't believe some of the damage you showed me. It just doesn't make sense that it is worse down deep than it is near the surface. That suggests something like an oil spill or chemical contamination from careless transport." He shook his head, one lock of wavy hair flopping into his eyes in a way Beka found ridiculously endearing. "And I'm happy to help, especially if the answers lead us to something that would explain the reason the fish have disappeared."

A spasm of guilt made Beka wince. She was still struggling to deal with Kesh's admission from last night. She really liked the Selkie prince, and she knew he was doing his best to protect his people from what he rightfully saw as the Human threat, but she couldn't allow him to purposely throw off the natural balance as he'd been doing. Distress from her divided loyalties had kept her up tossing and turning most of the night, almost feverish with worry. Even now, her stomach was twisted into knots and she shook her head at the apple Marcus offered her. Hopefully Kesh listened to her, and would send the fish back where they belonged, and she wouldn't be forced to choose between her new friend and her responsibilities as Baba.

"I know you're worried about your father not catching enough fish," she said sympathetically. "It must be hard to watch him struggle to keep the boat going when he is this sick."

Marcus shrugged. "My father is a tough old goat; he'll be fine. I'm more worried about some of the other folks who depend on fishing to keep their families fed and a roof over their heads." A distant look flitted over his face, as if for a moment he wandered through long-forgotten days, revisiting the path once trod by his own younger, more innocent feet.

"My mother left us when I was seven and my kid brother was five," he admitted. "My father wasn't much good at being a da; he absolutely sucked at being both mother and father. A lot of the fishing folk picked up the slack; the women made sure we had clean clothes for school, instead of a bunch of patched and outgrown rags, and that there was real food in the fridge from time to time, instead of just frozen dinners or big pots of leftover fish stew.

"Anyway, these are good people, most of them the same folks that looked out for us when we were growing up. If I can find any way to return the favor, I will. I'm not planning to stick around once my father doesn't need me anymore, but I'd like to help out while I'm here." He visually shook off his old memories, shoving them down deeper than the cold, dark waters they'd just been diving in, and favored her with one of his rare and powerful grins. "Besides, somebody has to keep an eye on you; otherwise who knows what kind of trouble you'll get yourself into."

Beka grinned back, vowing to get those fish back for him if she had to steal Kesh's seal skin and hold it for ransom, like in the old tales. "Who, me?" she said innocently. "When have you ever known me to get into trouble?"

They both laughed, the unaccustomed activity making Marcus suddenly seem younger and less unyielding. Beka had a thought. Marcus worked so hard on the boat for his father, and never seemed to do anything for fun. Maybe she could repay him for his help by getting him to actually relax and have a good time for a change. Although she fully expected that the suggestion that he could have fun in her company would meet with an argument, to say the least.

She leaned forward a little, and hid a tiny smile as she caught him looking down the front of her bathing suit. *At least she knew he was not completely oblivious to her charms. Such as they were.* Perversely, that knowledge gave her the courage to make her suggestion.

"You're an impressive diver," she said. "You must have spent a lot of time in the water when you were younger."

He nodded. "Kind of hard to avoid, growing up on the bay."

"Ever go surfing?" she asked. "Because I have an extra board; I just thought maybe I'd thank you for all your help by taking you out on the waves some morning."

His expression turned to stone, and their temporary camaraderie seemed to slide through her grasp like the fish that got away. Shadows filled his eyes as the past swallowed him up.

"I did surf, when I was younger," he said, his voice flat. "I was okay at it. Not great. Even then, I was really too big to ever be supple enough for anything other than simply powering through the water. My brother Kyle, though, he was a wizard." He shook his head. "You should have seen him; he rode the waves like he was a part of them, as if that board were just an extension of his body. I swear, some days it was as if the water were dancing with him. The sheer joy of it used to radiate from his whole being. Even the other surfers used to stop what they were doing just to watch, if they weren't racing out into the breakers to try and imitate him. It was really something to see."

"It must have been," Beka said softly. "Chico told me he died. I'm sorry."

Marcus grimaced. "It was a long time ago. But no, I don't surf. I haven't since Kyle was killed. After he drowned, the water just didn't seem that friendly to me anymore. Hell, I went halfway across the world to work in the desert, just to get away from it." He looked around at the ocean surrounding the dinghy, as if he couldn't quite figure out how he'd gotten back there.

"Maybe it is time to make your peace with it," Beka said, venturing a small smile. "Since you seem to be stuck here with all this water, for a while, at least."

She tilted her head, thinking out loud. "I suspect Kyle would like it if you went back out on a surfboard, doing the thing he loved so much. I know you'll probably think I'm just being a flaky New Age nut, but I'd bet that if you rode the waves with joy, the way you used to, you might even feel him out there, riding along by your side."

Marcus was silent for a moment, and then he stunned Beka by leaning forward and kissing her with fervor. He wrapped one big hand around the curve of her shoulder and the other around the back of her head, pulling her in close as his lips pressed firmly against hers, both soft and rough at the same time. Heat blossomed between them, roaring up out of her core like a wildfire, fierce and magical and completely unexpected.

The kiss only lasted a minute or two, but it felt like an eternity of bliss. Beka felt strangely bereft without his arms around her.

"Wow," she said, blinking rapidly.

Marcus gave her a wicked grin. "Sorry about that," he said, clearly not sorry at all. "I just wanted to thank you for giving me a way to reconnect with my brother. I never would have thought of it like that." He paused, and then added, his smile widening, "Not being a flaky New Age nut, and all."

Beka rolled her eyes, pleased that her idea had gone over so well. And wondering what on earth she could suggest next to elicit the same reaction. Her heart still hadn't stopped beating fast, and she thought her kneecaps might actually be trembling.

"Does that mean you'll come surfing?" she asked.

"It means I'll think about it," Marcus said, back to his usual serious self.

And for a moment, it seemed as though he was going to lean forward and kiss her again, until a yell from off to their stern heralded the arrival of the *Wily Serpent*, with Chico waving wildly over the port side. Apparently they'd had a good day out on the water.

Beka rather felt that way herself.

TWELVE

"SO, YOU'RE GOING surfing with the fisherman," Chewie said. Of course, his doggy snout was halfway into one of Beka's specimen bags, so it sounded more like "Whrooworoomnn." Still, Beka had no problem understanding him, more's the pity.

"Maybe," she answered, trying for a light tone. "He said he'd think about it. It's no big deal. I just wanted to do something to thank him for helping me with the diving, and he hasn't been out since his kid brother died." She stuck her head into the small fridge to cool off her burning face and, while she was at it, look for something to eat. "I just told him to show up in the morning if he wanted to go with me."

She was *not* going to think about that kiss again. Twice in five minutes was more than enough time to waste obsessing about something that was almost certainly never going to happen again. She definitely wasn't going to tell Chewie about it. He'd never let her hear the end of it. But great Ziva, it had *really* been some kiss. She felt like steam was coming off of her, just thinking about it. Time to think about something else. Like the impossible task of figuring out what was poisoning the sea life in the trench where the Selkies and Merpeople lived.

"Get your nose out of there before you contaminate my samples," she added. Chewie might be more dragon-in-disguise than actual Newfoundland, but he liked to add the occasional bit of drool to the act for verisimilitude.

"Touchy today, aren't we?" Chewie said, sitting back on his haunches. "While you're in there, see if you can find me a nice filet mignon, will you?"

Like much of the rest of the school bus, the refrigerator was more magical than mundane, and it could produce pretty much anything either she or Chewie felt like eating. Thankfully, it wasn't nearly as temperamental as Barbara's hut-turned-Airstream trailer, which had once produced nothing but cherry pies for a week. Beka's residence was much more dependable; probably because it had been changed from a hut into a bus by her predecessor, and simply had never dared to argue.

Beka pulled out a ham and cheese sandwich and put it on a plate, placing Chewie's raw beef on another piece of hand-thrown pottery from one of her craft fair friends and setting it on the floor in front of him. She hoped it would divert him from the current topic under discussion, but no such luck.

"I can't believe that after all these years without so much as a date, you actually have two guys interested in you," Chewie said with his mouth full.

"Hey!" Beka said. "I had a date six months ago with that guy Herman set me up with." Herman was the dwarf that owned the land the bus was currently parked on.

"That wasn't a guy," Chewie argued. "It was a half-tame fire elemental. You barely made it through dinner without him setting your hair on fire." He shook his shaggy head. "I don't understand why you can't date within your own species once in a while."

Beka set her sandwich down, her appetite vanishing almost as fast as Chewie's dinner. "Right. Because most Humans are perfectly comfortable dating legendary witches who can change them into toads at the wave of a hand. Not to mention the insane responsibilities that come with the job, aging slower than Humans, and not being able to have children. Sure. Most guys are lining up to get a piece of that."

Chewie just stared at her with big brown eyes. "This Marcus seems tougher than most Humans," he said. "Maybe you are underestimating his ability to cope with the truth."

"Ha," Beka said. "I think you are overestimating his interest in me, outside of being a source of income for his father. He already thinks I'm a crazy, flaky hippie. Can you imagine what he'd say if I tried to tell him I'm a Baba Yaga?"

Depressed by the very thought of it, she sat down on the floor next to Chewie and put her sandwich on his plate. He breathed flames at it for a minute to melt the cheese the way he liked it, then swallowed the entire crispy, gooey mess in a single bite. The aroma of toasted bread and hot ham filled the bus; it should have made Beka hungry, but instead her stomach just churned and roiled like the sea during a summer squall.

"Well, you might have a point," Chewie said, "but I still like him better than that stuck-up Selkie prince. Something about that guy puts my scales on edge."

Beka's mouth dropped open. "What do you have against Kesh?" she asked. "You've never even met him."

Chewie gazed intently at his empty plate, not meeting her eyes. "I may have followed you down to the beach the other night. And, you know, overheard a little bit of your conversation." He gave the plate a halfhearted lick and then ate it, too, making crunching noises that *almost* distracted Beka from what he'd just admitted.

"You spied on me?" she said, not believing her ears. "Don't you trust me either?"

"Oh, be serious, Beka," the dragon growled. "It's not you I don't trust; it's that seal in man's clothing. There's something just not right about him. What kind of Selkie woos a Baba Yaga and doesn't come to formally introduce himself to her Chudo-Yudo?"

Beka could feel her face turning as red as the ocean at sunset. "He's not wooing me, Chewie. We're just hanging out together. He's a prince, for one thing."

"And you're a Baba Yaga. That trumps even a prince, you silly witch." Chewie snorted, spewing bits of pottery crumbs over the polished wooden floor. "And he is so woo-ing you."

"Well, I'm not interested, even if he is," Beka said firmly. She wasn't, was she? Yes, he was incredibly handsome and sweet and thoughtful. A girl would have to be crazy not to be flattered by his attentions. And she had always been more comfortable with magical creatures than with Humans, no matter that she'd been born one. So why *wasn't* she interested?

Chewie seemed to see into her heart, the way he so often did. Such was the relationship between a Baba and her Chudo-Yudo. For better or worse.

"You like the sailor," he said. "Even though he is Human. Even though you think he doesn't like you." He gave her a lick with his rough tongue; his version of a huge hug. Only wetter. "Good."

No, Beka thought bleakly. *Not good at all.*

THE OCEAN WAS blue the next morning when Beka walked down to the waves, a vivid blue-green that made the sky seem pale and shy in comparison. Exuberant whitecaps raced into shore as if beckoning her to play, and there were already two or three surfers out amid the azure curls, racing each other to the crest of the biggest wave.

Beka would have been out sooner herself, but she'd waited a little longer than usual to see if Marcus would show up. He didn't.

She was feeling a bit out of sorts anyway, tired and achy and a little nauseous, so she wasn't moving quite as rapidly as she usually did. But being out on the water would make her feel better. It always did. Marcus or no Marcus.

A quick tug pulled the zipper on her wet suit the rest of the way closed, and she tucked her board under one arm as she headed over the damp, gritty sand toward the water's edge. Time to get wet.

"Hey, wait up!"

Beka swiveled around to see Marcus loping toward her from the road, her spare board held under one muscular arm, and his tight wet suit molded to his tall, broad figure like a second skin. Her pulse sped up as if she were already riding the waves, and she couldn't help the wide grin that spread across her face.

"I thought you weren't coming," she said as he came up to her.

Marcus looked unusually flustered, his wavy hair curling every which way and his breathing rapid, as though he had run to catch up. "Sorry," he said, "I meant to get to your place earlier, but my da was having one of his bad mornings, and then we got into a fight when I insisted he wait for me to get back before taking the boat out."

He paused to take a deep breath and gave her a crooked smile. "And I confess, I hadn't really made up my mind whether or not I was going to come, right up until the last minute."

Beka was just glad he was there, with a depth of feeling she chose not to look at too closely. "I see you found the board all right." She'd taken it out in case he showed up, and then just walked away and left it leaning up against the bus when he hadn't.

His hazel eyes twinkled, green and brown, with a hint of copper. "Your dog said it was okay if I borrowed it."

Beka stiffened in shock. "Chewie talked to you?" She was going to kill that dragon.

Marcus let out a laugh, one of the first she'd heard from him. He already seemed more relaxed than usual, despite the dustup with his father, so maybe her plan was working.

"Well, he nudged the board with his nose and it fell on me. I took that as permission." Marcus shook his head. "I wasn't sure if he was supposed to be out, loose like that. Aren't you worried about him running away, or someone stealing him?"

Whew. "Uh, no, not really," she said. Chewie took his duties as guardian for the Water of Life and Death seriously; he rarely strayed far from the bus, even though the magical elixir was well hidden in a secret compartment, and locked behind a powerful spell to boot. He occasionally came for a brief romp in the water he loved so much, but he would never go far, or be away for long. Still, she couldn't exactly tell Marcus that.

"He's very well trained," she said, figuring it wasn't a lie if she didn't specify at what. "And you've seen him—do you actually think anyone could take him if he didn't want to go?" Marcus probably weighed at least 225 pounds, although all of it was lean muscle, without an extra ounce of fat. But Chewie outweighed him by twenty or thirty pounds, even so. And, of course, he was a damned dragon. But she couldn't say that either.

The former Marine gave her a wry look. "You've got a point there. I was just happy he let me take the board without so much as barking at me." He hefted the surfboard meaningfully. "Shall we see if I remember any of the things I used to know? I hope I don't make an ass out of myself. It's been a long time."

Beka smiled up at him. "Don't worry; it's just like falling off a bike."

"I was afraid you were going to say that," he said, but he grinned at her all the same as they paced down to the surf.

MARCUS COULDN'T REMEMBER the last time he'd felt this good. Years, probably. For once, he wasn't looking over his shoulder for the enemy to sneak up on him, or fretting about his da, or trying to figure out what the hell he was going to do with his life next. The early morning sun filled the sky with light, and the reckless waves pounded away all the stray thoughts until there was only water and man and board, in perfect balance.

Or not, he thought, as an unexpected breaker surged sideways and knocked him off the board. Laughing, he pulled himself back to the surface, spitting out salty brine and heaving himself back up again. He'd never admit it to Beka, but this had been a brilliant idea.

He'd been afraid that his brother's ghost would haunt him, out here in the misty spray, but instead, it was almost as though he could feel Kyle's spirit joined with his, like an echo of kinder days, colored blue-green like the water, and golden like the sun-touched clouds overhead.

"Having fun?" Beka appeared next to him, paddling with him toward an incoming swell.

Marcus nodded, amazed as always by the way his heart lifted at the sight of her. Even now, with her hair pulled back in an untidy braid and dripping wetly over one shoulder, bright blue eyes squinting against the spray, she was more appealing than any glamorous movie star. There was something just so *real* about her. She still wasn't his type, of course, but he had to admit, he was getting accustomed to having her around.

And if he'd been daydreaming about kissing her again, well, it wasn't as though he was going to do anything about it.

He opened his mouth to answer her, maybe even to admit that yes, he was actually having fun, but the words never made it past his lips. Another surfer slid up on Beka's other side, paddling over with effortless ease.

"Beka, darlin', what an unexpected pleasure, to meet up with you on such a fine morning. Surely the gods are smiling on me today." The stranger somehow managed to bow and paddle at the same time and look damned good doing it.

Marcus had a completely irrational urge to knock the other man off of his surfboard and hold him under the water for a minute or ten.

"Kesh!" Beka said, seeming delighted. "I didn't expect to see you until tonight."

Oh, great. So this was the guy she'd been seeing. The one she said she wasn't dating. Maybe someone should tell him that, since Kesh was gazing at Beka with an altogether too-proprietary air. Funny he should just happen to show up. And the morning had been going so well too.

They all spent another hour or so paddling out and then riding waves back in, although it was clear that both Beka and Kesh were much more experienced and proficient at it than Marcus was. Rationally, he knew that was to be expected. Hell, he hadn't been on a board in ages; really, he was doing damned well, all things considered, for a guy who'd spent most of the last twelve years in the middle of the desert. But he still hated that the other man was showing him up, doing fancy flips and turns, and generally being dazzling and handsome and charming.

Marcus shook his head, pushing wet hair out of his eyes as he headed back in to shore. He knew he was being irrational. It's not as though he and Beka were a couple, or ever likely to be one. She deserved a lot better than a burned-out Marine with a sick father and a bad attitude. And there was no place in his life for some New Age wisdom-spouting surfer chick who lived in a painted bus, for god's sake. It wasn't as though he wanted to be with Beka. He just didn't want some guy with an Irish accent and gleaming white teeth to be with her either.

Jaw tight, he laid his borrowed board upright in the sand and waited for Beka to finish riding her current wave. Her graceful form cut through the water as though she were a part of it, and for a moment he just watched and admired. As soon as she came in, he'd just tell her that he had to get back to the boat, and call it a day.

"A wonder to behold, is she not?" a lilting voice said in his ear.

Marcus practically jumped out of his skin. *How the hell had the guy snuck up on him like that?* For a moment, his heart beat wildly as he flashed back to a scorching-hot alley in Afghanistan—to a man with glinting black eyes and a viciously curved knife sliding silently out of a doorway, the smell of garlic and exotic spices and the dust underfoot, the sound of his own blood spattering onto the ground as they fought. Then he clenched his fists and jerked himself back to reality. He was home and safe. More or less.

"Yes, she is," he said, his tone even. But he had a feeling

the other man could sense how much he'd rattled Marcus, and was enjoying it.

You're being an idiot, he scolded himself. *You just don't like him because he's interested in Beka. That's hardly fair, since you're not.*

"It is kind of you to allow her to accompany you and your father out on your ship," Kesh said in the same casual voice Marcus had used. His eyes were aimed at the sea, and Beka, but his attention was firmly rooted onshore. "I find her current preoccupation misguided, however, and I think it might be best if you no longer encouraged it."

Marcus folded his arms over his chest. "I think that's up to her, don't you?"

Kesh turned his head and gazed into Marcus's eyes. Despite the fact that Marcus had about forty pounds on the other man, and was at least three inches taller, a slight chill ran down his spine. Not fear. Kesh didn't intimidate him, no matter how much he might be trying to. More like that feeling he got when he saw a scorpion or a coiled snake or a great white shark; that visceral gut reaction that said *predator*.

"You would be wise to tread carefully where Beka is concerned," Kesh said. "She belongs to me."

The HELL you say, Marcus thought. But out loud, he merely said, "She doesn't seem to know that. And Beka strikes me as a girl who makes her own decisions."

Kesh made a low sound in his throat, almost like a growl, as the woman in question bounded up the beach, grinning madly at them both as she rode the high that came from catching a great wave.

"Did you see that?" she yelled, still a few yards away. "I owned that wave! It was amazing! Unbelievable!"

"Leave her to me, fisherman. Or you will regret it." Kesh strode off toward Beka and pulled her into an exuberant hug.

"Definitely unbelievable," Marcus muttered to himself. This was *not* how he'd planned for his morning to go.

THIRTEEN

BEKA SPENT THE next couple of days trying to find answers and getting nowhere.

She called her friend from the university to check in, and see if any of his students could remember whatever results they'd turned up before the fire. *That* was a frustrating phone call.

"Everything," Bran said, unhelpfully.

"What the hell is that supposed to mean?" she asked. "How could they have found everything?"

She could practically see the shrug through the phone. "The ocean is a dirty place these days, Beka," he said. "They found traces of pesticides, petroleum distillates, heavy metals, even radiation."

"Radiation!" Beka had a vision of herself suddenly glowing in the dark.

Her friend laughed. "They've been detecting small amounts of radiation for the last year or so, washed across the Pacific from the Fukushima explosion in Japan. It's nothing to worry about. My guess is that you haven't found your 'ground zero' yet."

His voice grew more serious, as he added, "Be careful, Beka. Whatever is causing this, it is clearly capable of creating serious damage in plant and animal life. You may be tougher than the average girl, but that doesn't mean you'll be immune to its effects. Maybe you should report this problem to the government and let them take care of it."

She thanked him, then put the phone down with a bang. If only she could. Unfortunately, the government she reported to had already called in their supposed expert—and she was it.

To make matters worse, both Marcus and Kesh were acting weird. Well, weirder, really.

She'd thought the morning out surfing had gone really well, and Marcus seemed to have a great time. But ever since, he'd been even ruder and more distant than usual, barely speaking to her when they went out on the boat to dive.

And Kesh . . . she had no idea what was going on with Kesh. Suddenly he was everywhere. He showed up in the morning to escort her down to the dock, saying that then she didn't have to find a parking spot for the Karmann Ghia (like she couldn't tuck the tiny car into a corner and then hide it with magic so she wouldn't get a ticket), and then came to get her when she was done for the day. He carried her diving gear for her as if she were a schoolgirl, and brought her little gifts like flowers or some ancient trinket he'd found on the bottom of the sea.

Their sunset picnics on the beach seemed to have become an every night affair too. She knew she should be grateful for his attention—he was a prince, after all, and a very handsome one at that—but she was getting to the point where she missed her quiet nights burning marshmallows by a bonfire with Chewie in front of the bus.

But she couldn't figure out a way to tell Kesh she wanted a night off from his company without hurting his feelings (or offending his royal father, which would have been worse). So she spent her mornings with a grumpy ex-Marine and her evenings with a too-charming Selkie, and she was rapidly becoming sick of it all.

In fact, she just felt sick in general. She blamed too much diving, deeper than was truly comfortable even for her, and too much rich food at her nightly banquets-by-the-sea. Not to mention too many nights spent wide awake and staring at the paneled ceiling of the bus, trying to figure out what she was going to do if she couldn't solve this problem and live up to her title as Baba Yaga. Or if she even wanted to be Baba Yaga at all. Her thirtieth birthday was rapidly approaching, and she still hadn't made a decision. Although she'd skipped her last couple of doses of the Water of Life and Death, mostly because she just didn't feel like she deserved to drink the rich and magical elixir that kept her young and boosted her magical ability.

KESH SAT IN the battered wooden chair as though it were a throne, his black silk shirt and expensive linen pants as out of place in the dingy, crowded office as an orchid in a field of dandelions. On the walls, faded maps of fishing routes were interspersed with photos of numerous generations of men in boats, men showing off gigantic fish, and the exterior of the building when it was new and shiny and proud.

Across an equally battered metal desk heaped with invoices, bills, and miscellaneous other bits of paper, all held down bits of flotsam reclaimed from the sea, Leo Koetke shook his head wearily. "I've told you, Mr. Kesh, I'm not interested in selling the processing plant. My grandfather started it with his brothers, my father ran it until the day he died, and I'm not about to give up on all that history. Yes, we've had a rough couple of years, what with the competition from out of the country and the crappy economy, but we're hanging in there. So I'm afraid you're going to have to find someplace else to build your luxury condos."

Kesh leaned back in a chair that creaked in protest, and smiled benignly at the other man. Neither the slightly run-down surroundings nor their short, balding owner impressed him much. But he had plans that would change all that. Power on land was all about money, and Kesh was discovering he enjoyed playing the games that brought him more of both.

"I have heard that the fish are not running well this year and you have had to cut back on hours and staff," Kesh said in a conversational tone.

Leo shrugged, calloused fingers fiddling restlessly with a chunk of old iron that might have once been part of an anchor. "Some years the fishing is good, some years it isn't. That's the nature of the business. In a couple of weeks, it could all turn around." He started to rise from his seat. "If we're done here, I have to get back to work. I've got a machine down that I have to jury-rig a part for, and it isn't going to get done while I'm sitting here talking. Like I've told you before, I have no plans to sell."

Kesh didn't move and the smile never left his lips. But malice gleamed out of his gray eyes. "I have also heard you are behind on paying your workers, you owe money to suppliers, and you had to take out a large loan on the property. What a shame, when your family has owned the building for so long."

The shorter man subsided back into his chair and glared across the cluttered expanse of his desk. "I don't know where you're getting your information, but none of that is any of your business."

Kesh raised one eyebrow. "It is true, though, is it not? Just as it is true that if the fish do not return quickly, you will be forced to close your doors whether you wish it or not." He leaned nearer, suddenly projecting an aura of menace that had been previously hidden from view. "Would it not be better to sell to me now than to wait until you are forced to shut down and get nothing?"

Leo bit his lip, running one hand through already rumpled hair. "I can't just sell up. It isn't only that the business has been in the family for three generations. I'm one of the biggest employers in the area; if I shut down, where will my people get work? They depend on me, on this place. Your condos aren't going to provide jobs for more than a few gardeners and maids. I can't do it, I tell you." The piece of iron he'd been toying with slipped through his fingers and fell unnoticed onto the gouged linoleum floor.

"Oh, I am certain we could find employment for a few of your workers," Kesh said with a leer. "I noticed a number of reasonably attractive women when I came through before. I have a new venture—floating casinos located on boats just over the line into international waters. They are proving to be surprisingly profitable, and I can always use pretty women to provide entertainment to my predominantly male and wealthy clientele."

"You want to use my workers as *prostitutes*?" Leo got up so fast his chair fell over with a clatter. "You're crazy!"

Kesh lifted his hands in the air. "How is being a paid companion any worse than cleaning fish for a living?" He rose in a more leisurely fashion and headed for the door, turning around before he went out to add, "It would be best to accept my offer sooner rather than later, Mr. Koetke. The price will go down every day you wait. And I do not believe you have much time left."

He shut the door softly behind him and stopped to wink at the cute redhead sitting at the reception desk. She blushed a becoming pink that matched the strand of little pearls she wore around her neck. Her fingers reached up involuntarily to touch them.

"Good meeting, Mr. Kesh?" she asked.

"All my meetings are good," he said with a grin, laying on the charm even thicker than usual. "I wouldn't have it any other way, darlin'."

The secretary giggled and gazed up at him with open admiration. "I guess that's why you're so successful, huh?"

Kesh leaned over and kissed her lightly on crimson lips. "It helps to have friends in all the right places," he said, barely managing to conceal his distaste. The woman was far below him, and not his type, but an endless font of useful information.

She giggled again. "Will I be seeing you again soon? That last restaurant you took me to was so fancy." She sighed in memory.

"You can be sure you will, darlin'," Kesh said. *And you can also be sure that you will be the first one I send to work on the casino boats after I raze this dump to the ground.* "You have no idea how much I am looking forward to it."

FINALLY, IT WAS Sunday, and that meant the *Wily Serpent* wouldn't be going out. She'd told Kesh last night that she needed the day to herself to do some magical work, and he'd agreed, however reluctantly, to give her some space.

So first thing after the breakfast of toast and tea that was all her twitchy stomach seemed willing to tolerate these days, she'd pulled out a bunch of arcane supplies, the bits and pieces she needed to work with the powers of Earth, Air, Fire, and Water, and a dozen tiny glass dishes filled with the various samples she'd collected over the last week. Chewie sat off to the side to "supervise" (she'd made him stay at least three feet away from her during complicated magical workings ever since the time he sneezed and melted the enchanted necklace she'd been making as a wedding gift for Barbara).

Most of the magic that a Baba Yaga did was instantaneous and relatively effortless; the snap of her fingers could summon a book from across the room or turn a cloudy day into instant rain. But she was trying to achieve something much more delicate, examining the essence of each frond of seaweed or fish's fin, so she'd decided to go the more traditional route of casting a ritual circle to contain and focus her power and whatever showed up during her explorations.

It would have been easier to have done the work outside, in a larger space, but Beka wasn't in the mood to drag everything out to someplace private and then do even more magic to ensure that some tourist didn't stumble upon her and get the surprise of his or her life. (The windows of the bus were already enchanted so that no one could see in; a hand-me-down from her mentor Brenna.)

So she just made do with the patch of clear floor in front

of the sofa, sprinkling sea salt around herself and her supplies to create a ritual circle. Once that was in place, she sealed it with a drop of her blood by using one of her sharpest knives to prick her thumb, letting the salt in her own fluids join the beginning and the end of the white crystals.

A humming in her bones, too low to hear, told her that the circle was in place. That meant it was safe to call in the elementals: the swirling red-hot salamander that represented Fire, the mythical golden Bird of Paradise who represented Air, the tiny goat-legged faun who represented Earth, and a delicate sea horse swimming in its own bubble of seawater that stood for Water.

"Thank you for coming," she said, bowing slightly to the elementals. "You are welcome here."

All the small creatures bowed back from their places at the quarters: Air in the east, Water in the west, Fire in the south, and Earth in the north.

Beka gestured at the bowls that contained the selections of damaged and mutated sea life. "Can you tell me what caused this?" she asked.

Each elemental took a turn hovering above the collection of glass bowls, sending that same subliminal humming sensation through Beka's bones. Finally, the salamander said in a fierce sizzling voice, almost too high-pitched to hear, "It comes from the sun, the great cauldron."

The faun said hesitantly, in tones that rang clear like bells in a forest clearing, "It comes from deep under the earth, Baba Yaga, from the great untapped veins below."

The Water and Air elementals just shook their heads.

Beka forced herself to smile and thank the elementals for their aid, giving them the tiny gifts she had gathered for them—bits of shiny crystal for the faun, a perfect miniature shell for the sea horse, a small candle for the salamander, and for the Bird of Paradise, a vial of air from the moment when the first rays of light hit the ocean, one of its favorite meals.

She had no idea what their words meant, but at least they'd tried.

As the elementals examined their gifts, Beka placed some of her samples into the black marble mortar and pestle she had inherited from Brenna. It was a bit of an "in joke" for the Baba Yagas, of course, since the earlier Babas in Russia and the surrounding Slavic countries actually rode around in enchanted mortars that were steered by huge pestles, but it was also a handy tool for magical work.

The marble was beautiful—dark porous stone with white swirls like clouds in a midnight sky—but it was also charmed so that whatever was ground within it would meld together in new and powerful ways. Beka was hoping that if she combined some of the pieces she had brought up on her dives, they would tell her something together that she hadn't been able to discern from the individual bits on their own.

She crumbled some grayish kelp, a sad cousin of its healthier vibrant green relatives, and added the briny remains of tiny krill. But as she reached for a faded off-orange branch of coral, Chewie suddenly sat up and looked at the door.

"You have company," he said in a low rumble.

Oh, bother. Beka suppressed a groan. If Kesh had ignored her request for time by herself and shown up with another damned picnic, she was going to turn him into a toad, son of the King of the Selkies or no.

A brisk knock on the door was accompanied by a slightly more hesitant, "Beka?" But the voice belonged to Marcus, not Kesh.

Surprise made her drop the pestle with a clatter, and that was obviously too much for the elementals, all shy creatures to begin with. They each disappeared from sight with a slight popping noise and a buzzing sensation that made Beka's ears ring. Chewie rolled his big brown eyes at Beka, although whether at their behavior or hers, she couldn't tell.

"Beka? Are you home?" The knock on the door was repeated, a little louder this time.

She sighed, rubbing her palm through the line of salt nearest to her so that the power of the circle faded away with a slightly disappointed *whoosh*, like the curtain falling after a less-than-successful play.

"Coming," she yelled, looking helplessly at the collected jumble of esoteric tools in front of her. It looked like exactly what it was: a witch's ritual circle. How she would explain that, she had no idea. She'd just have to keep him outside.

She walked over to the door of the bus, Chewie padding along on his gigantic furry black paws behind her as if he were a shadow of impending doom. Her stomach knotted for a moment before she opened the door, but she couldn't tell if it was due to nerves or anticipation. Or maybe just frustration; she'd almost been getting somewhere. Or nowhere at all.

"Hey," Marcus said as she peered out at him. As usual, he looked tall and strong and calm, and made her heart beat ridiculously fast for a moment. "Are we interrupting anything?"

"We?" she said, and then smiled as she saw Tito standing next to him, the skinny boy practically lost next to the large ex-Marine. "Tito, dude! This is a surprise!" She put up her hand and he high-fived her with glee.

"Hi, Beka," he said, his voice cracking on the last part of her name. "I hope it's okay we came to your house." He glanced around him at the outside of the bus. "Which is *way* cool, by the way. I can't believe you actually live in a bus, man."

"We were down on the beach below with Tito's mom," Marcus said in his much deeper tones. "And I was telling Tito about how we went out surfing the other day, and he told me he'd never been and really wanted to try it. So I thought maybe we could borrow a board, if that would be okay."

Beka swallowed hard, fighting back a moment of jealousy. She knew that the boy's mother was single, and she tried to tell herself that they were all just hanging out together for Tito's sake. And that even if they weren't, it was none of her business.

Then she met Marcus's eyes and saw the sadness there, and realized with a shiver that he was afraid that if Tito didn't get to try surfing soon, the boy might never be able to do it. Looking at Tito, she saw the same fear, bravely held beneath the surface, but there nonetheless.

"Of course you can borrow a board," she said, suddenly not caring about her failed magical experiment. "I've got a smaller one that should be easier for you to start out on. I'm sure you'll pick it up in no time."

Tito's face lit up as if he had swallowed the sun. "Cool! Marcus said he taught his brother when they were younger, so he can definitely teach me."

Beka raised an eyebrow at Marcus. She'd gotten the impression he didn't talk about his brother much. Tito must really be getting under his skin. "I'm sure Marcus will do a great job teaching you." She grinned mischievously. "He's very patient."

The former Marine made a decidedly undignified face at her. "Ha," he said. "Just because *some* people drive me crazy doesn't mean that everyone does." He held out a hand in invitation. "Why don't you come with us? You can meet Tito's mom, and give him pointers if I leave out anything important." He almost looked like he wanted her to come, although she was pretty sure he was just being polite in front of the boy.

"Oh, please say you'll come, Beka!" Tito said, practically jumping up and down with excitement. "It'll be great! My mom even packed us a picnic to eat on the beach."

Beka's stomach did acrobatic flips at the thought. Or maybe it was the notion of spending the afternoon on the sand watching Marcus and Tito's mother, who was undoubtedly lovely and unmagical and completely Human.

"Uh, no, that's okay," she said. "You guys go ahead. I don't want to horn in on your day out."

Her treacherous dragon-dog butted her in the back of the knees with his huge head, almost sending her flying down the step. Marcus reached out one large hand to steady her, laughter chasing away the shadows that had been lurking in his hazel eyes.

"It looks like Chewie thinks you should come with us," he said, lips twitching. "And even I know better than to argue with Chewie."

Tito's face was a study in amazement as he looked at Beka's companion. "What the heck kind of dog *is* that? He's humongous!"

"He's a Newfoundland," Marcus said, at the same time Beka said, "That's because he's part dragon." They all laughed.

"Can he come to the beach with us?" Tito asked, a little wistful. "My mom and me can't have a dog in our apartment, but I really like them."

Beka patted Chewie regretfully on the head. "Sorry, dude, but someone has to stay here and guard the bus from marauding pirates. Besides, he's really too big to take out when there are innocent bystanders. Believe it or not, some people find him kind of intimidating."

Chewie woofed in indignation, sounding like a train in a long, winding tunnel.

"Maybe next time," Marcus said gravely to Chewie. "This time, we'll just borrow Beka, if that's all right with you?"

Chewie woofed again, and gave Beka another not-very-subtle shove. She glared at him, to no noticeable effect.

"I guess I'm going," she said, trying to act as though that wasn't exactly what she wanted. "Let me go grab that board for you." She hadn't been able to give Tito the treasure he wanted the day they'd been out on the boat, but at least she could give him this.

"Whoo hoo!" Tito shouted.

Marcus grinned at her. "Ooh-rah."

Beka rolled her eyes. It was going to be a long day.

DOWN ON THE beach, Tito's mother Candace was just as lovely as Beka had imagined, despite the dark circles under her brown eyes and the lines of strain that worry had etched around her generous mouth. But her enthusiasm when she greeted Beka seemed quite genuine, and her gratitude made her hard to dislike.

"It's very kind of you to let Tito use your surfboard," Candace said in a soft voice that was almost lost behind the raucous sounds of the beach at midday.

Beka was so used to the quieter morning setting, when the only people out and about were serious surfers, people walking their dogs, and a few folks practicing Tai Chi on the hard-packed sand, the noise and commotion of the afternoon crowd caught her by surprise. Children raced up and down the beach, shrieking and laughing, and groups of women clustered under umbrellas chatted as they compared recipes or talked about the latest books on their Kindles. Gulls swooped overhead, competing for the abundant treats left behind by careless snackers, almost louder than the gathered Humans below. The smell of sunscreen overwhelmed the more delicate briny air of the sea. It was like being in a different universe.

Beka didn't much like it. But she wasn't here for herself, so it didn't really matter.

She and Candace sat on a striped beach blanket, watching Marcus show Tito the basics of how to catch a wave and balance on a board. The guys were still practicing on the damp area toward the edge of the water; the ocean itself would wait until Tito had gotten the hang of things, and even then they would stay in the shallow bit for today. Tito looked to be having a grand time anyway.

"I suppose you think I'm crazy for letting a kid who is in the middle of chemotherapy try to learn how to surf,"

Candace said. Her shoulders were hunched and she gazed anxiously at her son as he toppled over again, giggling madly.

Beka shook her head. "Are you kidding? Look how much fun he is having. I'd think you were crazy if you didn't let him come down here today." She took a deep breath, breathing in a moist and salty lungful. "Besides, I can't think of anyplace more healing to be than here."

Candace gave her a grateful smile, relaxing a little. "It sure beats hospitals," she said, gazing at Tito sadly. "Do you have any kids, Beka?"

"No," Beka said, watching the children racing around on the beach. As always, the sight made her heart clench at the thought of never having one of her own.

"Ah," Candace said. "I hadn't planned to have any, myself. Tito was a 'whoops.' His father never even bothered to meet him. And sometimes it has been tough, doing things on my own. But I wouldn't trade him for anything." Tears shimmered in her eyes, refusing to fall. "Marcus has been just great, ever since he met Tito and me in the waiting room at the chemo center. He's a real sweetheart. You're lucky to have him."

Beka watched Marcus help Tito find the right stance on the board, one large hand on the boy's narrow shoulder, the other pointing out to sea. She tried not to stare at his wide shoulders and tight butt, thankful for the dark glasses that hid her gaze. Marcus might be cranky and rigid with her, but he was patience personified when it came to Tito.

"Uh, I don't. Have him, I mean." Beka could feel herself flush and hoped the other woman would blame it on the heat of the sun. "That is, we're not a couple. I'm just paying him and his father for the use of their boat, that's all."

Candace arched one dark brow. "Really? I thought I picked up on a vibe."

Beka played with the sand next to their blanket, building a tiny castle complete with an impenetrable moat. Some things were only possible in fairy tales. And not the kind of fairy tales that Baba Yagas featured in; those tended not to have happy endings.

"Nope. No vibe," she said lightly. "If you're interested, go for it."

Candace gave her a wide-eyed look. "Me? God, no! I mean, he's a great guy and all, but not my type. A little too much of a good thing, if you know what I mean. I prefer my guys on the skinny, geeky side, to be honest." She laughed. "Tito looks just like his father, minus about a foot in height and a pocket protector."

Beka tried to convince herself she wasn't relieved. After all, it wasn't as though it made any difference. Hell, there was a whole beach full of women who probably all liked the tall, rugged, impossibly manly type. It wasn't his fault he was by far the sexiest guy on the beach.

"No vibe, huh," Candace muttered with a snort. "Better tell your hormones that, girl, 'cause from where I'm sitting, there's vibe all over the place."

"Mom! Hey, Mom!" Tito had progressed as far as the shoreline and waved at his mother madly. "Come see what I can do!"

Candace gave Beka a wry smile, but there was a bounce to her walk as she went down to join Tito and Marcus. It was clear that she needed this day out as much as her son did.

Beka couldn't imagine what it would be like to have a child who was sick and not be able to do anything about it. Motherhood was a tough job. Of course, Candace struck her as a pretty tough woman, but still. Beka wasn't sure how she'd handle things, under the same circumstances.

She watched the three of them playing amid the waves. Marcus, Tito, and Candace looked like a not-so-unusual California family, the dark-skinned boy and his mother romping alongside the tanned sailor. Beka wondered what it felt like to be a family; that wasn't something she had ever experienced. Obviously, no family was perfect; Tito only had a mom, albeit one who clearly adored him, and Marcus and his father barely spoke most days. Still, Marcus had come back to take care of the older man when he was needed, because that was what family did.

Beka couldn't imagine having someone who would do that for her. Her own family was long gone. Brenna had followed a silent call of magic one day twenty-five years before and found Beka at the other end, crying piteously next to her dead mother's stiffening body in the back corner of a dank, abandoned building full of empty-eyed druggies. No one had known who Beka's father was or cared that Brenna was taking her away. Even her original name was lost in misty memories of hunger, loneliness, and vague fears that probably meant something to her four-year-old self.

Brenna had renamed her Beka and raised her in the hut-turned-painted bus as they traveled around the country. The old Baba Yaga had trained Beka to be her successor, and taught her everything she'd deemed important for a Baba to know—but she hadn't taught her anything about what it meant to be a part of a Human family. Sometimes, Beka thought it was probably far too late for her to figure it out on her own.

MARCUS LEFT TITO and his mother giggling as they took turns being knocked off the surfboard into the low break-ers near the shore. He'd turned around to wave at Beka, and there was something so sad about the way she was sit-ting all by herself on the blanket watching them romp, he'd moved without thinking about it, drawn to her like a magnet to a lodestone.

Her eyes were hidden behind the dark lenses of her sun-glasses, and her thoughts were hidden behind her usual cheerful expression, but something about the way she sat, still and silent, made him certain that her thoughts were less than pleasant. He didn't know why, but he didn't ques-tion it either.

"Heya," he said, plopping down next to her on the wide woven cloth, its bright black and yellow stripes making it look like she was riding a giant bumblebee. Considering the bizarre effect she seemed to have on him, maybe it would be more appropriate to envision her riding a broom. God knows, she had cast some kind of spell on him; he hadn't stopped thinking about her since the day they'd pulled her up in the net, like a Mermaid captured from the arms of the sea.

"Heya," she said back, stretching her long legs out in front of her and distracting him even further with the sight of all that tanned, sleek flesh.

"Penny for your thoughts," he said, reaching into the cooler for a bottle of iced tea. The elusive scent of strawberries briefly triumphed over the suntan lotion emanating from the baking bodies next to them, then disappeared like a mirage. He peered deeper into the cooler. No strawberries.

"I'm not sure they're worth that much," Beka said, flashing him a pale imitation of her typical grin.

"Really, what were you thinking?"

She tilted her head down the beach at Tito and his mom. "Just that they're good people."

"They are," Marcus agreed. He'd been drawn to the boy since the day they met. The military shrink would probably say it had something to do with losing his brother at an age not much older than Tito was now, and maybe that was part of it. But he respected the way the kid was handling a tough situation; he didn't wallow in self-pity, tried to keep a positive attitude, and worried more about his mother than he did himself. Not bad for someone who hadn't even hit puberty yet.

Beka stole Marcus's iced tea and held the cold bottle against her neck, letting droplets of condensation trickle down into her cleavage. He shifted slightly, his denim cutoffs suddenly tighter. Luckily, Beka was still gazing out at the water and didn't seem to notice the effect she was having on him. Of course, she never did. Clearly, the intense physical attraction was all on his side. Just as well, really, under the circumstances, although it was hard not to feel a twinge of disappointed male ego.

He grabbed another iced tea for himself and they sat there for a moment in companionable silence.

"You're good people too," Beka said after a minute. "I think what you're doing for them is really terrific. I know you've already got your hands full dealing with your dad's illness and the boat and everything. It's nice of you to take the time to treat them to a day at the beach. Poor Candace looks like she hasn't done anything fun in ages, and Tito is having a blast."

"Good people, huh?" Marcus felt the edge of his mouth curving up in a smile and forced it back, giving Beka an exaggerated scowl instead as she turned to look at him. "I thought you considered me to be cranky and unpleasant. I believe the term 'stick-up-the-butt' might have been used."

She snorted. "You've got to admit, we got off to a rocky start. But you're kind of growing on me."

The smile slid out despite his best intentions. "Yeah, you're kind of growing on me too."

Marcus could see that Tito and Candace were getting ready to head back to the blanket, and he had a sudden urge to make this rare moment of détente last a little longer.

"Are you planning to come out and dive tomorrow?" he asked. "We're pulling out of dock at dawn. My da has a feeling that the fish will be running near the spot you usually go in, so it's no trouble if you want to tag along."

She shrugged one tanned shoulder. "I'm not finding what I'm looking for at the depth I've been diving. I'm going to have to go quite a bit deeper the next time, and that means a longer dive, since I'll have to come back up slowly to compensate. Is that going to be a problem?"

Only for his nerves, waiting for her to come back up from the dark and treacherous depths of the ocean. "No, not at all. As long as I can be back on board in time to help them pull in the nets when they're done, the guys and my da should be able to manage the rest without me."

He watched Tito's progress out of the corner of one eye, trying to gauge how much time he had left before the other two rejoined them.

"Uh, do you have any plans for tomorrow evening?" He braced himself to hear her say she was going out with that guy Kesh again; it seemed like he was always around these days. Staking out his territory, which just happened to include Beka, apparently.

"Nothing definite," she said. "Why?"

"It's no big deal, but a couple of the guys I knew from high school asked me to meet them in Santa Carmelita tomorrow night. There's some sort of barbeque on the beach, with fireworks and stuff, and they've been asking me to get together and do something since I got back, so I really couldn't say no." He took a deep breath. "The thing is, I'm not great with crowds these days, and explosions, well, they make me kind of edgy. I thought if you went with me, it would help remind me that I wasn't in Afghanistan anymore."

She lifted an eyebrow in question, but he didn't know how to explain to her that something about being with her seemed to ground and calm him—even when she was frustrating the living crap out of him. It was as though the sunlight in her soul shined a light into the dark places in his. But there was no way he could put that into words without sounding like a complete idiot.

"Please?" he said instead. "It might even be fun. We don't have to hang out with my friends the entire time."

Beka nodded at Candace and her son, who were nearly back to where they were sitting. "Why don't you ask them? I'm sure Tito would love fireworks."

Marcus shook his head. "Past his bedtime, and I'm sure Candace has to work. Besides, I'd rather go with you. It'll impress the hell out of my friends if I show up with a gorgeous blonde on my arm."

Beka rolled her eyes at him, the movement barely visible behind her sunglasses, but a big grin slid across her face and a hint of a blush touched the top of her high cheekbones. "I suppose you want me to wear something low-cut with a short skirt too," she said, choking back a laugh.

"Well, if you insist," Marcus said. "I wouldn't try and talk you out of it." He held his breath, trying to remember that he didn't really care if she came or not, that it was just to keep him from jumping every time they set off a sparkler. "So you'll come?"

Her smile would have set the showiest fireworks display to shame. "It sounds like fun," she said. "And I've got the perfect dress. It's going to knock your socks off."

Marcus wasn't sure if that was good or bad, but he couldn't wait to find out.

FOURTEEN

BEKA WAS FEELING ridiculously cheerful when she arrived back at the bus. Anticipation and excitement effervesced in her blood like bubbles in a champagne glass; sparkling and popping against the edges of her aura. A rosy glow seemed to suffuse her vision, rendering the mundane world unusually bright. A seagull's raucous cry sounded like Mozart as she climbed the steep bluff with her surfboard on her shoulder, and the ragged, hardy weeds that grew to either side of the path were suddenly more beautiful than the loveliest hothouse orchids.

By the sea god's beard, you have got to get a grip, she told herself sternly. *It's not a date. Marcus just needs someone to ground him in a tricky situation and you were the easiest person for him to ask.* It didn't matter. The stupid grin wouldn't leave her face anyway.

She tucked the board away on its rack in the storage space under the bus and, giving in to impulse, spun around in an impromptu dance around the clearing, only stopping when she grew dizzy.

"What the hell has gotten into you?" Chewie was sitting

in the open doorway of the bus, his mouth gaping open to display an impressive array of very sharp, very white teeth and a lolling black tongue. "Are you drunk? Or, I don't know . . . possessed?"

Beka didn't even care that her dragon was laughing at her, that's how good a mood she was in.

"I'm fine," she said, pushing him out of the way so she could go inside. "I just had a really nice afternoon, that's all. It was a lot of fun watching Marcus teach Tito the basics of surfing. He's great." She plopped on the couch, noticing in passing that Chewie had actually put away all her magical supplies. It truly was a red-letter day.

"Who's great?" Chewie asked slyly. "Marcus or Tito?"

Beka sat up straight. "Tito. I meant Tito, of course."

"Of course."

"Although it turns out that Marcus maybe isn't *quite* as big a pain in the ass as I thought he was." Beka fiddled with a blue-green cushion embroidered with bright orange fish. "He was really patient with Tito today."

"Uh-huh."

"And he kind of asked me to go into Santa Carmelita with him tomorrow night for some barbeque thing they have on the beach," Beka added in what she hoped was a convincingly casual tone. "Some old friends of his asked him to come, and he's apparently not too comfortable with the fireworks they're having later in the evening and thought he'd do better if he had someone to, uh, hold his hand. Metaphorically speaking."

"Right," Chewie said dryly. "Metaphorical hand holding. You should be good at that. As long as there's no *actual* hand holding." He snorted, tiny flames shooting out to singe the edge of the couch. Beka extinguished the flames and repaired the damage without even thinking about it, since such things were a common occurrence when one lived with a dog who was mostly dragon.

"I think he has a bit of post-traumatic stress disorder, even though he would never admit it," Beka explained. "Mister tough guy. But obviously he can sense my Baba nature, and realizes subconsciously that I can help him to stay more in control." She could feel that silly grin still flitting in and out of existence like sunspots during a flare; trying to keep it off her face was as impossible as catching a rainbow. Hopefully Chewie wouldn't notice.

Fat chance.

"Maybe he senses your great boobs and fabulous legs too," Chewie said, leering at her.

"Oh, shut up," Beka said. Fat chance of that too.

Chewie gave her a long, considering look. "Oh, oh," he said.

"What?" Beka looked over her shoulder, wondering if something had somehow snuck through the hut-bus's defenses. She had been neglecting her protective magics lately, what with everything else that had been going on.

"I don't believe it," Chewie said. "You're in love with him."

That wiped the grin off her face. "I'm what? Don't be absurd."

"You are," the dragon insisted. "You've finally fallen in love. It's about damned time."

"Have you been chewing on my salvia plant again?" Beka asked. "Because I think you're having hallucinations."

"You wish," Chewie said. "I saw you—you were *dancing*. It's a classic symptom. You're in love."

"I can't be," Beka said in a whisper. "He's a Human. A Human who dislikes everything I stand for."

Chewie shrugged, knocking over a chair in the process. "Better him than that damned Selkie prince. And hey, you never know. It worked out for Barbara. She and her sheriff have settled down together and she's happily training little Babs to be a Baba Yaga. If it can happen to her, why not you?"

Because I'm no Barbara, Beka thought. And Liam might have learned to deal with the fact that the woman he loved was a powerful witch straight out of Russian fairy tales, but somehow, she couldn't imagine Marcus dealing with her special brand of weirdness nearly that well.

"It doesn't matter," she said firmly. "You're wrong. I'm not in love with Marcus. I'm not in love with anyone. I was just in a good mood. Which you have now ruined, thank you very much."

She stalked over to the refrigerator and glared at it until it offered up a nicely chilled bottle of sauvignon blanc. Then she pulled a couple of her favorite knives down off the wall and proceeded to sharpen them until they practically glowed.

Chewie very wisely made himself scarce.

IF MARCUS HAD been wearing socks, they definitely would have been knocked off. As it was, his toes curled in their sturdy sandals, and he had to fight the impulse to stand up even straighter and salute.

Beka looked amazing.

In the slowly gathering twilight of the summer evening, there was something haunting and magical about the dress she wore. As promised, it dipped low in the front, highlighting her abundant feminine curves. Capped sleeves ended in wide ribbons of silk that matched the panels of the skirt below, seeming to flow around her as if the dress were a living thing. The length of the skirt gave the illusion of modesty, until she took a step forward and the panels parted and swirled, revealing long swaths of shapely leg.

The fabric itself was a watercolor swirl of yellow and gold and amber, and a few hues he didn't even have a name for, like the sunrise on a foggy day. It set off perfectly the glorious glossy fall of her blond hair, which flowed loose and shimmering over her shoulders and down her back. The only adornment she wore was a simple gold necklace in the shape of a dragon, and the matching earrings he'd noticed the first day he'd seen her. He'd thought then that she was some miraculous sea creature. Now, he thought she was a goddess. Much too good for a mere mortal like him—but man, was he going to have fun showing her off.

"You're staring," Beka said, a tiny wrinkle appearing between her brows. "Is it too much? I could go change."

"Don't you dare," Marcus breathed. "You look incredible.

I was just trying to figure out if I should charge people just for the privilege of being on the same beach with you."

"Oh. Uh, thanks, I guess."

For the first time since he'd met her, Beka was at a loss for words. If he didn't know any better, he would have said she'd been worried about what he thought. But this was Beka; so clearly that wasn't true.

"Shall we go?" he asked, gesturing toward his Jeep. "I'm sorry I don't have a carriage that does justice to that dress, but I wasn't expecting Cinderella."

Beka laughed and patted Chewie on the head before heading toward the car. "I'm more like the fairy god-mother than I am Cinderella, but that's okay—I'm not in the mood for Prince Charming tonight anyway."

Take that, handsome Irish surfer guy. Marcus felt an unaccustomed trickle of happiness swirl around his heart like the way Beka's dress eddied and flowed over the ground. Her hand felt warm in his as he helped her into the passenger side.

"That's good," he said. "Since I am neither a prince nor charming. But I'll do my best to be a little less crabby than usual."

"That's what I was hoping for," she said with a laugh, "Prince Hardly Crabby At All. Dude, this is going to be a great night."

AND IT WAS. Marcus hadn't expected much more than to just get through the experience; show up, be as sociable as he could manage, pretend to still have something in common with guys he hadn't seen since he was a teenager, try not to make an ass out of himself in front of Beka, eat some food, drink a beer or two, and go home.

So far, none of it had gone the way he'd expected, except for the eating and the beer. Maybe Beka's magical dress had turned *him* into Cinderella, because he was actually having a ball. Even the crowds weren't bothering him as much as he'd thought they would, probably because he was too busy watching Beka to pay much attention to anyone else.

His old high school friends turned out to still be pretty nice guys, all married to attractive and pleasant women who went out of their way to try and make him welcome in what was obviously a tight-knit group. He'd worried that he wouldn't have much in common with the men, since their lives had taken a much different path than his. He was fairly certain that none of them had ever killed an enemy in battle and watched the life seep out of his body.

But everyone else was happy to keep the conversation going, occasionally stopping to ask him a question about his father's health or what it felt like to be back after all these years. Those he mostly sidestepped, so as not to bring down the mood. Still, it was more fun than he'd expected to hang out on the beach and eat decent barbeque with a cold beer in his hand and Beka by his side, making him look good merely by being there.

If he was going to be completely honest with himself, Beka was most of the reason why the evening was going so well. She'd already charmed all of his friends and their wives, and subtly filled in the spaces in the conversation when he couldn't think of an acceptable answer to things like, "So, how are you and your father getting along these days?" One of the women recognized her from a craft fair where Beka sold her jewelry every year, and that got them chatting about all sorts of female-centric topics that Marcus eventually tuned out.

Instead, he studied the beautiful woman next to him. In the flickering lights of the torches set out by the restaurant hosting the barbeque, she seemed almost ethereal, as if she might vanish between one moment and the next. She gave every appearance of having a good time, but he'd noticed that she hardly ate anything, pushing the food around on the plate but rarely bringing the fork to her lips. He thought she looked pale, too, although it was hard to say in the tremulous torch light.

Of course, maybe she was just thinking about her work

and her lack of progress finding answers. Dave, the guy who invited Marcus in the first place, had already mentioned that he was planning to finally give up the fishing boat he'd inherited from his dad—too few fish to keep going, he'd said. And Frank, who loved the sea almost as much as Marcus's father did, confessed that he was worried about having the money to send his kid to college, since he'd already taken out a second mortgage on his house. Frank's wife, Nancy, laughed and said if necessary, she could always take up prostitution. But you could tell that, under their cheery exteriors, they were all worried.

They changed to more pleasant topics of conversation, but Beka just looked grimmer and grimmer. Marcus wasn't having any of that.

When there was a break in the chatter, he leaned over and said quietly in her ear, "Are you okay? If you're not having a good time, we don't have to stick around for the fireworks."

She gave him a startled look, blue eyes wide. "I'm having a great time," she said. "I'm just a little tired from the dive earlier. It took more out of me than I thought, I guess."

Marcus wasn't surprised. He wasn't sure how deep she'd gone, but her return journey to the surface seemed to take forever. By the time her head had broken through the water by the dinghy, he'd been on the verge of jumping in to make sure she was okay. Only her periodic tugs on the rope between them kept him from doing so, and by the end he'd been sweating and agitated from the wait.

"You should probably take a couple of days off," he suggested, although he hated the thought of not having her on the boat. When had he grown so addicted to her company?

"Maybe," she said. "I could use the break to do some research. I'm not sure I can learn anything more from diving anyway. I've replaced all the samples I got originally, and I can't dive any deeper than I did today."

The fact that she didn't argue with him made him even more concerned. Beka *always* argued with him. She must be feeling lousy indeed. Maybe she was coming down with one of the summer colds that was going around. They'd warned his father at the hospital to stay away from anyone who showed signs of being sick. All the more reason to keep her away from the boat, dammit.

Marcus suddenly had enough of being social. "This has been great," he said to the group they were sitting with. "It's been really nice to see you all again. But I think we're going to take off for now. Thanks again for inviting us." He stood up and Beka stood with him, smiling at everyone and adding her thanks.

"Aren't you going to stick around for the show?" Frank asked. "It starts soon."

His wife Nancy elbowed him in the ribs. "I think maybe Marcus would like to spend a little time with Beka without all us old married people cramping his style." She nodded toward the bonfire where a local band played an eclectic mix of rock, swing, and jazz. A dozen couples had kicked off their shoes and were dancing on the sand. "I'm guessing he'd rather dance with his beautiful date than sit around talking over the good old days, most of which you guys made up anyway."

Frank studied Beka a little too earnestly, about one beer over his limit. "Hell yeah, I see what you mean." Nancy elbowed him again, harder this time, and everyone else guffawed. Eventually they managed to get away, and Marcus could feel his face burning like the fire they were heading toward.

"Sorry about that," he muttered. "They meant well. We don't have to dance, of course."

Beka stopped walking and put one hand on his arm. Electricity shot through him where her flesh touched his. "Does that mean you don't know how to dance?" she asked, a sly twinkle in her eye.

"I'll have you know that I am the best former Marine–fisherman dancer on this beach," Marcus said stoutly. The fact that he was probably the only one didn't make it any less likely that he would step on her feet, of course, but if the music stayed slow enough, he could probably keep up without making an ass of himself.

Her laugh trilled lightly above the notes of the flute player, flying up like lightning bugs into the night sky. When they reached the circle around the band, the tune changed to something quiet and slightly mournful from the eighties; Billy Joel, maybe. He wasn't sure. All he knew for certain was how right Beka felt in his arms, her face turned up toward his with a smile, the silk of her hair brushing against his skin as he twirled her around.

The rest of the world vanished into the distant background, until there was nothing left but the salty breeze off the ocean, the warmth of Beka's presence, and a music that seemed to come as much from the stars and the moon and the rare bubble of happiness in his chest as it did from any human hands.

Until someone tapped him on the shoulder and a familiar voice said, "May I cut in?"

FIFTEEN

WHAT THE HELL was he *doing here?* Marcus spun around to face Kesh, his hands balled into fists as he fought the almost uncontrollable urge to pound the other man into dust.

Beka said, "Kesh!" But Marcus thought he detected more surprise than pleasure in her voice.

"Did you invite this guy to join us?" Marcus asked through gritted teeth. This was taking "three is a crowd" to whole new levels.

Beka shook her head. "No, I did not. In fact, I haven't seen him since the day before yesterday; I'm not even sure how he knew I would be here." The look on her face was distinctly unwelcoming, which made Marcus relax just enough to start thinking instead of simply reacting.

"Did you follow us here?" he asked, taking a half step in front of Beka. *Great. The guy was a stalker. Well, if he wanted Beka, he was going to have to go through Marcus to get her.*

Kesh shrugged elegantly. "I was concerned when Beka did not arrive for our usual dinner on the beach," he said. "When I arrived at her home to make sure that she was not ill, I saw you driving away. So yes, I followed her. But merely to ensure her safety."

Beka scowled at him, for once clearly not impressed by his charm. "We don't have a 'usual dinner,' Kesh. Just because we got together a few nights in a row doesn't mean that it is going to happen every day." She crossed her arms over her chest, making that magical dress do dangerous things. "And I certainly don't need you to keep me safe." She gave him a glare that was steeped in meaning. "Have you forgotten who I am?"

Marcus felt like he was missing something, but he wasn't going to worry about it right now. "Beka, this guy is stalking you. He could be dangerous. Maybe you should report him to the cops." *Or let me beat the crap out of him.*

Beka shook her head, hair pale in the moonlight. "You're overreacting, Marcus. He's from a background that's . . . different from ours. He just doesn't understand about boundaries, that's all."

How different could Ireland be? Marcus breathed out through his nose, trying to rein in his temper. "Is that why he told me to stay away from you? And said that you belonged to him? That's not a cultural difference, Beka, that's just arrogance."

She slid across the sand to stand between the two men, her gaze swinging back and forth. "He *what*? When?"

"That morning we were all surfing together." *Come to think of it, he'd shown up out of nowhere that day too.*

Beka narrowed her eyes at him, and he suddenly thought that maybe he should have just kept his mouth shut.

"You mean *that's* why you were acting so rude and cranky? Because Kesh warned you off?" She rolled her eyes in his direction, and then turned that piercing blue gaze on Kesh. The temperature on the beach seemed to drop ten degrees, and Marcus realized that the few times he'd thought he'd seen her angry, she'd merely been a tad peeved. This was Beka angry, and it was a truly impressive sight.

"And you, Your Highness," she bit off the words as she poked one finger into Kesh's slim chest. "I do not belong to you. I do not belong to *anyone* except myself, and you would do well to remember that. You are not my ruler. You are not my lover. And if you ever pull anything like that again, you won't be my friend either. Have I made myself perfectly clear?"

Kesh actually took one step backward, alarm flitting across his handsome face for a moment before it was replaced by his usual composure, and then by what was no doubt supposed to be an endearingly sheepish grin.

"You are quite right, my darling Beka. I overstepped, and for this I am very sorry." He bowed over the hand that had jabbed him and kissed her fingers.

Marcus gritted his teeth until he thought he would crack a molar.

Big brown eyes with absurdly long, dark lashes topped a crinkled smile. "Please say that you will forgive me, Beka. I shall be crushed otherwise."

Beka stared at Kesh for one long moment, until her anger slid away like frost on an autumn morning. "Fine, you're forgiven."

Marcus opened his mouth to protest, then closed it again. She didn't belong to him either, and he couldn't tell her what to do. So much for a great evening.

Kesh shot him a triumphant look out of the corner of his eyes and turned to bow again to Beka. "Then may I have this dance, my lady?"

"No," she said.

Marcus wasn't sure which one of them was more surprised, him or Kesh.

"No?" repeated Kesh, a baffled expression on his face. "But I apologized."

"And I accepted your apology," Beka said in a calm voice. "But I promised this evening to Marcus, and that didn't include sharing it with you. After all, you wouldn't like it if I invited him to join our picnics on the beach now, would you?"

Marcus almost laughed, watching Kesh try and figure a way to wiggle out of that one. He had to bite his lip as Kesh sputtered his way through the beginnings of three different sentences, only to end up saying, with less than his customary poise, "As you wish. Perhaps you will dine with me tomorrow," and then stalked off across the sand without a backward glance, almost knocking over a woman who happened to be in his way.

"Sorry about that," Beka said, putting her hand back in his and resuming their interrupted dance. The band had switched to something faster with a Latin beat while the three of them had been absorbed in other matters, but Marcus stuck with the slow sway that was his only speed.

"Not a big deal," Marcus said. After all, he was the one who'd ended up with the girl. He could afford to be gracious in victory. Although he couldn't keep himself from adding, "I'm still worried about that guy, Beka. He might be dangerous."

"Kesh is just from a very different culture," Beka said, although she softened the disagreement by moving in even closer as they danced. "He's kind of, um, privileged, where he comes from, and he's not used to people saying no to him. But he'd never hurt me." She tilted her head up and smiled into his eyes. "Although it is sweet of you to worry."

With Beka in his arms, Marcus felt anything but sweet. She set his blood on fire and made him want to scoop her up and carry her off to someplace lonely and private and dark. Part of him actually sympathized with Kesh, although that didn't make him like the spoiled rich guy any better. There was something not right about him, but now wasn't the time to push the issue. Not when there were so many better things to do.

"I'm sorry he interrupted such a lovely evening," Beka said, echoing his thoughts. "Let's just pretend he never showed up, and we can move on to whatever was next on the agenda."

Marcus gave her a slow, wicked smile, feeling the smoldering heat rise to the surface like molten lava, irresistible as a force of nature. "If you insist," he whispered, and bent his head to capture her lips with his own. He put all his yearning, all his gratitude for the gifts she'd given him, all that heat bubbling up within him into the kiss, feeling her lips yield beneath his.

She returned his fire with fire, kissing him back with a wild abandon that left them both trembling and enraptured, wrapped around each other in the midst of a crowd, focused only on each other.

Overhead, fireworks lit the sky, but neither of them noticed.

FROM A STAND of straggly trees overlooking the beach, Kesh watched them embrace and thought about death.

Bad enough that Beka had shamed him in front of that peasant. But for her to choose a mere Human fisherman over him—this he could not forgive. Or permit to go unpunished.

Yes, he was already poisoning her with the radiation-tainted fish he fed her at every romantic moonlit dinner. But he had never really intended it to kill her. When she had grown ill and weak and given in to his wishes, he would simply have suggested that she take an especially large dose of the Water of Life and Death. She was a Baba Yaga; it should have been sufficient to drive the poison from her body. Then, even more grateful, she would have been his to use as he pleased.

Now, though, a cold rage filled that place where his soul would have been, had he cared to possess such a useless thing. She had the audacity to reject him. Him—a Prince of the Selkie people. Baba Yaga she might be, but she was still merely a woman, and a foolish one at that. Look how she had fallen for his lies, swallowed up each charming twist of the truth as he slowly used her own weakness against her. He had had such hopes for their future; him as a king on the land, with her power at his beck and call.

But he would have to find another way. He did not need her magic. Not after tonight. No, now he needed only one thing from the Baba Yaga—her screams as she died in agony, calling his name.

BEKA CALLED MARCUS'S name as she came into sight of the *Wily Serpent* the next morning, and he raised a hand in greeting, his usual scowl replaced by something that looked like it might grow up to be a smile.

She ducked her head, hiding one of her own, as she swung about with her gear. Chico and Marcus Senior were there, checking the nets over one more time before setting out.

"Morning, Beka," Marcus's father said gruffly. "Joining us again, I see." Despite his pallor and the dark shadows under his eyes, he was clearly still the captain of the ship. He pretended to be annoyed, but it was just a game they played. Chico winked at her as she walked by; her presence on the ship always seemed to put the old man in a better mood, and that made life easier on everyone.

Everyone except Marcus, who'd only mellowed a little where his father was concerned, although to be fair, his father hadn't mellowed back any either. They were at least being civil to each other, which was more than could be said for when she first started going out with them, but it was as if neither one wanted to be the first to bend and show affection to the other.

Beka sighed a little but refused to let the old wounds between the two men ruin her lovely mood. Despite Kesh's unexpected arrival, she and Marcus had enjoyed a wonderful evening, far beyond anything she'd imagined when she'd agreed to go to the barbeque with him. She still thought Chewie was out of his mythical mind, suggesting that she'd fallen in love, but she had to admit, the kiss she and Marcus had shared on the beach had been . . . remarkable.

Legends had been written about less.

He'd kissed her again when he'd brought her home around midnight, but that time had been gentler, quieter.

Maybe he'd begun to regret the passion he'd revealed in that first one. Or maybe it was just the inhibiting presence of Chewie, standing by the door of the bus waiting for her like a giant furry chaperone, his dark mass barely visible against the backdrop of the summer night.

Either way, there had been a glimmer of something like hope in his voice when he'd asked her casually, "So, are you coming out with us in the morning?"

She hadn't actually intended to; the odd weakness and fatigue she'd been feeling were starting to make diving difficult, and she'd meant it when she told him earlier that she didn't think there was anything to be gained by gathering more samples. But the thought of not spending the day in his company was almost painful, so she decided that maybe one more day of easy exploration near the surface wouldn't hurt anything. She could always start her research when she got home in the late afternoon.

Marcus came down from the prow to give her a totally unnecessary hand with her equipment and a brief, secret smile that caused butterflies to flutter around inside her already unsettled stomach.

"We're going out to the same spot as yesterday," he said as the boat pulled away from the dock. "My father was really happy with the mackerel haul we brought in, so he's going to see if they're still around."

The huge catch had made Beka happy, too, mostly because it meant that Kesh had done what she'd asked and stopped chasing the fish away from the Humans' boats. She hoped he was feeling as benign after she'd made him leave last night. Still, she thought she'd made her point, and he was a reasonable man. It wasn't as though he was actually interested in her; he and Marcus just had one of those competitive testosterone things going on.

She wasn't sure if Marcus was actually interested either, but she was working hard at convincing herself that she didn't care. Much.

As usual, she and Marcus put on their diving gear and

lowered the dinghy into the water. The *Wily Serpent* moved off slowly, nets lowered to glide through the nearby seas in search of fish. Rather than try and make awkward conversation, she slid into the water right away, a few sample bags tucked into her belt pouch. Marcus gave her the thumbs-up and she dove down, although not nearly as far as she had been going.

So far, there was still no sign of an issue this close to the surface, other than the usual bits and pieces of flotsam that floated out from the shore or were dumped by careless boaters. That was good news for fishermen like Marcus, but it meant that the problem was almost certainly limited to the Selkie and Mer home trench, far below.

This baffled her, since the mystical creatures were normally excellent custodians of their watery realm; it was literally their entire world, and there was no other for them to go to. Not that this stopped Humans from destroying their own environment, but sea beings had a close connection to the ocean they lived in, and generally treated it with respect and care.

Beka swam lazily back up toward the dinghy, wondering if it was possible that one of the court wizards could have done some sort of magical working that had gone wrong, and then been afraid to confess it to his or her ruler. She wasn't looking forward to broaching the question with either the King of the Selkies or the Queen of the Merpeople, but it was worth looking into.

Despite the rich oxygen mix in her tanks, even this brief dive had left Beka feeling tired and short of breath. Maybe she would risk the potentially unsettled atmosphere, stuck in a tiny boat with Marcus, and give herself a break. Or even let him take a turn diving instead, although he'd be doing it for fun, not to try and keep an impossible promise and save an entire supernatural homeland.

A huge shadow blocked out the light from the surface for a moment, and she glanced up to see if she'd misjudged the location of the dinghy. What she saw sent adrenaline rushing through her veins and made her heart skip a beat as she grabbed for the knife she always wore in a waterproof sheath strapped to her calf.

Above her, a great white shark circled, its belly only six feet from the top of her head, its massive body between her and the surface.

$\mathfrak{S}$IXTEEN

THE SHARK SWAM through the currents, its vast maw open as if tasting the water for hints of something edible. Beka desperately hoped it would find something other than her and swim away.

It didn't.

Instead, it turned its blunt, bullet-shaped snout in her direction, revealing multiple rows of sharply serrated teeth. Beka froze, knife in hand, trying to estimate her chances of getting past the beast to the surface without being noticed. Considering that it was at least twenty feet long and had the ability to sense electromagnetic fields as well as movement, she didn't count the odds as being in her favor.

A brief, regretful thought of Marcus and what might have been flashed through her mind, and then she focused all her attention on trying to stay alive.

The shark circled, closing in on her in an ever-tightening loop. Beka gripped the knife so hard her fingers ached, the sound of her own breathing reverberating loudly through the regulator in her mouth. She had to force herself to take slow, calm breaths; panicking underwater would get her killed with or without the shark's assistance.

Something about its behavior struck her as odd; sharks usually came up on their prey fast, attacking from below. Despite what you saw in the movies, they didn't usually lurk about, looming ominously. Maybe this one hadn't read the rule books, because it was doing a damned good job of doing just that.

For a moment, she thought she caught a glimpse of an impossible oddity—a thin golden chain around its massive neck. And then it attacked and she stopped thinking and just reacted.

It roared at her like a jet plane, its bulk displacing the water forcefully, its jaws gaping wide, one dark eye staring into her soul. The power of its passage spun her around, and she was untouched but disoriented for a moment, unable to distinguish up from down in the murky depths.

Just as she glimpsed a hint of sunlight from above, the shark came back again. Its own length was all that saved her for the moment; the necessity of a wide turn bought her an extra second to get her knife in position for a wild slice across its gills. Clearly hurt, the shark lashed around in the water, almost missing her entirely. Only the jagged edge of one tooth tore through wet suit and skin, leaving blood leaking out from a wound in her left calf.

It wasn't much. But in the end, it would probably be enough.

MARCUS SAT IN the dinghy and looked at his waterproof watch for the third time. According to the timepiece, which had always been reliable up until now, Beka still had four minutes until her next check-in. Four minutes until he felt that tug on the rope that meant she was okay. Much longer than that before her tanks started to get low and she should be heading for the surface.

But his skin prickled across the back of his neck in a way that hadn't happened since Afghanistan. A soldier learned the hard way not to ignore that feeling. Not if he wanted to survive to fight another day, and all his buddies with him.

Muttering a curse, Marcus pulled on his mask, grabbed the spear gun he'd tucked into the dinghy just in case, and slid into the water. Better to look foolish than to spend one more minute in that tiny boat, sure that something had gone wrong in the blue-green depths below.

Heading directly down, along the path of the rope that Beka should be following back up, he didn't have far to go before he came upon a scene that seared itself on his brain, joining the worst horrors of the battlefield to forever haunt his dreams like reels of black-and-white movies.

The largest shark he'd ever seen was just ahead of him, its colossal body almost hiding Beka from sight. She was backed against a rock formation, knife held iron-steady in one hand while the other clamped desperately around a seeping gash in her leg. Blood oozed viscously into the water, like a watercolor brush tossed into a jar.

He could tell the second she spotted him. The clear seawater between them showed her eyes widening behind her mask, first in hope, then in terror as the shark's snout swung ponderously in his direction.

Arming the spear gun, Marcus held up three fingers, and then pointed to the surface. Beka shook her head frantically, attracting the great white back in her direction. Its huge head moved back and forth between them, hesitating, and Marcus held up three fingers again, gesturing at her bleeding leg. Reluctantly, she nodded, and braced herself against the rock.

He aimed the spear gun at the shark, released the safety, and held up one finger, then two, then a third. As Beka launched herself toward the surface, swimming as rapidly as she could, Marcus moved even closer to the shark and fired the spear directly into its dark and malevolent eye. It gave a massive heave, thrashing around in a frenzied dance of teeth and fins and tail, spiraling down toward the bottom of the ocean. In the twilight depths, gray-black blood stained the water.

Once Marcus was sure the shark wasn't coming after them, he eeled his way to the surface, the muscles in his thighs burning as he pushed himself to his limits. Beka clung to the side of the dinghy, taking great gasps of air, a look of almost comic relief lighting up her face as he broke through next to her. He tossed the spear gun carefully into the bottom of the boat, and then lifted her in after it. Adrenaline got him out of the water almost without effort, although once they were both in and safe, he could feel the aftereffects pulsing through his system. Battle had always been like that—the rush, followed by the backlash.

His heart threatened to burst through his rib cage as he gazed at Beka's bleeding leg. Closer examination showed him that the gash was deep but clean, and the shark seemed to have missed anything vital. They'd been lucky. Very, very lucky.

"Well, that was an adventure," Beka said in a shaky voice as he pulled out the first aid kit and started to bandage her leg, brushing aside her protest as he cut through the expensive wet suit to expose the wound. The suit was ruined anyway. "Oh, and by the way, thanks for saving my life."

"No problem," Marcus said, keeping his tone casual and his eyes focused on her injury, so she wouldn't see the emotion he couldn't quite keep off his face. "All part of the friendly service. But don't be surprised if my father adds on an extra charge."

"It's a good thing we went to that barbeque last night," she said with an unsteady laugh. "I'm not sure I'll be doing a lot of dancing in the near future."

Marcus tucked the end of the bandage securely into place and reached for the radio to call his da to turn the *Serpent* around and come get them. But first, he gave in to irresistible impulse and kissed Beka so hard their teeth clashed.

"Just so long as you save a dance for me," he said. "I'll wait as long as it takes."

MARCUS INSISTED ON driving her home, even though she told him—repeatedly—that she was perfectly fine. The extensive first aid kit aboard the *Wily Serpent* had done a perfectly good job of taking care of the gash, which looked worse than it was, and she'd refused to go to a hospital to have it looked at. As a Baba Yaga, she healed considerably faster than most Humans, and once she was able to put some of Barbara's supercharged herbal wound cream on it, it would vanish in no time.

Of course, Marcus's father had griped about their mishap interrupting his fishing, and threatened to bill her for the loss. But since the nets were empty, it looked like the fish had gone elsewhere again anyway. Beka thought guiltily of her argument with Kesh and hoped it wasn't her fault. Marcus Senior still looked tired and wan, and he was due for another chemo session later that week, so he didn't give more than a token protest when Marcus suggested that they should take the ship back in to shore.

Back at the bus, Marcus stowed her gear while she went inside, barely limping at all.

"What the hell happened to you?" Chewie barked.

"Nothing. I just got a little nibbled on by a shark," Beka said, sinking down on the futon and running her hands through his soft fur.

"Nibbled on by a shark doesn't sound like nothing," Chewie said. "In fact, it sounds like a lot of something. I don't like it."

"Well, to be honest, I didn't like it much either," Beka said. "Remind me not to repeat the experience." She wondered if she should mention the gold chain she thought she saw the shark wearing—but she had to have imagined it in the heat of the moment.

Marcus came up the stairs into the bus, shaking his head. "You know, it sounds for all the world like the two of you are actually having a conversation. Too bad I don't speak Dog."

"I was just explaining to Chewie what a hero you are," she said. "He saved my life," she told Chewie. "Shot the shark with a spear gun so I could get away."

"Aw, shucks, ma'am, it weren't nothin'," Marcus said with a smile, coming to sit down next to Beka.

Chewie made a gagging noise. "I don't think I can take any more of this," he said, giving Beka an affectionate swipe with his tongue before heaving himself up in a mass of dark fur and dust motes. "I'm going to go out and pee on something." He padded over and opened the door with his teeth, leaving it to Beka to get up and shut it, grateful that Marcus couldn't actually understand him.

"Talented dog," Marcus commented.

"You have no idea," Beka said. She sat back down next to Marcus and gazed into his hazel eyes for a moment without speaking. Every time she looked at them they were different. In the diffuse afternoon light streaming through the bus windows, they seemed almost green, with hints of brown and copper and amber, like a piece of polished agate washed up by the sea.

"Thank you again," she said quietly. "You know, for saving me. You really are my hero."

"I'm just glad I got there in time," Marcus said. In that simple statement lurked the unspoken memory of all the times he hadn't, the men he hadn't been able to save. She could see the pain of it in those gorgeous eyes although he never said a word. "I've kind of gotten used to having you around." He reached out and picked up one of her hands, holding on to it lightly.

Beka could feel a smile tugging at the corners of her lips. "I was under the impression that you thought I was a flaky tree-hugging hippie chick."

"You mean, like you think I'm a cranky, rigid, stick-up-his-butt former Marine?" He laughed. "It turns out, shockingly enough, that I actually like flaky tree-hugging hippie chicks."

Beka could feel her heartbeat start to race, fluttering butterflies seeming to chase one another around her belly. "Really?" she said in a teasing tone. "*All* flaky tree-hugging hippie chicks?"

Marcus paused as if considering. "No. In fact, there is one in particular who has somehow gotten under my skin." He leaned in closer, as if he was going to kiss her, but then pulled back, leaving her feeling bereft. The laughter slid off his face, replaced by a serious look.

"Can I ask you one question?"

She looked down at their joined hands, pondering all the questions he might ask that she wouldn't be able to answer—at least not with the complete truth. Looking back up at him, she took a deep breath.

"Sure, what's the question?"

Marcus scanned her face as if he could read the answer before he'd even formed the question. "Is there something going on between you and that guy Kesh?"

Beka almost giggled in relief. Yes, there had been a point when she thought that there might be some potential there . . . but that point was long past. If she was going to be honest with herself, she couldn't imagine being with anyone other than Marcus. She didn't for a moment believe that there was any way that they would be able to make things work together, but he was all she thought of. Kesh didn't even come into the equation.

"No," she said decisively. "We're just friends. Nothing more, in the past *or* in the future."

"Good answer," Marcus said, and then he did kiss her, leaning in to touch her lips with his, at first gently, and then with a firm and assertive pressure that urged her to return the kiss with interest. So she did, sliding forward into the protective circle of his arms, which tightened around her in response.

The heady scent of him filled her nostrils, that particular blend of salt and sea and musk that was his alone. Just the smell of him made the blood rush to her core; the feel of his strong arms, the sweet taste of his mouth made her whole body pulse with need and longing.

Marcus made a groaning noise deep in his throat and started to pull away.

"Don't you dare," she breathed in his ear. "If you stop kissing me, I'll . . . I'll bite you."

"You can bite me anyway," he suggested, nibbling on her neck and sending shivers of anticipation and sensation sliding down her spine. "But we should stop. You have a hurt leg." He loosened his arms reluctantly.

Beka gazed into his eyes, so dark with desire they seemed to go on forever, capturing her soul in their depths. "My leg is fine," she said, standing up to show him. "Look, no limp."

"What are you doing?" Marcus asked in a husky voice, getting up too. He looked like he wanted to grab her and pull her back into his arms, but didn't quite dare.

"I'm going to show you a magic trick," she said, grinning.

"A what?"

She gestured him back and leaned down to tug on the futon, which glided out smoothly to reveal its other form.

"Voila," Beka said. "A bed."

"Oh, thank god," Marcus said, scooping her up and laying her out on the bed, and then pulling his shirt off over his head in a quick motion before joining her there. "I want you so much I feel like I'm going to explode."

"I hear that Marines are good with explosions," Beka said, turning sideways so their bodies faced each other. She ran eager hands over his chest, marveling at the strength and breadth of him and the crisp hair that tickled her palms, then up his shoulders and down his strongly muscled arms. His lips found hers again, and everything dissolved into a delirious blur of touch and taste and blissfully erotic sensation; his fingers and tongue explored her, discovering secrets she never even knew she had.

Their clothes flew away as if enchanted, and the feel of his naked body on hers drove her almost mad with desire. As they joined together, she could feel her nails biting into his back, but that only made him move faster and deeper and wilder inside her, the floodwaters of passion rising up to drown them both in waves of ardor, intensifying and ebbing, swirling and racing, ever higher, ever stronger, until together they crested with a moaning, throbbing crescendo that made their two bodies into one, gloriously united in joyous celebration.

Afterward, they lay in each other's arms, panting and sweating and laughing. Beka rested her head against

Marcus's chest, listening to the strong beat of his heart, and had a sudden, appalling realization: Chewie had been right. Somehow, no matter how impractical, no matter how improbable, she had fallen in love with this man. And that meant that she had no choice—she had to tell him the truth. Even if it meant she lost him forever.

SEVENTEEN

MARCUS TRIED TO remember the last time he felt even remotely as good as this, and failed completely. Lying there with Beka in his arms, spent after a passionate bout of love-making he had never expected, the summer sun sliding in past slanted shades to bathe them both in buttery yellow warmth, was as close to nirvana as he ever expected to get.

His life up until now had mostly been about survival, nothing more. He'd survived his mother's abandonment, survived his father's harsh and brutal approach to parenting, survived the loss of his beloved younger brother—though that one only barely. Then he'd gone on to join the Marines and survived boot camp and twelve years in the harsh desert.

For the first time since he was a kid, he felt something almost like . . . hope. A shimmer of happiness, a glimpse of optimistic possibilities. Clearly, Beka was not the craziest one in the room. And yet, despite all that he had seen and learned in his years on this planet, he suddenly felt as though a curtain had opened and revealed a future he could never have hoped to achieve.

All because of Beka.

He looked down at her; this unexpected miracle. Her head was pillowed on his shoulder, that glorious blond sheaf of hair falling in a tumble of silken strands over both of their naked bodies. One tanned leg was thrown on top of his in comfortable abandon, and her arm was flung over his chest as if she lacked the energy to move it. It was a position he could get used to.

In fact, it was with some shock that he realized he could get used to the entire package: Beka, sex, curling up together . . . forever.

Forever was never a word he had considered before. Everything in his life had always been temporary. Living with his father until he was old enough to get away, staying with the Marines until he couldn't stand the killing anymore, coming back to take care of his sick da until the old man died or got better enough to manage without him. But suddenly, he found himself thinking of the long term; settling down, finding something to do with the rest of his life that actually meant something to him, and maybe, just maybe, sharing that with someone.

He laughed a little, knowing that he was getting ahead of himself. *Way* ahead, where one completely inappropriate but bewitching hippie surfer girl was concerned. There was no way that things could work between them. They were so different, and he came with so much baggage. Why would a woman so full of light and life ever be interested in a man as dark and haunted as he was?

And yet, for a moment, he actually dared to hope. There was something so real and true about Beka, it made him feel as though he could find whatever was real and true in himself and bring it to the surface. He'd been accused of having trust issues—and no wonder if he did, between a mother who'd left when he was a kid, a father who had allowed his only brother to be killed, and a dozen years spent living in a war zone. But with Beka, he felt as though somehow he might find a way to learn how to trust. Now *there* was a crazy thought.

"What's so funny?" Beka asked, a strange shadow coming over those glorious blue eyes as she tilted her head back to look at him. "Something you'd like to share with the class?"

Marcus smiled at her. "Just thinking. Mostly about how wonderful you are."

She flushed, and he enjoyed watching the pink tide moving across her face and down her chest.

"I'm not wonderful," she said. "Although that certainly was."

He bent his head to kiss her. "Yes, it was. And yes, you are, Beka. I know I don't always seem to appreciate your quirkier side, but I don't want you to think that doesn't mean I don't like you just the way you are."

For some reason he didn't understand, her face grew even sadder, the shadows moving from her eyes to overtake those luscious lips, which no longer smiled in relaxed contentment.

"What?" he said in alarm, raising himself up on one elbow. "Beka, honey, I'm just trying to tell you how much you've come to mean to me. I know I'm not good at showing it, but I didn't want you to think this was just some adrenaline-fueled roll in the sack. It meant something." He smiled at her, tugging on one golden tress. "I swear, you've cast a spell on me. I've never felt like this before."

Beka sighed, sitting up in bed and pulling the light blanket that had been thrown over the back of the futon up to cover most of the amazing body he'd just made love to. Twice.

"For the record," she said, "I'd like to make it clear that I didn't. Cast a spell on you, I mean."

Marcus blinked, feeling like he'd missed something. "What are you talking about, Beka?"

"I have something to tell you," she said, squaring her shoulders as if facing a firing squad. "But first I need you to know that it meant something to me too. That you mean something. And I definitely didn't cast a spell on you; not at any time."

He was starting to get a little irritated, and more than a little worried. "Beka, there is no such thing as spells—we both know that. What the hell are you talking about?"

"There's something I've been keeping from you," she said. "Something important. I didn't tell you before because I knew you wouldn't like it, and really, it wasn't something you needed to know. But now everything has changed." She bit her lip, already red and swollen from their lovemaking. "I hope in the end, you can still say that you like me just the way I am."

"Beka," Marcus said, "you're scaring me. Please don't tell me that you're married. Or dying from an incurable disease. Or . . . a lesbian, or something." He stared at her anxiously.

She giggled at that last one, humor for a moment washing away the somber expression that had come over her features. Then she sighed, her entire body drooping. "No, none of those. Definitely not a lesbian." She stared straight at him, as if daring him to run. "I'm a witch."

"What?" Marcus almost laughed, too, practically giddy with relief. "You mean you're a Wiccan? Hell, Beka, I don't care what kind of tree-hugging religion you follow." Yes, he thought most of the New Age goddess worship stuff was kind of silly, but it wasn't as though it bothered him. Hell, one of the guys in his unit was a Wiccan, and he'd been just as tough and dependable as everyone else, even if he wore a pentacle around his neck instead of a cross.

She shook her head. "Not Wiccan, Marcus. A witch. You know: flying broomstick, bubbling cauldron, turns people into toads." She sighed again, which made her breasts do interesting things under the blanket, distracting him for a moment. "Let's do this a different way. Have you ever heard of Baba Yaga?"

Marcus tried to focus, although having her nearly naked next to him made it difficult. "Um, I think there was a story my ma used to read us when we were young that had someone by that name in it. Didn't she eat children or something? And lived in a weird hut that ran around on chicken legs?" He stared at her. "Why are we talking about fairy tales now?"

"We're not," Beka said flatly. "We're talking about me. I'm a Baba Yaga."

"What?"

"A Baba Yaga. It's not so much a person as it is a job title," she said, as if she were talking perfect sense and not gibberish. "They were best known in Russia and the surrounding Slavic countries, but there have always been Baba Yagas throughout Europe, and eventually they moved to the Americas too. There are three of us here now: me and my sister Babas, Barbara and Bella. Babas are powerful witches who are responsible for watching over the doorways to the Otherworld and maintaining the balance of the natural world." She scowled. "*That* used to be a lot easier in the old days, believe me."

"Is this some kind of joke?" Marcus asked. He could feel himself pulling back, the world turning gray again. If there was one thing he couldn't stand, it was foolish fairy tales like the ones his da used to tell them when he and Kyle were kids. "Because if it is, it isn't funny."

Those damned stories of magical sea creatures had made Kyle feel safe and invincible on the water. And that had gotten him killed, as much as the stoned-out-hippie flake his father had hired had.

Beka rolled stormy blue eyes at him, like the sea before a big blow. "You don't believe me. I don't blame you. Hell, I wouldn't believe me either." She gestured widely. "I don't expect you to take my word for it, any more than I would expect you to accept that this bus used to be a hut on chicken legs."

He glanced around the bus. It was unusual, certainly, but there was nothing enchanted about it. "Look, Beka—I should tell you that I can't deal with this kind of paranormal nonsense. My father brought us up on idiotic tales of Selkies and Mermaids and sea monsters. Hell, he even told us that a Mermaid had rescued him once during a storm. My brother believed all that shit. I don't. The world isn't a romantic place full of magic. It's a hard, dangerous jungle, which will kill you if your head is in the clouds. So if we're going to continue to get along, I'm gonna have to ask you to drop it, okay?"

"I can't," Beka said in a small voice. "Because it's all true."

"And next I suppose you're going to tell me that Chewie really is a dragon," he snapped.

"Actually," Beka said, almost managing a smile, "he is. But I don't expect you to believe that either. Not without proof."

"Fine," Marcus said. He would be patient. He would be calm. And when she failed to come up with her so-called proof, he would patiently and calmly drag her off to see the best shrink he could find. "Are you going to turn me into a frog?"

She made a face. "Not while you're sitting in my bed, I'm not. I like frogs just fine, but ew."

Before he could decide if she was taking a joke too far, or just plain crazy, she snapped her fingers with a decisive motion, and her surfboard appeared in the middle of the kitchen with a crisp *pop*. It spun lazily in midair for a moment before gently coming to rest on the polished wooden boards.

"Your mouth is open," Beka said, a tad acerbically. "Need something else?"

He closed his mouth with a snap and nodded, completely speechless. He had to have imagined that. Or it was some kind of trick. That was it—it was a trick. Crazy people did all sorts of things to support their version of reality. She must have somehow arranged that stunt ahead of time.

"How about if I pick something?" he asked.

"Sure," she said, cool as a rock. "Go for it."

"Okay," Marcus said, wracking his brain to come up with something completely impossible. Maybe if he could get her to face reality, it would help her to snap out of this. He leaned down and picked up a pillow from where it had fallen—or been shoved—onto the floor during their passionate love-making. "Can you turn this into, oh, I don't know, a bird?"

She raised an eyebrow, but took the pillow out of his

hands. "I can't change an inanimate object into a living being; no witch has that kind of power," she said.

Aha!

"But I can make it seem like a bird, if that would help." She tossed the pillow up into the air, making some kind of swirling gesture with two fingers on her right hand as she did so. As he watched in stunned amazement, the pillow became a vivid crimson cardinal that flew across the room before coming to rest on a countertop and returning to its original form. It even sang a few melodic notes along the way.

"What the—"

"I'm sorry," Beka said. "I know it is a lot to take in. But if we were going to have any chance together at all, you had to know the truth."

Marcus felt like he'd been standing too close to a mortar strike; as if the ground underneath his feet suddenly shook and disintegrated, filling what had moments before been clear air with sharp and deadly debris. Nothing was what he had thought it was. Least of all Beka.

"The truth?" he said, raising his voice as he got out of bed and started pulling on clothing as fast as he could. Shock made his head spin. "You wouldn't know the truth if it hit you over the head with a brick. I can't believe you let things get this far without telling me you're some kind of magical creature out of a storybook. Does anyone else know?" He spun around and stared at her, tee shirt crushed in his hand. "Does Kesh?"

Beka dropped her gaze. "Yes. Kesh knows. But I didn't tell him. I mean, he's always known."

Marcus jammed the shirt on over his head, not caring that it was inside out. "What, is he a Baba Yaga too?"

"No," Beka said. He could tell he was upsetting her, but at the moment, he couldn't bring himself to care.

"Baba Yagas are always women," she said. "Kesh is a Selkie."

"A Selkie. Like the people who can turn into seals. My da used to tell stories about them too."

"More like seals that can turn into people," she said,

then brushed away the correction with a wave. "It doesn't matter. But yes, Kesh is a Selkie. Um, a Selkie prince, actually. So he knows what I am. But nobody else does. I mean, nobody who isn't magical."

A freaking prince. It figured. He never had a chance, did he? "Well, I'm sure as hell not a prince," Marcus growled, shoving his feet into his shoes. "But I can do magic."

"You can?" Beka looked startled, confused, and hopeful, all at once.

He took one more moment to look at her, so beautiful, so treacherous. Thank goodness he hadn't let her get any closer to his heart.

"Yes," he said. "I can make myself disappear out of your life."

He turned and walked away, stomping across the bus to the door and slamming it open with a shuddering crash. He turned around long enough to see one shimmering tear glide over pale skin to hang, quivering like a frightened faun, before falling in slow motion to the half-empty bed.

"And I expect you to stay away from me, my father, and the boat," he said. "Whatever the hell you're really up to, I want nothing to do with it. Or you."

He should have known better, he told himself as he got into his Jeep, feeling shocked and betrayed by the magnitude of the secrets she'd been keeping from him, just when he thought he was coming to know the real Beka. All the things he'd been sure were lies were true. And the one thing he'd been sure was true was a lie.

If life was a fairy tale, his was never going to have a happy ending.

BEKA GOT DRESSED methodically and folded the futon back into a couch. The air inside the bus smelled like passion and heat and exertion; her skin still held the scent of Marcus. Every time she moved she could feel the pleasant ache of unaccustomed activity between her legs and in the heaviness of her breasts. It should have been glorious.

Instead, it was hell. Finally, she just gave up and sat on the floor in the kitchen, hugging her legs and letting the tears seep into her already sodden tee shirt.

She should have known better. There was a reason that Baba Yagas didn't allow themselves to get close to Humans. But Barbara had managed to make it work, and so for one brief moment, Beka had convinced herself she could do it too. She *really* should have known better.

Heaving clumping steps and a deep woof heralded the return of Chewie before he slid the door open and ambled inside. She brushed away tears and tried to look normal.

"Heya, Beka," Chewie said, "I saw the sailor's car was gone so I figured it was safe to come back." He gave a doggy smirk. "Did you have a nice afternoon?"

Then he took a closer look, sniffed the air, and wandered into the kitchen where she was sitting next to the surfboard she hadn't bothered to whisk back into its storage space.

"Okay, I'm confused," he said. "Either you've taken up indoor surfing, or you've come up with some kinky new way to have sex. Which is it?"

"Neither." Beka sniffed. "I was proving to Marcus that I could do magic. I tried telling him about being a Baba Yaga, and he didn't believe me, so I brought the board in, and then turned a pillow into a bird."

Chewie peered at her red eyes. "Either the sex really sucked, or telling him you're magical didn't go over well."

Beka sniffed again, another couple of errant tears escaping and plopping onto the floor like a mini rainstorm. "The sex didn't suck."

"Ah." Chewie sank down next to her, his giant head resting on her feet in a gesture of furry solidarity. "So he wasn't thrilled and excited to discover that he was living in a fairy tale."

"Not exactly," Beka said with a sigh. "More like pissed off and freaked out. He obviously felt like I'd been lying to him by not telling him all along."

Chewie growled. "Well, that's just stupid. It's not like

you can go around telling everyone you're a powerful witch out of Russian legend."

"I know, I know," Beka said. "I'm not saying his reaction was fair. But maybe I should have told him *before* we made love and not after. Or before he told me that he was serious about me." She scrubbed at her eyes with her hands, tired of crying, but not sure how to stop. "*Was* being the operative word, I'm afraid."

"Are you serious about him?" Chewie asked, lifting his head to stare into her face.

She shrugged. "It doesn't matter now. He told me to stay away from him. It's over. I just need to concentrate on doing my job and get on with my life. I'm sure Kesh will be happy to console me."

Chewie growled again, louder this time. "Stick to chocolate; it might be safer." He perked up. "Hey, at least you finally got laid. That's something."

"Oh, shut up," Beka said, but she gave a watery laugh nonetheless, and rested her head against the cabinet behind her. The weight of the dragon leaning against her was comforting; almost enough to make her forget about her burning eyes and the relentless fatigue that made her bones feel like they were filled with lead.

The sound of a brisk knock on the half-open door made her stand up so fast, her head swam, and she had to grab the counter to keep from passing out.

"It's not him," Chewie said with quiet compassion. He stood on his hind legs to peer out the window. "Whoever it is doesn't smell Human."

"Oh." Beka scrubbed at her face and straightened her clothes before walking over to the door with Chewie on her heels. She thought about grabbing one of her knives, but no paranormal creature would be foolish enough to try and harm a Baba Yaga inside her own hut. Er, bus.

When she pulled the door open the rest of the way, she could see their visitor standing just out of the sunshine; the shade from the bus seemed to cause his form to flicker and change. One moment he looked like a skinny Human of indiscriminate age and medium height, with sandy brown hair and no notable features. The next, the light shifted into a suggestion of pointed ears and something that resembled a lashing tail. And possibly an extra arm or two.

The not-quite-a-man gave a low bow, holding out a curled-up parchment in pale twiggy fingers. The antique paper bore a few thin scores that might have been made by claws clutching it a bit too tightly as its bearer traveled between two worlds.

"Baba Yaga," the messenger said in a scratchy voice like wind creaking through gnarled tree limbs. "I bring you greetings and solicitations from my mistress, the Queen, and deliver to you this summons to her most August Presence." He bowed again, so deeply that the invisible points on his seemingly Human ears scraped twin lines in the sand and gravel surface of the lot.

Beka swallowed hard. "Uh, when you say the Queen, I don't suppose you mean the Queen of the Merpeople."

The messenger blinked too-large, wide-set eyes. "No, Baba Yaga. The High Queen of the Otherworld is She who requests and requires your attendance." He placed the parchment into Beka's outstretched palm. Which, she was happy to see, hardly shook at all.

Chewie whined deep in his throat as she unrolled the heavy paper and read the elegant scrawl of ink etched into its surface with a quill-tipped pen. The ink itself was bright red, as ominous as the summons it inscribed.

My dearest Baba Yaga,

> *It is Our wish that you attend Us at a meeting in the Otherworld, wherein the King of the Selkies and the Queen of the Mer will discuss their continuing difficulties and seek solutions to the same. Please come prepared to explain your lack of success so far in ameliorating this problem. We expect to be given a positive report of your progress. Or We shall be Most Unhappy.*

There is also an additional issue that requires your attention and to which We shall expect an immediate solution, without fail.

Come to Tir fo Thuinn at the hour of midnight, traveling by the usual way.

Affectionately,
Queen Morena Aine Titania Argante Rhiannon

Beka looked up from the missive to ask the messenger a question, but he was already gone, his errand completed. Only the dust of his passage hung in the air like a harbinger of rapidly oncoming doom. She sighed and showed the letter to Chewie, who read it through and then said, with feeling, "Shit."

Her sentiments exactly.

EIGHTEEN

BEKA NERVOUSLY ADJUSTED the draped neckline of her outfit, tweaking it so it lay just right. It didn't do to look less than perfect when you went before the Queen of the Otherworld. Very big on pomp and circumstance, was the Queen. And woe betide the person who didn't live up to her idea of proper attire. Members of the court still talked in whispers of the lady-in-waiting who had accidentally worn mismatched stockings to an afternoon tea. They said she made a lovely rosebush, always festooned with stunning flowers in two slightly different colors of peach.

Beka didn't aspire to be a rosebush.

She checked the mirror one more time, just to be certain she wasn't missing anything. Her skirt was made from raw silk, purchased from a woman at the Renaissance Faire who hand-dyed it in various shades of blue and green and then embroidered the hem with scenes of undersea life, so when Beka walked, the skirt swirled around her ankles and fish seemed to dart behind coral reefs and in between waving fronds of emerald seaweed.

Her top was woven of linen so fine, it flowed with the

lines of her body; its pale cerulean tint was like an echo of a fading evening sky. She'd cinched the waist in with a wide leather belt adorned with snowy white pearls and purple-blue abalone and paua shell, iridescent and gleaming with subtle highlights. A matching decorative wire mesh restrained her long hair at the back of her head, and her gold dragon earrings and necklace revealed the jewels usually hidden by a simple glamour—a pearl on the mouth of one earring's dragon, a black tourmaline in the mouth of the other, and the claws of the dragon on the necklace wrapped around a bright red ruby. These were her version of the more showy tattoos that Barbara wore, and enabled her to summon the three Riders when she needed them.

Lastly, she tucked her favorite ornamental dagger, honed to a sharpness that could almost cut you if you simply looked at it, into the sheath that hung from the leather belt. Dark blue slippers on her feet (and no stockings at all, mismatched or otherwise) meant that she was ready to go.

Physically, anyway. Psychologically was something else altogether. The Queen scared the sparkly paint right off her toenails.

"You look fine, Beka," Chewie said from the side of the bedroom, where he'd been banished lest he accidentally get a stray clump of dog fur on her clothing. "Stop worrying. You'll go report to Her Majesty about all the things you've been working on to try and track down the problem, she'll scold you for not having solved it already, and you'll come home. And then we'll eat s'mores."

"Right," Beka said, not at all convinced things would go that smoothly. She'd rarely had to deal with the Queen herself, but she'd been with Brenna a few times when she'd been summoned to the Otherworld. It had seldom been a pleasant experience.

The Queen was incredibly beautiful, and could be quite kind, but she was as mercurial and changeable as the sea, and just as deadly when aroused to anger. After ruling the Otherworld for more years than anyone could count, her power was immense and her rule absolute.

While technically the Baba Yagas were Human, and therefore not her subjects, their unique position juxtaposed between one world and the next meant that they reported back to the Queen. And the Water of Life and Death that gave them their extended lives and increased their magical abilities was a gift from the Queen that came with the job. She might not have been their sovereign, but in a very real way, she was their boss.

"Maybe I should take a sword too," Beka mused fretfully, fingering her dagger. "Just for balance."

Chewie sighed, gnawing on a bone to soothe the nerves he couldn't quite hide. "Don't be silly. You're going to court, not to war."

"I'm not sure it isn't the same thing," Beka muttered. "At least in this case." But she straightened her back and faced the mirror. Behind it was the closet where her clothes hung . . . unless the door was opened in just the right way, in which case it was the entrance to a passageway that led to the Otherworld.

It was part of a Baba Yaga's duties to guard that doorway from use by anyone other than herself and anyone sent through from the other side. The Queen had the power to create temporary passages—like the one the parchment-bearing messenger had undoubtedly come through—but for everyone else, the only way into or out of the Otherworld was through one of these doorways.

In the olden days, before the Otherworld had been permanently separated from the mundane plane where Humans lived, there were many places where the two worlds touched; a mortal might accidentally find himself spending a lifetime in what seemed like an hour, dancing with maidens whose unearthly beauty would haunt him forever, or a mischievous sprite could wander through to lure a passing stranger into a murky bog.

These days, though, there were a few remaining natural entrances, all carefully safeguarded by the Queen's hand-picked protectors, and the doorways that existed inside each Baba Yaga's travelling home.

"It's time, Beka," Chewie said. "You wouldn't want to keep the Queen waiting."

Goddess forbid.

Beka took a deep breath and put her hand flat against the door in a spot precisely three inches above the crystal knob, and two inches inward. Then she sent a carefully measured pulse of energy into the living matrix of the gateway; sort of the energetic equivalent of a secret knock—two long, three short, two long. The door swung open to reveal a sparkling curtain of mystical light, like a thousand fireflies darting and glowing in a swirl of ever-changing motion.

She formed a strong mental picture of where she wanted to go: Tir fo Thuinn, the underwater portion of the Queen's realm, where her sea-dwelling subjects could visit in comfort. Then she gathered up her skirts and her courage and took one giant step forward.

A SWIRLING GRAY fog enveloped Beka as soon as she stepped through the doorway. Tiny glowing purple and gold lights flitted and flew around her, finally forming a shimmering path that led onward into the depths of the Otherworld. With each footstep, a faint musical chime resounded through the seemingly endless mists, growing louder as she moved in the direction she was meant to go.

Slowly, plants appeared on either side of the path—bright yellow asters, daisies, and tulips, all growing higher than her head. Softly swaying ruffle-edged ferns rubbed their green borders against sparkling ebony trees draped with hanging vines that bore bejeweled fruits and, occasionally, emerald lizards whose tails were barbed and sharper than any of Beka's swords.

Tinkling laughter echoed from the direction of the castle grounds, and Beka wished that she could go and watch the well-dressed courtiers playing croquet upon the perfect lawn that surrounded its timeless stone walls and sky-touching spires. Unfortunately, her path led in a different direction.

The destination at the end of her short journey looked like a vast cavern at the edge of an underground sea. It was lit by thousands of phosphorescent crystal clusters that grew out of the walls and lofty ceiling, some as tiny as her pinky, and others larger than her head. Their eerie bluish-white radiance made the water lapping at the shore look dark and mysterious and cast haunting shadows on the faces of the assembled company.

The Mer Queen stood in her Human guise on the gleaming black sand of the beach, along with the Selkie King and a well-dressed man who looked enough like him to be one of his many children. Beka looked, but she didn't see Kesh, either standing with the few Mer and Selkies who had assumed the two-legged form of their rulers, or among the ones who kept to their natural shapes and swam nearby in the miniature ocean.

On a slightly raised patch of ground near the shore, the High Queen and her consort sat on ornate benches that only just missed being thrones through their lack of arms and high backs. The seats were formed from the stark white bones of some gigantic underwater creature, every inch carved with intricate detail, and adorned with pearls, shells, and jewels that twinkled dully in the dim and muted light of the cavern. The Queen sat upon a luxurious purple silk cushion, her feet resting on a matching ottoman. The King disdained such pampering and sat directly on the bench's unyielding surface, lounging as though it were the most comfortable seat in the palace.

The King looked powerful and impressive—his darkly handsome good looks set off by black velvets and silks, a strong nose and arched brows adding to the impression of dignity and grace. A tiny hint of a smile greeted Beka's entrance.

The Queen was as light as the King was dark. Long silvery-white hair was gathered in a complicated arrangement of braids atop her swanlike neck, twisted with strands of delicate pearls and silver chains dripping with diamonds. Soft pink silk, the color of a baby's first blush, flowed in fluid layers to drape her tall, slim figure, and kissed the tips of her white fingers with pointed edges dripping with delicate lace. High cheekbones and pale translucent skin made her look as dainty and fragile as a china cup. But Beka knew better.

"Your Majesties," she said to the Queen and the King of the Otherworld, curtsying low the way Brenna had taught her on her first visit to court as a child. She nodded her head in the direction of the Queen of the Mer and the King of the Selkies for good measure. "Your Majesties. Greetings."

"Welcome, Baba Yaga," the High Queen said in a voice like choral bells ringing. It echoed off the high ceiling and scattered a few colorful winged creatures, not quite birds, in a flutter of feathers and sharp, pointy beaks. "Thank you for coming. Queen Boudicca and King Gwrtheyrn have been enlightening Me with their woeful tales regarding the sad corruption of their watery realm that has forced them to leave their homes and endangered their citizens." She narrowed icy amethyst eyes in Beka's direction. "Have you news to give Us regarding the cause of this unfortunate predicament? Or better yet, some cure for this malady?"

"Not as yet, Your Majesty." Beka did her best to look confident as she turned toward Gwrtheyrn and Boudicca. "I assure you, I have been working on the problem every day. I haven't found the answer, but I have eliminated a number of possibilities, and I'm sure I must be getting close." Her heart thudded in her chest as she waited for someone to expose her as a fraud, but no one did.

She bit her lip, seeing lines etched deep in both the royal faces that hadn't been there when they'd first come to her for help. "Are the sick folk any better, now that you've moved to different waters?"

Gwrtheyrn shook his head, his straight black hair slicked back like a seal's short fur. "They are not, Baba Yaga. In truth, they grow worse, especially the children. They cannot eat; whatever they do take in is returned with dire results. Some are losing fur or scales, and others their hair. Their cries tear at my soul. The water people are at their weakest at the time of the full moon, when the tides pull on us most strongly, causing our two different natures to fall out of harmony. We are greatly feared that should there be no solution by the next waxing of the moon, some of the most vulnerable will succumb to this illness."

"Gracious, how repulsive." The High Queen made a moue of distaste, her perfect lips curved downward. She waved one dismissive hand, obviously not interested in hearing anything more involving unpleasant physical symptoms.

"Mortal bodies are so fragile; I do not know how you abide them. Well, I am sure that the Baba Yaga will find a solution in time." The Queen sat up even straighter, her posture as rigid and unforgiving as her rule.

"Unfortunately, it has come to Our attention that We have an even more pressing problem," Queen Morena said.

Beka felt her stomach sink down to the level of her slippers. *Now what?*

Gwrtheyrn growled a little at the Otherworld Queen's abrupt dismissal, and the suggestion that there was something more important than the welfare of his people, but Boudicca pressed a cautioning hand to his arm and he subsided.

"Um, what is this new crisis, Your Majesty?" Beka asked with a growing sense of dread. She hadn't even been able to come up with a solution for the first disaster; how the hell was she supposed to fix another one?

"And why call us here if not to discuss our calamity at greater length?" Gwrtheyrn added, bitterness coloring his voice.

The Queen gave him a sharp glance, clearly not liking his tone, and two of the crystal formations on the wall cracked and went dim. Overhead, a massive stalactite creaked ominously and a few of the courtiers who had accompanied the royal couple looked up anxiously before sidling unobtrusively a few feet to the left.

"This new issue concerns your people as well, Gwrtheyrn," she said, her incandescent purple stare circling around to include all of the Selkies and Mer in the great cavern. "You would appear to have renegades in your ranks."

"Renegades, Majesty?" Boudicca repeated, but Beka got the impression that the Mer Queen wasn't entirely as taken aback as she tried to seem. "Surely not."

The High King shifted on his bench, no longer smiling. "Are you questioning the Queen's word, Boudicca?" His expression grew as dark as his neatly pointed beard.

"Certainly not, Your Highness," Boudicca said, hurriedly dropping a curtsy and bowing her head. "I was merely expressing dismay at the thought that any of our subjects might be behaving in ways that have offended Your Majesties."

Nice save, Beka thought. *But what the hell is going on, and why am I the one who has to fix it?*

"We have received reports," the Queen continued, ignoring the interruption, "telling of magical creatures who are actively working against the Humans in the region. Not many, as yet, but those who are doing so are breaking Our rules, which specifically forbid malicious behavior that might draw attention to the existence of those of Us who are Other."

Beka swallowed hard, remembering her conversation with Kesh about how he and his friends were driving away the fish from their normal routes. Surely that wasn't worthy of the Queen's ire—it wasn't as though the fishermen had blamed anything other than the weather or bad luck for their lack of good catches. And Kesh was the King's son; there was no way he would be involved with renegades. She'd talk to him when she got home. But surely not.

"Uh, is there some reason that you believe that there are Selkies and Mer involved?" Beka asked.

The Queen shrugged, one elegant shoulder moving barely more than a millimeter in a rustle of silk. "Those are the tales We are told by those who remain in the mundane world. Your own mentor Brenna returned from a recent visit and spoke of a Mermaid who was spotted singing to men on a boat and trying to lure them onto the rocks, as in the days of old. And let Us speak true here—most of those remaining on that side of the doorway are Selkies and Mer, who could not come with the rest when We withdrew the majority of our people back to the safety of this world. Who else could be responsible for this disturbance?"

"If this is so, why bring the Baba Yaga into it?" Gwrtheyrn asked, his proud face haughty and affronted. "Do you not trust us to control our own people?"

The King held up a pacifying hand. "It is not a matter of trust, King Gwrtheyrn. But We have heard that some of these renegades may have ties high up in your government and deep into the remaining local paranormal community as well. We thought it best to have someone from the outside look into this, so you might avoid conflict within your court at a time when you need most to come together in unity."

"Ah," Gwrtheyrn said, subsiding. Boudicca just looked depressed.

"Baba Yaga," the Queen said, standing up and speaking loudly, so that her voice rang clearly throughout the chamber. "We call on you to discover the identity and whereabouts of these troublemakers who threaten to expose the existence of the underworld dwellers in your territory, and to either put a stop to them yourself or bring the information here to Us so that We might summarily deal with them Ourselves." The expression on her wintery visage left no doubt of the finality of her brand of justice.

"In addition, We expect you, with no further delay, to find and resolve the problem with the Merpeople's and Selkies' home waters, so that they might return there in all due haste, since it is Our opinion that it is likely that the disruption to their heretofore stable lives has led to this most unwise and potentially destructive behavior."

The Queen drew herself up to her full height, looking even more glorious and more imposing than usual, and stared directly at Beka. "Do *not* fail me in this, Baba Yaga. I will not tolerate anything that threatens the safety of Our secrets, which We have sacrificed so much to keep hidden from the Humans all these long years. Have I made myself clear?"

Beka nodded, afraid to speak. She prayed her silence

would be perceived as calm strength, instead of the para-lyzed abject terror that it was.

"I realize that this is much to ask of one so young and new to her position," the Queen said in a less oratory voice. There was even a hint of kindness, and something like re-gret as she added, "But this is too important to be left un-resolved. If you cannot manage the tasks I have given you, I shall be forced to allow Brenna to come out of retirement to handle it." She sighed. "I assure you, this is the very last thing I would wish; Brenna was becoming somewhat . . . problematic . . . in her later years, and it was only with great difficulty that I persuaded her to retire at all. She insisted until the very end that you were not prepared to assume the mantle of Baba Yaga. I sincerely hope that you do not prove her right."

With this last soul-searing statement, she held out her hand to her consort and they swept out of the cavern, their retinue trailing behind them, twittering like a tree full of sparrows at dusk.

Beka stood stock-still, watching them go, feeling as stunned as if she had been hit by a ten-ton truck. She couldn't be certain, but she was pretty sure that she'd just been told that her failure to fix these two crucial issues would mean the end of her days as a Baba Yaga. Until a moment ago, she would have guessed that her reaction to such an edict would have been more relief than sorrow—what a time to find out that assumption would have been wrong.

It turned out that she wanted more than anything to suc-ceed, and remain a Baba Yaga. Too bad it looked like that was going to be completely impossible to pull off.

NINETEEN

BEKA WALKED OVER to Boudicca, Gwrtheyrn, and the young man with them. They looked only slightly less shell-shocked than she did, although Beka caught the Mer Queen and Selkie King exchanging furtive glances before she reached them. She had the feeling again that they knew something about these renegades that they weren't admitting to. Of course, with their populace in the midst of such upheaval, perhaps they were simply feeling overwhelmed, and the guilty looks were all in her imagination. Brenna had always accused her of being too quick to jump to conclusions.

Apparently Brenna had criticized her for that and more to the Queen of the Otherworld. Wasn't that terrific. As if Beka didn't feel insecure enough already. She was beginning to wonder why Brenna hadn't simply decided she'd made a mistake in taking in Beka in the first place, and started all over with a new apprentice Baba. She wondered if that was what would happen if the Queen took away her role as Baba and gave it back to Brenna.

"Your Majesties," Beka said. "I am so sorry to hear that

the children are even sicker." She felt just awful about that; Baba Yagas tended to be particularly protective of children, ancient tales notwithstanding. In truth, the stories of Baba Yagas "eating" children were mostly a metaphor for their removing defenseless youngsters from abusive or neglectful homes.

"It is most upsetting, Baba," Boudicca said. "My own grandchild, a girl not yet a year old, is sick nigh on to death. I fear greatly for her. Have you truly no idea at all what has poisoned our waters?"

Beka hung her head. "I'm sorry," she said, barely louder than a whisper. "I'm sure that Brenna would have solved this long ago. Perhaps the Queen was right to consider bringing her back." What was the point of having all this power if she couldn't help the very people who depended on her?

To her surprise, Gwrtheyrn came to her defense. "You are too hard on yourself, Baba Yaga. After all, our own shamans and wise men could not discover the source of the toxins either, and our very best healers have been able to do nothing more than merely ease the symptoms in those affected. And they had considerably longer to work on the problem than you have. We have no complaints about your efforts on our behalf."

She stood up a little straighter, gratified and relieved at the same time. And even more determined to find the answer, so that Gwrtheyrn and Boudicca's faith in her would not be proven to be misplaced.

"Ah," Gwrtheyrn said. "I do not believe that you have met my son and heir, Tyrus."

Tyrus bowed over her hand, almost as handsome and charming as his brother, but with more warmth in his gray eyes and a cheerful, almost eager demeanor, despite the dire circumstances. "I am most honored to meet you, Baba Yaga. I look forward to working together for many years to come." He glanced at his father and grinned. "Not that I will be ascending to the throne any time in the near future; thankfully, my father is still most healthy and hale."

"I'm pleased to meet you too," Beka said. "Although I

wish it were under better circumstances." She turned back to the King. "I'm surprised that Kesh didn't tell me your people were still getting sicker. I guess because he didn't mention it, I just assumed that they'd begun to improve once you removed them from the affected areas."

Gwrtheyrn stiffened and Tyrus gave him a darting look out of the corner of his eyes, keeping his face expressionless with what seemed like a conscious effort.

"You have been speaking with my son Kesh, Baba Yaga? How did this come about?"

Beka felt like she was missing something, a feeling to which she was becoming all too accustomed. She didn't much like it. "He hasn't mentioned spending time with me, Your Majesty?" *Was Kesh ashamed of her?*

Gwrtheyrn just grunted and it fell to Tyrus to explain. "My father and Kesh had a falling-out, alas. We have not seen him in our lands in many months, as you surface dwellers mark time. We had not even been certain he remained in the area. It was thought that perhaps he returned to our original home waters off of the land of Eire."

"Oh," Beka said. She tried to remember if Kesh had ever mentioned a rift between him and his family; she thought not. Perhaps he was embarrassed. To creatures like the Selkies, family and clan were all-important. Or maybe he was afraid that she would be uncomfortable spending time with him if she knew he and his father weren't talking, since she was working on a mission for the Selkie King.

No wonder he had been so persistent in his pursuit of her, and so jealous of the time she spent with Marcus. Poor Kesh, he was probably terribly lonely without his people, and she was the closest thing he could find to one of his own.

Of course, said a little voice in the back of her head, maybe he is hiding something. He already admitted to manipulating the fishing routes . . . what if he and the friends he'd mentioned were involved in something worse?

Then she felt terrible for even thinking such a thing. Kesh had been nothing but sweet to her, and so supportive about her fears of not being good enough to do what was expected of her. She resolved to be more patient with him, and somehow find time for another picnic or two, despite the pressing need to find answers to both the old problem and the new one the Queen of the Otherworld had just dropped in her lap. After all, she had to stop and eat sometime, despite her constantly roiling stomach and lack of appetite.

"Please don't worry about him," she said reassuringly. "He's got plenty of acquaintances among the surfing community, so he isn't completely alone. And we've become friends, I think."

Boudicca and Gwrtheyrn exchanged another one of those weighted glances, making the air between them seem heavy with unspoken words.

"Kesh always was overfond of Humans," Gwrtheyrn muttered. Tyrus cleared his throat meaningfully, and the King added belatedly, remembering to whom he was speaking, "Nothing against Humans, of course. I merely meant that he could have better occupied his time and energy by attending to those who looked to him for leadership under the sea."

Boudicca sighed. "Shut up, Gwr, you old bull. Before you swallow your flippers so deeply they come out your earholes."

Beka swallowed a smile. She so rarely thought of herself as Human these days, having more in common with most paranormal creatures than she did the race she was born to. His words hadn't bothered her at all. This sense that they were keeping secrets from her, however, bothered her a great deal.

"I was wondering, Your Majesties, Tyrus, if perhaps you knew anything about these renegades that you hadn't, er . . . felt it wise to share with Queen Morena?"

More guilty looks. Beka tried to channel her inner Baba and simply stared at them wordlessly, putting the force of her office, if not her own personality, behind the implacable silence.

Tyrus broke first. "Father, you really should tell the Baba Yaga all we know. How is she to help us if we keep her in the dark?"

The Selkie King grimaced, but after a moment he nodded in agreement. He walked away from the edge of the water so they could talk without being overheard by the Selkies and Merpeople still waiting patiently for their sovereigns.

"It is not so much that we *know* anything, Baba Yaga. I assure you, if we did, we would have informed the Queen no matter what the possible . . . repercussions." They all looked at the broken crystals and the still-quivering stalactite and shuddered in unison at the thought of the Queen in one of her rages.

"We have simply been hearing rumors," Boudicca put in, her voice melodic and gentle compared to the gruff old Selkie. "You know how such things swirl about in a court; at first we thought them merely gossip and the mutterings of a disaffected and unsettled populace."

"And just what were these rumors?" Beka asked, a touch grimly.

Tyrus had the grace to look guilty, where his father did not. "Some said that there was a mysterious stranger who had come to lead the underwater people back to glory. No one ever admitted to speaking to this man, or knowing anyone who had. It was always a friend of a friend of a friend. But everyone agreed that this person was attempting to recruit members of the Mer and Selkie communities to his cause."

"This rabble-rouser made ridiculous, impossible promises," Gwrtheyrn said bitterly. "He spoke of driving the Humans from the sea and allowing our people to live openly on the wide ocean as we once did, feared and worshipped rather than dismissed as tales for children. Anyone with any sense would know that such things could never happen. They are too many and too powerful, and we are too few, and vulnerable to the brutal weapons you landdwellers are constantly inventing."

"No offense," Boudicca said with a rueful eye roll.

Beka smiled at her. Gwrtheyrn's mostly well-deserved anti-Human bias didn't bother her nearly as much as discovering that the outlaw leader the Queen had tasked her to uncover had already been hard at work sowing dissention and recruiting followers among the undersea people.

"How many of your people do you think have chosen to follow this agitator?" Beka asked. "And do you think they are dangerous?"

Boudicca sighed, her abundant bosom heaving. "It is impossible to say. The rumors are everywhere. The renegade himself seems to be nowhere. As for dangerous . . . how dangerous are Humans when they are feeling threatened and helpless and frightened, and some forceful figure comes along and tells them exactly what they want to hear?"

That was exactly what Beka had been afraid of. Queen Morena's fears that this renegade and his followers would do something that would irrevocably reveal the existence of magical creatures to the entire Human race had apparently not been an overreaction.

If Beka couldn't find and stop these people before they went too far, Humans could get hurt or even killed. And then the backlash, should the paranormal world be discovered, would be unspeakable. The best they could hope for would be dissection tables, zoos, and internment camps. The worst—the witch hunts all over again.

She had to find these renegades fast, and not just because the Queen was going to take her job away from her if she didn't.

Beka said her good-byes to Boudicca, Gwrtheyrn, and Tyrus, and made her way back to the pathway that would return her to the doorway between the worlds. Frantic plans tumbled through her brain as she walked. She would try to find Kesh and see if he had heard anything about this renegade leader, or even been approached to join the group. She would send a message to Marcus's father (hopefully without Marcus finding out and ripping her head off) asking him to warn the other fishermen to be alert for trouble. Although that one was tricky, since she couldn't exactly explain what forms the trouble might come in.

And she thought it was time to call in some help.

As soon as she got home, she was going to summon the Riders.

JUST AS THERE had always been Babas, there had also always been the Riders. No one seemed to know if they were immortal creatures who chose to look like men, or if they were simply a series of creatures who took on the same guise when one took over for another. Brenna had insisted that the Riders she knew had been the same ones that *her* mentor Baba knew, and between them, they covered hundreds of years of experience.

No matter what manner of being they truly were, the Riders were dedicated to the service of the Baba Yagas. Attractive, powerful, and completely dependable (as long as you didn't mind some collateral damage along the way), the White Rider, the Red Rider, and the Black Rider had ridden their magical horses through the old Baba Yaga stories, inspiring awe and fear. If a Baba Yaga had a problem too big to handle on her own, she could call in the Riders.

As far as Beka was concerned, this particular set of problems definitely qualified.

Apparently Chewie agreed.

"It's about damned time," he muttered as she changed out of her finery and detailed her plan to him. "There is no shame in admitting you need help." He was stretched out on the floor next to her bed, taking up most of the rest of the space in the small room. "Are you going to call them now?"

Beka nodded, tossing on a simple sundress and sitting on the edge of the bed. "Right this very minute, if you could stop bitching long enough for me to concentrate."

"I am a male," Chewie growled. "I don't *bitch*." But he sat up alertly, adding only, "I really like that Alexei. It will be good to see him again."

Beka snorted. "Of course you do. You're both insanely

large, furry, and like to eat anything not nailed down. You're practically twins."

Taking off the dragon earring with the black tourmaline in it, she held it in cupped hands and closed her eyes, summoning as clear a picture of Alexei Knight as she could, building a bridge to his essence with her memories and her desperation. A huge bear of a man, at least six foot eight, and massively built, Alexei was the berserker of the three, who lived to fight and drink and eat, and did all of them with joyous abandon. She could see him now as if he stood before her—his coarse brown hair wild as brambles, his beard braided, his eyes lit from within as if by fire. He usually wore black leathers that jangled with chains, and rode a black Harley that roared almost as loudly as he did.

I need you, Alexei. Come to me.

Replacing the tourmaline earring, she took out the one with the pearl and thought about her favorite of all the Riders. Mikhail Day, the White Rider, had always been kind to her when she'd been a child, and she'd had an avid crush on him as a teen. Little wonder, when he looked like a Tolkien elf; his long blond hair worn loose to drift over his broad shoulders, dressed in pristine white jeans and a linen shirt, so handsome that otherwise sensible women tended to lose their heads when he walked into a room. His white Yamaha purred like a panther, and he had a weakness for sweets and damsels in distress. Surely Mikhail could help her, if anyone could.

Mikhail, I need you. Please come right away.

Lastly, she held the necklace with its blood-red ruby. The Red Rider had always intimidated her a little, although she was glad to have him on her side. Gregori Sun was as serene as Alexei was turbulent; shorter than the others, with long black hair pulled back in a tail and the flat cheekbones, dark, slanted eyes, and Fu Manchu mustache of a Mongol warrior, Gregori moved with the grace of an assassin and wore a red skintight leather jumpsuit that matched his silent red Ducati. Beka had never quite figured him out—she thought he was probably the deadliest of the three, which was really saying something, and yet he always seemed so calm and never said a harsh word. He was a puzzle she wasn't sure she really wanted to solve.

Gregori, I need you. Come to me.

She hung the necklace back around her neck and opened her eyes with a sigh. Hopefully it wouldn't take the Riders long to get here. The last she knew, they'd finished helping her sister Barbara with something across the country in New York State. But their magical motorcycles, transformed from the enchanted steeds they'd once ridden, could get them from one place to the next much faster than should have been possible. With any luck, they would be here in the next day or two.

Which was good. Because she needed all the help she could get.

MARCUS LOOKED AT the dripping nets they'd just hauled back aboard and ran through every curse word he'd learned in the military. Then he made up a few more on the spot. Chico and Kenny gaped with disbelief, their mouths hanging open like the fish they'd expected to be unloading, and his father was so pale that Marcus was afraid he was going to pass out on the deck.

He moved unobtrusively to stand next to the old man, who was so upset, he didn't even bother to say something sarcastic about not needing to be babied like a sick child.

"It's shredded," Marcus Senior said in a lifeless voice. "There isn't even enough of it left to mend."

"What could do that?" Kenny asked, glancing fearfully over the side of the *Wily Serpent.* "Some kind of giant squid?"

Chico rolled his eyes and spat. "You watch too many late night movies, *mi hermano.* There are no monsters under the sea waiting to eat you."

"Well, something sure as hell tore the crap out of that net," Kenny retorted. "Unless you think maybe the tuna have learned to fight back."

Marcus ignored their familiar squabbling and squatted

down to take a closer look. His father knelt down next to him, fingering the tangled and tattered remains of what had been perfectly woven fibers not three hours before.

"Have you ever seen anything like this before, Da?" Marcus asked.

"Never," his father said. He'd been as stubborn and strong as ever through his diagnosis and cancer treatment, but now there were undercurrents of defeat in his cracking voice. He picked up one segment to look at it and it fell apart in his hand. "Look at that. It's garbage. It's as though something gnawed through parts of it and cut other sections with a knife. Garbage," he repeated, letting it fall back to the wooden planks with a slithering thump.

"Could a shark have gotten tangled up in it somehow?" Marcus asked, thinking of the one he and Beka had come up against just a couple of days before. The thought of her made his chest hurt and his head ache. It hadn't been that long since he'd seen her, but it seemed like without her presence his spirit was as shredded as this net. Ridiculous. Intolerable. But there it was.

"I don't see how a shark could do this," his father said, standing up slowly. "But I can't think of any other explanation either." He gazed down at the mess, the lines in his face carved by years in the sun and the wind seeming to grow deeper as Marcus watched.

"I can't afford a new net," his da admitted reluctantly. "The fishing has been that bad this year. There's no money for a replacement." His eyes skittered over the ship, taking in all the places where he'd skimped on repairs or touch-ups. Marcus had been working on a few of the smaller ones when no one was around, but the ship still looked a lot less polished and trim than it had when he was growing up. As far as he could tell, his father hadn't noticed any of the improvements; all the old man saw was the imperfections. He'd always been that way.

"Maybe I'm too old for this," Marcus Senior said, his gnarled hands twisting around each other. "Maybe I should just give it up."

"Is that what you want?" Marcus asked quietly. His father had always loved the sea more than anything. More than his mother, which is probably why she left. More than his children, although ironically, Marcus's brother had loved the ocean almost as much as their father had, a connection that had bonded them together until the day that ocean killed him. Marcus had always imagined that the old man would die at the wheel of his boat one day, happy in the arms of his watery mistress.

His father shrugged, what was left of his former vibrancy draining away as Marcus watched. "I don't see that I have any choice."

"I can help," Marcus said. "I want to help." He was stunned to discover it was even true. "I've got plenty of money saved up from when I was in the Marines. Nothing to spend it on in the desert, after all. Let me buy you a new net."

His father shook his head. "My boat. My problem. I don't need your help."

Marcus could feel the rage rising up like bile in his throat, choking and fiery, as if he'd swallowed some circus performer's flaming baton.

"You never change, do you?" he said, the words forcing themselves out through his clenched teeth. "You would never listen to anyone else. You'd sure as hell never listen to me. I told you that Kyle was too young to be working the boat. I told you that the new guy you'd signed on was a stoned-out flake who was going to get someone hurt. But you couldn't find anyone else willing to work for you, because you'd alienated every damned sailor in the port with your lousy temper and bad attitude, and so you let him stay anyway, and Kyle died. Because heaven forbid you actually ever listen to a word I said."

His father's face turned red, and then white, but Marcus couldn't seem to stop himself from shouting. "Now I come halfway across the world to help you when you're sick, and you'll let me haul in fish with the hired help, but you won't let me actually *do anything* to make this easier on you. I could fix up the boat, but you won't let me. I could buy you a new net, but then you'd have to admit you needed me for something, and you'd rather go broke and give it all up than take anything from me."

He kicked the net, causing more bits and pieces to subside into ruin. "Did you really think I didn't realize you were broke? The harbormaster came to me days ago, asking for his back docking fees."

"Well, I hope you didn't pay them," his da shouted back. "Them's my debts, and I'll pay them myself."

"How?" Marcus asked. "Beka's not coming back to give you any more bags of salvaged coins. Your net is in shreds. How do you expect to pay *your* debts if you can't fish?"

"Beka's not coming back?" his father said, looking shocked, and surprisingly unhappy. "What did you do, boy?"

Marcus felt a sudden desire to revert to childhood and stamp his feet on the worn deck. "What makes you think it was me that did something? Did it not occur to you that maybe your precious Beka was the one at fault?"

Across the way, Chico and Kenny exchanged glances.

"She lied to me," Marcus said stubbornly, as though someone were arguing with him. "She wasn't who she said she was at all." He wasn't going to mention that his da had been right about mystical creatures actually existing—not only would that give the old man something more to feel superior about, but Marcus was still doing his best to pretend he'd never learned the truth about dragons and Selkies and Mermaids. Oh my.

Marcus Senior shook his head. "You're as big a fool as I am, boy," he said in a marginally quieter voice. "I lost your mother because I was too prideful to go after her when she left. Don't you make the same mistake I did. That Beka, she's one in a million. Even I like her, and that's saying something."

Chico snorted into his mustache. Marcus glared at them both.

"She's gone, and she's not coming back. You'd better

just get used to the idea." *Like he would—any day now.* "And in the meantime, you still need a new net, and I'm going to go get you one. So you'd better get used to that idea too."

The old man opened his mouth, but Marcus didn't wait around to see what he had to say, striding off to the front of the boat and taking the wheel to steer them back into shore. The sooner he got off this boat and away from his father, the better. There was a beer at the Cranky Seagull with his name on it. And if there was any luck left in his life at all, it would have brought plenty of its relatives.

TWENTY

"BEKA. BEKA. YOU should get up and see this."

Chewie's voice was like a hammer beating against the anvil of her headache. The sun peeking through the blinds provided the flames for the forge. She wasn't asleep; hadn't slept much at all, lately. Some of it was worry, of course. And feeling like crap. But most of it was missing Marcus like crazy.

You would think they'd been together forever, the way she missed him, instead of just spending a couple of weeks on the same boat, and one brief moment of passion together. Before it all blew up in her face. And yet, she ached for him. Half a dozen times in the last couple of days, she'd almost swallowed her pride and gone to him. Begged him to listen. To understand. But what was the point? They came from two different worlds. There was no way their separate stories could share the same ending.

"Beka." Sharp teeth tugged at the long tee shirt she slept in. "Are you getting up? There's something on TV you need to see."

Beka brushed away tears with a hand that shook and

tried to paste a disgruntled expression on her face as she rolled over to face her dragon-dog. "Fine, I'm coming. But if this is another rerun of *The Lord of the Rings*, I don't want to hear about how Smaug isn't really a bad guy at heart."

Chewie shook his massive head, not at all convinced by her show of normalcy, but clearly willing to let it slide. For now, anyway.

"No, it's the local news. Not nearly as much fun as *Lord of the Rings*, but almost as educational."

Beka forced herself to get out of bed, ignoring her pounding head and churning stomach. She followed Chewie into the living room, where the TV showed a chipper blond weather girl predicting warm weather and no rain. What a surprise. Beka spun her hand counterclockwise, and the scene on the television rewound slowly.

"Stop there!" Chewie demanded, settling down on his haunches.

Beka snapped her fingers, and the picture started moving forward again at normal speed, showing the news from a few minutes before. A perky female reporter, nearly identical to the one who'd been doing the weather, stood on a dock with a microphone and an intently serious expression.

"We have multiple reports of odd occurrences out here at the harbor," she said, showing a lot of very white teeth and very tanned cleavage. "Some of the fishermen have told me that their nets are being chewed up and destroyed in a way that none of them has ever seen before. A couple of men I talked to claim to have seen mythical creatures, such as Mermaids or sea serpents, and one even insisted that some kind of mysterious force is responsible for this season's poor fishing."

"Gee, Kelly, that all sounds pretty far-fetched," the anchorman back at the station said. "Have you seen anything unusual yourself?"

Kelly shook her head, although her hair didn't move at all. "No, Bob, I haven't. But these guys are mostly experienced fishermen, and as tough as old nails. It is unusual to see them this rattled. And I did see one of the nets they were talking about, and it did kind of look like something had chewed on it."

"So, Kelly, do you think we are dealing with some kind of sea monster out there in the beautiful Monterey Bay? Could these fishermen be onto something?" The anchorman's cheery demeanor made it sound like someone was about to declare a new national holiday.

"Well, Bob, this is California, so anything is possible," Kelly said, the sun nearly blinding as it bounced off her teeth. "But Mermaids? Really?" She smiled at the camera as if inviting the audience in on the joke. "I think it's more likely that they're *on* something than *onto* something. But I'll let you know if I run into a talking dolphin. Back to you, Bob."

Beka scowled so hard at the television, smoke started seeping out the back. Chewie hurriedly hit the "off" button with his paw.

"Gah," she said, stomping off to the kitchen to make tea. "I guess it is a little too late to try and get Marcus's father to warn the other fishermen to watch out for things that are odd and dangerous."

"I'd say so." Chewie looked slightly depressed under all his fur. "What are you going to do now?"

Besides kiss my career as a Baba Yaga good-bye? Beka sniffed the rejuvenating tea, slightly scented with the blue roses that formed its base. It seemed like her stomach was always upset these days, but the magical tea still made her feel a little bit better. It didn't do anything to help the fatigue that had suddenly started to make her feel as though gravity was heavier wherever she happened to be standing, but she blamed that on the sleepless nights and too much diving. If she'd been fully Human, she would have suspected the flu. But Babas didn't get sick.

Too bad the same thing didn't apply to being lovesick.

She sighed. "I guess I'll try some more magical work to see if I can get a better idea of what is at the bottom of the poisoning problem. And track down all the paranormal creatures I know, so I can ask them if they've heard or seen anything of our mystery renegade. I'll be happy when the Riders get here."

Chewie suddenly picked up his head and gave a reasonably doglike woof.

"Timmy in the well again?" Beka asked sarcastically.

"Someone at the door," Chewie said. "Or at least there was."

Beka didn't know if it was just her pounding head, or if the damned dragon was making even less sense than usual. But she made her way over to the door anyway and swung the handle to open it.

She looked out, but all she saw was an empty parking lot and a view of the sea across the road. *Damn. Just for a moment, she'd thought that maybe Marcus had come to apologize. As if that was ever going to happen.*

"There's no one here, Chewie," she said.

He woofed again, and knocked something over that had been leaning next to the door. It was a huge bunch of roses, orchids, and lilies in various shades of dainty pink and blushing peach. Not exactly her colors, but very pretty in a completely over-the-top kind of way. The overpowering odor made her stomach flip-flop, or maybe that was due to a momentary spurt of hope. Seconds later, though, she realized that Marcus wasn't the flower-giving type.

"There's a note," Chewie pointed out helpfully. "Are they from the sailor?"

"Don't be stupid," she said, disappointment making her crabby. She looked at the note. "They're from Kesh."

"Oh. Swell." Chewie scowled. "Put them back on the ground. I'll pee on them."

Beka rolled her eyes. "You will do no such thing. I told you he's had some sort of falling-out with his family. He's just lonely and needs a friend."

"He *needs* to leave you alone. You're busy."

Beka ignored him and read the note out loud. If she didn't, the dragon would just bug her until she told him what was in it anyway.

"Dearest Beka," the note read. "These flowers are but a pale reflection of your beauty, but I hope you will accept them as a token of my regard. I have missed you these past days, and it is my fervent hope that you will honor me with your presence at dinner tonight. I will be on the beach at the usual place, eagerly waiting for you to join me and put the moon to shame with the glow of your smile. Yours, Kesh."

Chewie made gagging noises. Loudly.

"Oh hush, you," Beka said, secretly agreeing with him. She really wasn't the flattery type either. Maybe that's why she'd liked Marcus so much; he'd never tried to flatter her. Or said anything nice at all, for the most part. It was kind of restful.

"You're not going to go, are you?" Chewie asked, following her back inside. "You have mysteries to solve and a bad guy to track down. You don't have time to waste on Prince Not-As-Charming-As-He-Thinks-He-Is."

Beka stood with the flowers in her hands, trying to figure out where she could put them where they wouldn't stink up the place. Finally, she opened the door to the Otherworld and tossed them inside, before the smell could make her throw up. Some pixie would love them. Hell, considering the size of the bouquet, a whole tribe of pixies.

"I need to talk to him anyway about this renegade issue. He must know *something* about it." She tried again to ignore that nagging voice that said he'd already admitted to working against the Human fishermen. A few childish pranks didn't make him a villain.

A COUPLE OF hours later, there was a brisk knock on the door. Beka looked up from studying an ancient tome on magic and almost dropped the priceless relic on the floor when the door clattered open to reveal a plump woman with long, frizzy, gray-streaked hair and a brightly flowered tunic over puffy-legged tie-dyed pants. Multiple lengths of colorful beaded necklaces were tangled around her neck, and the scent of patchouli preceded her like a trumpeter announcing her presence.

"Hello, sweetie," Brenna said, sailing into the room. "I hope you don't mind me letting myself in, but it still seems strange to be knocking on my own door." She gave a trilling laugh, looking around the place with a critical eye.

"Goodness, you've changed a few things around, haven't you?" Pursed lips suggested a marked lack of approval. "Where are all my throw pillows? The place looks positively drab."

Beka lowered the book with a sigh and tried to muster up some enthusiasm for this unexpected visit. Brenna had raised her, after all, and taught her everything she knew. Beka was pretty sure that meant she should be happy to see her old mentor. So why could she feel her stomach knotting and her shoulders hunching?

"Hello, Brenna. This is a surprise," Beka said. "Last I'd heard, you were off enjoying your retirement in some tropical corner of the Otherworld." She got up and went over to Brenna. They didn't hug. For all her earth-mother exterior, Brenna didn't do hugs. "Can I get you some tea?"

"Stand up straight, dear," Brenna said, settling herself into a chair. "And yes, thank you, something herbal, please."

"I hear nightshade is a nice herb," a low voice growled from behind the couch. Chewie sauntered into view and gave Brenna a slit-eyed look. "How about some of that?"

The gray-haired woman chuckled. "Oh, Chewie, you always did love to tease me. I've missed you." A flitting glance bounced over to where Beka stood, juggling mugs and a bottle of honey. "You, too, of course, sweetie."

"Of course," Beka murmured. She handed Brenna a steaming cup of tea and sat down nearby with her own.

"What are you doing here, Brenna?" Chewie asked with his usual bluntness. With an equal lack of subtlety, he settled onto the floor at Beka's feet, making it clear that his loyalties lay with the current Baba, not the old one.

Brenna merely raised an eyebrow, clearly unaffected. "I'm checking in on Beka; I would have thought that was obvious. I heard that she was having some difficulty dealing with her first big task, and I thought I'd just pop in to see if there was anything I could do to help. Offer support and encouragement, you know, that kind of thing."

Chewie snorted and Brenna pressed her lips together until they made a thin red line. "If you're going to be unpleasant, dear, why don't you go take a walk? Beka and I have Baba Yaga business to discuss. Your presence is not required." She made a shooing motion.

Beka opened her mouth to protest, but the dog just shrugged his massive shoulders and muttered, "I need some fresh air anyway. I forgot how much I hated the smell of patchouli oil." He gave Brenna a measured look. "I won't be gone long. I'm assuming this won't be a lengthy visit."

Beka's head swung back and forth between her mentor and her dragon-dog. How had she never noticed before how much they disliked each other? She sighed, wishing Chewie was staying, but knowing that she had to be able to face her predecessor on her own.

"So," Beka said when the door had swung shut with a particularly sarcastic clang, "who told you I was having problems?"

Brenna waved one hand languidly through the air, her many rings flashing. "Oh, sweetie, everybody knows. The paranormal community here, people back at the Queen's court; it's not exactly a secret now, is it?" She reached out and patted Beka's arm. "You mustn't feel bad. Everyone knows you're trying your best. Nobody blames you for failing. You're just in over your head."

Beka's stomach knotted even tighter, and she hoped she wasn't going to add to the ignominy of the situation by throwing up on the floor at her mentor's feet. She pulled her arms in and wrapped them protectively around her middle. "I haven't failed yet, Brenna," she said, trying to sound more confident than she felt. "There's still time for me to find the answers that will allow me to fix the situation."

"Of course there is, sweetie. After all, the water people don't reach their weakest point until the night of the full moon, when the tides pull hardest against their magic.

That's probably when most of the really sick ones will start to die, and you've still got days until then."

Brenna peered over at the stack of books Beka had been desperately searching through before Brenna arrived. "Oh dear. You're still doing research? I thought for certain you would have found the cause of the problem by now and been working on a cure." She made a *tutt*ing noise with her tongue, shaking her frizzy head before slurping more tea.

Beka bit her lip. She hated more than anything to ask, but clearly, she didn't have any choice. "Brenna, do you think you could help me? You have so much more experience than I do. I'm certain if we worked together—"

Brenna's sad laugh echoed through the bus, making a set of wind chimes peal a discordant tune. "Oh dear, you know the High Queen has forbidden me to take on any Baba Yaga duties. I'm sure she wouldn't approve at all of me helping you out."

Beka's shoulders drooped even further. She hadn't really expected a different answer, but it had been worth a try, with so many people depending on her to get this right.

"Oh," she said. "Probably not. I understand."

Brenna tapped one finger against her lips thoughtfully. "You know, there might be one solution . . . but no, it wouldn't be fair to even ask you to consider it."

"What?" Beka sat up a little straighter at the thought that there might be something she could do. "Tell me what it is? I'd do anything to help the Selkies and the Merpeople." *Not to mention the Human fishermen, but she didn't think Brenna would be impressed by that. She'd never been all that fond of Humans, for all that she'd been born one of them.*

"Well . . . you could give up being the Baba Yaga. I know you've been having second thoughts lately about whether or not to continue on, and if you left the position open, then the Queen would have no choice but to let me come back and take up my mantle again." She smiled brightly at Beka. "I'm sure I could find a solution in no time if I was allowed to do so."

Beka's head was buzzing, filled with confusion and doubt.

How did Brenna even know that Beka had been thinking of giving up being a Baba? Did everyone know? Was that the only choice she had left—the only way to save the water folk? Surely there was some other option. But right this very minute, she couldn't think of what that might be.

Brenna put her mug down on the table with a decisive click that sounded like a death knell. "I should be on my way, sweetie. Things to do, people to enchant, you know how it is. If you want to get in touch with me, simply send out a magical call; I won't be far away. You just think over what I said. I'm sure you'll do what's best. That's how I raised you."

Beka wasn't sure how long she sat there after Brenna left, huddled on the couch with her knees drawn up to her chest and her hands over her face. Her own breath seemed too loud in the silent bus, but her thoughts were even louder. *Give up. Don't give up. Give up. Don't give up.*

When Chewie came back, she didn't even bother to raise her head. She was just so tired.

"I take it the reunion was less than a shining success," the dog said in a grumpy tone as he plopped down next to her. The couch groaned in protest. "I knew I should have stayed."

"It wouldn't have made any difference," Beka said. She sighed as she straightened out her cramped legs. "Your being here wouldn't have changed the truth of what she said to me. Everyone knows I'm failing as a Baba Yaga, and it isn't fair to the Selkies and the Merpeople."

"Oh, for the love of—" A thin stream of smoke slid out of Chewie's nostrils and curled in an undeserved halo around his head. "You don't seriously believe that, do you? Shit. I knew that woman was going to undermine your confidence, just the way she always did. I should have stayed and eaten her."

Beka was so shocked she almost fell off the couch. "Chewie! A Chudo-Yudo can't eat a Baba Yaga—that's just wrong!"

"She's an ex–Baba Yaga," the dragon muttered. "And it might be wrong, but I still think I should have done it. Look at how much she upset you."

Beka gave him a halfhearted smile. "You can't go around eating everyone who upsets me, Chewie. If nothing else, you'd get indigestion."

He woofed at her, licking her face affectionately. "It would be worth it. Besides, I know a really good cure for indigestion. Works for discouragement too."

Beka looked at him doubtfully. "Really? What's that? Some kind of magical remedy?"

Chewie shook his head. "S'mores." He gave her an unsubtle butt with his large head. "And if you make me some, I'll help you with your research. I just don't want to hear anything more about you failing. You only fail if you give up."

He walked toward the kitchen and Beka followed, but she couldn't help thinking that maybe giving up was the only way *not* to fail.

"HOW WAS YOUR visit?" Kesh asked. "Did it go the way you had hoped?"

"Of course it did. The poor girl is probably rehearsing her resignation speech for the High Queen as we speak."

"Good," he said. "I was quite put out when you sent that shark after her without speaking to me first. And the storm was simply unnecessary. I told you I had the situation under control."

"If you had it under such good control, I wouldn't have had to go have my little heart-to-heart with her now, would I? Still, maybe this way neither of us will have to kill her. I suppose that would be best."

"As long as she does not interfere with my plans," Kesh said.

"Our plans, you mean."

"Right. Our plans. That is what I meant to say."

"Of course you did, sweetie. Of course you did."

"HEY! DO YOU hear that?" Chewie bounded back over to the door.

Beka hoped to hell it wasn't a singing telegram or a mariachi band sent to serenade her. But unless they'd started traveling on motorcycles, she figured she was probably safe. So she was right on Chewie's heels as he yanked the door back open with his teeth.

Pulling up in front of the bus was a red Ducati and a black Harley. The Harley had fringed saddlebags, lots of bright silver chrome, and an engine that sounded like a roaring ogre. The giant that swung his leg over the saddle as soon as the bike had come to a halt roared almost as loudly.

"Beka!" Alexei Knight bellowed, coming over to pick her up and swing her around as if she were still a four-year-old child. He planted an enthusiastic kiss on each cheek, his beard tickling her chin, and walloped Chewie affectionately on the head. "Chewie old pal, how are t'ings?" His thick Russian accent made Beka think of borscht and potato dumplings.

"Unhand that poor woman, you hairy behemoth," Gregori Sun said, coming up behind his friend and bowing to Beka with his hands pressed together in front of his heart. "Greetings, Baba Yaga. It is a pleasure to see you again. It has been too long." His accent was barely discernible as a slightly musical lilt to his speech.

"It has," Beka agreed with a smile. "The only downside to staying out of trouble is that I don't get to see my Riders nearly often enough."

"You have trouble now, though, yes?" Alexei said. "Or you would not have called us."

Beka let out a huff of air. "Yes, I have trouble now." She glanced around, looking for a third motorcycle. "Where's Mikhail? Isn't he with you?"

Gregori shook his head, his shining black tail of hair swinging against his back. "We finished up with Barbara's latest crisis a few days ago and each went our own way. Alexei and I met up along the road, but I'm sure Day will be here soon."

He glanced at her with a critical eye. "In the meanwhile,

perhaps you would like to put some clothes on and tell us about this problem you are having."

Beka blushed, tugging down on her long tee and trying to make it cover a little more of her thighs. The Riders had watched her grow up, and were sort of like slightly odd uncles to her, but still, she would like to have presented a slightly more dignified appearance when they showed up.

"Do not change on my account," Alexei said with a leer. "I always like a Baba with good legs. There are only so many old crones one can look at in a lifetime as long as mine."

Gregori smacked him on the back of the head as he walked by, having to reach up to do it. "Come on, you Cossack. You'll scare the girl, and then she won't conjure up any of those wonderful melty things for us." He looked at Baba hopefully. "What do you call those?"

"S'mores," Chewie said helpfully.

"Yes," said Alexei. "I would like some more, too, whatever you call them."

Beka's load felt lighter already. It was good to have family. Even if they were loud, ate her out of house and home, and spent most of their time arguing with each other. When they weren't breaking things. Or people. Yup. It was definitely good to have family.

A CRESCENT MOON hung over the nearly deserted beach like an enchanted lantern, casting both light and shadow over Kesh as he sat across the blanket from Beka. As usual, he'd brought a veritable feast of delicacies from the sea, as well as the requisite bottle or two of heady champagne. Beka sipped at hers and tried to stop wishing he were someone else. Like maybe a cranky ex-Marine with broad shoulders and a way of kissing that made her tingle just thinking about it. It was hard to believe that only three weeks before, she hadn't known either one of them. Life had been much simpler then.

Farther down the beach, a boisterous group of college-age kids were drinking beer around a flaming bonfire; the sounds of their laughter and the deep rhythmic beat of their music made for a pleasant backdrop when separated by half a mile of sand and rocks. Other than that, there was only the *whoosh*ing of the waves coming in and going out and the occasional bird calling on its way back to its nest for the night.

Their own smaller fire crackled and snapped, sending embers dancing up into the sky like tiny firefly messengers. The smell of the smoke gave a pleasant tang to the sea air, and Beka inhaled deeply, trying to draw the energy of the elements into her core. She was so tired. But it meant so much to Kesh that she be there, she hadn't had the heart not to show up.

As if echoing her thought, the Selkie prince said, "I am so pleased that you could join me tonight, Baba Yaga. You have been very busy of late." It *almost* didn't sound like scolding. He handed her a plate laden with dainty, perfectly presented bites of food that she had no desire to eat.

"Well, I *am* trying to save your people's home, Kesh." She mustered up a smile to ease the sting of her words. After a moment's consideration, she confessed, "I should probably tell you that I spoke to your father."

The darkness made the shadows seem to creep into Kesh's gray eyes. "Oh?" he said cautiously. "And what did my progenitor have to say?"

"He told me that the children who'd fallen ill hadn't gotten any better since the Selkies and Merpeople moved to their new temporary grounds," Beka said, wishing there was some way to soften the blow. "I'm so sorry."

"Ah," Kesh said. "That is unfortunate." A smile flickered over his lips; he was no doubt trying to put up a brave front for her, so she wouldn't feel worse about it than she already did.

"I'm working as hard as I can, I promise you," she said. "I've *got* to be close to an answer. I feel as though it is right in front of me, and I just can't see it." Frustration made her stomach hurt even more than usual, and she shifted the food around on her dish without eating it.

"I have every faith in you," Kesh said. He bit off a piece of bright red salmon with sharp white teeth. "So, did my father say anything else of interest?"

Beka played with the sand, not wanting to meet his eyes. The coarse grains felt unusually harsh against the sensitive tips of her fingers. "Well, your brother did mention that you and your father had some kind of falling-out and you'd left home."

"Indeed, that is true, Baba Yaga," he said, his voice soft against the sound of the ocean. "However, I am sure it is but a temporary estrangement. Do not worry yourself on my account."

Beka looked at him, impressed that even during a difficult time he still concerned himself for her feelings. A lock of dark hair had fallen over his forehead, giving him an endearingly childlike charm, and his admiring smile glinted at her across the salty air. She waited to feel something, anything, other than friendly affection, but her heart stubbornly refused to cooperate.

He still wasn't Marcus, dammit.

"There's a new problem too," she said, giving up on her plate and laying it down on the striped blanket. She took a sip of champagne instead; the bubbles seemed to calm her uneasy insides, and the expensive wine soothed her frayed nerves. "Something you might be able to help me with, in fact."

He bowed slightly regally as always. "Anything I can do, my dear Baba. What is this new problem, pray tell?"

Beka explained about the renegade the Queen had tasked her with finding, and then took a deep breath. "Kesh, I need you to tell me the truth. Are you involved with this man? You told me you and some friends had been acting against the Humans. If you are mixed up in this, I can help you, but I need to know."

Kesh looked hurt. "I cannot believe you would think me capable of such a thing; to betray my own people. Yes, I have played a few harmless tricks on the local fishermen, but surely you would not condemn me for such a small mischief." His dark eyes gazed at her earnestly.

Beka felt just awful. Kesh had been nothing but supportive, and here she was accusing him of being in league with criminals. She should have known better. "I'm sorry, Kesh. It's just, well, in all the times we talked, you never even mentioned that you weren't living under the sea with your family anymore. I thought . . . I don't know what I thought. That maybe you were hiding something."

The Selkie gave her a wan smile. "Perhaps I was only hiding my concern that you would not wish to be associated with me, if you knew I was no longer a prince of the realm."

"Kesh, how could you think that?" Beka patted his hand where it lay next to hers on the blanket. "I don't care if you are a prince or not! I like you for you." She was so relieved to discover her friend wasn't guilty, it made her dizzy. Or maybe that was the wine. "You'll tell me if you hear anything, right? After all, you have all sorts of connections with the local paranormal folk."

"No one has approached me as yet, alas," he said. "But I will make some enquiries amongst my friends, if you think that would be useful."

It was nice to feel like she wasn't alone. Between Kesh and the Riders, surely she could satisfy the Queen's demands and fulfill her obligations to the paranormal community.

"That would be great, Kesh," she said enthusiastically. "The Queen has threatened to bring Brenna back to replace me if I can't figure out who this mystery man is and stop him."

Kesh's long fingers tapped the side of his glass for a moment, then stilled. "Is that so? I thought that Brenna was out of favor with their majesties."

"What? I don't think so," Beka said. "I thought the Queen just insisted she retire because she'd been a Baba Yaga for so long, and it was time for her to have a break. I was taught that eventually all Babas had to step down, because otherwise continuing to drink the Water of Life and Death would have unpleasant side effects. For those who started out Human, anyway. Mind you, after over two hundred years, you would think anyone would want to stop working."

"Hmmm. Perhaps I heard wrong," Kesh said. "Either way, it would be a great shame for you to be replaced by anyone. Unless, of course, that was what you wished. Are you, perhaps, considering giving up your role as Baba Yaga? You are still young enough to start another life. I might even have some suggestions, should you find yourself in such a position."

Beka snorted. "I don't think so, although the thought has certainly crossed my mind. The Riders are here now—two of them, at least—and with their help, I'm sure to be able to fix this mess before the High Queen loses her patience." She hoped so, anyway. The Queen wasn't known for her tolerance of failure.

"The Riders are here? How nice to know." He gave her a smooth, sweet curve of the lips, and held out a morsel of succulent lobster. "You have a great deal to do, my darling. You must keep your strength up. Drink some more of your lovely champagne and try a piece of this rare blue lobster. I caught it for you myself, just this afternoon."

The moonlight seemed ensnared by his glinting eyes, captured and reflected in a distorted double vision of matching crescents as sharp as knives. Beka blinked, thinking he was right. She really needed to keep up her strength. Smiling, she opened her mouth and took a bite.

KESH FOLLOWED BEKA back home, pausing at the edge of the clearing where the bus was parked to ponder the evening's conversation. He was tempted to go closer and look through the windows to see if she was working on some new magical experiment, but he did not wish to attract the attention of the Riders or that cursed Chudo-Yudo. For some reason, the monster had taken against him. Suspicious beast.

Of course, he was poisoning the dragon-dog's mistress, and plotting to kill her, but his charm *always* worked on stupid animals, paranormal or otherwise. And it wasn't as though Chudo-Yudo had any way to know what Kesh was up to. Thankfully, that charm still seemed to be working on the Baba Yaga, although she mysteriously continued to refuse his romantic advances. Something to do with that damned sailor, no doubt, although why anyone would choose a coarse Human fisherman over a refined Selkie prince was beyond his comprehension.

He pouted into the darkness, annoyed by the way her stubbornness had forced him to change his plans. It seemed that Brenna's attempts to discourage Beka had failed. And now the Riders were here. *That* truly was unfortunate. He might be able to take advantage of Beka's relative youth and inexperience, along with her idiotically trusting nature (so un-Baba-like), but the Riders would not be so easy to fool. Nor were they likely to be willing to join in his efforts to torment the Humans who despoiled his ocean.

No, it was time to move on to his end game. Ahead of schedule, but what was one to do? And there was one bit of good news amidst the bad: that the Queen was actually considering giving Brenna back her position as Baba Yaga if Beka could not prove herself capable of doing the job. Kesh thought it was easily possible that the Queen had never intended to follow through on the threat, but nonetheless, Brenna would be very pleased to hear of it.

Almost as pleased as she would be when her adopted daughter was dead and unable to thwart her plan to return to the power and influence of being a Baba Yaga. With an ally like Brenna, Kesh could not fail to win.

Such a pity about Beka, but all wars had their incidental casualties. And she would only be the first of many.

TWENTY-ONE

WHEN THE MUTED rumble of a vehicle came in through the open window the next morning, both Beka and Chewie's heads swiveled in that direction.

"*Now* who's here?" Beka exclaimed in disbelief. Normally she could go months without anyone coming near her bus. Lately it seemed like Grand Central Station. Of course, it didn't help that she could tell from the sound that it wasn't Marcus's Jeep.

"Maybe I should put in a revolving door and start selling tickets," Chewie muttered. "At least it would pay for more chocolate and marshmallows."

Beka moved to open the door, and what she saw made her feel better than she had in days.

"I don't believe it!" she said, running down the steps and over to the large silver Airstream. A tall woman with a cloud of long, dark hair climbed out of the passenger side of the silver Chevy truck pulling the trailer. She moved with the dangerous grace of a panther. Or a Baba Yaga.

"Barbara! What are you doing here?" Beka asked, screeching to a halt with Chewie on her heels. "You're supposed to be on your honeymoon."

"I *am* on my honeymoon," her sister Baba said with a wide smile. "We just happened to be in the area and I thought we'd stop in and say hi, since you couldn't make it to the wedding."

A slim, attractive man with sandy brown hair came around from the other side of the truck, followed by a small, solemn-looking pixie of a child who peered at Beka from behind his long legs.

"This is Liam," Barbara said, putting one proprietary hand on his arm. "And this is Babs, my adopted daughter." Her pride in them both softened her usually severe countenance in a way that Beka had never seen before.

"Hey," Liam said, a good-natured grin lighting up his face. "I'm glad we finally get to meet. Barbara has told me all about you."

Beka grinned back. "Not as much as she's told me about you, I'll bet. Is it true that you are more powerful than a locomotive and can leap tall buildings in a single bound?"

"I think you're confusing me with Superman," Liam said. "I'm just a small-town sheriff. Barbara is the one with the superpowers in this family."

"Are you kidding? You got Barbara to marry you. If that isn't a superpower, I don't know what is."

Liam laughed. "You might have a point there. She wasn't exactly easy to woo."

Barbara scowled. "I was easy." She thought about it. "I didn't kill you and bury you in the backyard. It could have been worse."

Little Babs stuck her head out from behind Liam's knee to say, in a piping tenor voice, "You lived in the Airstream. You didn't have a backyard."

Barbara laughed. "Don't mind Babs; she's very literal. That's what spending the first few years of your life in the Otherworld will get you." She turned to the girl. "This is

Beka, one of the other Baba Yagas I told you about. Can you say hi?"

"Hi," the girl said, pushing a hank of short, dark hair behind one ear. "I'm going to be a Baba Yaga when I get bigger. But I'm only five, so today I get to see the Pacific Ocean. That's good, right? I've never seen an ocean before." She looked at Beka, tilting her head to one side like a crow eyeing something shiny. "Barbara says you get to see the ocean every day. Is it nice?"

Beka nodded, completely enchanted. "It is nice," she said. "Are you going to go swimming?"

Babs looked up at Liam. "I am, right? You're going to teach me to swim and I'm going to wear my special clothes for getting wet in." She gazed at Beka with a slightly baffled expression. "Barbara says there are clothes for getting wet in, and clothes for staying dry in. That seems silly to me. Does it seem silly to you?"

Barbara smothered a laugh under one hand. "Babs is still getting used to being in the mundane world. A lot of our rules don't make a lot of sense to her."

Beka squatted down so she was on Babs's level and said in a whisper, "Don't tell anyone, but I think some of those rules are silly too."

A tiny smile tugged at the edge of the little girl's rosebud lips. "Okay," she whispered back. "I won't tell." And then added in a louder voice, "I like her. Can we go swimming now?"

BEKA AND BARBARA sat on a blanket on the beach and watched Barbara's new husband patiently showing little Babs how to float. They'd left their respective Chudo-Yudos up at the bus getting reacquainted and catching up on whatever dragons gossiped about. It was distinctly possible that their two erstwhile huts were gossiping, too, but it was always hard to say with semi-aware buildings. Especially once they acquired wheels.

"So," Barbara said after a while. "What's going on?"

Beka tried to remember what she'd put in the letter she'd sent, apologizing for not being able to make it to Barbara and Liam's wedding. "Well, there's a problem with the trench the Selkies and Merpeople live in; something is poisoning the water, and I've been tasked to find out what and fix it. And apparently there is a renegade riling up the local paranormal community and risking exposure of all our secrets." She looked down, playing with a tiny shell. "I'm, um, not making a lot of headway."

Barbara sighed. "That's not what I'm talking about. I'm talking about *you*. I got a message from Chewie saying that you were having a crisis and needed someone to talk to—it's pretty unusual for one Baba's Chudo-Yudo to contact another Baba, so I thought I'd better come by in person instead of just calling."

Oh, great. She couldn't believe her dragon had interrupted Barbara's honeymoon because he thought she couldn't handle the situation. There might have been another moment in her life that had been more humiliating than this one, but she couldn't think of it offhand.

"I'm *so* sorry," she said, dropping her head into her hands. "I can't believe he dragged you all the way out here for this. I'm fine, really." Other than being completely mortified, that is.

"We really were in the area," Barbara said, patting Beka clumsily on the shoulder. She wasn't all that comfortable with Human gestures, having been raised by a Baba who'd been at the end of her career and not very good at being Human anymore. But she was trying. "We've been traveling across the country so we could show Babs some of her new world. And of course, with the Airstream being magical, it doesn't take as long to get from place to place as it should. I'd already promised to show her the ocean, so coming here was no big deal, although we need to get back on the road later today."

Barbara looked at Beka, studying her demeanor and posture. "And I'm not buying that 'I'm fine' shit, just in case you were wondering. You look terrible." She bit her lip. "I mean, you look tired and depressed. Liam says I need to be less blunt with other people, but you're a Baba—I'm not sure that counts."

Beka choked on a laugh. She didn't get to spend much time with either of her fellow Babas, but she liked them both. Barbara's sharp tongue was part of her charm. And at least it meant you didn't have to play any games with her.

"I'll admit, things have been a little tough," Beka said. "This is my first big solo job since Brenna left, and I'm kind of feeling like I'm in over my head. Brenna actually came to visit me recently and suggested that I resign and let her take over." It was the first time she'd said the words out loud, and they sounded weighty and final, like a heavy door closing with a thud.

"Did she?" Barbara said. "That explains a lot." She chewed on fingernail thoughtfully. "And are you considering it? Resigning, I mean."

Beka shrugged. "I don't know. I mean, I'd already been thinking that maybe this wasn't the life for me." She pointed down at the water, where Babs was splashing around in the shallow waves on the shore, a faint smile adorning her normally solemn face. "I keep thinking that I'd like to have a kid of my own." Her heart contracted at the sight, feeling as though there were slivers of jagged rock piercing her to her core. "It will be years before I'm advanced enough to be training someone like you are."

"That's true," Barbara said. "But that doesn't mean you can't find a way to have children in your life. Every Baba's path is different. To be honest, I put it off as long as I could, thinking I would be as bad with kids as my mentor was. But as it turns out, I really like having Babs around." She gave a rueful grin. "Of course, it helps that I have Liam. He's really great with her. With both of us."

Beka stifled any thoughts of Marcus, trying not to picture him in Liam's place, laughing and playing in the sunlit waters. "I'm really glad you found him," she said.

"Me too," Barbara said. "Is there anyone special in your life?"

Yes. No. Maybe. "It's complicated," Beka said.

Barbara snorted. "You're a Baba Yaga. It always is."

They sat in companionable silence for a moment, and then Beka asked, "Did you ever consider walking away before it was final? Being a Baba, I mean."

Barbara gave her a startled look. "And give up magic? Never." She narrowed her amber eyes. "Don't tell me you're really thinking about quitting—that's crazy."

"Brenna said—"

"Screw Brenna," Barbara said, scowling at her friend. "She was way out of line saying you should resign, and you know it."

"But—"

"There are no buts here, Beka," Barbara said, "other than the big, fat, hippie butt I'd like to kick into next week. For one thing, retired Baba Yagas don't ever get to come back. There's a reason they retire, and it usually has to do with them being too old or too crazy to do the job anymore. Or too dead, I suppose, but that's another issue. For another thing, *all* Babas struggle with their first assignments on their own. I did, and Bella did; that's the nature of the job. You'll do fine in the end, I promise."

A tiny blip of hope felt like a hiccup in Beka's chest. "Really? *You* felt overwhelmed by your first task too?"

Barbara threw back her head and laughed so loud, Liam glanced up the beach at her and smiled quizzically. She waved at him before turning her attention back to Beka. "Honey, during my first solo task, I blew up a volcano. The very volcano I was supposed to stop from erupting, in fact."

"Holy crap," Beka said, feeling perversely better. "What happened?"

"After it blew up, it stopped erupting," Barbara said. "Problem solved. There was just a bigger mess to clean up than I'd planned on." She put one arm around Beka's shoulders, awkwardly but kindly. "You're going to be fine. I don't care what Brenna said. She wouldn't have chosen you to train as her replacement if you didn't have what it took to be a Baba Yaga. You just need to have a little faith in yourself."

Beka sighed. "That's not always easy."

Barbara shook her head. "If it were easy, everybody would do it. And you're not everybody; you're a Baba Yaga. That's *way* better."

MARCUS SAT IN the hospital waiting for his father to finish up his chemo. Since the incident with the shredded nets, his da seemed to fade away day by day, as if the fight had drained out of him like air from a leaky balloon. Marcus had held true to his promise to replace the nets, but he might as well not have bothered. All they brought up was seaborne debris—a dismal harvest of empty plastic bottles, bubble-edged once-white plastic cooler lids, and bedraggled bits and pieces of sunken ships that had suddenly been imbued with a mysterious desire to return to the surface. Every once in a while there was a fish or two, but they were all dead or diseased, with blank staring eyes and ragged fins.

Marcus was a little depressed, too, although only part of that could be blamed on the lack of fish or his da's ill health. Truth be told, he missed Beka. He missed having her around the boat, always there to lend a hand with cheerful enthusiasm. He missed seeing her bright smile and gleaming hair, missed the way he felt when he was around her. The *Wily Serpent* seemed to have lost some of its little remaining shine without her aboard. Hell, the whole world was darker without her daily presence in his life. He was an idiot.

An idiot for having fallen for her so hard. But an even bigger idiot for having let her go.

He still found it hard to believe what she'd told him— that she was some kind of magical being, like out of the stories his da used to tell. But her demonstration had been unmistakably real, and it certainly explained a few things that had baffled him, including how she ended up in the middle of the ocean to be caught in his nets in the first place. And a man didn't survive a dozen years in a war zone without seeing a thing or two that couldn't be explained away by the rational mind.

She was a witch. An honest to god, magical witch. Hell. He couldn't decide if that was worse or better than thinking she was just some flaky surfer chick. Either way, she was completely unsuitable for him. Completely, totally, and irrevocably not his type. So why did he miss her like a phantom limb?

He'd turn a corner and see some woman with a fall of long yellow-gold hair, and for a moment, his heart would seize up in his chest, thinking it was Beka. Or he'd catch a whiff of strawberries, impossible on the ocean breeze. At night, she haunted his dreams; swimming, laughing, scowling at him with those big sapphire eyes, or naked, writhing in pleasure beneath him, all tanned flesh and glowing joyfulness.

Waking alone and realizing he'd lost her—that was the worst.

Well, that and wondering if she was seeking comfort in the arms of that damned too-good-looking Kesh, who no doubt had been just waiting for Marcus to do something stupid, like walking away from the best woman on the entire planet.

He was an idiot squared. An idiot times infinity. He'd kick his own ass if the universe wasn't already doing such a good job of it. Damn, he missed that woman.

DAMN, SHE MISSED that man. Beka tried to focus on Alexei's report, but she was feeling even sicker and shakier than ever, and having a hard time focusing. That was the only reason she couldn't seem to keep her mind on topic. It had nothing to do with Marcus.

"Beka, are you listening to me?" Alexei rumbled, his deep basso voice bouncing off the paneled walls of the bus. "I haven't spent the last three nights crawling through every dive bar in town where paranormal creatures are known to hang out just for my health, you know." He gave her a broad grin that was almost lost within his beard. "Of course, I did have a bit of fun breaking heads and twisting arms so people would tell me the truth."

Gregori rolled his eyes at his larger comrade. "A bit of fun? We're banned from half the bars down by the wharf now. And the other half are just too scared of you to try it. Why can't you learn to ask politely?"

"Like you do?" Alexei said with a snort. "I seem to recall one poor Selkie lad you held up over your head for an hour while you drank beer with the other hand."

"Well, I didn't need both hands to hold him up there; why not drink beer? And he did eventually tell us what we needed to know."

"Boys," Beka interjected, not up to listening to any more gleeful recaps of the Riders' unique methods of information-tion gathering. "I assume that you actually did learn something from all this carousing and harassing of the locals, beside which tavern serves the best ale."

"The Cranky Seagull," they both said in unison.

Swell. The one place she could never go again, for fear of running into Marcus or his father. It figured.

"Lovely," she said in an uncharacteristically snappy voice. "I'll be sure to pass along your recommendation to the Queen. Now, if we had something a little more helpful to tell her at the same time, that might be good too."

Gregori raised one feathery eyebrow, the color of ink. "Are you all right, little one? You don't quite seem yourself."

"Yes," Alexei agreed, grabbing another handful of chips from the bowl on the table between them. "You are acting almost as crabby as Barbara. But on you, it is not so natural. What is the matter?"

A black mountain shifted underneath them, nudging the table an inch or two to the left. "She's pining for her fisherman," Chewie said morosely. "And so am I. I liked him, even if he was Human. Also, I think she's sick. Pass me the chips, will you?"

Alexei put the bowl on the floor. "Sick? Baba Yagas don't get sick."

"I'm fine," Beka said, propping her aching head on one hand and trying to look perkier than she felt. "I'm just tired."

"This is more than just tired," Gregori said, peering at her more closely. "I have been watching you, and you move like your whole body hurts. There are dark circles under your eyes, and you hardly eat anything at all. Surely this is not all because of some man."

Beka nudged Chewie with one bare foot and muttered, "Thanks so much for sharing, buddy."

"You're welcome," he muttered around a mouthful of chips. "But she doesn't smell right either. She's sick."

Gregori and Alexei both sniffed at her. Beka couldn't figure out whether to laugh or cry, burying her face in her palms for a moment before pushing her chair back from the table.

"Guys, I'm fine. Can we just focus on the matter at hand?"

Alexei settled back with a grunt, grabbing another bag of tortillas off the counter behind him without bothering to turn around. It helped to have the longest arms in the room. But Gregori still gazed at her, his dark eyes calm but concerned.

"When is the last time you had some of the Water of Life and Death?" he asked. "That should cure whatever is wrong with you."

Beka couldn't remember off the top of her head. Things had been a little crazy, and her brain felt like mush. Babas usually drank a small amount of the magical elixir once or twice a month, so it couldn't have been that long ago.

"I don't know," she said. "Last week? The week before? I'll have some later, okay? Right now, I'd really like to know what you've come up with, so we can deal with this problem once and for all. Do you have any idea yet who this mysterious renegade is?"

Surreptitiously, she crossed her fingers.

"We do have an idea, yes," Alexei said with a smirk, his enthusiasm making his accent even thicker than usual. Bits of tortilla scattered as he spoke, and Gregori sighed, cleaning a speck of food off his immaculate red pants.

"You do?" Beka said.

"We do." Gregori almost looked pleased; on him, it was the equivalent of an ear-to-ear grin. "At least, we have a description, and a likely place to look. One of the Merpeople we talked to last night—well, early this morning, really, since it was about three a.m. by the time we'd finished our little chat—was eventually convinced to share the information that our unknown pal has an appointment at an abandoned dock tonight. The only reason our informant knew anything about it was because he apparently uses that place to make his transformation when he comes onto land, and this mystery man warned him to stay away this evening. Or else."

"He seemed quite frightened by our mysterious friend," Alexei added with a certain relish. "But for some reason he found us even more intimidating. Go figure."

"You did have your big, meaty paw wrapped around his family jewels at that point in the conversation," Gregori pointed out. "This might have had something to do with it."

"Nah," Alexei said. "It vas my delightful personality."

Beka laughed. She loved working with the Riders. They always cheered her up.

"So, you have a place to look for him, and you said you know what he looks like too? That's great." She could almost feel hope creeping up on her like a sunrise over the ocean. "Is he an ogre? Some kind of Nixie?"

Chewie gave a great barking laugh. "You know ogres aren't smart enough to plan anything. And no one would follow a Nixie; they're just too unpleasant. All those sharp teeth, ugh."

"Look who's talking about sharp teeth," Beka muttered. But she patted him on his massive head anyway, and gave him most of her sandwich. They were having their meeting over an early dinner for her, more like a late breakfast for the Riders, since they'd been up most of the night and hadn't woken up until after two that afternoon.

"We're not completely sure what kind of creature our renegade is," Gregori said, looking thoughtful. "He has only appeared to people in his Human-seeming form. But everyone we've talked to paints the same picture: tall, dark hair, gray eyes, very handsome, very charming and charismatic, speaks with an Irish accent, acts like he owns the world. And by all accounts, he is very bitter about what Humans have done to the sea, so we're assuming he is some kind of ocean being."

Beka closed her eyes, shaken to her core. She knew someone who matched that portrayal exactly, right down to the attitude. But it couldn't be—could it? She couldn't have been that wrong about him. Besides, that description could apply to plenty of people—almost all the Selkies had black hair, gray eyes, and a dislike for the Humans who had despoiled their oceans.

Chewie gave a great roar and sprang to his feet, causing the table to rock back and forth until Gregori caught it in a steadying hand. "Aha!" the dragon said, looking around as if for someone to bite. A very particular someone. He gave Beka an accusing glare. "I *told* you I didn't like him. Didn't I? I told you there was something off about that damned Selkie."

Alexei and Gregori exchanged puzzled glances, turning to Beka with identical expressions of confusion written on their very different faces.

"Wait," Alexei said, scratching his beard and producing a rain of crumbs. "You *know* this person?"

"Maybe," Beka said with reluctance. "If it is the same man. It might not be."

Chewie grumbled low in his throat. "What are the odds of two handsome, arrogant, black-haired, black-hearted scoundrels showing up at the same time? Face it, Beka, you've been tricked. He has probably been hanging around you to keep an eye on what you're doing and make sure you don't interfere with his plans."

Beka shook her head. "No. I don't believe it. Kesh cares about his people, and he cares about me."

"That wouldn't necessarily stop him from trying to cause trouble for Humans, Beka," Gregori pointed out gently. "So, I take it you know someone who might be our renegade?"

She pressed her lips together, as if talking about it might somehow make it true. But just because she liked someone didn't mean they couldn't be guilty of bad decisions, bad behavior, or worse. Brenna had always warned her that she was a terrible judge of people. Of course, Brenna thought she was terrible at pretty much everything.

"His name is Kesh," Chewie informed the Riders flatly. "He's a Selkie prince, and he's been wooing our Beka for weeks. Leaving her stinky flowers, inviting her to romantic picnics on the beach. Showing up here, there, and everywhere. I never liked him."

"You not liking someone isn't exactly proof of wrong-doing," Beka pointed out. "You didn't like me when Brenna first brought me home, as I recall."

Chewie settled down, pillowing his head on her foot after giving it a consoling lick. "You smelled bad," he muttered. "And you kept crying on me and getting my fur all wet. But you grew on me."

"See," she said. "You might like Kesh if you got to know him better. The couple of times he's been here, you barely spoke to him."

"He was too damned charming. I don't trust charming people; they're always up to no good."

"Well, that's not proof of anything," Beka said stoutly. "And neither is a vague description that could be any of a dozen people I've met since I moved here. I asked Kesh if he was involved and he swore he wasn't. I'm not going to believe that he has anything to do with this until I've seen it with my own eyes."

"Fine," Gregori said, his tone mild. "Then come with us tonight when we go to this dock we were told of. If our renegade shows up, you can tell us once and for all if it is this Kesh or not. And either way, we will have him, and you can present him to the Queen."

"Alive or dead, your choice," Alexei added generously.

"Fine," Beka agreed. "But how do you know that your informant didn't just go running off to warn the man he spoke to you about as soon as you left?"

Alexei gazed innocently at the ceiling. "We might possibly have found a deep hole to drop him in. You know, temporarily. Just until we took care of this business."

At Beka's startled look, Gregori added, "Don't worry, Beka. We'll go back and fetch him out later."

"If we don't get busy and forget," Alexei said with a laugh. "He really was a very nasty creature."

Beka sighed. This wasn't turning out exactly the way she'd planned. But at least after tonight, she'd know, for better or for worse. She only hoped that Chewie was wrong, and it didn't turn out that her one friend was really her enemy after all.

"IT'S TOO BAD Mikhail isn't here," Alexei said in what passed for a whisper with him. It wasn't very quiet, but so far, no one had come anywhere near the bluff where they were situated, well above the dock, but with a clear view and an easy path they could use to descend upon the area if their guy ever showed. "He'd love this part. Skulking is one of his favorite things. Although I've never understood how he manages to hide so well while wearing white from head to toe."

"Hmm," Gregori muttered in his much softer voice. "I don't understand what is keeping him. It isn't like Day to miss a party. Or to let down a Baba Yaga when one needs him."

Beka nodded. She was starting to get worried about their missing Rider too. But at the moment, she had much more urgent matters on her mind. *Please don't be Kesh*, she thought. *Please don't be Kesh.*

She'd already lost Marcus. She didn't think she could handle losing Kesh too. Even if she didn't even really want him. She was so confused. Maybe she just didn't want to have been that wrong about someone she cared for.

"Look," Gregori said, pointing one slim finger down toward the road. A Mercedes SUV came slowly down the rutted path that led toward the deserted warehouse. It paused briefly by the dock itself, where a medium-sized man wearing expensive clothes and a disgruntled expression climbed out. He looked around and appeared even unhappier at not seeing whatever or whoever he was expecting, then opened the back of his vehicle and half rolled, half carried two canisters onto the splintery wooden surface. They weren't particularly large, but they must have been heavy, if his muttered grunts and curses were anything to go by.

He waited there for another long moment, then climbed back into his vehicle and backed it partway up the path again, obviously preparing to wait in greater comfort, or perhaps not wanting to be in the company of the canisters for any longer than was necessary. Or both.

"Is that him?" Beka whispered. She felt a brief burst of relief; that guy looked nothing like Kesh. He was too old, for one thing, and too pudgy to ever be mistaken for Kesh's whipcord slimness. Maybe Chewie had been wrong after all.

Gregori shook his head, one finger to his lips to remind them to be quiet. His reply was barely more than a breath on the quiet night air. "Not him. Must be he is meeting our guy."

As if on cue, a low sound cut through the silence. Little more than a mechanical purr, it heralded the arrival of a glossy black motorboat, low-slung and fancy, like the ones used by smugglers and pirates on bad TV shows. Maybe it was that kind of association that made Beka imagine an ominous, dangerous look to the boat and its occupant. But maybe not. A shiver ran down her spine, for all that the night was warm and pleasant.

Next to her, she could feel Alexei growl happily, always more comfortable with action than with waiting, but Gregori put a restraining hand on his gigantic bicep.

"Wait until he is out of the boat. We don't want him to spot us and run away."

Beka nodded. They had a boat of their own, procured by the Riders, tied up nearby. But it would be better if they didn't have to chase him. On the other hand, they'd already discussed the possibility of following their quarry, if it looked as though he wasn't the man they sought, so she'd prepared the boat with a "silence and invisibility" spell, just in case.

She held her breath, but the man just sat there, unmoving. His boat rocked gently, its polished ebony rubbing against the faded wood of the dock, making tiny creaking noises in the almost silent night. The nearly full moon didn't cast enough light for them to be able to make out his face, since the boat itself sat in the shadow of the old, falling-down warehouse.

Get out of the damned boat, Beka thought to the figure below. *Get out and let us see you.*

CHARLIE KELLY SHIFTED restlessly from one foot to the other as he waited for the diver to disembark from his black speedboat. But the guy just sat there, his craft butted up against the dock, his dark eyes seeming to reflect the night's eerie stillness.

What the hell was this? Was this ass playing games with him? Charlie had gotten a message, tucked under his windshield wiper in the supposedly well-guarded parking lot of the power plant, telling him to come tonight to meet his contact. Not asking him, mind, but telling.

Meet me at the usual spot. Midnight. Alone. For our mutual best interests.

That was all the note had said. Terse and unforthcoming, just like the man who had written it. Charlie had been so pissed, he'd seriously considered not going. After all, he was the boss in this relationship. Not some flunky to jump just because a hired hand told him to.

But in the end, it was less the contents of the note than

where he'd found it that had convinced him. Not just under the wiper of his car—bad enough the guy knew which car was his—but in the lot at the Diablo Canyon Nuclear Plant, behind barbed wire walls and electronic gates and armed guards. That could have meant it was an inside job. But Charlie ran the place. He knew every face of every employee who had ever walked through those gates, and the man at the end of the dock wasn't one of his.

Which meant instead that either the guy had some connection inside that Charlie didn't know about, or that he could somehow magically walk through walls. Charlie had the uneasy feeling he'd been played. Still, he'd had to show up to find out what the diver wanted, since the man clearly knew a lot more about Charlie than Charlie knew about him.

Finally tired of waiting, Charlie hunched his shoulders against the cool ocean breeze, got out of his car, and walked down to the dock. Two more canisters—all he could easily move by himself—already sat down there. It was too late for this nonsense. His wife thought he was out playing poker with some buddies, but he'd have to be home soon or she'd start suspecting him of sleeping around or something. The last thing he needed right now was anyone asking him suspicious questions, even his wife. Hell, especially his wife. The woman could be like a bulldog once she got her teeth into something.

"I hope you're not planning to ask me for more money," Charlie said, not bothering with polite hellos. People who stuck cryptic notes under windshield wipers didn't get polite. "I'm already paying you more than I should be."

One elegant eyebrow rose lazily. "Really?" the diver said, his Irish accent even heavier than usual. Probably because he'd figured out it annoyed the shit out of Charlie. "You t'ink that you are overpaying me to carry your poison down into the sea? Perhaps you would like to procure the services of another to do so for you." The arrogant smirk lurking around the corners of his lips said he knew just how difficult that would be.

Bite me. Charlie didn't say it out loud, though, as much

as he wanted to. Finding another diver who was capable of going down to the depths of the hidden trench to dispose of the canisters where they wouldn't be found—and who was willing to handle nuclear waste, no matter how safely it was packaged—would be a tall order indeed. Still, that didn't mean he was going to let the guy rip him off. After all, if he turned Charlie in to the authorities, he'd be in trouble too.

"What do you want?" Charlie asked, feeling weary. Just another five years, and he could take his bonuses and retire to the Caribbean, where most of the money was already socked away. Then the plant, all those people's jobs, and the damned government regulations could be somebody else's problem. "Your note said something about our mutual best interests?"

The diver's smile grew a smidgeon broader and somehow more sinister. It suddenly occurred to Charlie that maybe it hadn't been all that smart to come to this lonely spot in the middle of the night all by himself.

"I am afraid that the word *mutual* may have been something of a falsehood," the other man said, stepping gracefully onto the dock. "'Tis only my own interests that bring us together this night. You see, I have decided that I have no further need of your toxic refuse; what you have given me already has more than done its job."

Charlie gaped at him. What the hell was the man talking about?

An effortless stride brought the diver close enough that Charlie could smell the fish on his breath, although Charlie barely saw him move.

"And if I have no need of your poison, I have no need of you," the diver said, his voice as calm as if they discussed a favorite show or the best way to get from the highway to the nearest Denny's. "Which, alas, makes you more of a liability than an asset. You Humans, so undependable. You understand; I simply cannot take the risk."

Charlie felt a sudden sharp pain, like indigestion, only more intense, and looked down in amazement to see a long, thin knife protruding from his chest. No, not a knife, he thought muzzily as his knees buckled. It looked more like a tusk of some kind, or the barb from a swordfish.

He barely felt the diver scoop him up and toss him into the bottom of the boat, the deadly canisters following him in with a dull thud. The last thing he heard as the cold crept into his bones were the sweet notes of an old Irish lullaby about a sailor going to his final rest in the deep blue sea, sung by the man who'd just murdered him.

BEKA SAW THE man collapse, be caught in strong arms, then slung carelessly into the boat. There was a flash of moonlight on silver, and the canisters went in after him. A throaty roar of a motor, and their quarry was on his way. The glaring headlights of the abandoned Mercedes lit an empty dock.

"What the hell happened?" she asked no one in particular. "Did that guy faint?"

"Sure," Alexei said, grabbing her hand and dragging her rapidly down the slope to where their own transport awaited. "Right after he was stabbed. Being killed will do that to you."

Gregori lifted her gracefully into the boat and set off after the other vessel with the ease of one who had spent centuries handling every different type of transportation there was. Beka noticed with a numb sort of gratitude that her spell seemed to be working just fine; the boat they were in moved swiftly and silently, like a ghost upon the ocean.

"Killed," she repeated.

"I'm afraid so," Gregori said, steering through the night like a hunter unerringly tracking his prey.

Gregori looked at her, something like pity in his dark eyes, shining under the cold gaze of the moon. "So, was that your friend Kesh?"

Beka swallowed hard. Nodded. There had been no mistaking him, his proud carriage, the narrow arch of his nose, the shape of his sleek head. Once he'd walked into the beam of the headlights, she knew him instantly. "Yes. It was Kesh. *Not* my friend, apparently."

"Do not worry, my little Baba," Alexei said, sounding unusually grim. "I will tear him limb from limb for you. By the time I am done, there will be nothing left but scraps for the rats to feast on."

As much as she appreciated the sentiment, the imagery that came with it, coupled with the movement of the boat on the waves, didn't do anything good for Beka's already roiling stomach.

"I think we'd better keep him in one piece to give to the Queen," she said. "But if he happens to acquire a couple of bruises along the way, I won't complain."

Gregori flashed her a bloodthirsty edge of a smile, slowing the boat to a crawl, and then to a halt as they spotted Kesh's boat ahead, its streamlined shape a dark blot against an only slightly less dark sky.

"Baba? A little light would help, if you would," said Gregori.

Oh, right. Magic. Duh. Beka focused on what she needed and gestured with both hands, creating a clearseeing bubble around her and the two Riders. It enabled them to see out across the water as if someone had turned on a low-glowing lamp, but wouldn't be visible from the outside. By, say, a murderous Selkie prince.

They all looked out across the expanse of restless waves, Beka hiding her shaking hands between her knees so the others couldn't see how much even that relatively simple magical act had taken out of her. Made more difficult by the ocean that surrounded them, but still, it shouldn't have taken that much energy. She peered around, trying to figure out where they were. They'd come from a different direction than the one she usually took on the *Wily Serpent*, but based on the distance from shore and the shape of the distant city lights, she thought they weren't too far off from where she'd been diving all those days. What were the odds?

"Is something wrong, Baba?" Alexei asked.

She gave a short chuckle, decidedly lacking in humor. "You mean besides discovering that the man I've been having dinner with almost every night is a cold-blooded killer who is apparently leading some kind of paranormal guerrilla war against Humans and threatening the safety of all the water-dwelling magical creatures, not to mention my job?"

"Yes," Alexei said perfectly seriously. "Besides that."

"Well, it just occurred to me that my two problems might not be as unrelated as I thought."

Gregori lifted an eyebrow.

Beka pointed out toward Kesh's boat, where a dark figure was poised at the port side, slowly lowering the two canisters and what looked like a bulky, rolled-up sail into the water. Once they'd disappeared beneath the surface, Kesh dived in after them, his Human-shaped body cleaving the water neatly with barely a splash. After a moment, a sleek seal head bobbed into view then vanished under the waves with a flash of a ruffled tail.

"So?" Gregori said. "He is dumping the body and whatever is in those containers."

"Yes, but it is *where* he is dumping them that makes me think he might be involved with whatever is destroying the Selkies' and Merpeople's home waters, and making their people ill," she said. "I can't be certain, of course, but I am fairly sure that we are right above the trench where the contamination began."

"So whatever is in those containers . . ." Gregori's eyebrow rose even further.

"May very well hold the answers I need," Beka said. "The problem is, if he is taking them down as far as the bottom of the trench, I can't dive that far. I've gone down as far as I could and didn't see anything, but he must be tucking them away in some hidden spot. The Selkies and Merpeople looked for anything unusual before they had to abandon their homes, but they are too frightened to go back and search any further."

"Do you want us to try and grab him when he comes

back up?" Alexei asked, always happy to take the direct route. "We could beat on him until he tells us where he hid the rest."

Gregori snorted. "Use what little brains you have, my large friend. Trying to hold a Selkie on the ocean would be as much use as trying to hold a sunbeam on a clear day. To catch this one, we will have to wait until he is on land."

"Oh, right," Alexei said. "Then what will you do, Baba?"

"Don't worry," she said, a plan forming in her head as she watched the empty boat bob up and down on the swells. "I can't dive down that far, but I know someone who can."

WHEN THEY RETURNED to the shore where they had left Beka's Karmann Ghia and the Riders' motorcycles, Beka stared pensively at the fast but not very large boat they'd used to follow Kesh.

"I hate to say it, but I think we are going to need a larger boat than this for what I have in mind," she said.

Alexei looked vaguely guilty. "Uh, that is probably just as well, Beka. We, uh, sort of borrowed this one, and I should probably get it back to its owner before it is missed." He whistled a bar or two from an old Russian tune, gazing off into the distance so he wouldn't have to meet her eyes.

"Alexei! Gregori! Don't tell me you stole this boat!"

"Very well, Baba," Gregori said placidly. "We will not tell you. But Alexei is correct; we should probably return it soon."

Beka sighed. She was right back where she started, needing a boat, and only knowing of one she could use at a moment's notice. At least Marcus already knew about her mission. And about Chewie, who was her secret weapon.

"That's okay," she said. "I think I know where I can get a boat that will take me out there. Then it is just a matter of finding the canisters and figuring out what Kesh has done to poison the water. Once I know the cause, hopefully I'll be able to fix it. And then I can turn Kesh over to the Queen to face her wrath for everything he's done." She said it all so confidently, she almost convinced herself.

"It sounds like you have everything under control," Gregori said. Beka thought she detected a strange tone to his voice. "Perhaps you no longer need us after all?"

She peered at him, and then at Alexei, who still wasn't meeting her glance. This wasn't about the stolen boat, then. Or at least, not *only* about the stolen boat.

"Out with it," she said. "What's going on?"

Alexei shrugged, like a mountain shifting during an earthquake. "I have a bad feeling."

"A bad feeling?" Beka repeated. She scowled at Gregori, hoping he would be slightly more forthcoming than "a bad feeling."

Gregori let out a tiny sigh. "We are concerned about Day," he said. "He should have been here long ago, and we've had no word from him at all. We contacted Barbara and Bella, and neither of them has seen him. It is . . . worrisome."

"Worrisome, yes," Alexei said, absently chewing on the braided end of his beard. "I t'ink maybe that sonofabitch has gone and found some trouble without us. That is not right."

That was an understatement, Beka thought. She didn't really understand just how the Riders communicated with one another, but she'd never heard of one being lost without the others knowing where he was, and more or less what he was up to. And if Alexei said he had a bad feeling about Mikhail Day, bad enough that his accent was this thick, then he and Gregori had to be truly anxious.

"Look," Beka said, "you guys have been a huge help. I never would have tracked down Kesh's involvement without you. But I'm sure I can handle it from here. You two should go look for Mikhail."

Gregori gazed at her solemnly for a moment, assessing, and then he gave a small nod, his usually expressionless face hinting at equal parts remorse and relief. "When it comes time, do not try to tackle this Kesh by yourself, Baba. Tell the Queen your suspicions and she will send her guards to assist you."

"Um, okay," Beka said. She had really been looking forward to bringing Kesh to the Queen, all wrapped up like a nice, tidy present. But she'd cross that bridge when she came to it. "Don't worry about me. I'm going to prove myself to be worthy of the title of Baba Yaga, or die trying."

"It would be better if you didn't die," Alexei said seriously.

She rolled her eyes at him. "It's a Human expression, you goofball." She gave him a shove in the direction of his bike, but it was like trying to move a chunk of granite.

"Do not forget to use the Water of Life and Death as soon as you get back home," Gregori added, sounding like a Russian version of Mary Poppins. "You need to be at your full strength to deal with this, and I have begun to wonder if whatever has made the Mer and Selkies sick hasn't begun to have an effect on you as well. It would be best to be safe, and drink extra Water, just in case."

The same thought had occurred to her, once or twice. It simply kept slipping away in the confusion of events and the muddle that was her perpetually aching head. But she'd make sure to remember this time.

"You're right," she said. "Are you coming back to the bus with me?"

Alexei cast an openly longing glance toward the road above them. "We need to return this cursed boat," he said. "But then, perhaps, we could be on our way?" He gave Beka a big bear hug, making her ribs creak ominously. "If that is okay with you, little one."

In truth, Beka would have loved for them to stay, as much for the company as for the help. But they would never consider leaving in the middle of an adventure if they weren't seriously worried about Mikhail. Which made her worried too.

She mustered up the last of her strength, trying to make it seem like nothing, and grabbed their saddlebags from the bus, bringing them through the ether to materialize with a *pop* and a tumble of jangly chains on black leather and perfectly polished red.

"You boys go find Mikhail," she said with a cheeriness so forceful it rattled her teeth. "I've got this. And don't worry about the boat. I'll make an anonymous call to the cops and they can come fetch it back to its owner." She made a shooing motion. "Go on, get. And let me know when you find him, okay?"

Hopefully she'd still be a Baba Yaga when they did. She wasn't sure what the rules were about the Riders contacting a civilian.

Gregori gave her one of his graceful bows and then they were gone, the sound of their departing motorcycles fading before she could draw another breath.

Damn, she hoped her plan worked. Because if it didn't, without the Riders, she was screwed.

TWENTY-TWO

BEKA LET HERSELF into the bus as quietly as she could, but Chewie woke up anyway, lifting his head up from his paws where he was sprawled out over most of the kitchen floor like a dark, lumpy rug. She guessed he wouldn't be much of a guard dragon if she could sneak past him, but she'd really been hoping to go to bed and put off the inevitable argument until morning. Well, later morning. It was already after two.

He padded over to greet her, nails clicking on the wooden floor, and blinked rapidly as she turned on the light.

"How did it go?" he asked, looking around. "And where are the Riders?"

Beka grabbed a bottle of ice-cold water from the fridge, thinking she was forgetting something. Exhaustion dragged at her feet and fogged her mind, so overwhelming it made her want to weep with tiredness. She really needed to get some sleep, and soon. But first, she had some explaining to do.

She plopped down on the couch with a sigh, gesturing for Chewie to join her. "It went . . . well, it went. We didn't catch him, but we did see enough to be sure we had the right guy, and to also discover that he is probably behind the poisoning of the water people's homes, in addition to being the renegade the Queen wants caught."

"Huh," Chewie said. "We should have figured the two might be connected. It never occurred to me though."

"Me either," Beka said. "I guess I haven't handled this very well."

Chewie stared at her. "You've handled it just fine. No one else could have done any better. You're just hearing Brenna's voice in your head, telling you you're not good enough. It's as though she never left."

Beka sat up straight, taken aback by the unexpected vehemence in his voice. "What? What are you talking about? Yes, Brenna was always a little hard on me, but she criticized me for my own good, so I'd learn to be the best Baba Yaga I could be."

Chewie sighed, looking at her as though she were an idiot. "Your own good, my hairy black ass. She criticized you because she felt threatened by your youth and beauty and strength of character, and because she hated the idea of training anyone to replace her. I've always thought she picked you because you satisfied the requirement of magical ability, but your innate goodness made it easy for her to manipulate you. Look, you're still defending her, even now."

"She rescued me from a hellish fate," Beka said indignantly. "And she raised me to be a Baba. What more could I have asked for?"

"A little kindness, maybe? An occasional 'Well done, Beka'?" Chewie said, poking his cold nose into her hand and giving it a lick, as if to make up for his comments. "Never mind. This isn't the time for this conversation, although it is long overdue. You beat her at her game anyway, by turning out to be a lot stronger than she ever thought you'd be."

Beka had never loved that silly dragon more than she did at this very moment, although she thought he was vastly overestimating any strength she might have. Her whole body ached, and there was a tremor in her hands that made her quickly put down the bottle before he could notice.

"Yes, well, maybe," she said ruefully. "But it turns out that my taste in men is pretty lousy."

"Ah." Chewie sat back on his haunches. "It was the Selkie prince, then. I'm almost sorry to be right." He thought about it for a moment. "On the other hand, I told you so."

Beka rolled her eyes, a movement that hurt more than it should have. "Yes, you did. And since I actually watched him murder a man in cold blood a couple of hours ago, I can't even work up the will to argue with you. Dammit."

Chewie smirked, his black tongue lolling. "It could be worse, you know."

"Really? How?"

"You could have slept with him."

Beka shuddered. "Gah. True enough. Although I didn't do much better picking the one I *did* sleep with." *Dammit again. And now she had to go ask him for help. Maybe she could just throw herself in the ocean instead. Holding on to a big, heavy rock.*

"So what did you do with the sonofabitch? Is that where Alexei and Gregori are, taking him to the Queen?" Chewie asked.

"No. Kesh took a couple of mysterious containers and the dead body of the man who brought them to him, and drove his boat out to near where I've been diving. And he didn't come back up again while we were there. Not that it would have mattered, since as Gregori pointed out, there was no point in trying to capture a Selkie on the open water." She took a deep breath. "And the Riders left. They went to look for Mikhail; they're afraid something has happened to him."

"Wait, what?" Chewie's muzzle wrinkled. "You mean they just left you to deal with this by yourself?"

"Not by myself," Beka said, leaning forward and giving him a big hug. "I've got you. In fact, you're a vital part of my cunning plan."

"Oh, great," Chewie said. "You've got a cunning plan. Why do I have the feeling I'm not going to like it?"

Because you're not going to like it, Beka thought. But out loud, she said, "Are you kidding? You get to be the hero of the story for a change, instead of complaining that you're stuck here, guarding the Water of Life and Death and missing all the action."

He perked up a little at that, but still looked at her doubtfully, cocking his head to the side. "Uh-huh. And what exactly is it your plan requires me to do that is so heroic only I can manage it?"

Beka took a deep breath. Everything was riding on her being able to persuade Chewie to break one of the most basic rules of being a Chudo-Yudo. But without him, her plan had no chance at all, and she could kiss her career as a Baba Yaga good-bye.

"You're going to do what you were born to do, Chewie. You're going to go for a swim. A really long, really deep swim."

BEKA FORCED HER feet to move toward the pier where the *Wily Serpent* was docked, even though every fiber of her being wanted to run in the opposite direction. Or walk, maybe, since it was really early and she'd barely gotten any sleep.

It had taken almost two hours to convince Chewie that it would be okay for him to leave the bus and go with her out on the ocean. The main duty of a Chudo-Yudo was to guard the Water of Life and Death that his Baba Yaga was entrusted with by special favor of the Queen of the Otherworld. The Water was precious and rare, which was why it stayed hidden away in a special compartment. (Or, in the case of Beka's Baba-sister Barbara, tucked away behind the orange juice in her refrigerator. As Barbara liked to say, it was the last place anyone would ever look.)

Chewie took his duties very seriously and rarely left the bus if Beka wasn't there. He occasionally ran down to the beach below to sport amongst the waves, but even then he was close enough to sense if the magical defenses on the erstwhile

hut sent up a warning of an intruder. It took all of Beka's persuasive powers to talk him into going with her today, and if it
wasn't for the urgent nature of the mission, and the lives at
stake, she was sure he would have refused.

And it wasn't until after they left the bus that she realized she'd still forgotten to take the dose of the Water as
she'd promised Gregori. It would have been nice to get the
boost, but it would just have to wait until they got home.

They'd set out soon after the sun came up, because
Beka was afraid that the boat would have already gone out
if they waited too long, but when she reached the end of
the pier, there it was. She didn't see Marcus or his father,
but Chico and Kenny were hard at work, repainting the
fading trim and scrubbing the deck.

"Ahoy the boat," she said, standing by the short gangplank that connected it to the dock.

"Hey! Beka! Look Chico, it's Beka!" Kenny dropped his
scrub brush into his bucket with a splash and raced over to
meet her. "And her . . . um, what is that thing, anyway?"

Beka laughed, surprised by how pleased she was to see
Kenny's open, sunny face. "This is Chewie. He's a Newfoundland."

"*Hola, chica*," Chico said. "It is nice to see you back
here. Marcus told us that you were done with your diving,
and we thought maybe we weren't going to see you again."
He eyed Chewie with the admiration of a true dog lover.
"*Dios mio*, that is some big dog. We had donkeys in my
village back home smaller than him."

Chewie gave a proud woof and Beka whispered, "Stop
showing off. You'll scare the natives."

"I wasn't sure if I'd catch you," she said. "I didn't realize
it was cleaning day."

Kenny's face fell, his big grin sliding away like an eel
hiding from a hawk. "Yeah. Marcus Senior, he ain't doing
so good, and the fishing has been pretty bad. He's thinking
about maybe selling the boat, so he's got us spiffing it up a
little."

"Oh. Damn. I'm sorry to hear that." Her heart ached to

hear that Marcus's father was losing his battle; she'd actually grown to like the crusty old sailor. And, of course, without his father and the boat to hold him here, Marcus would be gone in a flash. Not that it made any difference to Beka's life. But still, she'd kind of liked the thought of knowing he was out on the Bay, even if she couldn't be with him.

Focus, Beka, focus.

"Uh, is he here? Marcus, I mean?" Beka could feel herself flushing and stared down at the oily water underneath the pier, watching the swirls of iridescence moving back and forth with the waves as boats chugged in and out of the harbor.

"He's here," Chico said. "Hang on. Kenny, you want to get Mr. Marcus for the lady?"

"Sure," Kenny said, and turned around to yell over his shoulder, "Hey, Marcus! Beka's here!"

Chico rolled his eyes and muttered something in Spanish. "I meant you should go and fetch him, *idiota*, not wake up everybody on the whole pier."

Kenny glanced up and down the dock, where most of the boats had already set sail for the day. "Oh. Right. Sorry."

Beka stifled a laugh at their antics, but her sense of humor fled when she caught sight of Marcus, coming around the starboard side of the ship. He looked just as amazing as he had the first time she'd seen him, his hair curling a little from the damp air, those broad shoulders straining his tee shirt. His hazel eyes had an amber hue as they gazed at her, the sun lighting him from behind like a corona. She fought the desire to run to him and throw herself into his arms. She knew she wasn't welcome there.

"Beka!" he said, sounding surprised. "I didn't expect to see you. Did you make some kind of arrangement with my da that he forgot to mention?"

She shook her head. This was the part she'd been dreading since she figured out last night that she was going to need to use the boat again. What was she going to do if he turned her down? For a minute, she was tempted to lie and say yes, she'd already talked to his father, but she'd lied to Marcus enough already. Look at where that had gotten her.

"Um, no," she said, "and I'm sorry to hear that he isn't doing well. Is he in the hospital?"

Marcus gazed from her to Chewie, obviously puzzled, but for now, he simply answered the question. "No. He's just tired and resting at home. It's hard to tell how much of his exhaustion is the cancer, how much is the treatment, and how much is plain old discouragement." He crossed his arms over his chest. "What are you doing here, Beka?"

She'd just been asking herself the same thing. She must have been out of her mind to think this would work. But Marcus already knew about her—and more importantly, about Chewie—and she didn't know how in hell her plan could work using a boat full of people she had to come up with some kind of reasonable explanations for.

"Can I talk to you?" she asked, trying to keep the pleading out of her voice. "Alone?"

Marcus stared at her for a minute, then turned to Chico and Kenny. "Why don't you guys take a lunch break." He pulled out a couple of bills from his wallet and handed them to Chico. "It's on me."

Kenny's face scrunched up in confusion. "But Marcus, it's only seven in the morning."

Chico grabbed the money and stuffed it in his back pocket, cuffing Kenny on the head and giving him a little push toward the gangplank. "You maybe would rather stay here and scrub the deck some more? Come on—we go get coffee. Maybe we can find someplace to buy you some brains too." The older man gave Beka an encouraging smile as he passed her. "*Buena suerte, chica.*"

Beka thought she was going to need more than good luck. She was going to need a miracle.

MARCUS HAD NEVER been so happy to see someone in his entire life. Even though Beka looked like crap; she was pasty white under her tan, and her dark circles had dark circles. If he had a little more ego, he'd think she'd been pining for him. But he was pretty sure that wasn't it. For the moment, he was just glad she was here. He'd find out why soon enough.

"You brought Chewie," he said, for lack of anything more intelligent to say.

"Yes. Actually, he's kind of why I'm here." If he didn't know Beka better, he'd swear she looked guilty. Obviously she was up to something, but it wasn't diving, because she didn't have any gear with her.

"Why don't you come on board and tell me about it," he said, and was rewarded by a shadow of her usual sunny smile. He realized with a shock that she hadn't even been sure he'd let her on board.

He gave her a hand onto the boat, the dog bounding after her with a thump that shook the entire ship. "Hey," he said softly, still holding on to her hand and gazing down into those amazing azure eyes. "You look terrible. Are you okay?"

Beka gave a tired laugh. "Still the charmer, eh?" Chewie woofed in what might have been agreement.

Marcus shook his head. "If you want charming, I'm afraid you'll have to stick with your friend the Irishman. Or prince, or whatever he is."

She pulled her hand out of his but didn't move away from him. "He's a rat and a murderer, actually. And he turns out to be behind both the problem I was trying to find a way to fix *and* the disappearing fish. That's why I'm here. I need your help to stop him."

Sonofabitch! He knew he didn't trust that guy. "I'd be happy to stop him. Permanently, if necessary. But maybe you'd better tell me what the hell is going on. Obviously, I've missed a part of the story." *His own fault, for walking away just when it was getting good. Not a mistake he planned on making again, if he could help it.*

Marcus guided Beka over to sit on a bench, Chewie sticking close to their heels.

"I'm sorry," he and Beka both said at the same time.

She looked startled, eyes so wide he could almost see the ocean in their depths.

"You're sorry?" she said. "What are you sorry for? I'm the one who didn't tell you the truth from the beginning and let you think I was a normal woman."

Marcus snorted. "I never thought you were normal, Beka. Hell, the first time I met you, I fished you out of the sea in a net. But normal is highly overrated." He wanted so badly to reach out and hold her, but he was afraid she'd pull away if he tried. "I'm sorry I overreacted when you told me who—what—you really are. You're still Beka, and I should have realized that."

"Oh, for the love of Poseidon, could the two of you please just kiss and make up and get it over with? I need to get out and back again as soon as possible; we don't have time for all this romantic crap," a deep voice said.

Marcus looked around, trying to figure out who the hell was talking. With a shock, he realized it was Chewie.

"Holy shit—your dog can talk!" He almost fell off the bench, and Beka tried not to snicker.

"Of course I can talk, you twit," Chewie said. "I'm not a dog. I'm a dragon disguised as a dog. Have you ever met a dragon that *couldn't* talk?"

Marcus glanced around to make sure no one else could hear them. "You're the first dragon I've ever met, as far as I know."

Beka took pity on him. "Don't worry. No one else can understand him unless he wants them to. But Chewie's right, we shouldn't stay away from the bus any longer than we have to. He's really not supposed to be gone at all. But I need him. And the *Wily Serpent*, if you're willing to take me out one more time."

She quickly explained to him what the Riders had discovered, finishing up with the events of the night before. Marcus swallowed hard, clenching his hands into tight fists when he thought about how close Beka had been to a man who could murder someone in cold blood. Since Marcus had come back from Afghanistan, he'd felt like a killer masquerading as a civilized person. But he suddenly realized that compared to some, he was very civilized indeed.

Although that could easily change, if he ever came face-to-face with Kesh.

"So what is this plan of yours?" he asked when she was done. "And what does it have to do with Chewie and my boat?"

Beka patted her not-a-dog on the head. "Do you know anything about Newfoundlands?" she asked.

"Only the stuff you told me that first day," Marcus said. "About how they're specially bred to work in the water, and that they can swim really well. I thought that was pretty cool."

"Damn straight," Chewie said, preening a little.

"You are the coolest dragon-dog in town," Beka said with a fond smile. But she got serious again when she looked back at Marcus. "There's a reason he picked this shape for his doggy guise," she said. "He's not just any dragon; he's a water dragon. Water is as much his element as it is mine. More, in fact, since the pressure below doesn't bother him at all, and he can dive much deeper than I ever could."

She took a deep breath as she told him the rest of it. "If you're willing to take us back out there, Chewie is going to dive down to the bottom of the Monterey Trench, and see if he can find whatever Kesh has hidden down there. Then he's going to bring it back up so I can figure out how to restore the water and the people to health, and prove to the Queen once and for all that I have what it takes to be a Baba Yaga. And it has to happen before the full moon, so I'm running out of time."

Marcus could see her desperation and her fear. He also saw her determination to see this through, no matter what it took. He thanked his lucky stars that she'd worked up the courage to come ask for his help, because he sure as hell wasn't letting her do this without him.

Not only did he want to kick Kesh's ass for chasing away the fish and driving a lot of good men like his father to the brink of losing everything, not to mention messing up their nets and whatever mischief he and his pals had been up to—although god knew, that was reason enough to go after the guy.

But he also wanted to sit on the slimy creep until he admitted to whatever he'd done to Beka and promised to fix it. Because no matter what she said, she really wasn't okay. And Marcus had the sneaking suspicion that Kesh had something to do with it.

"You bet I'll take you out there," he said with an only slightly bloodthirsty grin. "Any chance we'll meet up with your pal Kesh when we're there? Because I've got a couple of things to say to him the next time we meet."

Ooh-rah.

TWENTY-THREE

THE FRESH AIR and the feel of the spray on her face revived Beka enough that she actually enjoyed the trip out to the dive site. Although the fact that Marcus seemed to have gotten over being mad at her might have helped too. Just a little.

Once they'd arrived, Marcus looked at Chewie dubiously. "What now?" he asked.

"Now you stand back," Chewie said.

Marcus shifted about a foot and Chewie snorted, a small hint of flame briefly curling through the salty air.

"Seriously, dude. *Way* back."

Beka grabbed Marcus's arm, only momentarily distracted by the feel of his muscles under her hand. "Brace yourself," she said, grinning at him. She loved this part.

Marcus looked puzzled, then alarmed, then just plain stunned as Chewie began to shimmer and glow, the massive black Newfoundland replaced by a truly enormous dragon with a long, sinuous neck, tightly overlapping metallic-looking scales, and a tail that wrapped halfway around the front cabin. As a dog, he'd been impressive. As a dragon, he was magnificent; a vibrant royal blue starting at his wedge-shaped head and then shading down through aqua and into a deep green, all glimmering with a deep iridescence like the inside of a shell.

Beka beamed at the dragon proudly. "Kind of cool, isn't he?"

Marcus gazed from her to Chewie, his eyes wide and round, his jaw hanging. After a moment, he snapped it shut, shook his head, and said, "Kind of cool, Beka? Kind of cool? He's fucking glorious."

Chewie preened, as much as a dragon could be said to do so, and Beka hid a grin behind one hand. "Oh great," she said. "Now there will be no living with him at all."

"How can he do that?" Marcus asked, still staring at the gigantic dragon sprawled across his father's deck. "He was small. Well, he was huge for a dog, but still not . . ." He waved at Chewie's current form. "Not *this*. It shouldn't be possible."

Beka tried not to laugh. After all, this was his first dragon. It took some getting used to. "Says who?" she asked. "Einstein? He got a few things wrong. Physicists never enter magic into the equation."

Marcus opened his mouth, closed it again, then just shook his head. "Wow. First witches then dragons." He looked as if his entire worldview had changed in a second. Which it probably had. "I hate to think what that makes me—the talking frog?"

Chewie nudged him with one webbed foot, claws carefully sheathed. "It makes you in the way, dude." He nodded to Beka, then half climbed, half slithered over the side of the boat, disappearing under the water without so much as a splash.

"Holy crap." Marcus sat down rapidly on the nearest flat surface.

"Yep," Beka said, scooting him over so she could sit next to him. "Now you can see why I didn't want to try renting a different boat to take him out on. There's not a distraction big enough in the world to keep people from noticing him when he is in dragon form."

Marcus didn't say anything for a minute, so she turned to look at him.

"What?" she asked.

He shrugged broad shoulders. "Oh, I don't know. I guess part of me hoped that you'd come to me because you trusted me to help. And because maybe you missed me, just a little."

Beka took a deep breath. "Just a little? Hell, Marcus, it felt like I was missing half my soul." She felt like an idiot saying it, but at least it was the truth. After everything that had happened, she owed him that.

His hazel eyes stared into hers, as if he could read her mind, or maybe her heart, which stuttered and skipped as if it only half remembered how to beat.

Then he said in a low, fervent voice, "I think I found it for you." He pulled her into his arms, wrapping her in strength and warmth and longing, tugging her in close until his lips met hers. Soft yet firm, they pressed against her own until she parted for him without thought, his tongue dipping in for a moment as if to taste the words she hadn't said yet.

He drew back long enough to say, "God, I missed you, Beka." Then there was only the silken slide of his lips and the glory of his hands and the passionate heat and joy that came from being in his arms once more.

MARCUS FELT LIKE he could kiss Beka forever. It was as if the universe had granted him a second chance. And he sure as hell wasn't going to blow it this time. This time he was going to hold on to her and never let her go.

Or at least not until someone dumped a bucket of cold water over him.

Sputtering, he turned around to see Chewie, still amazing in scales and long, sharp teeth and shining, curved claws the purple-black of mussel shells. And water. Lots and lots of water.

Chewie shook himself again, like the dog he usually

was, and doused Marcus and Beka with another couple of gallons of seawater. "Oh, sorry," he said, glowing golden eyes innocent. "I didn't see you there. Did I get you wet?"

Beka pulled away, half laughing and half scowling, and leaving Marcus feeling absurdly bereft. He wanted to grab her and drag her back into his arms, but the moment had clearly passed. He'd just have to make sure there was another one. Soon.

She grew more serious as she noted Chewie's empty hands. Paws. Whatever.

"Weren't you able to find anything?" she asked, a hint of panic in her tone.

"Oh, I found things all right," Chewie said grimly. "Lots of things. Silver canisters, just like you said, cleverly tucked into crevasses where no one would ever think to look, and hidden under rockfalls disguised to look old, but actually quite recent. I wasn't sure if you wanted me to bring one up. They're slowly leaking whatever's inside— purposefully, I think—and I'm not sure you want to have one on the boat."

"Drat," Beka said. "Maybe I can give you a container to get me a sample in, and you could go back down and collect some for me to examine?"

Chewie shook his huge head, scattering more salty water like teardrops. "I don't think that will be necessary. All the canisters had the same symbol on them; I can draw it for you."

He took one claw and delicately scratched a triangle into the wooden deck. Inside the triangle, he added a trefoil design of three cones, their wide ends toward the outside edge, and flattened narrower ends meeting around a smaller circle in the middle. "There," he said. "It looked like that. The background was bright yellow, and the three inside bits were black. There was a black rim around the outside too. Does that mean anything to you?"

"Jesus Christ," Marcus said, feeling as if all the breath had been sucked out of his lungs.

"It looks kind of familiar," Beka said, tilting her head

sideways to look at it again. "Do you know what it is?" She glanced back at him, her brows drawn together as she clearly saw something on his face that alarmed her. "What is it? Is it really bad?"

Shit, shit, shit. "That's as bad as it gets, Beka," he said, glad beyond measure that Chewie had been smart enough not to bring one of those canisters back up with him. "That's the symbol for hazardous nuclear waste. And if the water in that trench is full of it, it is no wonder all those poor people are sick. They have radiation poisoning."

He got a sinking feeling in his stomach, looking at her pallor and shadowed eyes. "And I hate to say it, but I think you do too."

FOR A MOMENT, panic rose like bile in Beka's throat, but then she got a grip on herself. He didn't understand how impossible that was; what it meant to be a Baba Yaga. Fear slowly loosened the claws it had tightened around her heart.

"I believe that radiation poisoning is what is causing the illness in the Selkies and Merpeople," she said, thinking it out. "That actually makes sense with the vague information I got when I summoned some elementals. And it explains why I couldn't identify what was wrong with the water. I was looking for some kind of liquid or solid contaminant that had been added to the water; radiation is neither, although whatever is in those containers probably is. No wonder Kesh wanted to stop me from diving and finding them." She sighed. "But it can't be what is making me sick."

"But Beka," Marcus said. Anxiety and concern etched themselves as deep into his face as Chewie's claws had etched the deadly symbol into the deck.

"No, really, Marcus," Beka said. "First of all, the ones who got sick were those actually living in the trench. I never got anywhere near that deep. And even then, those affected are mostly the weakest and most vulnerable; the very young and the very old. As a Baba Yaga, my natural defenses and healing ability are much stronger than the average Human's. A few dives into the edges of the contaminated water wouldn't have had any effect on me at all. It has to be something else."

Chewie shook himself again, transitioning back into his Newfoundland form as he did so. His doggy face wore an expression as close to Marcus's as their different shapes would allow.

"I don't know, Beka," the dragon said doubtfully. "You first started getting sick right around the time you started looking into the water people's problem. That can't be a coincidence."

"I'm telling you both, it would take a lot more than a superficial dose of radiation to make me feel this sick," Beka insisted.

"*Kesh*," Marcus said, fury transforming him almost as much as Chewie's change from dragon to dog. "It was that damned Kesh and his fucking picnics by the sea." His hands clenched and unclenched, as though they could wrap themselves around the absent prince's neck. "I am going to kill that sonofabitch."

Beka could feel all the blood drain out of her face. "He couldn't," she said. "He wouldn't." But she remembered all those times he brought her special bits of fish or lobster, caviar and clams; things he insisted he'd found just for her and refused to share.

Her legs went out from underneath her as the magnitude of his betrayal hit her, and she would have fallen if Marcus hadn't scooped her up and returned her to the pile of rope they'd been sitting together on so blissfully only a few moments before.

"Great Aphrodite, risen from the sea," she muttered. "That sonofabitch fed me seafood from the trench and sweet-talked me while he watched me eat poison, all the while trying to convince me to stop looking into the problem. Goddess, I was such a fool!"

"You were trusting and kind," Marcus said, wrapping his arms around her. "That's not a bad thing. Hell—it's one of the things I love about you the most. Kesh is just a slimeball who took advantage of that. That's his bad, not yours."

Did Marcus just say he loved me? Sadly, Beka couldn't bring herself to focus on that right now. Suddenly, she had a thought that perked her up so much she jumped to her feet, leaving Marcus to follow, looking alarmed.

"I'm such an idiot," she said with a slightly shaky laugh. "We're freaking out for nothing."

"We are?" Chewie asked, sounding dubious. "Are you sure? Because I kind of feel like we're freaking out for something."

She shook her head. "No, Chewie—you're forgetting one important thing."

"I am?"

"The Water of Life and Death," she said. "The Water of Life and Death will cure anything, even radiation poisoning." In fact, she could kick herself. If she'd just remembered to take a drink at some point in the last week, she'd be feeling fine right now.

Chewie let out a gusty sigh of relief. "Of course! Belobog's balls—don't ever scare me like that again."

Marcus's rugged countenance bore a look of almost comic befuddlement. "What are you two talking about? You have a cure for radiation poisoning? How is that possible? Are you sure?"

Beka's weakness and queasy stomach almost vanished as relief washed over her like a wave. Here was the answer to another part of the problem too.

"The Water of Life and Death is an enchanted elixir that the Baba Yagas drink to increase their strength and magical ability. It also extends their lives so that they live longer than your average Human, and has miraculous healing properties in larger amounts," she explained to him. She'd tell him how much longer sometime when there wasn't quite so much going on. "If I'd been drinking it all along, the way I should have, I might not have gotten sick at all. Or at least, not as much as I have. But I've been having doubts about remaining a Baba, and Kesh must have figured out that I was slacking off on my dose while I was trying to make up my mind."

Marcus looked almost as relieved as she felt. "So all you have to do is go back to the bus and have a swig of this stuff, and you'll be as good as new?"

"Pretty much," said Beka. "What's more, it should work on the sick Selkies and Merpeople too. I'll have to get permission from the Queen of the Otherworld before I can share it with them, but under the circumstances, I think she'll probably allow it."

"The Queen of the what world?" Marcus asked.

"It's kind of a long story," Beka said.

Chewie rolled his eyes. "Here's the short version, dude. There is another plane of existence, kind of like the fairylands you read about in stories. It's called the Otherworld, and it's where most of the magical creatures went hundreds of years ago when it became too dangerous for them to stay here in the Human realm. The Otherworld is ruled by a King and Queen, and the Queen is kind of like Beka's boss. If your boss is drop-dead gorgeous, all-powerful, and turns people into swans at the drop of a hat. There—now you're all caught up. Can we get going, please? I for one will feel a lot better once Beka has taken her medicine and no longer glows in the dark." He turned and marched in the direction of the front cabin, just in case the other two had somehow missed his point.

Marcus hugged Beka before grabbing her hand and starting after Chewie. "You're sure this stuff will cure you?" he asked.

"Absolutely sure," Beka responded, feeling hopeful for the first time in days. "And if I can use it to cure the sick water dwellers, then I have fulfilled half of my assignment to the Queen, *and* my promise to the King of the Selkies and the Queen of the Merpeople. You know, I actually think everything is going to be okay."

TWENTY-FOUR

BACK AT THE bus, Chewie ground to a halt right inside the front door like a giant roadblock, causing Marcus and Beka to barrel into him. Beka, not as steady as she usually was, almost fell over his huge rear end and planted her face on the floor.

"What the hell is wrong with you?" she asked, grabbing onto Marcus for support.

Chewie lifted his black muzzle into the air, pulling it in through his nostril in great snorting gulps. "Someone has been here," he announced ominously.

"What? That's impossible." One of the reasons that Beka hadn't been too worried about dragging Chewie away and leaving the bus unguarded was because the former hut was perfectly capable of guarding itself. There were magical protections built into the very walls, handed down from Baba to Baba. Maybe she'd slacked off a little on refreshing them, what with everything that was going on, but they should still be more than capable of thwarting any would-be trespassers.

"Impossible or not," Chewie growled, "someone has been

here. I smell the sea, and fish, and . . ." he sniffed again. "I think that's Old Spice."

"Kesh!" he and Beka said at the same time, and exchanged equally alarmed glances.

Beka bolted for the secret cabinet where the Water of Life and Death was hidden. She didn't know how the hell Kesh had gotten past the defenses, but he couldn't have found the Water.

But he had.

The cabinet gaped, its own magical locks clearly breached, although there was no sign of either physical or supernatural tampering. When she opened the door all the way, the space inside seemed to mock her with its emptiness. Impossible maybe, but the Water of Life and Death was gone.

Marcus had gone ghostly pale as he realized that Beka's only cure was missing. "Shit," he said with feeling. "Can you ask this Queen of yours to give you some more?"

Beka shook her head mutely. "Not a chance. If I admit I was careless enough to let the precious gift she gave me slip through my fingers, not only will she undoubtedly strip me of my title of Baba Yaga on the spot, she'll probably turn me into something prickly and ugly to serve as an example to future Babas." She fought not to cry. It wouldn't help anything anyway.

"What's that?" Chewie asked, poking his snout a little deeper into the vacant cupboard.

Beka shoved his nose out of the way and discovered a piece of antique parchment paper that had blended in with the brown bottom of the cabinet. Her hand shook as she read it aloud, but she wasn't sure if the tremor came from fatigue or rage.

My darling Baba,

I am sorry that it had to come to this. But Brenna will make a much more powerful ally, and I have great plans I could not allow you to thwart.

> *When I am a king on land, ruling as I was meant to,*
> *I shall write lyrical songs to your beauty and grace,*
> *and remember you fondly. It is unfortunate that you*
> *will not be around to hear them, but in any war, there*
> *are always sacrifices to be made.*

> *You should have joined me when you had the*
> *chance. You shall not get another.*

Kesh

"Why that, that—" Marcus was so furious he was speechless. Beka thought he looked even more magnificent than usual, not that it mattered anymore. She was a dead witch walking. If the radiation didn't get her, the Queen would.

"Brenna," Chewie said with a snarl that bared lots of sharp white teeth. "That explains a lot."

Beka, startled out of her reverie, just stared at him. "What are you talking about, Chewie?"

He tilted his massive head toward the note. "Didn't you read what he said about Brenna making a better ally than you? *That's* how he got in here; she gave him some kind of magical key to give him safe passage through the defenses. After all, she was one of the ones who created them in the first place, and I'll bet you never thought to change them once she left. And she must have told him where the Water of Life and Death was hidden too. I wonder how long they have been working together. No wonder she came by and tried to convince you to quit."

"Who is Brenna?" Marcus asked.

"Brenna was my foster mother," she said, stone-faced. "The one who raised me from the time I was four to be a Baba Yaga and follow in her footsteps."

Marcus glanced around the bus, clearly remembering the funky painting on the outside. "The woman with the tie-dyed pillows? She's working with Kesh? Why?" That last bit came out a touch plaintively, as if they'd finally reached a part of the story that was beyond his comprehension.

Beka knew exactly how he felt.

"Brenna acted like she was a hippie earth-mother stuck in the sixties," Chewie said flatly. "But she never cared about anything other than herself, and I always suspected that toward the end, she was beginning to lose her grip. I'm not convinced she is completely sane anymore."

Beka didn't know if that made her feel better or worse. If Brenna had succumbed to the Water Sickness that sometimes beset a Baba Yaga who had overstayed her tenure, then maybe that could somehow excuse her betraying Beka to Kesh. On the other hand, if there was anything scarier than an insane woman with the power of a Baba Yaga, Beka couldn't think of it off the top of her head.

"Damn," she said. That seemed to sum things up nicely.

"Yeah, damn," Chewie agreed.

Marcus made a movement toward where he would have carried a gun in bygone days, looking warily around the bus. "Do you think this Brenna came here with Kesh? Maybe to get the Water of Life and Death for herself?"

Chewie shook his head, bits of drool flying off in every direction. "Nah. For one thing, I don't smell her here, and believe me, I'd recognize her scent after living with her for nearly two centuries."

"Two centuries?!" Marcus's eyes were wide and stunned. "How long can Baba Yagas live?"

Chewie waved the question off with a paw as incidental to the discussion. "Besides, I don't see Kesh as the type to share, no matter what kind of deal they have cooked up between them. The Water of Life and Death is one of the most precious substances on earth. There's no way he'd just give it to Brenna. No, my guess is that she gave him the information on how to get in here, knowing that if the Queen discovered you'd allowed the Water to be stolen, she'd be more likely to give Brenna back the position of Baba Yaga."

He looked at Beka with pity in his big, dark eyes. "It's possible Brenna doesn't even know about the poisoning, so maybe she isn't actually trying to kill you."

"Just get me kicked out of my job and banned from the Otherworld," Beka said bitterly.

"Yeah, that." Chewie shrugged. "So what are we going to do about it? Are we going to let Brenna and Kesh win?"

If it had just been her life on the line, Beka might have given up. But she'd made a promise, and Baba Yagas always kept their promises. She might not be one for much longer, but she'd be damned if she would let those little Selkie and Mer babies die because of Kesh's greed for a power that didn't belong to him.

Think, Beka, think. You're a Baba Yaga. No two-bit, too-handsome Selkie prince is going to beat you.

"No," she said, so firmly that Marcus blinked and Chewie took a half step backward. "No, we are not going to let them win. We are going to track down Kesh, take back the Water, and kick his ass from here to the Otherworld and back again."

"That's my girl," Marcus said. "Um. How?"

"Yeah," Chewie echoed. "How? He could be anywhere by now, and I can't follow his scent if he goes underwater."

"I'm guessing he's going to be holed up somewhere on land," Beka said. "If he has to avoid being seen by his father or any of his people, he'd have to stay onshore whenever possible. With all his talk about being a ruler here, I'm guessing he's found himself a posh mansion somewhere and is sitting around in luxury gloating over his upcoming triumph in true arch-villain fashion." *The fish-eating, double-crossing son of a kraken.* "And if he's on land, I can find him."

She crossed the room to root through an enameled box of miscellaneous shiny bits of crystal, old keepsakes, and the few pieces of jewelry she hadn't made herself. "Aha!" she said, pulling out a gemstone-encrusted pendant hanging from a thick gold chain. "I thought I'd thrown it in there."

"Are those diamonds?" Marcus asked, gaping at the sparkly necklace.

"Uh-huh. And some rubies, and I think maybe the blue

ones are sapphires," Beka said, walking back over to them. "Kind of over the top, if you ask me."

"Ah," Chewie said, a hint of laughter in his eyes despite his worry. "Let me guess: Kesh gave it to you."

"Yup. This was one of his 'little trinkets' he brought me when he was trying to woo me, back in the beginning." *Before he'd decided it would be easier to kill me.* "He told me he'd found it in an old wreck and thought of me, which is kind of a backhanded compliment, really. But the important part is that he carried it on him for an entire day before he gave it to me."

She favored the guys with an evil grin. "The moral of this story, boys and dogs, is never give a Baba Yaga something that once belonged to you—no matter how briefly— if you aren't going to want her to be able to track you down later."

Beka took down her favorite sword and started grabbing a few basic magical items out of her tool cabinet. "I'm going to create a spell to find Kesh, using this pendant as a focus, and then I am going to go get what he stole from me. If I have to kill him a little in the process, well, that's just too bad."

It all sounded very good, but it probably would have been more impressive if she didn't drop the salt because her hands were shaking so much.

"I have a better plan," Marcus said, looking grim. "You find him, and *I'll* kill him a little."

"Marcus, you're a Human. You can't be involved in this. Besides, you have no idea how dangerous Kesh can be."

Marcus raised one eyebrow. "I survived three stints in a desert hell-hole. I think I can take on one Selkie prince. And let's face it, Beka; you are too weak to do this on your own. You can barely lift that sword, much less use it to fight Kesh. I'm not letting you go alone."

"I'm coming too," Chewie said stoutly. "After all, there is nothing left to guard here. I might as well come help with the biting and clawing part of the program."

Beka shook her head. "I'll take Marcus with me, but I

have a more important task for you, old friend. Two tasks, actually." She held up a hand when he would have protested.

"I need you to go through to the Otherworld and get the Queen's permission to use the Water of Life and Death to heal the Selkies and Merpeople who need it. You can tell her I couldn't ask her in person because I was tracking down Kesh so I could bring him to her."

She paused, arranging the supplies in front of her without really looking at them. "That way, if something happens and we don't capture him," she added softly, "at least the Queen will know who is responsible."

"What about calling in the Riders to help?" Chewie asked, obviously not liking the odds any better than she did. Kesh was not only underhanded and dangerous, he almost certainly wouldn't be alone. A prince wasn't a prince without subjects.

"There's no time," she said. "The Mer Queen said the babies were getting sicker every day, and one elder has already died. And the Riders are still out looking for Mikhail. If they haven't contacted me yet, they haven't found him or he's in even bigger trouble than they thought. Either way, we can't wait for them. I could send for the Queen's guard, but then she would find out that Kesh stole the Water of Life and Death, and that would be the end of my chance to save those children. Or myself. This is the way it has to be, I'm afraid."

Chewie sighed. "Fine. I'll go. I'll even be polite. You said there were two tasks—what's the second one?"

"Once you've come back from the Otherworld," Beka said, "I want you to go to the Mer Queen and the Selkie King and explain what's happened." *She didn't envy him that conversation. She didn't know how the King would react when he found out that his own son had been responsible for the poisoning of their lands and peoples, but she suspected that he might rival the Queen of the Otherworld for explosive potential. Luckily, dragons were pretty tough.*

"Then ask them to gather all their sickest subjects and bring them to the beach down below us. If, by some miracle, we manage to find Kesh and get the Water back, we need to be able to get it to them as fast as possible."

Chewie hesitated, then nodded. "Okay, Beka. You're the Baba Yaga." He gave her a big lick across the face, and an affectionate head butt that almost knocked her over. "Kill him once for me, will you?" he said, then vanished through the door to the Otherworld without a backward look.

Beka appreciated his show of faith in her. In truth, she wasn't sure she shared it. But she didn't have the option of failure this time. She wasn't just fighting for herself, but for the lives of innocents who depended on her, and in a way, for the sea itself. It was time to prove Brenna wrong, once and for all.

TWENTY-FIVE

MARCUS WATCHED BEKA add one more knife to a sheath around her ankle and said, "Are you sure you don't want another three or four, just in case?" Maybe it came from being a Marine, but he kind of liked her fascination with sharp, pointy things.

Still, there was a limit to how many one person could carry. He'd chosen to borrow one extremely large bowie knife and a small, deadly switchblade, and call it a day. He dearly wished he had some of his old weaponry from Afghanistan. Sadly, the military hadn't foreseen that he'd be involved in a paranormal conflict at home, and had foolishly insisted he leave it all behind. But since that conflict was not only killing the woman he'd grown dangerously fond of, but threatening the livelihood of his entire community, too, he was going to take down the guy behind it if he had to use his bare hands.

Beka looked thoughtful, clearly not hearing the sarcasm in his voice. "Well, maybe just one more," she said, and stuck a long, thin blade disguised as a hair stick down the length of the braid she'd twisted her hair into. She was looking a lot better than she had, although still nothing like her normal perky self. She'd told Marcus that when she'd done the magical work on Kesh's pendant, she'd also cast a spell to give herself some more energy. But she'd warned him that it was only temporary—like the esoteric version of a large pot of black coffee—and it would wear off before too long.

They needed to be on their way soon.

"Ready?" Marcus asked. He wasn't sure he was comfortable yet with all this magical stuff, but if it led them to Kesh, he might just become a fan. The upcoming violence, on the other hand, he was completely on board with— especially if it ended up with Kesh lying on the ground bleeding profusely and begging for mercy.

Beka walked to the door, putting the pendant over her head so it nestled between her breasts. "Ready as I'll ever be."

They got into Marcus's Jeep. He'd already argued, successfully for a change, that she needed to keep her attention on the necklace instead of the road. And if they managed to capture Kesh, he'd never fit in the back of the Karmann Ghia. Even Beka couldn't dispute that one.

"Which way?" he asked as they pulled out onto the highway.

Beka, her expression intent, as though listening to a melody only she could hear, pointed to the right. "That way. He's at least a few miles away, I think."

Huh. "How does that thing work, anyway?" Marcus still couldn't quite decide whether to be freaked-out or fascinated by the discovery that magic was real, but he was definitely starting to lean in the direction of "Shit, that's cool."

"It's a little bit like that game kids play," Beka said. "You know, the one where when you get close, someone says you're getting hotter, and when you move in the wrong direction, they say you're getting colder." She sounded a little wistful, as if she'd only ever seen the game played by others but had never taken part herself. He supposed that little Babas-in-training didn't get to hang out with other kids much. Or ever.

"So the spell makes the pendant hot or cold?"

She shook her head, flipping her braid over her shoulder so that the knife hidden inside clunked on the headrest behind her. "Not exactly. The spell just strengthens the connection between the object, in this case the necklace, and the person it used to belong to. If I'd done the spell slightly differently, I could have tracked every owner it ever had, but for our needs, I just have it homing in on Kesh. When we head in the right direction, I can feel a kind of tug in my belly. When we go farther away, the tug lessens, so I can tell if we're off target."

Marcus whistled. "Wow—magical GPS. That's pretty snazzy."

"Mmm," Beka agreed, sounding distracted. "We need to go north from here, I think."

He found a side road that meandered more or less in a northerly direction.

"Ah, better," Beka said. "I think we're getting close." Her fingers tightened around the pendant, her knuckles turning white.

"Are you worried about facing Kesh?" Marcus asked. "Afraid you won't be able to hurt him if you need to? I know it can be tough when you're facing someone who used to be a friend." *Thankfully, he wasn't going to have that problem. At all.*

Beka pointed toward a sandy path, barely a road at all. "Hell no. More afraid that I won't be strong enough to beat the crap out of him. I can't believe he actually poisoned his own people and drove them from their homes. What a shit." Suddenly she stuck out a hand. "Stop here. Stop!"

Marcus eased the Jeep to a halt, pulling it over to the verge where scrubby grasses struggled to take over what little path there was. "Are we close?" he asked, wishing again for a gun. Any gun, although an assault rifle would have been preferable.

"I think so," Beka said. She indicated the road ahead of them, which looked like it led straight into the ocean. "I'm pretty sure he's right over that rise," she said. "I hope he didn't hear the car."

But when they crawled on knees and elbows to peer over the sandy hill, it was clear that Kesh was too preoccupied to have noticed the small sounds of the Jeep engine. Beyond them lay a small cove, too shabby and off the beaten path to get much use, from the look of it. At the moment, however, it seemed full to overflowing with a milling crowd that gathered in front of Kesh as he spoke to them from atop a rock outcropping.

Marcus was too busy assessing the enemy force to listen very closely to Kesh's speechifying, but he caught something about "strike a blow for water people and paranormals everywhere" and "are you with me?" There was a muted roar of cheering.

Great. Nothing like attacking an already revved-up adversary. He did a quick head count and decided that there weren't quite as many as he'd initially thought, although there were still a lot more than he was comfortable taking on with just him and Beka; maybe a dozen in all. They mostly looked Human to him, although he suspected that none of them were—some had the sleek black hair and round, dark eyes that Kesh had, as well as a few with the red or auburn tresses that Beka said often indicated a Mer.

"There are more of them than I expected," Beka said quietly. "If you want to back out, I wouldn't blame you." She pulled out one of her larger knives and grasped it tightly.

Marcus grinned at her. "And miss all the fun? No way. Besides, we've the element of surprise on our side. Piece of cake."

Beka gaped at him in amazement, and then grinned back, shaking her head. "You're really something, Marcus

Dermott Junior. I love you." She kissed him soundly on the lips, jumped up, and ran down the hill yelling, almost before he could take in either her words or her actions.

Then, like any good Marine, he put aside thinking and feeling, and just went to work.

For the first few minutes, it was all a blur, the way war usually was; all sound and fury and frantic confusion. Out of the corner of his eye, he could see Beka making elaborate, swooping hand gestures. Each time she carved a swirling shape in the air, it seemed to sparkle and hang there for a split second. Then a red-haired man or woman would let out a screech—whether of pain or wrath, Marcus couldn't tell—and where they had been standing, there was now a creature with a tail, stranded on dry land and unable to join in the fight.

He saw her take out four people that way, but he also saw that each time she did it, her newfound energy visibly ebbed away. By the time she'd returned the last one to his original form, Beka was back to being white and shaky, something that didn't escape Kesh's notice.

The Selkie prince had hung back while his people attacked Beka and Marcus, merely urging them on from atop his rocky podium. While Beka was working her magic, Marcus had taken out most of the others, Selkies, he thought, with knife and fists and sheer brute strength. Beka had warned him that the supernatural people could be unusually strong and fierce. But they weren't fighting for the woman they loved, and they hadn't had the benefit of Uncle Sam's training and twelve years of a never-ending battle for survival. The Selkies never had a chance.

Any of the rebels who weren't lying bleeding or unconscious on the once pristine sands had bunched up in front of Kesh, maybe to defend him, or maybe thinking he would defend them. Either way, he pointed at Beka and said, "Ignore the Human. Kill the witch. Kill her now." The three remaining Selkies headed across the beach to where Beka was standing, barely holding herself upright and visibly trembling.

Then Kesh jumped down and faced Marcus, a sly smile snaking across his handsome face like a cloud across the sun. "You'd better let me go and rescue your precious Baba Yaga. She's looking quite ill; I suspect she may not be up to defending herself. Such a pity."

Marcus wanted so badly to wipe that self-satisfied smirk off the Selkie Prince's face, he could feel the muscles in his thighs bunch as he prepared to spring. But he couldn't abandon Beka. Kesh had the advantage—there was no one in the fight that he cared about; it was clear that he would cheerfully abandon all those battling on his behalf. But as much as Marcus wanted to pummel Kesh, he couldn't do it if it cost him Beka.

He risked a quick glance over his shoulder, not quite taking his eyes off of Kesh, who was poised to make a break for the water, taking one sidling sideways step after another. Once the Selkie got to the sea, he'd be gone for good.

Beka was winded and gasping, bent over with her hands braced on her upper thighs as though she was about to collapse entirely. Two of the remaining paranormals stood in front of her, holding large pieces of driftwood they'd picked up off the beach. The third was circling around from behind.

Torn in agonized indecision, Marcus met Beka's eyes across the ground that separated them. As he watched, she sank even lower . . . and then closed one eye in an unmistakable wink.

Marcus smothered a laugh, spinning around to leap through the air and tackle Kesh, just as Beka whipped out a knife from each of the sheaths she'd glamoured to be invisible, and plunged them deep into the attackers in front of her, ducking under their flailing arms to sink the blades in. He'd just have to trust her to take care of the third. For now, he had his hands full.

Kesh fought dirty, which came as no surprise. He was supple and slippery, pulling out of Marcus's grasp time and time again, fingers shaped into claws to try and gouge out Marcus's eyes or jab at his windpipe. He bit and scratched, twisting like an eel, cursing all the while. Sometimes Marcus was on top, sometimes Kesh was.

Both of them punched and jabbed at each other, connecting more times than not. Sand flew into Marcus's eyes, and he blinked it away, his feet slipping on the uneven surface. Unwanted memories of other battles flashed before him, but he shoved them down, out of the way. There was only here. Only now. Only one target. Everything came down to Kesh.

By the time they staggered to their feet, facing each other, they were both cut and bleeding from over a dozen places. Marcus was pretty sure one of his ribs was cracked from a flying kick the other man had managed to get in, and the ornate silver knife clutched in the Selkie's hand cut just as well as Marcus's more utilitarian model.

"You cannot win," the Selkie panted, holding his knife out in front of him as he edged even closer to the sea. Tiny waves lapped at their feet, their soothing murmur a sharp counterpoint to the sounds of vicious struggle. "No matter what you do, Beka will die. Already she lies bleeding on the sand. You have lost, Human. Let me go, and perhaps you will still have time to save her. Unless of course she is dead already."

Marcus didn't dare turn away from his quarry, as much as his heart yelled out at him to check on Beka, to make sure that Kesh lied. He couldn't hear anything over the thudding of his pulse and his own harsh breathing.

"If she dies," Marcus said grimly, "so do you. Count on it." He took one step forward, and something in his face finally chased away the look of smug superiority on Kesh's.

"You cannot kill me," Kesh said with certainty, his back foot ankle-deep in salt water. "I am a Selkie prince."

Marcus pivoted on one heel, ignoring the stab of his rib as he spun around and kicked Kesh squarely in the stomach. The Selkie doubled over, and Marcus took one more step in, grabbed him by the hair, and smashed his fist into the other man's face with all of his might. The Selkie dropped like a stone, waves foaming whitely around his crumpled body.

"You might be a Selkie prince," Marcus said, gritting his teeth. "But no one, not even a Selkie prince, takes out a Marine."

And he hauled the unconscious man out of the surf and went to find his woman.

TWENTY-SIX

THE WORLD CAME back to Kesh in a blurry haze, half eclipsed by an eye that was rapidly swelling shut. He tried to move, but his arms and legs seemed to have cleaved to each other, and the best he could manage was an abbreviated wiggle, like a newborn pup just birthed into the sea.

A face swam into view, familiar save for the fierce grin that adorned its battered surface; an expression he had never seen before, and one that he would be happier not to be seeing now. Who knew the insecure little witch had it in her? She had been full of surprises from the beginning—not at all what Brenna had said, or what he had expected.

This final surprise was most particularly unpleasant. As was the shiny silver blade she held about an inch from his one working eye. Most insulting of all—the knife was his own. This had not gone at all as he had planned.

"Hello, Kesh," the Baba Yaga said calmly, as if she didn't have blood slowly trickling from a cut above her brow. "So nice to see you again. Sorry about the duct tape." White teeth showed in a smile that held nothing of apology.

"Ah, he's awake," a deeper voice said, and the Human

mate she had chosen over him appeared to gaze down at Kesh over her shoulder. Kesh took some satisfaction from the battered look of the man. He would have taken more had their positions been reversed.

"Should we kill him quickly, or carve off one piece at a time?" the man called Marcus asked, not seeming to have a preference either way. "I'm still kind of pissed about the way he poisoned you with those fancy picnics. I say we kill him slowly. I learned some stuff in Afghanistan you wouldn't believe. I can make it last for weeks."

Kesh swiveled his head toward Beka in alarm. Surely she would not allow this barbarian to harm him. They had been friends, after all. And she had always had a soft heart.

Beka reached out and patted him gently on the cheek with the hand not holding the knife. "I really don't think that's a good idea," she said.

There. He knew she would not allow him to be killed. Now he just had to find a way to speak to her alone, and surely he could persuade her to let him go.

She grinned at Marcus, wincing a little when the motion made a crack in her bottom lip open up again. "It would take way too much time and trouble to torture him, and we still need to figure out where he hid the Water of Life and Death. I say we just slice a few more holes in him and set him out where the sharks will find him."

Kesh's eye opened wide and he could feel his mouth gaping and closing like a fish out of water. "But . . . but . . . you can't do that!"

Beka raised one eyebrow. "Why not? You tried to kill a Baba Yaga, not to mention your own people. I don't think anyone is going to get too upset if we take justice into our own hands." She tossed the knife into the air and then caught it a mere inch above his nose, making him twitch.

"But Beka, darling—"

Marcus's face loomed close. "Call her darling one more time and I will rip out your tongue and feed it to the fish while you watch, you sonofabitch." Kesh tried to edge away from him on the sand.

Beka snorted. "I don't think your charm is going to work on anyone here, Kesh. You might as well save your breath. You know, for the screaming."

Kesh could feel his heart start to race as it finally dawned on him that she meant what she said. They were going to kill him. All his plans, all his scheming and hard work, all brought to naught by an untried Baba Yaga and a Human fisherman. The disgrace of it was almost enough to make him willing to accept death. Almost. But he reminded himself that as long as he lived, there was always a chance to start again.

"Wait!" he said. "I can help you!"

Marcus looked at him with disgust. "Don't listen to him, Beka. He'll say anything to keep us from killing him. Let's just get this over with." He grabbed Kesh by his bound legs and started hauling him toward the road, none too gently.

Kesh winced as a shell cut into his face, scrabbling with the hands tied behind his back to try and grab the shifting sands and slow his forward movement.

"No, Baba, you need me," he said in a rush. "I can lead you to the Water of Life and Death. You need it to cure your illness."

"You mean the radiation poisoning you gave me?" she asked, her expression cold. "That illness?"

He swallowed hard as he realized she'd somehow learned exactly what he had done. There was no way he would be able to convince her that he hadn't intended to kill her. Kesh looked from Beka to Marcus, taking in their matching hard stares and the grim set of their jaws.

He had lost, well and truly. The universe was cruel and unfair, to reward ones such as these over someone like him. But someday they would learn. If not at his hands, then at the hands of another.

"I will take you to the Water of Life and Death," he said, drooping. "Just let me live."

Beka sighed and stuck the knife through her belt. "Oh, okay. But you'd better lead us directly to it and fast. I've had a really rough week and I'm running out of patience."

"And I never had any to start with," the fisherman added. "And I *really, really* don't like you."

Kesh closed his good eye as the Human hauled him off the ground and threw him over one large shoulder, no doubt heading back toward their vehicle. *The feeling is quite mutual, fisherman.* But even he was not foolish enough to say it out loud.

WITH KESH FIRMLY trussed up and tossed in the back of the Jeep, and the Water of Life and Death safely retrieved, its decorative box held securely in both hands on her lap, Beka finally felt like she could take a breath. Everything on her hurt, but she was more worried about Marcus, who was clearly favoring his ribs, as well as dripping blood all over the driver's seat of the Jeep.

They were headed down Highway One, almost to the beach where she'd told Chewie to gather the sick Mer and Selkies. She worried that either one or both of Chewie's assignments hadn't gone as planned; that the Queen had said no, or that the water folk hadn't listened, or both. But there was nothing she could do about that now.

The fancy silver Camaro they'd been following for the last mile suddenly made a left turn into a parking lot, causing Marcus to jam on the brakes and throwing them forward against restraining seat belts. Beka clutched the box even tighter and listened to Marcus curse out everyone who ever got a license to drive without being instructed on the use of turn signals.

She started to laugh until she saw his face—pale and set, teeth gritted in obvious pain.

"What's the matter?" she asked. "Are you okay?"

"I'm fine," he said tersely, but then he coughed, holding on to his ribs and wincing, and she saw a bubble of crimson appear at the corner of his lips.

Hell. She wasn't a healer like Barbara, but even she knew a punctured lung when she saw one.

"We have to get you to the hospital," she said, feeling a

pulse of panic starting at the base of her throat. She'd been so terrified when he was fighting Kesh, and so relieved when they'd made it through with only minor injuries. Trust Marcus not to mention a little thing like a broken rib. Or ribs.

"I'm fine," he insisted, hands gripping the steering wheel so tightly his knuckles were white. "Tonight is almost the full moon; we have to get the Water of Life and Death to the Selkies and Merpeople as soon as possible." He gave a brief chuckle, cut short by a gasp for breath. "Ow," he said. "I can't believe that sentence just came out of my mouth."

"That's not the only thing coming out of your mouth," Beka said in a grim tone, using a tissue to blot away another bead of blood. "Pull over."

"Beka—"

"Pull the damned car over right now," Beka commanded. "Or would you rather start practicing saying *ribbit*?"

She couldn't do anything about whether or not Chewie's missions had been successful. There was, however, one thing she could fix. Even if it cost her the title of Baba. It would be worth it.

Marcus eased the car to the side of the road, ignoring the blare of a horn and raised middle finger from the battered green pickup that had been on their rear bumper. In the backseat, Kesh let out a muffled protest from underneath the blanket they'd thrown over his duct-taped body.

"I ought to turn you into a toad anyway, just for telling me you're fine when you're not," Beka said. "Unless you consider having a piece of your ribs intersecting your lungs 'fine.' I sure as hell don't."

Marcus gave an abbreviated shrug, stopping when the motion obviously caused him pain. He turned to face Beka, moving slowly and carefully. "I'm fine for now," he insisted. "Believe me, I've been in worse shape before. I'll go to the emergency room when we've dealt with the others."

Beka shook her head, taking the Water of Life and Death out of its box and reverently removing the cork from the polished turquoise glass bottle that held its precious liquid. The bottle was etched with arcane symbols that seemed to shift and change as she watched them, and a shadow swirled around the inside as if a genie lived within it. From the open neck came the scent of summer and exotic flowers and the ocean at the moment of dawn. Next to her, Marcus caught a whiff and gave an involuntary sigh.

"Here," she said, holding it out for him. "Take a sip. Just a small one. It ought to be enough to heal your wounds."

Marcus stared at her. "Is that allowed?" he asked. More muttering came from the backseat and he leaned back carefully and thumped the blanket until it subsided. "I don't want you to get into trouble."

Beka grimaced. "You fought to save a Baba Yaga from an evil Selkie prince and his followers; that should earn you dispensation. If it doesn't, well, I'll deal with the consequences." Nothing the Queen could do to her would be worse than living with herself if Marcus died. Not just because he'd been fighting on her behalf, but just . . . because. It was Marcus, dammit. And the Queen had allowed Barbara to share the Water with her new husband, Liam, so he might live an extended life at her side. It wasn't exactly the same thing, but she didn't care.

"Here," she said again. "Drink."

Marcus stared into her eyes, his expression stern. "You first."

"Don't you trust me?" Beka asked, shocked.

He snorted, clutching his side. "Ow. You idiot. I followed you into battle with a bunch of seals and Mermaids. If that isn't trust, I don't know what is. But you need that Water far more than I do, and I noticed that you still haven't had any either. So I'll drink if you do, and not otherwise." His features might have been carved out of granite.

Beka gritted her teeth. Why was it the man could never just do what she asked without disagreeing with her? "I'm not bleeding all over my vehicle, or coughing up lung tissue," she said. "Unlike some people I can name. I'll have mine later."

Marcus cocked his head to one side, considering her as if she were some kind of puzzle to be figured out. She could see his pupils contract when he figured it out.

"You're afraid there won't be enough," he said quietly. "So you're leaving yourself for last. And giving me your share, because you think I deserve it more than you do." He leaned forward and brushed a wisp of hair off her face tenderly. "You just don't get it—you deserve the world on a platter. I just wish I had it to give to you."

Beka sniffed. There was something in her eye. Sand or dust or something. That was it. She'd never had anyone look at her like that. Never had anyone who treated her like she was precious and valuable. She knew better than to get used to it, but still, it felt pretty wonderful.

"You give me plenty," she whispered.

"Good," Marcus said. "Then stop arguing with me and drink the stupid Water."

When she hesitated, he added, with his usual practical nature, "You can't take care of everyone else if you're about to fall on your face. This isn't over yet, and you're going to need all the strength you can get."

He was right, of course. Even if she managed to heal the sick Selkies and Merpeople, she still had to heal the ocean where they lived. Giving in, she tilted back the bottle and let a few precious drops slide down her throat. It tasted like sunshine, bright and vibrant and warm, with a hint of roses and an aftertaste of ashes, to remind the drinker of the essence of death within every moment of life.

As it hit her system, she could feel her body phasing and shifting, the damaged cells transforming themselves into something new and healthy. Energy and warmth flooded through her, making her fingertips—and other parts—tingle and spark. A sudden rush of desire roared through her; life reasserting itself in the most basic way possible. It was a pity there was no time to indulge in the feeling.

Although she was going to enjoy watching Marcus's face when he got his first taste of the magical elixir.

She handed him the bottle, carefully licking the last tiny bit of moisture off of her lips.

"Wow," he said, staring at her. "You look better already. You're practically glowing."

"They don't call it the Water of Life and Death for nothing," she said, laughing at his expression. "Go on. Just a little sip."

Marcus narrowed his eyes, but he took the bottle from her, holding it as if it were a bomb that might explode. Warily, he tipped it back so a couple of drops flowed into his mouth. For a moment, he just sat there, then amazement rolled over his face, like the sun coming out after a storm.

"Holy crap," he said, breathing deeply without wincing. As she watched, most of his wounds scabbed over and disappeared. A healthy color replaced the clammy paleness of his skin, and for just a second, a golden glow seemed to cover the surface of his hazel eyes. "That's some stuff."

Beka took the bottle back and carefully recorked it, placing it back in its box like the treasure it was. "Magic," she said. "Gotta love it."

"I'm starting to," Marcus said, not looking at her as he put the car back in gear and steered them back onto the highway. He was silent for a moment. Processing, she thought. Then he said hesitantly, "Beka, would the Water cure my father's cancer?"

She was afraid he'd think of that.

"It would," she said, hating the words that had to come next. "But I can't give it to him."

There was another pause, and he didn't speak again until they were pulling off the road into a parking spot near the beach. "Why not?" he asked.

"It's against the rules to use the Water of Life and Death to cure Human illness," she explained. "Otherwise a Baba would be tempted to use it all the time, and there isn't very much of it. How could we choose who to save and who not to? So it is simply forbidden."

Marcus stopped the car again and stared at her. "But you gave it to me anyway."

She blushed. "There's an exception for a Baba's mate, on the rare occasions when one is Human," she said, not meeting his eyes. "I was sort of hoping it would be covered under that. Because we, uh, you know." She could feel the heat in her face climbing to reach her ears. "If the Queen is pleased with me when this is all over with, she'll probably allow it. If she's not, I'll be in so much trouble, it probably won't matter."

"I see," Marcus said. He got out of the car without another word. She couldn't tell if that meant he'd simply accepted her explanation, or if he was angry with her because she'd refused to heal his father. And she didn't have time to worry about it, because night was falling and suddenly she could see Chewie on the beach, leading the King of the Selkies and the Queen of the Mer, along with a number of their people.

TWENTY-SEVEN

THEY WALKED OUT of the sea by the dozens; they must have transformed out behind the rocks that bordered the beach. A few of the adults stayed where the water was about chest high, holding babies too young to change their forms under the water where they could still breathe. It was an eerie sight; the very old and the very young and their silent friends and family supporting them if they were too ill to walk on their own. No one made a sound, and in the waning dusk it was as if the beach was some strange twilight place between the worlds.

The few regular folks who had lingered on the sands all packed up in a hurry and left, shaken and uncomfortable without knowing why. But Beka knew; she could see death in some of those waiting eyes, and prayed that she had not come too late.

The King of the Selkies and the Queen of the Mer held themselves very straight and proud as Beka and Marcus approached. Behind them, their guards shifted slightly at the sight of a stranger, but a gesture from the King made them settle into an alert but relaxed stance. Chewie bounded up to Beka, spraying gritty sand and woofing an enthusiastic greeting.

"Nice job, Chewie," she said, patting him on the head in gratitude. "How did the other half of your task go?"

She held her breath and crossed her fingers on the hand not holding on to the box. She wasn't sure what she would do if the Queen of the Otherworld had refused her request; there was no way Beka could simply let all those children die. It was a Baba Yaga's duty to protect the young, but it was more than that. Those young lives were so precious, so rare in a community that bore fewer and fewer children every year. Beka knew she would trade anything so save them. Even her own life, if that was what it took.

Chewie head-butted her leg, almost knocking her down. After most of a lifetime together (hers, anyway), he knew the way she thought.

"Stop worrying," he said. "I was very persuasive." He smiled his sharp-toothed doggy smile, and Marcus took half a step back involuntarily. Beka snorted. Chewie didn't realize that his smile didn't quite come across the way he meant it to. Of course, when he was in dragon form, it was much worse.

"The Queen said yes?"

"The Queen said yes." Chewie nodded his massive head toward the ornate box Beka held tucked carefully under one arm. "She said to tell you that under the circumstances, she would allow it, since the Selkies and Mer are her people, too, for all that they are forced to live out their lives on this side of the doorway between the worlds."

Beka snorted. That sounded like a direct quote from the Queen, who always had a certain amount of pity for any paranormal creatures not able to reside within the ethereally beautiful borders of her kingdom. Still, all Beka cared about was that she had permission to use the Water of Life and Death to save the people Kesh had poisoned.

The King of the Selkies had been politely listening from a few paces away, but now took a forceful step forward. "The Queen has granted your request?" he said with relief, his stiff back unbending just enough to show how tense he had been. "That is most welcome news." He looked at Beka and Marcus, taking in their somewhat battered appearance. "And may I also assume that you have found and vanquished the villain responsible for all of this?"

Beka widened her eyes at Chewie, and he gave a tiny shake of his black muzzle. *Great. He clearly hadn't told the King the identity of the person who had poisoned his realm.* She sighed. First things first.

"Yes," she said, leaving it at that. Marcus stared at her but didn't say anything.

"Oh, I'm sorry, Your Majesties," Beka said. "I would like you to meet my friend Marcus. He has been invaluable in helping to find the source of the illness, as well as helping me to capture the er . . . villain."

The King bowed his head, and the Queen of the Mer gave him a sweet but absentminded smile, most of her attention focused on the small child huddled in her arms.

"I'd like to start giving the Water to the sickest people first," Beka said, nodding to the Queen of the Mer.

Chewie dropped a small velvet bag in the sand at Beka's feet. "The Queen of the Otherworld sends these, with her compliments," he said, as Beka pulled out two silver spoons, one tiny and the other barely there at all. "She bid me to tell you that they are the exact amount needed for the treatment of the little ones and for the adults among the water people. You were instructed to give this amount; no more and no less."

Trust the Queen to control the situation, even when she couldn't be there in person. Still, no one knew the properties of the Water of Life and Death better, since the Queen was the one who created it through some magical process only she knew.

Boudicca held out her grandchild, her arms trembling noticeably as Beka tilted the minute amount of Water the smaller spoon contained into the limp Mer's open mouth. The aroma of flowers and sunshine drifted over the beach, and those still waiting for their own dose suddenly stood slightly taller.

A moment, suspended in time. The moon blinked out behind the clouds and returned. The Merchild giggled. "Yummy," she said to her grandmother. "More."

Boudicca clutched the little one tightly as they all watched the color return to tiny, chubby cheeks. "Thank you, Baba Yaga," she whispered. "All my gratitude and blessings upon you." She wept unabashedly and stepped aside for a haggard man bearing a Selkie elder, a shrunken woman so tiny and thin she seemed to weigh nothing at all.

One by one, Beka dispensed the Water to all those who needed it. One by one, they began to recover as soon as they swallowed the precious liquid. Only a single tiny infant Mer failed to improve, his cloudy green eyes fluttering for a moment and then closing forever. His parents enfolded him in grieving arms and swam slowly back into the sea. For him, the answers had come too late.

Beka wanted to weep, but there would be time for that later. For now, there was still work to be done.

Finally, only the royals and their guards remained, standing with Beka, Marcus, and Chewie on the deserted beach.

Boudicca turned to Beka. "Now that you have discovered the cause of the illness, this rade-ey-ashun your Chudo-Yudo told us about, will you be able to repair the damage to our homelands? Or will we be forced to remain in our new location, more vulnerable to discovery by Humans?"

"I am fairly certain I can come up with a magical solution," Beka said, happy to be able to impart good news. "It will take me a little research and experimentation, but I believe that I should be ready by tomorrow afternoon. If Marcus and his father will agree to take me out in their boat one more time, I hope to cleanse and purify your old home of the toxins that were poisoning both you and the water." She smiled at both of them, hoping that she wasn't promising more than she could deliver. "If you like, I can meet you here tomorrow night at this same time and report to you on my progress."

"That would be most acceptable," Boudicca said.

"Now, about the one responsible." Gwrtheyrn glared at Beka. "Please do not tell me you killed him in battle. I have been looking forward to having that pleasure myself."

Marcus and Beka exchanged glances. "I am afraid that the Queen of the Otherworld has commanded me to bring him to her," Beka explained. "She intends to pass judgment on him herself, for his crimes against both your people and hers." She swallowed hard. "But there is something you should know."

The King scowled. "What?" he barked, sounding more seal than man.

Beka bit her lip, and Marcus touched her lightly on the shoulder. "We'll be right back, um, Your Highness," he said. He and Beka walked back to where the Jeep was parked.

"The King isn't going to be pissed that we beat up his son, is he?" Marcus didn't sound all that concerned one way or the other. "Because I'd just as soon not get into another fight tonight if I can help it."

Beka shook her head, opening the rear door. "Honestly, I have no idea what he's going to say when he finds out."

She pulled the slightly musty blanket off of Kesh, who gaped up at them, sweaty and disheveled. The additional time spent in the backseat of the car hadn't been kind to him. One eye was swollen almost shut and turning remarkably vivid shades of green, blue, and purple. Other bruises and cuts decorated his face and arms, and his silk shirt was tattered and marred by bloodstains and dirt. He bore very little resemblance to the handsome, charming prince she'd first met. Under the circumstances, she couldn't bring herself to feel sorry for him.

Apparently, neither could Marcus, who yanked him roughly out of the car, banging the Selkie's head on the doorframe in the process. Probably accidentally. Maybe. Beka pulled out one of her knives and enjoyed watching the Selkie Prince's eyes widen, but she just used it to cut the duct tape off of his arms and legs. He wasn't going to make a break for it; after his cramped sojourn in the backseat, it was all he could do to hobble down to the beach between them, with Marcus holding one arm and Beka the other.

He was just starting a sputtering, indignant speech about their inexcusably rude treatment when they brought him to a halt in front of Boudicca and Gwrtheyrn. A couple of the Selkie soldiers pushed forward, then stopped, stunned, as they recognized Beka's captive.

It took Gwrtheyrn a second longer, perhaps because his heart was unwilling to see what his eyes could not deny. Beka saw the moment when he realized the truth; the King seemed to waver between forms, both bull seal and man letting out a roar of pain and fury and agonized betrayal that echoed down the empty beach. Then he steadied, backlit by the setting sun as it blazed its way into the darkening sea.

"Kesh," Gwrtheyrn said in voice thick with sorrow. "Tell me this is a mistake. Tell me you are not the one who rained terror and disease down on our own people." Boudicca grasped his arm in silent sympathy, but her eyes glittered at Kesh with an anger not tempered by grief.

"*Our* people, Father?" Kesh spat, yanking his arms free so that he stood alone on the sand. "They ceased to be *our* people the day you stole my birthright and gave it to my younger brother." He spat on the ground. "You are a foolish old man who allows puny Humans to lay waste to our seas and decimate the dolphins and the sharks who are our brothers. You and the other weaklings that follow you would have lost that land eventually; I merely accelerated the process."

"For what gain?" his father asked, fists clenched in frustrated rage. "To what end?"

Kesh shrugged. "I thought at first that I would persuade many of the Selkies and Mer who had been forced to leave their homes to follow me instead. When they did not, I took the few who were wise enough to listen to be my new subjects, and sat back to watch the rest of you die. You turned your back on me, so I turned mine on you. It was only fitting."

"Fitting?" Boudicca sputtered. "Fitting to kill babies and old people because your father decided that you were unsuitable to rule? He did not banish you from the kingdom; you did that to yourself, leaving when matters did not spin in the direction you wished. You are a spoiled child, for all your age, and you would never have been half the ruler Gwrtheyrn is, or your brother will be."

Gwrtheyrn shook his head, eyeing his eldest son with something almost approaching pity. "Do you not see, Kesh? All you have done is to prove that I was right: You are not nor could you ever be a proper king. A king cares for his people, and you care only for yourself."

The old King heaved a sigh, turning away from his son to face Beka, his movements heavy and slow. "Might I ask one more favor of you, Baba Yaga?"

Beka braced herself. "I cannot set him free, Gwrtheyrn. I know he is your son, but he must face the Queen's justice. She has commanded it, and I would not dare do otherwise."

Gwrtheyrn gave a harsh barking laugh. "Nor I, Baba Yaga. Nor I." He didn't look at Kesh at all; it was as though the younger Selkie had suddenly become invisible. "I do not wish to circumvent his punishment. He deserves everything she chooses to mete out and more. But as you say, he is my son, and therefore my responsibility."

The sadness in his deep black eyes almost undid Beka, but she could see what it cost him to stay strong in front of her and Marcus, and so she forced herself to sound as calm as he did.

"I see," she said softly. "You want to bring him to the Queen yourself."

"It is my duty and my shame," the King said. "I will not shirk it."

Beka rubbed her hand across her face, pondering his request. She had *really* been looking forward to taking Kesh to the Queen of the Otherworld herself, throwing him down at the Queen's feet in a grand gesture of triumph that would demonstrate her worthiness to be a Baba Yaga. But the Queen had only demanded that the traitor be brought to her; not who did the bringing. She would hear from Gwrtheyrn that Beka had been responsible for Kesh's capture and know that Beka had fulfilled that part of her assignment.

Gazing at the furious and heartbroken King of the Selkies, she knew he needed to do this—needed it even more than she did.

She looked at Marcus and he nodded, clearly agreeing.

"Very well," she said, with only a tiny pang of regret. "You may take him. See that he reaches the Queen alive." She glanced over at Kesh, who curled his lip and sneered at her. "Although if he collects a few more bruises along the way, well, the water passage can be rough, I hear."

Still ignoring his son, Gwrtheyrn gestured for his guards to come and take custody of Kesh, who was dragged away cursing voluminously and with greater imagination than Beka would have given him credit for. She suspected this was the last time she would ever see him. The Queen of the Otherworld was not known for her forgiving nature.

"You have earned the boon we promised you, Baba Yaga," Boudicca said. "Have you aught to request from us? Perhaps a chest of precious jewels, or ancient coins reclaimed from the broken ships that lie upon the floor of the sea?"

Beka shook her head. "Neither of those, thank you, although I appreciate the offer." She took a deep breath. "What I would really like is for you to make sure that the fish go back to where they belong, so that men like Marcus's father can make an honest living doing the thing they love."

Boudicca nodded gravely. "Easy enough to do, and little enough to ask after all that you have done for our people. Are you sure you desire nothing for yourself?"

Beka shook her head. She had almost everything she could wish for—and the only other thing she wanted, they didn't have the power to give her.

"I am well satisfied, Your Majesty. After all, I was merely doing my duty as a Baba Yaga. I expect nothing in return for that."

She expected the royals to leave, but Gwrtheyrn apparently had one more thing to say. He bowed low to Marcus, much lower than she would ever expect from a Selkie King facing a Human commoner. Boudicca came to stand again by his elbow and gave a small curtsy of her own.

"I am told by the Baba Yaga's Chudo-Yudo that we owe you a debt of gratitude as well, fisherman," the King said gravely. "He says that you have been of much assistance to the Baba in her search for the answers to our problem." He eyed the knife slices in Marcus's clothing and the fading remnants of the bruises on his knuckles. "And it is clear that you came to her aid in apprehending Kesh as well."

His voice only broke a little when he said his son's name, and everyone there carefully ignored it.

Marcus bowed back, only a tad awkwardly. "It was my pleasure, sir. No thanks required."

Gwrtheyrn pursed his lips. "Perhaps not, but you have them nonetheless. We promised the Baba three boons for her service to our people; one of these to be given to the person of her choice. Clearly, you have earned that boon and there is, perhaps, a way we could repay you, if you wish."

Marcus gave Beka a puzzled look, but she just lifted her eyebrows. She had no more idea what was going on than he did.

Boudicca cleared her throat. "The Chudo-Yudo told us of all you did. He also told us of your father's illness. The one Humans call cancer."

Beka could feel Marcus stiffen beside her. "Yes, my father is ill. But Beka—uh, the Baba Yaga—has already told me that she can't give him the Water of Life and Death."

"You misunderstand," the King said. "We have an offer of a different sort. You see, we water folk do not have this cancer; it is not an affliction that affects such as us."

"That's nice," Marcus said. "But what does that have to do with my father?"

"There is a Selkie magic," Gwrtheyrn explained, gazing at Marcus with something less than his usual stern expression. "It can change a Human into one of us. I have consulted my wisest and most learned healers, and it is their opinion that such a change might well eradicate the cancer now plaguing your father."

Marcus's mouth gaped open. Beka couldn't tell what he was thinking, beyond his obvious shock at the suggestion.

The King held up a cautionary hand. "You must understand, there is no guarantee that such a thing would work. It is merely our best supposition. And the change is irreversible. Should your father choose to become one of us, there could be no going back. And he would not have the ability to transform from seal to man. This is something that must be learned when one is young, or not at all. Once a Selkie, he would never be able to walk on land again. But he might live a long and healthy life, and our people would welcome him."

"I—I don't know what to say," Marcus said in a strangled tone.

"It is not a small thing to take in, I understand," the King said, not unkindly. "The decision is not an easy one, and your father must choose for himself. But we would gladly grant this gift, should he decide that he wishes it."

Beka grimaced in sympathy at the shocked expression on Marcus's face and bowed politely to Gwrtheyrn and Boudicca. "It is a generous offer, Your Majesty, and kindly meant. We thank you for it."

Belatedly, Marcus added his own, "Uh, yeah, thanks."

"It is the least we could do, after all that you have given to us, who are not your people or even your own race," the King said.

He turned to Beka. "We will return here tomorrow night to hear the tale of your attempt to cleanse our waters. It is fervently hoped that the results will be successful, but either way, we are most grateful for your efforts on our behalf, and for healing our sick." He gave her a serious look. "We had the utmost faith in you, Baba Yaga, even when you doubted yourself. So far, you have more than proven yourself worthy of the title."

Beka flushed, pleased beyond measure by his words,

while at the same time trying not to panic about the possibility of failing at the next part of her task.

"I endeavor to do my best," she said. "And it is my pleasure to serve."

They all bowed one more time, and the King and Queen and their guards turned to head back into the sea.

"We will be here at the downing of the sun tomorrow," Gwrtheyrn said over one bulky shoulder. "If your father wishes to join us, fisherman, he should attend us then. If the Baba Yaga can cure the waters as she cured my people, I suspect it will be long and longer before we come this way again."

TWENTY-EIGHT

ALONE ON THE beach with Beka, Marcus sat down on a large rock. It had been a long day, but he wasn't quite ready to go home yet. If nothing else, he had to figure out how on earth he was going to explain the Selkie King's offer to his father. Obviously he was going to have to start with something along the lines of, "Oh, by the way, Da, Selkies are real," and move on from there. He wasn't looking forward to it. He wasn't even sure he *wanted* to tell his father about the offer.

"How are you doing?" Beka asked softly, sitting down next to him. Her voice seemed to harmonize with the sound of the waves hitting the shore and the calls of the night birds as they winged on their way to their nests. Now that she was healthy again, she had regained her usual glow, the blond hair he loved so much loose now from its braid and falling in a shimmering wave down her back.

Marcus shook his head. "Honestly, I don't know. It had already been the most bizarre day in my entire life. And now this." He gazed at her in the near darkness, her lovely face made eerie by the rising nearly-full moon and the faint light from passing cars on the road above. "Things have certainly gotten interesting since I met you, Beka."

She winced. "Interesting good? Or interesting as in the ancient Chinese curse: 'May you live in interesting times'?"

He gave her a rueful smile. "A little bit of both, I guess." They sat in silence for a minute, and he hoped he hadn't hurt her feelings, but he wasn't going to lie to her and pretend that this was easy for him. He suspected she wouldn't believe him if he said it was.

"So what's bothering you right now?" she finally asked. "Clearly something is. I'd like to help, if I can." She put one hand on his bare arm, and the warmth of her skin touching his moved him more than he could say. It was as if all the caring and passion between them had been summed up in that one simple gesture. But he just wasn't in the right frame of mind to appreciate it right now.

"It was bad enough to discover that there are really such things as magic and Merpeople and Selkies," he said. "I'm not sure I could deal with having a father who was one."

Beka gazed into his eyes. Even in the near darkness, those blue irises were vivid and clear like sapphires, able to see through his surface fears down to the soul underneath.

"Which are you more afraid of?" she asked. There was no judgment in her voice. "That he will decide to take the King up on the chance to live life as a Selkie? Or that he won't?"

"I'll lose him either way," Marcus said, bitterness lying on his tongue like acid. "The chemotherapy has stopped working, and the doctors say there isn't anything else they can do."

He was surprised to find out how deeply he cared. Somehow during his days on the boat, sharing close quarters with the father he thought he'd hate forever, he'd come to terms with his anger and resentment toward the man. They would never be close, and what affection they had for each other would always have an element of strain to it, but affection there was nonetheless. And now . . . this. A choice between the devil and the deep blue sea.

"I can't tell you how to feel," Beka said, tucking her arm around him and leaning her head against his shoulder, so they both sat facing toward the changeable sea. "But you might want to think about this: the ocean is in your father's blood already. Maybe he would prefer a life lived in the element he loves to the prospect of a slow death on land."

"No matter how strange that life is?" Marcus couldn't even wrap his mind around the possibility.

"Aren't all things strange to us when they're new? I'm sure that life in the Marines seemed strange in the beginning."

She had a point. He remembered how alien it had all been, all rules and regulations, and well-ordered training. And no ocean, when that had been all he'd known his whole life. Then the military became normal, until he'd left it to come home, and had to adjust all over again.

Now the sound and the smell and the rhythms of the sea had gotten back under his skin. Just like the woman sitting next to him.

He turned to face her, pulling her in close, breathing in the scent of her and that strange, elusive hint of strawberries. One hand rose to caress the velvet of her cheek, and the other tangled in her silky hair as he bent down to press his lips against hers in a kiss that he'd intended to be gentle but that somehow turned to fiery passion as soon as their lips touched.

Her arms reached up to wrap around his neck, holding on as if she would never let go. She kissed him back with an ardor that astonished, gratified, and aroused him all at once, and for a moment, he lost himself in the kiss, and in the woman, thinking to himself, *now this, this is magic*.

She finally pulled away, leaving Marcus feeling as if she took all the oxygen with her as she went. The space within his arms where she had been felt strangely empty and cold.

Beka's smile glinted at him in the darkness. "What was that for?" she asked. "Not that I'm complaining."

Marcus stood up with a sigh, handing her the box containing the Water of Life and Death and then tugging her up with him and turning them both back toward the Jeep and the complications of reality.

"I have a feeling it is going to be a long night," he said. "And I wanted something pleasant to think about in the midst of all the craziness."

"I could give you even more to think about, if you like," she said in a throaty voice, and his pants were suddenly tighter than they had been. He was incredibly tempted to run away from all of his troubles and hide in the warmth of her arms. And her bed. Images flashed before his eyes of Beka, naked and lovely, smiling her bright smile, long lashes half hiding those remarkable eyes.

"Oh, believe me," he said, barely able to form coherent words. "You just did." He sighed again, a gusty protest against obligation and responsibility. "But I really need to get home and talk to my father."

"I know," Beka said. She hugged him quickly before walking him to the driver's side.

He slid into the seat and turned the key. "So I guess you have to spend the morning figuring out how to get the radiation out of the trench. Can you really do that?"

"I think so," Beka said. "I guess we'll find out. Can you really talk to your father about Selkies and Merpeople and witches?"

"I think so," Marcus said glumly. "I guess we're going to find out."

BEKA STOOD FOR a moment in the darkness, watching the lights of the Jeep recede into the distance. It felt symbolic somehow of what was yet to come. One way or the other, Marcus's father would soon no longer need him. And then Marcus would leave, and she would never see him again. The very thought made the night seem colder, and the stars less bright.

"It ain't over until it's over," Chewie said, materializing out of nowhere. Beka jumped, having almost forgotten he was there. Toe-tingling kisses could do that to a girl.

"What?" she said. "You mean solving the water people's problem? I know there's still a lot of work to do."

"That too," Chewie said, "but that's not what I was talking about." He shook his head, rolling big brown eyes in her direction. "You need to have a little more faith."

"I need to focus on doing my job," she said, trying to do just that. "Speaking of which, I need you to do one last thing for me."

He gave a dragonish snort, crisping the edges of a few nearby weeds. "If it involves chasing down a certain fisherman and sitting on him until he comes to his senses, I'm all in."

Beka ruffled his fur, not sure whether she wanted to laugh or cry. "No, you ninny. Not that. I've been thinking about those canisters Kesh put into the trench. It would be a lot easier to clean up the area if they were gone. But I can't risk moving them by boat because we'd contaminate everything they touched. Could you bring them all up to the surface for me, if I can figure out some place to stash them until I can make an anonymous call to the authorities?"

Chewie looked longingly across the road and up the bluff to where the bus sat waiting. "I'll do it," he said, "but then I swear, I'm never letting the Water of Life and Death out of my sight again. This has all been *way* too traumatic."

Tell me about it, Beka thought. "Fine by me," she said. "But where the heck are we going to put that radioactive mess where it won't hurt anyone?"

Chewie gnawed on his tail thoughtfully. "None of the canisters are leaking very badly, as far as I can tell. It was only the cumulative effect over time that caused such drastic problems for the underwater trench. Isn't there someplace out of the way where you could put them? Preferably right on the ocean, so I can stay in dragon form the entire time?"

Beka pondered. "Well, we could probably use the little cove where Marcus and I fought with Kesh. If he thought it was isolated enough to risk meeting his followers there, it would probably be a safe place to leave the canisters for a few hours until they could be picked up by a cleanup crew." She would be very happy when the containers were back in the hands of people who knew how to deal with them. Without using magic, that is.

She gave Chewie the directions so he would know how to get there, and reminded him to try and keep a low profile when he made his multiple trips back and forth between the trench and the cove. It wouldn't do to suddenly have a whole bunch of people report seeing a flying sea dragon, all on the same night.

Her companion batted long lashes at her, his brown eyes open wide. "I'm always careful," he said indignantly. "Besides, if someone sees me, I can always just eat them."

Beka was almost completely sure he was joking.

IT WAS NEARLY dawn when the door of the bus opened and a tired-looking dog padded in. Even for a supernatural creature, it had been a long night. Beka, who had been sitting in the dimly lit kitchen nursing a long-cold cup of tea, got up to give him a big hug around shaggy black shoulders. His dragon hide should have repelled any residual radiation, but she would have hugged him even if he glowed in the dark.

"Thanks, Chewie," she said. "I don't know what I'd do without you."

"You would have figured something out," he said, yawning wide enough to show off all his sharp white teeth. "What are you still doing up?"

He sat down at her feet, so large that his eyes were almost on a level with hers, even in that position. "Are you worrying about cleansing the trench? That should be a piece of cake now."

Beka laughed. "I don't know about a piece of cake, but I spent most of the night looking through some of my basic spells and figuring out how to adapt them for this, and prepping something special to use to contain the radiation. I'm actually feeling pretty confident."

Chewie raised a furry eyebrow. "Well, that makes for a nice change. And it's about time. So what's the matter?" He cocked his head and gazed at her in the diffuse light of the single lamp she'd left on. "You look sad. Are you sad?"

She clenched her fingers together, feeling foolish, and stared at the floor instead of meeting his eyes. "You're going to think I'm crazy," she muttered.

"So what else is new?" the dog asked, head-butting her knee until she met his eyes. "Spill it, sister."

"You watch too much TV," she said. "Listen to you talk."

"Hmph, Listen to you *not* talk. Are you going to tell me what's wrong or not?"

"It's about being a Baba Yaga," she said.

Chewie dropped to the floor with a thump, hiding his head under his paws. "If you're going to start in on that bit about not knowing if you are good enough, or thinking maybe you don't want to be a Baba anymore, I swear to Belobog, I am going to gnaw off my own ears so I don't have to listen."

"Nice to know I can always count on you for sympathy, big guy," Beka said with an ironic chuckle. "And in fact, no, that's not it. Kind of the opposite."

"Huh?" He picked himself up again, apparently done with being a dragon drama queen for the moment. "Color me confused."

Beka didn't blame him. She was confused as hell herself. That was part of the problem.

"If I've learned anything these last few weeks, it is just how much I *do* want to be a Baba Yaga," she said. "Coming so close to losing it really made me see that this is what I was meant to do. As much as I'd like to have a child of my own, I realized I can help so many more children if I am a Baba. And I even think I might be good at it, with a little less avoiding trouble and a little more practice."

Chewie snorted. "I don't think you need to worry about avoiding trouble. It always seems to find you if you're a Baba Yaga." He tilted his head. "You're not still worrying about the Queen taking away the job and giving it back to Brenna, are you? Because last I heard, Queen Morena still wants to ask her some pointed questions about the possibility she was working with Kesh, and no one has seen hide nor frizzy hair of her. Besides, you've already cured the sick sea people and captured Kesh. Once you cleanse the Merpeople and Selkie's home in the trench you will have done everything the Queen asked of you. You should be fine."

Beka took a deep breath, feeling as though her heart were breaking in two. The air felt too thick, and gravity too heavy. "I don't think I'll ever be fine again, Chewie. I've done something really stupid."

His eyes widened. "You didn't lose the freaking Water of Life and Death again, did you? I've only been gone for a few hours!"

Beka laughed, sniffling at the same time. "No, no. The Water is safe and sound, locked up in the cupboard where it belongs."

"Holy Hekate," the dog said. "If I weren't immortal, you probably would have given me a heart attack. So what have you done that is so stupid?"

She bit her lip. "I fell in love."

"And this is bad how?"

"Don't be ridiculous." Beka kicked him lightly with one bare foot. It hurt her foot, as usual. You'd think she'd learn. "I'm in love with Marcus. I realized it earlier, when I saw him coughing up blood."

"How romantic," Chewie said sarcastically. "You're even weirder than I thought."

"You know what I mean," she said. "While the fight with Kesh and his followers was going on, I was mostly too busy trying to stay alive to worry about Marcus. Besides, he's the toughest guy I've ever known. It mostly didn't even occur to me to be concerned until after it was all over, and then he seemed to be okay, other than some relatively superficial wounds."

Beka gritted her teeth, remembering the moment when

she'd looked up and seen the ominous sign. Even now, her stomach flip-flopped in horror. "Then I saw him coughing up blood and knew he was really hurt. And it hit me that I couldn't even imagine living in a world that didn't have him in it. I love him, Chewie. I love him so much it makes my heart hurt."

Chewie scrunched up his muzzle. "So, that's good, right? I mean, I'm not an expert on Humans, but I'm pretty sure he likes you too. I saw that kiss on the beach tonight; that didn't look like indifference to me."

A single tear slid down her face, like the first raindrop that heralds the oncoming storm. She brushed it away without even really noticing it. "Don't you see, Chewie? Marcus may like me, but he doesn't like the magical world, or any of the things about it. He couldn't even decide if it would be worse for his father to be dead or to become a Selkie. If I choose to stay a Baba Yaga, I'll lose him. But if I give up being a Baba Yaga to be with him, I'll lose so much more. Including you."

Chewie licked her hand, shoving his big head under her arm for a rare affectionate cuddle. "You never know, Beka. People can surprise you."

"Sure," Beka said, feeling more tears prickling behind her eyes, hot and full of pressure, like a geyser ready to burst through to the surface. "They can. But most of the time they do exactly what you expect them to."

"Really?" Chewie said, sitting back and looking at her pensively. "Because you know, I would have sworn that if I came back from *hours and hours* of heavy labor on your behalf that you would have gone to the trouble of getting a little snack out for me. You know, like a T-bone steak or a couple of whole chickens. And yet, here we are, sitting around talking about some guy who may or may not love you back no matter what choices you make, and *surprise*—there's no snack!"

Beka gave him a watery smile, knowing he was trying to distract her, and letting him succeed, at least for the moment. She'd get through the last of her tasks and deal with it all then. For now, she had a dragon-dog to feed. And as he'd so forcefully reminded her, that always came first.

"How about a steak *and* a couple of chickens?" she asked as she got up to walk to the refrigerator. "Would that be enough of a snack for you?"

"Maybe," Chewie answered. "What else ya got?"

Beka snapped her fingers, and a plate full of s'mores appeared from where she'd hidden them in the bedroom. "Surprise!"

Chewie gave her a huge lick, practically a one-dog bath. "Dude, that's what I'm talking about. Forget about that Marcus—he smells like fish anyway. Stick with dragons; they're way more reliable." He sat down and started happily munching, blowing tiny sparks at each s'more to warm it up.

Beka patted him on the head and got the remainder of his food out before she went to bed to rest up for what promised to be another long day. She didn't expect to sleep though. Not when all she could think about was Marcus's face when he said, "It was bad enough to find out there was such a thing as magic."

Should she give the magic up? Could she?

TWENTY-NINE

THE LATE MORNING sky was pewter gray, a color that matched Beka's mood so well she almost thought she'd summoned it up. Storms flickered farther down the coast, visible over the vast, open expanse of the water, but so far the only thunder in the bay came from the sound of her heart when she saw Marcus waiting by the *Wily Serpent*.

Why did he have to be so handsome? She should have turned him into a toad after all. Toads didn't have broad shoulders and strong chests, and muscles on their muscles. Toads didn't have one wavy lock of brown hair that refused to curl in the direction of all the others, or hazel eyes that were as changeable as the sea.

Those eyes looked tired, as if their owner had gotten about as much sleep as she had. He helped her on board without saying much and went off to start the engines and take them out of the harbor.

His father came out of the cabin, his face pale and pensive, and walked over to stand by the rail with Beka.

"So," he said. "Selkies and Mermaids. And witches. He wasn't making any of that up, was he?"

"I'm afraid not," Beka said.

They stood there in silence for a moment, then Marcus Senior said, "I saw one once, you know. A Mermaid."

"What?" Somehow Beka had expected more resistance to the idea.

"When I was a young man, the ship I was crewing on got caught in a storm," he said. "I thought I saw this woman in the water, pointing us away from the rocks. The captain laughed at me, but he listened anyway, and steered us safely past. I used to tell the boys about it, when they were young. I'd almost forgotten, until Marcus came and talked to me last night."

Beka didn't know what to say. For the first time since she'd met him, Marcus Senior looked every year of his age, plus some. The skin hung loosely on a frame that had once been as muscular and broad as his son's, and his face was the color of chalk. His hands, leaning on the rail for support, trembled slightly.

"It's beautiful," she said. "The Selkie's kingdom under the sea. It's different from up here, but it is really beautiful." She wasn't trying to persuade him—just reassure him, if she could.

"I'd be amazed if it wasn't," he said, looking out over the surface of the ocean, its greens and blues muted by the overcast day. "There isn't anything about the ocean that I don't find beautiful. Even after it killed my son, I couldn't stop loving it."

He didn't meet her eyes, almost didn't seem to be talking to her at all. She thought he was just thinking out loud, but she was wrong.

"I knew Marcus was right, you know," the old man said abruptly. "He told me that the man I'd hired was unreliable. Flaky, he said. A stoner. Whatever. I knew, but it was hard to get people to work on boats in them days; all the kids who grew up on the water were leaving to work behind desks in the city, instead of following in their fathers' footsteps like they used to.

"I let the man stay, so I could keep the boat running,

and feed my children. Give them a livelihood they could hold on to. And my youngest son died, and I lost the older one anyway. It was all for nothing."

Beka knew the old man wasn't looking for sympathy, but she slid her hand over to cover one of his nonetheless. "Not for nothing," she said. "When you needed him, Marcus came back."

He gusted out a sigh that was lost on the freshening wind. "He did. And I thanked him by being the same grumpy bastard he ran away from in the first place. To be honest, I didn't want his help. Didn't feel like I deserved it. In a way, it felt like the cancer was my punishment for letting his brother die. I had nothing to lose anyway."

Beka gave his hand a squeeze, feeling the finger bones fragile under hers. "Only now you do." She knew how he felt.

"I can't tell you what to do," she said softly, as the boat slowed near the spot where she would be diving. "Or what the future holds." She laughed, only a little off key. "I'm afraid I don't know the answer to that one either. All I can tell you is that you need to make the decision that is right for you, without guilt or recrimination. I'm pretty sure that Marcus has forgiven you. Maybe it is time for you to forgive yourself."

THE UNDERWATER WORLD was silent and peaceful, enfolding her in its grace and ethereal loveliness the way it always did. Kelp forests taller than a house undulated in the mischievous currents, and tiny, brightly colored fish played hide-and-seek within their welcoming fronds.

Today there were no sharks; the only enemy was invisible and much more deadly, invented by men who had no place in these waters, and brought here by one who had forever forsaken his.

Beka intended to clean up the mess he'd made.

No matter what happened after today, she needed to finish what she had started that day on the beach when Boudicca and Gwrtheyrn had asked for her help and she had given them her sacred promise in return.

So much had happened since then, she hardly felt like the same woman who had made that promise. Still, it was up to her to fulfill it, and prove—not just to the Queen of the Otherworld, but more importantly, to herself—that she had the skills and power to make her worthy of the title Baba Yaga.

She floated weightlessly in the murky perpetual twilight of the ocean, as deep as she could safely go. The bulk of the trench lay beneath her flipper-wearing feet, but if what she had in mind worked the way she intended it to, that wouldn't matter.

From out of the waterproof bag she'd carried down with her, she pulled out the enchanted sphere she'd been up half the night creating. It looked as light and delicate as a soap bubble, but it was created from the essence of the element of Air, which could uproot huge trees and tear the roofs off of buildings when it chose to.

It would be strong enough. And so would her magic.

Beka let herself sink into a semi-trance, her breathing slowing until her heart seemed to beat in rhythm with the sea's own pulse. Slowly, she reached her magic out and began to gather the impurities from the water around her. Like limitless fingers of light and energy, the rays of magic drew radiation out of the water and into the glistening iridescent sphere, where it took on almost a solid form, swirling and glowing. No longer bound by fatigue and self-doubt, she finally let her powers soar.

More and more she pulled, from farther and farther away, until she was gathering in not only the radiation from Kesh's toxic canisters but also the scattered remnants of Fukushima's disaster.

As the enchanted sphere filled, it glowed brighter and brighter, until its presence lit the ocean like a beacon of hope. In the distance, Beka saw a Mermaid floating by; she couldn't be sure, but she thought it was the same woman who had come to her for help on that fateful day. She waved, hoping the Merwoman understood the meaning of a thumbs-up. Not that it mattered. It was already obvious that she would have good news to impart to the King of the Selkies and the Queen of the Mer when she saw them later.

She'd done it. The water below was as clean and clear as it ever had been, and the water people could return to their homes. Their long nightmare was over.

MARCUS COULD TELL that Beka had succeeded as soon as she pulled her mask off. Her smile could have lit up a day even gloomier than this one, and triumph exuded from every pore. He helped her over the side of the boat, wincing away from the bright light of the globe she carried tucked under one arm.

"What's that?" he asked, not sure he wanted it on his father's boat.

Beka followed his glance and mercifully stowed the glowing orb away in her bag. "That's all the radiation that used to be in the water," she said, as if that was a good thing.

"Jesus Christ!" Marcus took a step away from her, and even his father looked alarmed, for all that he was already dying. "Is that safe?"

Beka smirked. "Safer than your driving," she said. But she took pity on them and added, "No, seriously, the sphere is completely impermeable; it only takes things in, and doesn't let them out."

"Oh." Marcus let out a breath he hadn't realized he was holding. "That's good. What the hell are you going to do with it?"

"I'll take it with me to the Otherworld when I go to see the Queen," she said, like other people mentioned they were going to Santa Carmelita to catch a movie. "There are creatures there who will consider it a tasty treat."

He was never going to get used to all the weird.

"Great," Marcus said. "That's just great. You did it. I'm so proud of you."

And he was. So why did his heart feel like he'd swallowed fifty pounds of lead?

Standing there in her wet suit, hair dripping seawater onto the deck below, she looked just like the crazy surfer chick he'd pulled out of the ocean not so long ago. But she wasn't the same girl at all. She was so much more—and so much more to him—than he would have ever dreamed possible. And way out of his league. It was almost enough to make him wish he didn't know who and what she really was. Not quite, but almost.

"Here," his da said, opening a cooler. "I thought we might want this." He pulled out a bottle of champagne and three plastic cups. His smile wavered a bit around the edges, but he was clearly doing his best to put aside his usual crusty, growling demeanor, so it seemed like Marcus should do the same.

"Great," he said again.

Beka winced, but he couldn't tell if it was because of the champagne—a staple at Kesh's seaside picnics, so she'd said—or because his "happy voice" was unconvincing in the extreme. Overhead, a passing gull dropped a load of guano, missing him by inches. Fabulous—even nature was critiquing his efforts.

"Great," she echoed, not sounding any more sincere than he had. Luckily, his da didn't appear to notice, and took up his cup in a shaky hand when Marcus poured them each a tiny bit.

"To Beka," Marcus Senior said. "The heroine of the hour."

Beka blushed a becoming pink tint that stained her cheeks and accented her bright blue eyes. "Oh, please. I am not."

Marcus's father nodded his head. "You are, young lady, and in more ways than one. You saved those sea people's homes from poisonous radiation, which was nothing short of a miracle from where I'm standin'. You brought the fish back to where they belonged, which is going to save a lot of people here on land." He gave her a tremulous grin, rusty from disuse. "And you helped me and my boy here reconnect, which I reckon was an even bigger miracle."

"Hey," Beka protested, waving her hands. "You guys did that yourself. I don't get any credit for that one."

"Yes, but you kept us from killing each other long enough to do it," Marcus Senior said, winking at her.

"You can't deny the truth of that, Beka," Marcus said. And neither could he. The fact was, he and his father were barely speaking to each other at the point when she'd appeared out of the sea like a mythic goddess sprung from the waves. Somehow just by having her around, they'd both been transformed into kinder, less aggressive versions of themselves. Beka did that to people, and that was the biggest miracle of all.

"You brought the light back to this boat after too many years of darkness," his da said, raising his glass to Beka again. "I thank you for that, and for brightening up my last days upon the earth."

They all fell silent, the specter of the old man's illness hanging over their attempt at celebration like a ghost at a wedding feast.

"It has been my pleasure," Beka said, getting up and giving his da a hug. The old sailor actually looked pleased, which was almost as shocking as his toast had been.

"Speaking of darkness," Marcus said, all the naked emotion making him twitch worse than a hill full of snipers. "That sky is looking pretty ominous. I'd better get us headed into port before we are hit by a storm and get sent to the bottom, taking all that nasty radiation right back down there."

He headed for the cabin to start the engines, and as he walked rapidly away, he heard his father say, "That boy sure is cranky. I can't imagine where he got that from."

Beka's laughter pealed out over the sea like clarion bells in a church, calling the faithful to worship.

BACK AT THE bus, Beka and Chewie stared at the radiant globe on the table between them. It pulsed and shone as if a shard of the sun had been captured within it, looking so glorious it was hard to believe its contents offered death instead of life.

"So that's it," Chewie said, sounding pensive. "Mission accomplished. Day saved. Live to fight another battle. And like that."

"Pretty much," Beka said, trying to muster up the appropriate enthusiasm. "All I have to do is take that through to the Otherworld, make my report to the Queen, then go tell Boudicca and Gwrtheyrn it is safe for them to go home. Then life gets back to normal."

"Great," Chewie said.

"Yeah. Great." She sighed.

"So, no more long days stuck out on the boat with Marcus and his father," Chewie added. "You must be so relieved." She couldn't decide if he was being sarcastic or not. With dragons, it was often hard to tell.

"Right. Definitely." She thought about no more days filled with overlarge fishermen, bantering arguments, or sacks full of coins handed over to wily curmudgeons. No more teasing Kenny about his freckles, or listening to Chico brag in loving detail about his large family back home in Mexico. No salty breezes blowing through her hair as she sat on the bow with Marcus next to her, telling her ridiculous stories of the fish that got away to make her laugh. No watching hazel eyes turn from brown to green to amber in the midday sun as they hauled in nets or polished the fittings or sat in the dinghy waiting to be picked up by the *Wily Serpent* on its way back in to dock.

No, she wasn't going to miss any of that at all.

"I think we should go away," Beka said abruptly. "After all, Baba Yagas are supposed to travel around. What's the point of living in a bus if you always stay in one place?"

"But I thought you hated moving around all the time," Chewie said, his furry face perplexed. "You were ecstatic when Brenna finally settled us here for a while. And Baba Yagas travel when they get a magical summons that tells them they are needed somewhere. Did you get a vibe and not tell me?"

"No," Beka said. "No vibe. I just thought it might be good to have a change of scenery." She didn't know if she could face staying here without Marcus nearby. Once his father was gone—one way or the other—Marcus would be gone too. He'd told her from the start that he'd never intended to stay. As soon as his father no longer needed him, he would be on his way to whatever his life held next, leaving the Bay just too empty for Beka to contemplate.

There was no way she was going to try and explain all that to Chewie though. It sounded crazy even to her. Who knew love made so little sense? No wonder Humans wrote all those sad songs about it. From now on, she was sticking to paranormal creatures and meaningless trysts. It was a *lot* easier on the heart.

"I'm going to go get changed so I can visit the Queen," she said, jumping up from the table. "I won't be able to relax until I've gotten through my obligatory visit without being turned into something with feathers, scales, or thorns."

"There's nothing wrong with scales," Chewie called after her as she walked toward the bedroom. "And don't forget to take your Orb o' Death with you—that thing gives me the willies."

BEKA BREATHED A sigh of relief as she stepped back through the closet that hid the doorway between the Human realm and the Otherworld. Tiny purple sparkles swirled around her feet as she crossed the border, and high-pitched giggles like silvery wind chimes followed her for a moment before disappearing into the distance. She shut the door behind her and put her back against it. She had the utmost respect for the Queen of the Otherworld— but holy crap, that was one scary lady.

Still, the Queen and her consort had seemed quite pleased with Beka's report and her solutions to the problem. The Queen had even invited her to stay for high tea, an hours-long ritual involving dozens of stunningly beautiful ladies-in-waiting in gauzy dresses, exotic tea blends served in elaborately bejeweled golden teapots and poured into porcelain cups so delicate you could see through them, and dainty cakes so light that occasionally one simply floated away.

Beka rather enjoyed the spectacle of it all, basking in the Queen's rare approval, but in the end she was happy to return home without having broken anything or spilled bright crimson jam onto her white lace court dress with its low neckline, flowing sleeves, and tiny embroidered flowers. Other than a small mishap with a couple of errant cloth rosebuds that forgot they were merely decorative in the heady atmosphere of the Otherworld, she'd come through the entire experience no worse for wear.

Now she planned to hang up her ornamental sword, take off this lovely but impractical outfit, slip into some jeans, and pour herself a glass of wine. She'd had enough tea to last her a month.

Humming some haunting but catchy tune the court musicians had played during tea, Beka meandered out into the main area of the bus to put the pure silver sword back onto its empty rack before changing her clothes. Always take care of your weapon first, even if it was never used for anything more lethal than attending a fancy dress ball, so she'd been taught.

"Hey, Beka, look who's here," Chewie said cheerfully as she entered the living room. "It's Marcus."

She dropped the sword on the floor with a melodious clang. Stooping to pick it up, she hoped the dim interior would hide her burning cheeks. While she'd been gone, the storm had hit in earnest, and the sky outside was almost as dark as night. Inside the bus, only a few lamps glowed warm against the fury of the gusting winds and driving rain.

Marcus had been lounging on the futon, drinking a beer and looking way too at home for Beka's peace of mind. His hair was damp from the rain, and the rumpled forest-colored shirt he wore brought out the green in his eyes, which glinted when he saw her.

"Wow," he said, standing up so fast he almost spilled

his beer. He set it down on the floor with a thump. "You look incredible."

The open admiration on his face made her heart beat even faster. "Thanks," she said. "I was at court, visiting the Queen. She isn't a big fan of hippie-dippy tie-dyed skirts and tank tops."

One corner of Marcus's mouth curved up. "Neither am I. Unless you're the one wearing them."

"I'll just, um, go for a walk in this nice rain, shall I?" Chewie said, heading for the door. Beka barely heard him go.

"What are you doing here?" she asked Marcus quietly, putting the sword down on the counter and taking a couple of hesitant steps forward. "I would have thought you'd be spending the rest of the day with your father. Or has he chosen not to take the Selkies up on their offer?"

He shook his head. "As far as I know, he hasn't made the decision yet. I tried to talk to him about it and he just muttered something about having important errands to run and bolted for the door." He gave a short laugh. "I suspect he was headed straight for the Cranky Seagull, where men are men and emotions aren't allowed."

"Ah," Beka said. "None of that namby-pamby communication crap for you stalwart fishermen types, is that it?"

"Something like that, yeah," Marcus said. He stared at her across the foot or more of wooden floorboards that separated them, but made no move to get any closer. Of course, a lot more separated them than physical space, and they both knew it.

"So what are you doing here?" she asked, suddenly too tired to play their usual games. If he'd come to say goodbye, she wanted to get it over with as fast as possible—like pulling a Band-Aid off of a cut. Only multiplied by a power of a hundred.

Figuring there wasn't much point to pretending to be normal anymore, she snapped her fingers and a glass of wine manifested out of the air. She took a long swallow.

"Neat trick," Marcus said, not even fazed. "And I came to say thank you."

Beka blinked and took another drink. "Thank you for what?" she asked. "I'm the one who should be thanking you. I never could have done all this without your help. You know, even without the part where you saved my life and beat the crap out of the evil prince." She mustered up a grin. "That was my favorite bit, by the way."

"Mine too," Marcus said with sincerity. "It was my freaking pleasure." He scowled at her glass. "That isn't champagne, is it?"

Beka shuddered. "Goddess, no. I may never drink the stuff again. Although it was really sweet of your father to bring some out today to celebrate my success. I can't believe he did that."

"Me either," Marcus said. "That's part of what I came to thank you for. He's really changed since you've been around, and no matter what happens, I'm grateful for the chance to have made my peace with him."

"That would have happened anyway," she said, making her nearly empty glass vanish back to where it had come from. The conversation was making her head spin enough all by itself.

"I don't think so, Beka," he said, taking a step forward and gazing into her eyes. "I don't think you understand the power you have."

"What? Of course I do. I'm a Baba Yaga; I'm all about the power." She wondered if she should pop in an entire vineyard, if the single glass wasn't enough to impress him.

That crooked smile she loved so much snuck up on her and mugged her heart. "I'm not talking about your Baba magic, although I admit, that's pretty damned impressive. I'm talking about your own personal magic," Marcus said, his tone softer than usual.

"You have this amazing ability to make the people around you blossom into their best possible selves; you make people *want* to be better, to do better, just so you'll give them that smile full of sunshine that you get when someone has done something nice."

"I don't know what you're talking about," Beka said.

She moved a little closer, as if drawn by a magnet that connected his soul to hers. "I don't do that."

"You do though," Marcus said, suddenly right in front of her. He was so tall, so large, he should have felt intimidating. But she only felt sheltered by his nearness, a solid bulwark against the harsh realities of the storm that raged both inside and out.

"You don't even see it, but everyone you touch is happier because of you. Poor Kenny was so shy; he couldn't bring himself to say two words to a woman. But you were kind to him, you made him feel strong and confident, and he actually asked out this waitress he's liked for years. They're going on their second date tonight.

"And Chico, he's been missing his family so much, but he always felt like he had to work here to send money back home, and because he's illegal, he never dared to go back to visit. Talking to you all those times about his daughters, and the grandchildren he's never met, he finally decided to go back to Mexico. I was able to get him a job down there with one of my Marine buddies who opened a hotel in Mazatlan after he got out."

"That's wonderful," Beka said. "But they would have done those things eventually anyway, if they really wanted them."

"I don't think so, Beka," Marcus said, putting one hand gently under her chin and tipping her face up so she couldn't look away. "Because you made me a better person, too, and I would have said that was as impossible a task as cleaning radiation out of the ocean. When I left the Marines, I had been a killing machine for twelve years. It felt like I was some kind of monster, masquerading as a normal human being."

She made an inarticulate sound of protest, but he shook his head.

"I went through the motions, but something inside me was broken, I thought forever. I'd loved being in the Marines, but the endless war and death and the constant need to look over my shoulder made it impossible for me to stay. But what it had done to my soul had rendered me unsuitable for any other kind of life.

"You changed all that. I'm not even sure how, but you showed me the way back to myself. I may not be a perfect human being, but at least now I feel like I have a chance of becoming someone I can face in the mirror every morning. So I had to come and say thank you, before we disappear out of each other's lives forever."

The thought of it made the room seem unbearably cold, and she moved forward without thinking, wrapping her arms around his waist and resting her head on his chest. The thump of his heartbeat steadied her whirling thoughts and focused them on one suddenly clear and undeniable aim—to make love to Marcus one more time, no matter what came after.

THIRTY

BEKA PUT HER head on his chest, and something inside Marcus turned to molten fire. It was crazy the way she affected him; he couldn't even be in the same room with her without feeling the need to kiss her, touch her, hold her. Having her this close and not doing those things was just impossible. Suddenly his plan to go off and lead adventure tours seemed a lot less inviting.

A loud crash of thunder rocked the bus, and the lights flickered briefly, then went out.

"Shit," Marcus said.

Beka giggled and snapped her fingers, and candles burst into flame all over the bus. Fat red candles on windowsills, slim silver candles on tables, honey-scented beeswax candles on what was probably an altar. Light glimmered from tiny tea lights and tall tapers, casting mysterious shadows and making the bus into a cozy refuge from the storm.

Huh. Maybe this witchcraft thing had something going for it after all.

Marcus grinned down at Beka, who looked deservedly pleased with herself. "Nice trick," he said. "What else you got?"

She cocked her head to one side for a moment, thinking, and then reached up to kiss him softly, biting his bottom lip playfully when she was done. Marcus almost forgot to breathe, undone by the sheer glory that was Beka.

She seemed to be having a tough time breathing, too, blue eyes dilated and wide. "Your turn," she said. "Surely you know a magic trick or two."

He grinned and scooped her up, tossing her onto the futon and then pulling it out into a bed with her still riding along. She shrieked with surprise, giggling up at him in an irresistible combination of innocence and smoldering sexiness that went right to his head. He flopped down next to her, kissing her neck and wandering up to nibble on her earlobe.

"I learned that one from you," he whispered in her ear. "But I've got a few tricks of my own that I'll be happy to show you."

Thunder shook the bus, echoing the pounding of his heart as he sat up and slowly unfastened every button on the front of her white lace dress. There must have been thirty or forty of them, all tiny and slippery under his large fingers, but he didn't care; what lay beneath was worth the wait. He stared into her eyes as he went, loving the way she watched him back, clearly wanting him as much as he wanted her.

Finally, he slid the dress off of her, revealing all that enticing, tanned, soft, silky skin. No bra restrained the full, pale mounds of her breasts, and he smiled at that, leaning down to suckle gently at their rosy tips.

"The Queen of the Otherworld doesn't believe in underwear?" he said, both aroused and amused by the unexpected sight.

Beka gave him a mischievous grin. "What would faeries want with underwires and thongs?" she asked, and then let out a small gasp, closing her eyes as he sucked a little harder.

They gave up on speaking after that, too enraptured by the touching and scent and the sounds of the pleasure they gave each other, small gifts of demand and response, all accompanied by the forceful, rhythmic music of the storm that seemed to rage as much within them as it did in the sky without.

Marcus explored every inch of Beka's lovely long and supple body, marveling at each dip and curve, the gentle swell of breast and hip, the perfect indentation of her belly button, the hidden mysteries below.

And in return, she ran greedy fingers and tongue over all of him, until they were both gasping and clutching and kissing with such ardor that it seemed the candles were the smallest flame, the tiniest light in the room.

Beka shone beneath him like the ethereal luminosity of the full moon, like the sun on a perfect hot July afternoon, like hope at the end of the darkest hour. Together, it seemed that they could reach new heights that neither could have achieved alone.

Finally, finally, he sank himself deep inside her, rocking and thrusting and stroking until they reached those heights in a fiery climax of passion and glory and joy, accompanied by one final clap of thunder that seemed to rock the entire world.

As they lay together in a sprawl of damp limbs and satisfaction, the storm eased to a gentle rain, and one by one, the candles guttered out until only a few remained. Beka heaved a sigh and snuggled closer, slipping into a relaxed drowse with the hint of a smile lingering on her lips.

Marcus pulled her tight, not willing to sleep and miss a single minute of the best interlude of his entire life. Especially since he had no idea if he would ever come close to this kind of happiness ever again.

What they'd shared had been magical—more magical than dogs that were really dragons, or enchanted beings out of storybooks. But what it meant, he had no way of knowing.

Had they been saying "yes" to each other or saying good-bye?

THE RAIN EASED to a drizzle and then stopped just as the sun was going down. Beka woke after a while, looking as dazed and unsettled as he felt, and made them a dinner that neither of them tasted.

Chewie came back in as they were pushing the food around on their plates and finished off the lot, muttering dire imprecations all the while about Humans and idiocy and something that sounded like s'mores. Marcus ignored him, and Beka just patted him absently on the head, alternately smiling at nothing and frowning into space as though looking at a future she didn't like. He had a feeling she wasn't envisioning anything that wound up with "and they all lived happily ever after."

He'd tried calling his father, but the phone at the house just rang and rang. So he'd stayed with Beka, feeling alternately guilty and relieved, but mostly just happy to have a few more moments in her company.

Finally, when the late summer evening drew to a close and the sun was dipping into the hills, they headed down to the beach to meet the Mer Queen and the Selkie King. Chewie stayed behind to guard the Water of Life and Death, although none of them really thought there was anyone left to come after it, now that Kesh was gone.

Gwrtheyrn and Boudicca both looked tired but hopeful as they stood on the beach, backlit by the setting sun.

"How are your people doing?" Beka asked after they'd exchanged formal greetings. "Is everyone fully recovered?"

"Completely," the King said. "Thanks to you, Baba Yaga. Our gratitude knows no measure."

Queen Boudicca clasped her hands together, an abbreviated version of what would have been a more frantic motion in someone less regal. "And our lands under the ocean, Baba Yaga?" she asked hesitantly. "Were you able to cleanse them?" Gwrtheyrn closed his eyes for a moment in what might have been a silent prayer.

"Yes," Beka said simply. "Your water is free of poison or taint. You and your people can return home tonight."

Boudicca and Gwrtheyrn looked at each other, the Queen's eyes brimming with unshed tears, and the King suddenly returned to the vibrant, powerful being Marcus imagined he'd been before all of this started.

They both bowed deeply to Beka, and thanked her with voices that shook, their joy overflowing to cover the sands like sparkling diamonds. Behind them, their guards stayed in formation, standing straight and alert, but their fierce faces were transformed by grins into something much less threatening and much more celebratory.

"We can never thank you enough," Gwrtheyrn said, his voice gravelly with emotion. "If there is ever aught you need from the people under the sea, you have but to ask and it will be given to you."

A voice from behind Marcus said, "I hope that goes for me too," and his father walked down from the dunes.

Marcus forgot to breathe, and Beka grabbed his hand, squeezing tight as if to remind him that he was not alone.

"Da," he said. "You can't mean it. You're not going to let them turn you into a seal, are you?"

"A Selkie," Gwrtheyrn corrected, and added, "Indeed, our offer to you still stands, fisherman. You are welcome to join us if you wish."

Marcus opened his mouth to protest, but his father shook his head. "I'm dying, son, and you know it. If I stay, my ending is certain, and not a pleasant one. I would rather spend whatever time I have left living in the waters I have always loved." He gave a genuine laugh; the first Marcus ever remembered hearing. "And whether or not the change to Selkie can cure me, I can be sure that it will be the adventure of a lifetime. How can you argue with that?"

He couldn't, really. But Marcus was surprised to discover how much he was going to miss the old man.

"I never could win an argument with you, Da," Marcus

said, feeling emotion rising up in his throat and threatening to choke him. He walked over and gave his father a hug, the first they'd exchanged since he was a small child, trying to put everything he was feeling into the act. "I guess I'm not likely to start doing it now."

His da hugged him back, his bones feeling as fragile and hollow as a bird's. "Nay, that you're not." The older man stood back and gazed at him, although even now it was clear that half his attention was fixed on the sea beyond.

"I'm sorry I was so hard on you, son. I wasn't a very good man, or a very good father, and there is no making up for that now," Marcus Senior said, brushing away Marcus's feeble attempts at denial. "But I want you to know that I've left you the boat; signed it over to your name this afternoon, and all that I've got with it, the little that there is." He glanced from Marcus to Beka, now standing by herself on the sand in front of the King and Queen.

"You make a good life for yourself, boy. That's all I ever wanted for you anyway. Whether you choose to stay on the water or not, find whatever makes you happy and grasp it with both hands. I love you." He patted Marcus surprisingly gently on the cheek and walked toward the water people.

Gwrtheyrn shook out a leather pouch, and a vibrant emerald pendant the color of the ocean slid into his palm. "This will keep you safe until we are home and my wizards can make the transformation permanent," he said, handing it to Marcus's father. "Put it around your neck right before you go under, and you'll be able to swim and breathe like one of us until we can change your form."

The King and Queen nodded one more time at Beka and vanished under the waves with their guards. Marcus Senior hesitated for a moment, then smiled at Marcus and Beka.

"Take care of each other," he said, and walked into the sea.

BEKA SAT ON the damp sand and watched the foam curl lace-edged on the sand and then retreat. Just like life—something always coming, always going. Beautiful, unpredictable, implacable in its perpetual and constant change. No matter how much you wanted things to stay the same, they never did.

Sometimes they changed for the better. Sometimes they changed for the worse. But they always changed.

Marcus had been standing by the surf, staring out over the water as if he could see into the secret realms underneath. Or maybe just brooding; it was hard to tell. Either way, she couldn't blame him. After a while, he wandered over and sat next to Beka.

"You're crying," he said, sounding a little surprised. "You never cry."

She shrugged a little, her tee shirt and jeans feeling strangely constricting after the long, flowing dress she'd worn earlier. Her heart felt constricted, too, as if metal bars had formed around it, tightening into bands so firm she could feel them crushing into the flesh, making her pulse seem ragged and uneven.

"Are you crying for my da?" he asked. "Because I think he's going to be okay, one way or the other."

"I think so too," Beka said, looking at his face under the moonlight, so beloved and so strong. How could she choose a life where she would never gaze on that face again? How could she not?

Marcus scooted a little closer, brushing away a tear as it slid slowly down her cheek. "If you're not crying about my da, then what's wrong, Beka?" He leaned over and kissed the spot where the tear had been, making the iron bars tighten even further. "Can I help?"

"I don't think so," she said. "You see, tomorrow is my birthday."

He blinked at her. "And you don't like birthdays?"

She gave a tiny laugh. "I love birthdays, usually. But tomorrow I turn thirty, and I will have been a Baba—or a Baba-in-training—for twenty-five years. If I keep drinking the Water of Life and Death, there is no going back. I'll be a Baba Yaga, and a powerful witch, for the rest of my life. So you see, this is my last chance; I have to choose once and for all whether to be magical or to be Human, like everyone else."

"You could never be like everyone else," Marcus said solemnly. "And that's a good thing, not a bad one."

Beka sniffed, wiping the back of her hand across her eyes. *Damn him, the last thing she needed right now was him being sweet.* "I thought I didn't want to be a Baba Yaga anymore. I wanted a regular life, and kids of my own. But the last few weeks have shown me I really want to be a Baba after all. I feel like that's the role I was meant to play."

"Then what's the problem?" he asked, obviously confused.

She looked him in the eye. "I love you," she said. "That's the problem. I love you more than I ever thought I could love anyone, and I don't want to give you up. But I know you hate all this magical stuff, and you'll only want me if I am Human. So if I want to keep you, I have to give up the magic, and I can't bear the thought of losing it either. That's why I'm crying."

To her amazement, Marcus let out a huge laugh, leaning in to put his arms around her. His hazel eyes crinkled at the corners as he said, "You're wrong, Beka. I know I've been kind of freaked out about finding out that life really *is* like the fairy tales, but I've learned a lot over the last couple of weeks too."

He kissed her lightly on the lips, so she could feel the curve of his smile, and then pulled back to say in a voice that rang with truth, "The most important thing I learned is that I want you just the way you are—the whole crazy, magical, enchanting, infuriating package. That's who I fell in love with, even if I didn't know it at the time. And that's who I'm going to love for the rest of my days. No matter which path you choose, I want to walk it with you.

"As for me, I want to stay here on the Bay and go out fishing on my father's boat. But I also want to start a program to help kids like Tito, the ones who are poor and sick and need to get out into the fresh air and do something fun. I could take them out for a day on the boat and give their parents a break. But I'm going to need another crew member to help, now that my father is gone, and Chico is on his way back to Mexico."

To her amazement, he knelt before her on one knee and took her hands in his. "I know you're going to be off some of the time, doing Baba things, but when you're around, I was wondering if you'd maybe agree to work the boat with me. And, you know, marry me. If you don't mind being stuck with a slightly grumpy ex-Marine fisherman with a beat-up old boat and no money to speak of."

He let go of her hands and pulled a battered black velvet box out of his jeans, and she gaped at him in disbelief.

"I know," Marcus said with a grin. "I was kind of surprised, too, when my father slipped it into my pocket when he was hugging me good-bye. But it was his mother's, and I guess he thought you should have it."

The lid popped open to reveal a single luminous pearl, set in gold filigree. Beka thought it was the most perfect thing she'd ever seen.

One more tear danced down her face, melting the tightness around her heart as she felt her world filling up with unexpected joy.

"Beka?" Marcus said, sounding uncertain. "Is that a no?"

She plucked the ring out of its velvet bed and slid it onto her finger, where of course it fit as if it was made for her. Because everything about Marcus was made for her.

"That's a hell yes," she said, smiling. "And as long as you don't mind being married to a witch who lives with a gigantic dragon-dog and is a little bit flaky, I suspect things will work out just fine."

And she kissed him soundly, just because she could.

$\mathbb{E}$PILOGUE

Dearest Bella,

    Thanks so much for the lovely wedding gift. Marcus said he never heard of anyone giving a couple matching knives before, but he is sure that his will come in handy on the boat. He only hopes that none of the boys he is teaching will mock him for the mother-of-pearl handles. Personally, I think they are just perfect!

    I'm sorry for the short notice, but we wanted to go ahead and tie the knot now, in case his father doesn't get better after all (although he was looking pretty good under the moonlight, swimming around the floating dock we used for the ceremony). Barbara and her Liam flew out for the day. I can't believe how happy she looks and how adorable little Babs is. I'm just sorry you couldn't be here too.

    But I am relieved to hear that you've found a clue as to the whereabouts of our missing three Riders. I know they've all been around for over a thousand years, but they've never disappeared like this before, and I can't help being worried. How on earth do you suppose they all ended up in Montana? Do you think it has anything to do with all the wildfires you've been struggling with lately? Or that cryptic message the Queen of the Otherworld sent, calling us all to an urgent meeting?

Anyway, keep me posted, and I'll see you soon.

Much love,
Your sister Baba,
Beka

TURN THE PAGE FOR A SNEAK PEEK
AT THE FIRST BABA YAGA NOVEL

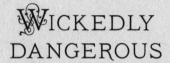

WICKEDLY
DANGEROUS

AVAILABLE NOW
FROM BERKLEY SENSATION!

THE CRACKLE OF the two-way radio barely impinged on Liam McClellan's consciousness as he scanned the bushes on either side of his squad car for any sign of a missing seven-year-old girl. He'd been down this same narrow country road yesterday at dusk, but like the other searchers, he'd had to give up when darkness fell. Like the rest—volunteers from the nearby community and every cop who could be spared, whether on duty or off—he'd come back at dawn to pick up where he left off. Even though there was little hope of success, after six long days.

His stomach clenched with a combination of too much coffee, too little sleep, and the acid taste of failure. Liam McClellan took his job as sheriff very seriously. Clearwater might be a tiny county in the middle of nowhere, its population scattered between a few small towns and a rural countryside made up mostly of struggling farmers, overgrown wilderness, and white-tailed deer, but it was *his* tiny county, and the people in it were his to protect. Lately, it didn't seem like he'd been doing a very good job.

Mary Elizabeth Shields had disappeared out of her own

backyard. Her mother had turned her back for a moment, drawn by the flutter of a bright-hued bird. When she turned around, the girl had vanished. Such a thing would be alarming enough on its own, but Mary Elizabeth was the third child to go missing in the last four months. To a lawman, that meant only one thing: a human predator was stalking the children of Clearwater County.

There had been no trace of any of the missing children. No tire marks, no unexplained fingerprints, no lurking strangers seen at any of the places from which the children had disappeared. No clues at all for a tired and frustrated sheriff to follow. And this time it was personal; Mary Elizabeth's mother was one of his deputies. A single mother who adored her only child, Belinda Shields was beside herself with grief and terror, making Liam even more discouraged over his inability to make any headway in the case.

A rabbit bounded out of a tangle of sumac, and Liam slowed to avoid hitting it, his tires sending up a spray of dusty gravel. In his rearview mirror, he thought he caught a glimpse of an old woman walking by the side of the road with a basket of herbs over one gnarled, skinny arm. But when he looked again, no one was there.

The gauzy fog of an early summer morning gave the deserted back road a surreal quality, which only heightened as he came around the bend to his destination to find a totally unexpected sight.

When he was out here last night, the wide curve of road that ended in a patch of meadow overlooking the Clearwater River had been empty. This morning, there was a shiny silver Airstream trailer parked in the middle of the crabgrass and wildflowers of the meadow, along with the large silver Chevy truck that had no doubt hauled it there. Liam blinked in surprise as he eased his squad car to a halt a few yards away. He didn't know anyone in the area who had such a fancy, expensive rig, and he couldn't imagine a stranger being able to navigate his way into the back-of-beyond corner on a bumpy tertiary road in the dark.

But clearly, someone had.

Swinging his long legs out of the driver's-side door, Liam thumbed the radio on and checked in with Nina in dispatch, hoping fervently she would tell him the girl had turned up, safe and sound.

No such luck.

"Do you know of anyone around here who owns an Airstream?" he asked her. "Any of the gang down at Bertie's mention seeing one come through town?" Bertie's was the local bakery/diner/gossip central. Nina considered it part of her job to swing by there on the way to work every morning and pick up muffins and chitchat to share with the rest of the sheriff's department.

"A what?" Nina asked. He could hear her typing on her keyboard in the background. The woman was seventy years old and could still multitask with the best of them. The county board kept pressuring him to make her retire, but that was never going to happen. At least, not as long as he still had a job.

"It's a big fancy silver RV trailer," he explained. "I found one sitting right smack-dab in the middle of Miller's Meadow when I got here just now."

"Really?" She sounded dubious. "In Miller's Meadow? How the heck did it get there?"

"Your guess is as good as mine," Liam said, scratching his head. He made a mental note to get his hair cut; it kept flopping into his eyes and annoying him. It seemed like a trim was never enough of a priority to make it to the top of his overburdened to-do list. "Drove here, I guess, although I wouldn't want to haul a big vehicle down this road if I didn't have to."

He told her to hang on for a minute, then walked around and checked the license plate on the truck. Returning to the car, he read off the numbers. "California plates, so someone is a long way from home. Hard for me to imagine anyone driving all that distance to upstate New York in order to park out here at the ass end of nowhere, but I suppose we've had tourists do stranger things."

"Huh," was Nina's only response. Clearwater County

didn't get much in the way of tourism. A few folks staying at the bed and breakfast in West Dunville, which had both a tiny winery and an antiques shop, as well as an old mill that housed a surprisingly good restaurant. Campers during the summer who used the small state park outside of Dunville proper. Other than that, the only strange faces you saw were those of people driving through on their way to someplace more interesting.

More tapping as Nina typed in the information he'd given her. "Huh," she said again. "There's nothing there, Sheriff."

"No wants and warrants, you mean?" He hadn't really expected any; not with an Airstream. But it would have been nice if the gods of law enforcement suddenly decided to smile on him and just hand over a suspect. Preferably one who still had all the children alive and well and eating cookies inside a conveniently located trailer. He sighed. There was no way he was going to be that lucky.

"No anything," Nina said slowly. "There's nothing in the system for that plate number at all. And I can't find any record of a permit being issued for someone to use the spot. That's county property, so there should be one if our visitor went through proper channels and didn't simply park there because he got tired."

Liam felt his pulse pick up. "Probably a computer error. Why don't you go ahead and check it again. I'll get the inspection number off the windshield for you too; that should turn up something." He grabbed his high-brimmed hat from the passenger seat, setting his face into "official business" lines. "I think it's time to wake up the owner and get some answers."

The radio crackled back at him, static cutting off Nina's reply. Any day now, the county was going to get him updated equipment that worked better. As soon as the economy picked up. Clearwater County had never been prosperous at the best of times, but it had been hit harder than most by the recent fiscal downturn, since most people had already barely been getting by before the economy slid into free fall.

Plopping his hat on over his dark-blond hair, Liam strode up to the door of the Airstream—or at least, where he could have sworn the door was a couple of minutes ago. Now there was just a blank wall. He pushed the hair out of his eyes again and walked around to the other side. Shiny silver metal, but no door. So he walked back around to where he started, and there was the entrance, right where it belonged.

"I need to get more sleep," he muttered to himself. He would almost have said the Airstream was laughing at him, but that was impossible. "More sleep and more coffee."

He knocked. Waited a minute, and knocked again, louder. Checked his watch. It was six a.m.; hard to believe that whoever the trailer belonged to was already out and about, but it was always possible. An avid fisherman, maybe, eager to get the first trout of the day. Cautiously, Liam put one hand on the door handle and almost jumped out of his boots when it emitted a loud, ferocious blast of noise.

He snatched his hand away, then laughed at himself as he saw a large, blunt snout pressed against the nearest window. For a second there, he'd almost thought the trailer itself was barking. Man, did he need more coffee.

At the sound of an engine, Liam turned and walked back toward his car. A motorcycle came into view, its rider masked by head-to-toe black leather, a black helmet, and mirrored sunglasses that matched the ones Liam himself wore. The bike itself was a beautiful royal blue classic BMW that made Liam want to drool. And get a better-paying job. The melodic throb of its motor cut through the morning silence until it purred to a stop about a foot away from him. The rider swung a leg over the top of the cycle and dismounted gracefully.

"Nice bike," Liam said in a conversational tone. "Is that a sixty-eight?"

"Sixty-nine," the rider replied. Gloved hands reached up and removed the helmet, and a cloud of long black hair came pouring out, tumbling waves of ebony silk. The faint aroma of orange blossoms drifted across the meadow, although none grew there.

A tenor voice, sounding slightly amused, said, "Is there a problem, Officer?"

Liam started, aware that he'd been staring rudely. He told

himself it was just the surprise of her gender, not the startling Amazonian beauty of the woman herself, all angles and curves and leather.

"Sheriff," he corrected out of habit. "Sheriff Liam McClellan." He held out one hand, then dropped it back to his side when the woman ignored it. "And you are?"

"Not looking for trouble," she said, a slight accent of unidentifiable origin coloring her words. Her eyes were still hidden behind the dark glasses, so he couldn't quite make out if she was joking or not. "My name is Barbara Yager. People call me Baba." One corner of her mouth edged up so briefly, he almost missed it.

"Welcome to Clearwater County," Liam said. "Would you like to tell me what you're doing parked out here?" He waved one hand at the Airstream. "I assume this belongs to you?"

She nodded, expressionless. "It does. Or I belong to it. Hard to tell which, sometimes."

Liam smiled gamely, wondering if his caffeine deficit was making her sound odder than she really was. "Sure. I feel that way about my mortgage sometimes. So, you were going to tell me what you're doing here."

"Was I? Somehow I doubt it." Again, that tiny smile, barely more than a twitch of the lips. "I'm a botanist with a specialty in herbalism; I'm on sabbatical from UC Davis. You have some unusual botanical varieties growing in this area, so I'm here to collect samples for my research."

Liam's cop instincts told him that her answer sounded too pat, almost rehearsed. Something about her story was a lie, he was sure of it. But why bother to lie about something he could so easily check?

"Do you have some kind of ID?" he asked. "Your vehicle didn't turn up in the database, and my dispatcher couldn't find any record of a permit for you to be here. This is county property, you know." He put on his best "stern cop" expression. The woman with the cloud of hair didn't seem at all fazed.

"Perhaps you should check again," she said, handing over a California driver's license with a ridiculously good picture. "I'm sure you'll find that everything is in order."

The radio in his car suddenly squawked back to life again, and Nina's gravelly voice said, "Sheriff? You there?"

"Excuse me," Liam said, and walked over to pick up the handset, one wary eye still on the stranger. "I'm here, Nina. What do you have for me?"

"That license plate you gave me? It just came back. Belongs to a Barbara Yager, out of Davis, California. And the county office found an application and approval for her to camp in the meadow. Apparently the clerk had misfiled it, which is why they didn't have it when we asked the first time." Her indignant snort echoed across the static. "Misfiled. Nice way to say those gals down there don't know the alphabet. So, anything else you need, Sheriff?"

He thumbed the mike. "Nope, that will do it for now," he said. "Thanks, Nina." Liam put the radio back in its cradle and walked back over to where his not-so-mystery woman waited patiently by her motorcycle, its engine pinging as it cooled.

"Looks like you were right," he said, handing her license back. "Everything seems to be in order."

"That's the way I like it," she said.

"Me too," Liam agreed. "Of course, it kind of comes with the job description. One half of 'law and order,' as it were." He tipped the brim of his hat at her. "Sorry for disturbing you, ma'am."

She blinked a little at the polite title and turned to go.

"I'm going to leave my squad car here for a bit," Liam said. "I'm continuing a search down the riverside. Unless you were planning on pulling the Airstream out in the next couple of hours, the car shouldn't be in your way."

Stillness seemed to settle onto her leather-clad shoulders, and she paused for a second before swiveling around on the heel of one clunky motorcycle boot. "I wasn't expecting to leave anytime soon." Another pause, and she added in a casual tone, that mysterious hint of an accent making her words musical, "What are you searching for, if you don't mind my asking?"

The wind lifted her hair off her neck, revealing a

glimpse of color peeking out from underneath the edge of her black tee shirt.

Liam wondered what kind of a tattoo a BMW-riding herb researcher might have. A tiny rose, maybe? Although in Barbara Yager's case, the rose would probably have thorns. Well, not likely he'd ever find out.

"I'm looking for a little girl," he answered her, dragging his mind back to the task at hand. "A seven-year-old named Mary Elizabeth who disappeared six days ago. I don't suppose you've seen her?"

Barbara shook her head, a small groove appearing between the dark arches of her brows. "Six days. That's not good, is it?"

She pulled off her sunglasses to reveal startling clear amber eyes surrounded by long, dusky lashes. For a moment, staring into them, Liam felt like he was falling. Up into the sky, or down into a bottomless pool of water, he couldn't tell which. Then she blinked, and was just another woman with beautiful eyes in an oval face with sharp cheekbones and a slightly hawkish nose.

Liam shook himself and thought longingly of coffee again. He didn't know what the hell was wrong with him this morning. Stress, he figured. And too little sleep.

"No, it's not," he said. "Neither is the fact that she is the third child to go missing in recent months." The muscles in his jaw clenched, hating to say it out loud. It was bad enough to have the numbers racing around in his head all day, and haunting him all night. Three kids, four months, six days, seven years old. It was like a demented counting book used to scare disobedient children. Or incompetent sheriffs.

Barbara gave him an odd look; some indecipherable mix of anger, concern, and resignation. He had no idea what it meant, other than that she clearly didn't like the idea of little girls disappearing any more than he did.

"Well," she said shortly. "We can't have that, can we?"

No, he thought, *we really can't.*